Gerald's
Game

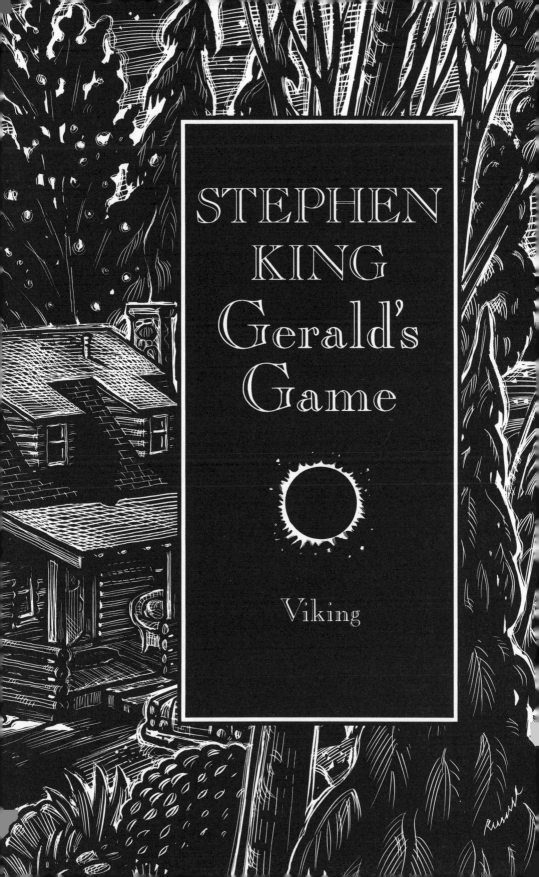

VIKING
Published by the Penguin Group
Viking Penguin, a division of Penguin Books USA Inc.,
375 Hudson Street, New York, New York 10014, U.S.A.
Penguin Books Ltd, 27 Wrights Lane, London W8 5TZ, England
Penguin Books Australia Ltd, Ringwood, Victoria, Australia
Penguin Books Canada Ltd, 10 Alcorn Avenue, Suite 300,
Toronto, Ontario, Canada M4V 3B2
Penguin Books (N.Z.) Ltd, 182–190 Wairau Road,
Auckland 10, New Zealand

Penguin Books Ltd, Registered Offices: Harmondsworth, Middlesex, England

First published in 1992 by Viking Penguin, a division of Penguin Books USA Inc.

Grateful acknowledgment is made for permission
to reprint excerpts from the following copyrighted works:
"Can I Get a Witness," by Eddie Holland, Brian Holland, and Lamont Dozier. Published
by Stone Agate Music, © 1963. All rights reserved. Used by permission.
"Space Cowboy," lyrics and music by Steve Miller and Ben Sidran. © 1969 Sailor Music.
Used by permission. All rights reserved.
"The Talkin' Blues," words and music by Woody Guthrie. TRO—© Copyright 1988
Ludlow Music, Inc., New York, N.Y. Used by permission.
"Come now, my child," from *But Even So,* by Kenneth Patchen. Copyright 1968 by
Kenneth Patchen. Reprinted by permission of New Directions Publishing Corporation.

ISBN: 978-0-7394-8534-7
Printed in the United States of America

This book is dedicated, with love and admiration, to six good women:

Margaret Spruce Morehouse   Anne Spruce Labree

Catherine Spruce Graves   Tabitha Spruce King

Stephanie Spruce Leonard   Marcella Spruce

{Sadie} gathered herself together. No one could describe the scorn of her expression or the contemptuous hatred she put into her answer.

"You men! You filthy dirty pigs! You're all the same, all of you. Pigs! Pigs!"

—W. Somerset Maugham,
"Rain"

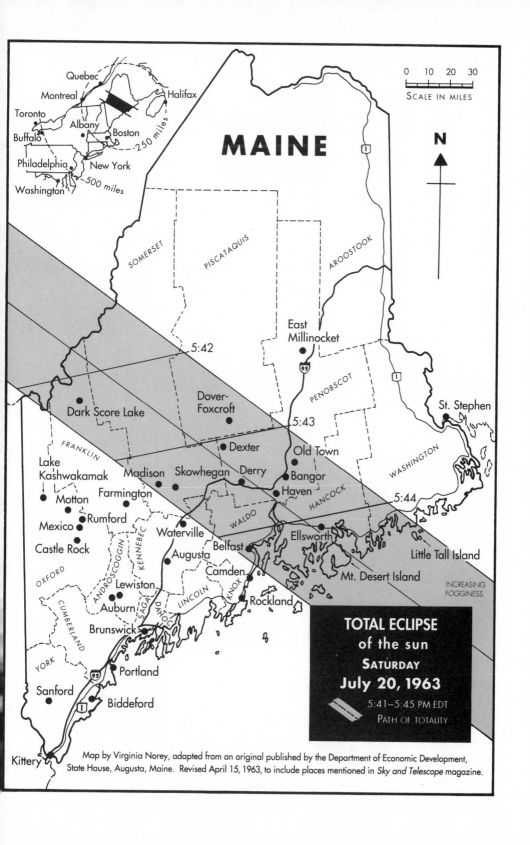

Quebec
Montreal
Halifax
Toronto
Albany
Boston
Buffalo
Philadelphia
New York
Washington

250 miles
500 miles

0 10 20 30
SCALE IN MILES

N

MAINE

SOMERSET
PISCATAQUIS
AROOSTOOK

5:42

East
Millinocket

PENOBSCOT

Dover-
Foxcroft

5:43

Dark Score Lake

St. Stephen

FRANKLIN

Dexter

Old Town

Lake
Kashwakamak

Madison
Skowhegan
Derry
Bangor
Haven

WASHINGTON

Motton

Farmington

WALDO

HANCOCK

5:44

Mexico
Rumford

Waterville

Castle Rock

ANDROSCOGGIN

KENNEBEC

Belfast

Ellsworth

Little Tall Island

OXFORD

Augusta

Camden

Mt. Desert Island

INCREASING
FOGGINESS

Lewiston

SAGA

LINCOLN

KNOX

Rockland

CUMBERLAND

Auburn

Brunswick

TOTAL ECLIPSE
of the sun
SATURDAY
July 20, 1963

YORK

Portland

5:41–5:45 PM EDT
PATH OF TOTALITY

Sanford
Biddeford

Kittery

Map by Virginia Norey, adapted from an original published by the Department of Economic Development,
State House, Augusta, Maine. Revised April 15, 1963, to include places mentioned in *Sky and Telescope* magazine.

Gerald's
Game

1

Jessie could hear the back door banging lightly, randomly, in the October breeze blowing around the house. The jamb always swelled in the fall and you really had to give the door a yank to shut it. This time they had forgotten. She thought of telling Gerald to go back and shut the door before they got too involved or that banging would drive her nuts. Then she thought how ridiculous that would be, given the current circumstances. It would ruin the whole mood.

What mood?

A good question, that. And as Gerald turned the hollow barrel of the key in the second lock, as she heard the minute click from above her left ear, she realized that, for her at least, the mood wasn't worth preserving. That was why she had noted the unlatched door in the first place, of course. For her, the sexual turn-on of the bondage games hadn't lasted long.

The same could not be said of Gerald, however. He was wearing only a pair of Jockey shorts now, and she didn't have to look as high as his face to see that his interest continued unabated.

This is stupid, she thought, but stupid wasn't the whole story, either. It was also a little scary. She didn't like to admit it, but there it was.

"Gerald, why don't we just forget this?"

He hesitated for a moment, frowning a little, then went on across the room to the dresser which stood to the left of the bathroom door. His face cleared as he went. She watched him from where she lay on the bed, her arms raised and splayed out, making her look a little like Fay Wray chained up and waiting for the great ape in *King Kong*. Her wrists had been secured to the mahogany bedposts with two sets of handcuffs. The chains gave each hand about six inches' worth of movement. Not much.

He put the keys on top of the dresser—two minute clicks, her ears seemed in exceptionally fine working order for a Wednesday afternoon—and then turned back to her. Over his head, sunripples from the lake danced and wavered on the bedroom's high white ceiling.

"What do you say? This has lost a lot of its charm for me." *And it never had that much to begin with*, she did not add.

He grinned. He had a heavy, pink-skinned face below a narrow widow's peak of hair as black as a crow's wing, and that grin of his had always done something to her that she didn't much care for. She couldn't quite put her finger on what that something was, but—

Oh, sure you can. It makes him look stupid. You can practically see his IQ going down ten points for every inch that grin spreads. At its maximum width, your killer corporate lawyer of a husband looks like a janitor on work-release from the local mental institution.

That was cruel, but not entirely inaccurate. But how did you tell your husband of almost twenty years that every time he grinned he looked as if he were suffering from light mental retardation? The answer was simple, of course: you didn't. His smile was a different matter entirely. He had a lovely smile—she guessed it was that smile, so warm and good-humored, which had persuaded her to go out with him in the first place. It had reminded her of her father's smile when he told his family amusing things about his day as he sipped a before-dinner gin and tonic.

This wasn't the smile, though. This was the *grin*—a version of it he seemed to save just for these sessions. She had an idea that to Gerald, who was on the inside of it, the grin felt wolfish. Piratical, maybe. From her angle, however, lying here with her arms raised above her head and nothing on but a pair of bikini panties, it only looked stupid. No . . . *retarded.* He was, after all, no devil-may-care adventurer like the ones in the men's magazines over which he had spent the furious ejaculations of his lonely, overweight puberty; he was an attorney with a pink, too-large face spreading below a widow's peak which was narrowing relentlessly toward total baldness. Just an attorney with a hard-on poking the front of his undershorts out of shape. And only moderately out of shape, at that.

The size of his erection wasn't the important thing, though. The important thing was the grin. It hadn't changed a bit, and that meant Gerald hadn't taken her seriously. She was *supposed* to protest; after all, that was the game.

"Gerald? I mean it."

The grin widened. A few more of his small, inoffensive attorney's teeth came into view; his IQ tumbled another twenty or thirty points. And he still wasn't hearing her.

Are you sure of that?

She was. She couldn't read him like a book—she supposed it took a lot more than seventeen years of marriage to get to that point—but she thought she usually had a pretty good idea of what was going through his head. She thought something would be seriously out of whack if she didn't.

If that's the truth, toots, how come he can't read you? How come he can't see this isn't just a new scene in the same old sex-farce?

Now it was her turn to frown slightly. She had always heard voices inside her head—she guessed everyone did, although people usually didn't talk about them, any more than they talked about their bowel functions—and most of them were old friends, as comfortable as bedroom slippers. This one, however, was new . . . and there was nothing comfortable about it. It was a strong voice, one that sounded young and vigorous. It also sounded impatient. Now it spoke again, answering its own question.

It isn't that he can't *read you; it's just that sometimes, toots, he doesn't want to.*

"Gerald, really—I don't feel like it. Bring the keys back and unlock me. We'll do something else. I'll get on top, if you want. Or you can just lie there with your hands behind your head and I'll do you, you know, the other way."

Are you sure you want to do that? the new voice asked. *Are you really sure you want to have any sex with this man?*

Jessie closed her eyes, as if she could make the voice shut up by doing that. When she opened them again, Gerald was standing at the foot of the bed, the front of his shorts jutting like the prow of a ship. Well . . . some kid's toy boat, maybe. His grin had widened further, exposing the last few teeth—the ones with the gold fillings—on both sides. She didn't just dislike that dumb grin, she realized; she despised it.

"I *will* let you up . . . if you're very, very good. Can you be very, very good, Jessie?"

Corny, the new no-bullshit voice commented. *Très corny.*

He hooked his thumbs into the waistband of his underpants like some absurd gunslinger. The Jockeys went down pretty fast once they got past his not-inconsiderable love handles. And there it was, exposed. Not the formidable engine of love she had first encountered as a teenager in the pages of *Fanny Hill* but something meek and pink and circumcised; five inches of completely unremarkable erection. Two or three years ago, on one of her infrequent trips to Boston, she had seen a movie called *The Belly of an Architect.* She thought, *Right. And now I'm looking at The Penis of an Attorney.* She had to bite the insides of her cheeks to keep from laughing. Laughing at this point would be impolitic.

An idea came to her then, and it killed any urge she'd had to laugh. It was this: he didn't know she was serious because for him, Jessie Mahout Burlingame, wife of Gerald, sister of Maddy and

4

Will, daughter of Tom and Sally, mother of no one, was really not here at all. She had ceased to be here when the keys made their small, steely clicks in the locks of the handcuffs. The men's adventure magazines of Gerald's teenage years had been replaced by a pile of skin magazines in the bottom drawer of his desk, magazines in which women wearing pearls and nothing else knelt on bearskin rugs while men with sexual equipment that made Gerald's look strictly HO-scale by comparison took them from behind. In the backs of these magazines, between the talk-dirty-to-me phone ads with their 900 numbers, were ads for inflatable women which were supposed to be anatomically correct—a bizarre concept if Jessie had ever encountered one. She thought of those air-filled dollies now, their pink skins, lineless cartoon bodies, and featureless faces, with a kind of revelatory amazement. It wasn't horror—not quite —but an intense light flashed on inside her, and the landscape it disclosed was certainly more frightening than this stupid game, or the fact that this time they were playing it in the summer house by the lake long after summer had run away for another year.

But none of it had affected her hearing in the slightest. Now it was a chainsaw she heard, snarling away in the woods at some considerable distance—as much as five miles, maybe. Closer by, out on the main body of Kashwakamak Lake, a loon tardy in starting its annual run south lifted its crazed cry into the blue October air. Closer still, somewhere here on the north shore, a dog barked. It was an ugly, ratcheting sound, but Jessie found it oddly comforting. It meant that someone else was up here, midweek in October or no. Otherwise there was just the sound of the door, loose as an old tooth in a rotted gum, slapping at the swollen jamb. She felt that if she had to listen to that for long, it would drive her crazy.

Gerald, now naked save for his spectacles, knelt on the bed and began crawling up toward her. His eyes were still gleaming.

She had an idea it was that gleam which had kept her playing the game long after her initial curiosity had been satisfied. It had been years since she'd seen that much heat in Gerald's gaze when he looked at her. She wasn't bad-looking—she'd managed to keep the

5

weight off, and still had most of her figure—but Gerald's interest in her had waned just the same. She had an idea that the booze was partly to blame for that—he drank a hell of a lot more now than when they'd first been married—but she knew the booze wasn't all of it. What was the old saw about familiarity breeding contempt? That wasn't supposed to hold true for men and women in love, at least according to the Romantic poets she'd read in English Lit 101, but in the years since college she had discovered there were certain facts of life about which John Keats and Percy Shelley had never written. But of course, they had both died a lot younger than she and Gerald were now.

And all of that didn't matter much right here and right now. What maybe did was that she had gone on with the game longer than she had really wanted to because she had liked that hot little gleam in Gerald's eyes. It made her feel young and pretty and desirable. But . . .

. . . *but if you really thought it was you he was seeing when he got that look in his eye, you were misled, toots. Or maybe you misled yourself. And maybe now you have to decide—really, really decide—if you intend to continue putting up with this humiliation. Because isn't that pretty much how you feel? Humiliated?*

She sighed. Yes. It pretty much was.

"Gerald, I *do* mean it." She spoke louder now, and for the first time the gleam in his eyes flickered a little. Good. He could hear her after all, it seemed. So maybe things were still okay. Not great, it had been a long time since things had been what you could call great, but okay. Then the gleam reappeared, and a moment later the idiot grin followed.

"I'll teach *you*, me proud beauty," he said. He actually *said* that, pronouncing *beauty* the way the landlord in a bad Victorian melodrama might say it.

Let him do it, then. Just let him do it and it will be done.

This was a voice she was much more familiar with, and she intended to follow its advice. She didn't know if Gloria Steinem would approve and didn't care; the advice had the attractiveness of the completely practical. Let him do it and it would be done. Q.E.D.

Then his hand—his soft, short-fingered hand, its flesh as pink as that which capped his penis—reached out and grasped her breast, and something inside her suddenly popped like an overstrained tendon. She bucked her hips and back sharply upward, flinging his hand off.

"Quit it, Gerald. Unlock these stupid handcuffs and let me up. This stopped being fun around last March, while there was still snow on the ground. I don't feel sexy; I feel ridiculous."

This time he heard her all the way down. She could see it in the way the gleam in his eyes went out all at once, like candleflames in a strong gust of wind. She guessed that the two words which had finally gotten through to him were *stupid* and *ridiculous*. He had been a fat kid with thick glasses, a kid who hadn't had a date until he was eighteen—the year after he went on a strict diet and began to work out in an effort to strangle the engirdling flab before it could strangle him. By the time he was a sophomore in college, Gerald's life was what he described as "more or less under control" (as if life—his life, anyway—were a bucking bronco he had been ordered to tame), but she knew his high school years had been a horror show that had left him with a deep legacy of contempt for himself and suspicion of others.

His success as a corporate lawyer (and marriage to her; she believed that had also played a part, perhaps even the crucial one) had further restored his confidence and self-respect, but she supposed that some nightmares never completely ended. In a deep part of his mind, the bullies were still giving Gerald wedgies in study-hall, still laughing at Gerald's inability to do anything but girlie-pushups in phys ed, and there were words—*stupid* and *ridiculous,* for instance—that brought all that back as if high school had been yesterday . . . or so she suspected. Psychologists could be incredibly stupid about many things, almost willfully stupid, it often seemed to her, but about the horrible persistence of some memories she thought they were bang-on. Some memories battened onto a person's mind like evil leeches, and certain words—*stupid* and *ridiculous,* for example—could bring them instantly back to squirming, feverish life.

She waited to feel a pang of shame at hitting below the belt like this and was pleased—or maybe it was relief she felt—when no pang came. *I guess maybe I'm just tired of pretending,* she thought, and this idea led to another: she might have her own sexual agenda, and if she did, this business with the handcuffs was definitely not on it. They made her feel demeaned. The whole idea made her feel demeaned. Oh, a certain uneasy excitement had accompanied the first few experiments—the ones with the scarves—and on a couple of occasions she'd had multiple orgasms, and that was a rarity for her. All the same, there had been side-effects she didn't care for, and that feeling of being somehow demeaned was only one of them. She'd had her own nightmares following each of those early versions of Gerald's game. She awoke from them sweaty and gasping, her hands thrust deeply into the fork of her crotch and rolled into tight little balls. She only remembered one of these dreams, and that memory was distant, blurred: she had been playing croquet without any clothes on, and all at once the sun had gone out.

Never mind all that, Jessie; those are things you can consider another day. Right now the only important thing is getting him to let you loose.

Yes. Because this wasn't *their* game; this game was all his. She had gone on playing it simply because Gerald wanted her to. And that was no longer good enough.

The loon voiced its lonely cry out on the lake again. Gerald's dopey grin of anticipation had been replaced by a look of sulky displeasure. *You broke my toy, you bitch,* that look said.

Jessie found herself remembering the last time she'd gotten a good look at that expression. In August Gerald had come to her with a glossy brochure, had pointed out what he wanted, and she had said yes, of course he could buy a Porsche if he wanted a Porsche, they could certainly *afford* a Porsche, but she thought he might do better to buy a membership in the Forest Avenue Health Club, as he had been threatening to do for the past two years. "You don't have a Porsche body just now," she had said, knowing she wasn't being very diplomatic but feeling that this really wasn't the time for diplomacy. Also, he had exasperated her to the point where she hadn't cared a whole hell of a lot for his feelings. This had been happening more and more frequently to her lately, and it dismayed her, but she didn't know what to do about it.

"Just what is that supposed to mean?" he had asked stiffly. She didn't bother to answer; she had learned that when Gerald asked such questions, they were almost always rhetorical. The important message lay in the simple subtext: *You're upsetting me, Jessie. You're not playing the game.*

But on that occasion—perhaps in an unknowing tune-up for this one—she had elected to ignore the subtext and answer the question.

"It means that you're still going to be forty-six this winter whether you own a Porsche or not, Gerald . . . and you're still going to be thirty pounds overweight." Cruel, yes, but she could have been downright gratuitous; could have passed on the image which had flashed before her eyes when she had looked at the photograph of the sports car on the front of the glossy brochure Gerald had handed her. In that blink of an instant she had seen a chubby little kid with a pink face and a widow's peak stuck in the innertube he'd brought to the old swimming hole.

Gerald had snatched the brochure out of her hand and had stalked away without another word. The subject of the Porsche had not been raised since . . . but she had often seen it in his resentful We Are Not Amused stare.

She was seeing an even hotter version of that stare right now.

"You said it sounded like *fun.* Those were your exact words: 'It sounds like fun.' "

Had she said that? She supposed she had. But it had been a mistake. A little goof, that was all, a little slip on the old banana peel. Sure. But how did you tell your husband that when he had his lower lip pooched out like Baby Huey getting ready to do a tantrum?

She didn't know, so she dropped her gaze . . . and saw something she didn't like at all. Gerald's version of Mr. Happy hadn't wilted a bit. Apparently Mr. Happy hadn't heard about the change of plans.

"Gerald, I just don't—"

"—feel like it? Well, that's a hell of a note, isn't it? I took the whole day off work. And if we spend the night, that means tomorrow morning off, as well." He brooded over this for a moment, and then repeated: "You said it sounded like fun."

She began to fan out her excuses like a tired old poker-hand (*Yes, but now I have a headache; Yes, but I'm having these really shitty premenstrual cramps; Yes, but I'm a woman and therefore entitled to change my mind; Yes, but now that we're actually out here in the Big Lonely you frighten me, you bad beautiful brute of a man, you*), the lies that fed either his misconceptions or his ego (the two were frequently interchangeable), but before she could pick a card, any card, the new voice spoke up. It was the first time it had spoken out loud, and Jessie was fascinated to find that it sounded the same in the air as it did inside her head: strong, dry, decisive, in control.

It also sounded curiously familiar.

"You're right—I guess I *did* say that, but what really sounded like fun was breaking away with you the way we used to before you got your name up on the door with the rest of the type-A's. I thought maybe we could bounce the bedsprings a little, then sit on the deck and dig the quiet. Maybe play some Scrabble after the sun went down. Is that an actionable offense, Gerald? What do you think? Tell me, because I really want to know."

"But you said—"

For the last five minutes she had been telling him in various ways that she wanted out of these goddam handcuffs, and he still hadn't let her out of them. Her impatience boiled over into fury. "My God, Gerald, this stopped being fun for me almost as soon as we started, and if you weren't as thick as a brick, you would have realized it!"

"Your mouth. Your smart, sarcastic mouth. Sometimes I get so tired of—"

"Gerald, when you get your head really set on something, sweet and low doesn't come close to reaching you. And whose fault is that?"

"I don't like you when you're like this, Jessie. When you're like this I don't like you a bit."

This was going from bad to worse to horrible, and the scariest part was how fast it was happening. Suddenly she felt very tired, and a line from an old Paul Simon song occurred to her: "I don't want no part of this crazy love." Right on, Paul. You may be short, but you ain't dumb.

"I know you don't. And it's okay that you don't, because right now the subject is these handcuffs, not how much you do or don't like me when I tell you I've changed my mind about something. I want *out* of these cuffs. Are you hearing me?"

No, she realized with dawning dismay. He really wasn't. Gerald was still one turn back.

"You are just so goddamned *inconsistent*, so goddamned *sarcastic*. I love you, Jess, but I hate the goddam *lip* on you. I always have." He wiped the palm of his left hand across his pouting rosebud of a mouth and then looked sadly at her—poor, put-upon Gerald, saddled with a woman who had gotten him out here in the forest primeval and then reneged on her sexual obligations. Poor, put-upon Gerald, who showed no sign whatever of getting the handcuff keys off the bureau by the bathroom door.

Her unease had changed into something else—while her back was turned, as it were. It had become a mixture of anger and fear she could remember feeling only once before. When she was twelve or so, her brother Will had goosed her at a birthday party. All her friends had seen, and they had all laughed. *Har-har, preety fonny, senhorra, I theenk.* It hadn't been funny to her, though.

Will had been laughing hardest of all, so hard he was actually doubled over with one hand planted above each knee, his hair hanging in his face. This had been a year or so after the advent of the Beatles and the Stones and the Searchers and all the rest, and Will had had a lot of hair to hang. It had apparently blocked his view of Jessie, because he had no idea of how angry she was . . . and he was, under ordinary circumstances, very much aware of her turns of mood and temper. He'd gone on laughing until that froth of emotion so filled her that she understood she would have to do something with it or simply explode. So she had doubled up one small fist and had punched her well-loved brother in the mouth when he finally raised his head to look at her. The blow had knocked him over like a bowling pin and he had cried really hard.

Later she had tried to tell herself that he had cried more out of surprise than pain, but she had known, even at twelve, that that wasn't so. She had hurt him, hurt him plenty. His lower lip had split in one place, his upper lip in two, and she had hurt him plenty. And why? Because he had done something stupid? But he'd only been nine himself—nine that day—and at that age *all* kids were stupid. No; it hadn't been his stupidity. It had been her fear—fear that if she didn't do something with that ugly green froth of anger and embarrassment, it would

(put out the sun)

cause her to explode. The truth, first encountered on that day, was this: there was a well inside her, the water in that well was poisoned, and when he goosed her, William had sent a bucket down there, one which had come up filled with scum and squirming gluck. She had hated him for that, and she supposed it was really her hate which had caused her to strike out. That deep stuff had scared her. Now, all these years later, she was discovering it still did . . . but it still infuriated her, as well.

You won't put out the sun, she thought, without the slightest idea of what this meant. *Be damned if you will.*

"I don't want to argue the fine points, Gerald. Just get the keys to these fucking things and *unlock me!*"

And then he said something which so astounded her that at first she couldn't grasp it: "What if I won't?"

What registered first was the change in his tone. He usually spoke in a bluff, gruff, hearty sort of voice—*I'm in charge here, and it's a pretty lucky thing for all of us, isn't it?* that tone proclaimed—but this was a low, purring voice with which she was not familiar. The gleam had returned to his eyes—that hot little gleam which had turned her on like a bank of floodlights once upon a time. She couldn't see it very well—his eyes were squinted down to puffy slits behind his gold-rimmed spectacles—but it was there. Yes indeed.

Then there was the strange case of Mr. Happy. Mr. Happy hadn't wilted a bit. Seemed, in fact, to be standing taller than at any time she could remember . . . although that was probably just her imagination.

Do you think so, toots? I don't.

She processed all this information before finally returning to the last thing he'd said—that amazing question. *What if I won't?* This time she got past the tone to the sense of the words, and as she came to fully understand them, she felt her rage and fear crank up a notch. Somewhere inside, that bucket was going down its shaft again for another slimy dip—a scumload of water filled with microbes almost as poisonous as swamp copperheads.

The kitchen door banged against its jamb and the dog began to bark in the woods again, sounding closer than ever now. It was a splintery, desperate sound. Listening to something like that for too long would undoubtedly give you a migraine.

"Listen, Gerald," she heard her strong new voice saying. She was aware that this voice could have picked a better time to break its silence—she was, after all, out here on the deserted north shore of Kashwakamak Lake, handcuffed to the bedposts, and wearing only a skimpy pair of nylon panties—but she still found herself admiring it. Almost against her will she found herself admiring it. "Are you listening yet? I know you don't do much of that these days when it's me doing the talking, but this time it's really important that you hear me. So . . . are you finally listening?"

He was kneeling on the bed, looking at her as if she were some previously undiscovered species of bug. His cheeks, in which complex networks of tiny scarlet threads squirmed (she thought of them as Gerald's liquor-brands), were flushed almost purple. A similar swath crossed his forehead. Its color was so dark, its shape so definite, that it looked like a birthmark. "Yes," he said, and in his new purring voice the word came out *yeh-usss.* "I'm listening, Jessie. I most certainly am."

"Good. Then you'll walk over to the bureau and get those keys. You'll unlock this one"—she rattled her right wrist against the headboard—"and then you'll unlock this one." She rattled the left wrist in similar fashion. "If you do this right away, we can have a little normal, painless, mutual-orgasm sex before returning to our normal, painless lives in Portland."

Pointless, she thought. *You left that one out. Normal, painless, pointless lives in Portland.* Perhaps that was so, or perhaps it was just a little overdramatization (being handcuffed to the bed brought that out in a person, she was discovering), but it was probably just as well she'd left that one out, in any case. It suggested that the new, no-bullshit voice wasn't so indiscreet, after all. Then, as if to contradict this idea, she heard that voice—which was, after all, *her* voice—begin to rise in the unmistakable beats and pulses of rage.

"But if you continue screwing around and teasing me, I'll go straight to my sister's from here, find out who did her divorce, and call her. I'm not joking. *I do not want to play this game!*"

Now something really incredible was happening, something she never would have suspected in a million years: his grin was resurfacing. It was coming up like a sub which has finally reached friendly waters after a long and dangerous voyage. That wasn't the really incredible thing, though. The really incredible thing was that the grin no longer made Gerald look harmlessly retarded. It now made him look like a dangerous lunatic.

His hand stole out again, caressed her left breast, then squeezed it painfully. He finished this unpleasant bit of business by pinching her nipple, a thing he had never done before.

"*Ow,* Gerald! That *hurts!*"

He gave a solemn, appreciative nod that went very strangely with his horrible grin. "That's good, Jessie. The whole thing, I mean. You could be an actress. Or a call-girl. One of the really high-priced ones." He hesitated, then added: "That's supposed to be a compliment."

"What in God's name are you talking about?" Except she was pretty sure she knew. She was really afraid now. Something bad was loose in the bedroom; it was spinning around and around like a black top.

But she was also still angry—as angry as she had been on the day Will had goosed her.

Gerald actually laughed. "What am I *talking* about? For a minute there, you had me believing it. *That's* what I'm talking about." He dropped a hand onto her right thigh. When he spoke again, his voice was brisk and weirdly businesslike. "Now—do you want to spread them for me, or do I have to do it? Is that part of the game, too?"

"Let me *up!*"

"Yes . . . eventually." His other hand shot out. This time it was her right breast he pinched, and this time the pinch was so hard it fired off nerves in little white sparkles all the way down her side to her hip. "For now, spread those lovely legs, me proud beauty!"

She took a closer look at him and saw a terrible thing: he knew. He knew she wasn't kidding about not wanting to go on with it. He knew, but he had chosen not to *know* he knew. Could a person do that?

You bet, the no-bullshit voice said. *If you're a hotshot shyster in the biggest corporate law-firm north of Boston and south of Montreal, I guess you can know whatever you want to know and not know whatever you don't want to. I think you're in big trouble here, honey. The kind of trouble that ends marriages. Better grit your teeth and squint your eyes, because I think one* bitch *of a vaccination shot is on the way.*

That grin. That ugly, mean-spirited grin.

Pretending ignorance. And doing it so hard that later on he would be able to pass a lie-detector test on the subject. *I thought it was part of the game,* he would say, all hurt and wide-eyed. *I really did.* And if she persisted, driving at him with her anger, he would eventually fall back to the oldest defense of them all . . . and then slip into it, like a lizard into a crack in a rock: *You liked it. You know you did. Why don't you admit it?*

Pretending *into* ignorance. Knowing but planning to go ahead anyway. He'd handcuffed her to the bedposts, had done it with her own cooperation, and now, oh shit, let's not gild the lily, now he meant to rape her, actually *rape her* while the door banged and the dog barked and the chainsaw snarled and the loon yodeled out there on the lake. He really meant to do it. Yessir, boys, hyuck, hyuck, hyuck, you ain't really had pussy until you've had pussy that's jumpin around underneath you like a hen on a hot griddle. And if she *did* go to Maddy's when this exercise in humiliation was over, he would continue to insist that rape had been the furthest thing from his mind.

He placed his pink hands against her thighs and began spreading her legs. She did not resist much; for the moment, at least, she was too horrified and amazed by what was going on here to resist much.

And that's exactly the right attitude, the more familiar voice inside her spoke up. *Just lie there quietly and let him shoot his squirt. After all, what's the big deal? He's done it at least a thousand times before and you never once turned green. In case you forgot, it's been quite a few years since you were a blushing virgin.*

And what would happen if she didn't listen and obey the counsel of that voice? What was the alternative?

As if in answer, a horrid picture rose in her mind. It was herself she saw, testifying in divorce court. She didn't know if there still were such things as divorce courts in Maine, but that in no way dimmed the vividness of the vision. She saw herself dressed in her conservative pink Donna Karan suit, with her peach silk blouse beneath it. Her knees and ankles were primly together. Her small clutch bag, the white one, was in her lap. She saw herself telling a judge who looked like the late Harry Reasoner that yes, it was true she had accompanied Gerald to the summer house of her own free will, yes, she had allowed him to tether her to the bedposts with two sets of Kreig handcuffs, also of her own free will, and yes, as a matter of fact they *had* played such games before, although never at the place on the lake.

Yes, Judge. Yes.

Yes, yes, yes.

As Gerald continued to spread her legs, Jessie heard herself telling the judge who looked like Harry Reasoner about how they had started with silk scarves, and how she had allowed the game to go on, progressing from scarves to ropes to handcuffs, even though she had quickly tired of the whole thing. Had become disgusted by it. So disgusted, in fact, that she had allowed Gerald to drive her the eighty-three miles from Portland to Kashwakamak Lake on a weekday in October; so revolted she had once again allowed him to chain her up like a dog; so bored with the whole thing that she had been wearing nothing but a pair of nylon panties so wispy you could have read *The New York Times* classified section through them. The judge would believe it all and sympathize with her most deeply. Of course he would. Who wouldn't? She could see herself sitting there on the witness stand and saying, "So there I was, handcuffed to the bedpost and wearing nothing but some underwear from Victoria's Secret and a smile, but I changed my mind at the last minute, and Gerald knew it, and that makes it rape."

Yes sir, that would do her, all right. Bet your boots.

She came out of this appalling fantasy to find Gerald yanking at her panties. He was kneeling between her legs, his face so studious that you might have been tempted to believe it was the Bar Exam he was planning to take instead of his unwilling wife. There was a runner of white spittle coursing down his chin from the center of his plump lower lip.

Let him do it, Jessie. Let him shoot his squirt. It's that stuff in his balls that's making him crazy, and you know it. It makes them all crazy. When he gets rid of it, you'll be able to talk to him again. You'll be able to deal with him. So don't make a fuss—just lie there and wait until he's got it out of his system.

Good advice, and she supposed she would have followed it if not for the new presence inside her. This unnamed newcomer clearly thought that Jessie's usual source of advice—the voice she had over the years come to think of as Goodwife Burlingame—was a wimp of the highest order. Jessie still might have let things run their course, but two things happened simultaneously. The first was her realization that, although her wrists were cuffed to the bedposts, her feet and legs were free. At the same moment she realized this, the runner of drool fell off Gerald's chin. It dangled for a moment, elongating, and then fell on her midriff, just above the navel. Something about this sensation was familiar, and she was swept by a horribly intense sensation of *déjà vu.* The room seemed to darken around her, as if the windows and the skylight had been replaced with panes of smoked glass.

It's his spunk, she thought, although she knew perfectly well it wasn't. *It's his goddam spunk.*

Her response was not so much directed at Gerald as at that hateful feeling that came flooding up from the bottom of her mind. In a very real sense she acted with no thought at all, but only lashed out with the instinctive, panicky revulsion of a woman who realizes the trapped thing fluttering in her hair is a bat.

She drew back her legs, her rising right knee barely missing the promontory of his chin, and then drove her bare feet out again like pistons. The sole and instep of her right drove deep into the bowl of his belly. The heel of her left smashed into the stiff root of his penis and the testicles hanging below it like pale, ripe fruit.

He rocked backward, his butt coming down on his plump, hairless calves. He tilted his head up toward the skylight and the white ceiling with its reflected patterns of sunripples and voiced a high, wheezy scream. The loon on the lake cried out again just then, in hellish counterpoint; to Jessie it sounded like one male commiserating with another.

Gerald's eyes weren't slitted now; they weren't gleaming, either. They were wide open, they were as blue as today's flawless sky (the thought of seeing that sky over the autumn-empty lake had been the deciding factor when Gerald had called from the office and said he'd had a postponement and would she like to go up to the summer place at least for the day and maybe overnight), and the expression in them was an agonized glare she could hardly look at. Cords of tendon stood out on the sides of his neck. Jessie thought: *I haven't seen those since the rainy summer when he pretty much gave up gardening and made J. W. Dant his hobby instead.*

His scream began to fade. It was as if someone with a special

Remote Gerald Control were turning down his volume. That wasn't it, of course; he had been screaming for an extraordinarily long time, perhaps as long as thirty seconds, and he was just running out of breath. *I must have hurt him badly,* she thought. The red spots on his cheeks and the swath across his forehead were now turning purple.

You did! the Goodwife's dismayed voice cried. *You really really did!*

Yep; damned good shot, wasn't it? the new voice mused.

You kicked your husband in the balls! the Goodwife screamed. *What in God's name gives you the right to do something like that? What gives you the right to even joke about it?*

She knew the answer to that one, or thought she did: she'd done it because her husband had intended to commit rape and pass it off later as a missed signal between two essentially harmonious marriage partners who had been playing a harmless sex-game. *It was the game's fault,* he would have said, shrugging. *The game's, not mine. We don't have to play it again, Jess, if you don't want to.* Knowing, of course, that nothing he could offer would ever cause her to hold her wrists up for the handcuffs again. No, this had been a case of last time pays for all. Gerald had known it, and had intended to make the most of it.

That black thing she had sensed in the room had spun out of control, just as she had feared it might. Gerald still appeared to be screaming, although no sound at all (at least none she could hear) was now coming from his pursed, agonized mouth. His face had become so congested with blood that it actually appeared to be black in places. She could see his jugular vein—or maybe it was his carotid artery, if that mattered at a time like this—pulsing furiously beneath the carefully shaved skin of his throat. Whichever one it was, it looked ready to explode, and a nasty jolt of terror stabbed Jessie.

"Gerald?" Her voice sounded thin and uncertain, the voice of a girl who has broken something valuable at a friend's birthday party. "Gerald, are you all right?"

It was a stupid question, of course, incredibly stupid, but it was a lot easier to ask than the ones which were really on her mind: *Gerald, how badly are you hurt? Gerald, do you think you might die?*

Of course he's not going to die, the Goodwife said nervously. *You've hurt him, indeed you have, and you ought to be sorry, but he's not going to* die. *Nobody is going to* die *around here.*

Gerald's pursed, puckered mouth continued to quiver soundlessly, but he didn't answer her question. One of his hands had gone to his belly; the other had cupped his wounded testes. Now they both rose slowly and settled just above his left nipple. They settled like a pair of pudgy pink birds too tired to fly farther. Jessie could see the shape of a bare foot—*her* bare foot—rising on her husband's round stomach. It was a bright, accusatory red against his pink flesh.

He was exhaling, or trying to, sending out a dour fog that smelled like rotting onions. *That's tidal breath,* she thought. *The bottom ten per cent of our lungs is reserved for tidal breath, isn't that what they taught us in high school biology? Yes, I think so. Tidal breath, the fabled last gasp of drowners and chokers. Once you expel that, you either faint or . . .*

"Gerald!" she cried in a sharp, scolding voice. "Gerald, *breathe!*"

His eyes bulged from their sockets like blue marbles stuck in a clod of Play-Doh, and he did manage to drag in a single small sip of air. He used it to speak a final word to her, this man who had sometimes seemed made of words.

". . . heart . . ."

That was all.

"*Gerald!*" Now she sounded shocked as well as scolding, an old-maid schoolteacher who has caught the second-grade flirt pulling up her skirt to show the boys the bunnies on her underpants. "*Gerald, stop fooling around and breathe, goddammit!*"

Gerald didn't. Instead, his eyes rolled back in their sockets, disclosing yellowish whites. His tongue blew out of his mouth and made a farting sound. A stream of cloudy, orange-tinted urine arced out of his deflated penis and her knees and thighs were doused with feverishly hot droplets. Jessie voiced a long, piercing shriek. This time she was unaware of yanking against the handcuffs, of using them to draw herself as far back from him as possible, awkwardly curling her legs beneath her as she did so.

"Stop it, Gerald! Just stop it before you fall off the b—"

Too late. Even if he were still hearing her, which her rational mind doubted, it was too late. His bowed back arched the top half of his body beyond the edge of the bed and gravity took over. Gerald Burlingame, with whom Jessie had once eaten Creamsicles in bed, fell over backward with his knees up and his head down, like a clumsy kid trying to impress his friends during Free Swim at the YMCA pool. The sound of his skull meeting the hardwood floor made her shriek again. It sounded like some enormous egg being cracked against the lip of a stone bowl. She would have given anything not to have heard that.

Then there was silence, broken only by the distant roar of the chainsaw. A large gray rose was opening in the air before Jessie's wide eyes. The petals spread and spread, and when they closed around her again like the dusty wings of huge colorless moths, blocking out everything for awhile, the only clear feeling she had was one of gratitude.

2

She seemed to be in a long, cold hall filled with white fog, a hall that was canted severely to one side like the halls people were always walking down in movies like *A Nightmare on Elm Street* and TV shows like *The Twilight Zone*. She was naked and the cold was really getting to her, making her muscles ache—particularly those of her back and neck and shoulders.

I've got to get out of here or I'll be sick, she thought. *I'm already getting cramps from the fog and the damp.*

(Although she knew it was not the fog and the damp.)

Also, something's wrong with Gerald. I can't remember exactly what it is, but I think he might be sick.

(Although she knew that sick wasn't exactly the right word.)

But, and this was odd, another part of her really didn't want to escape the tilted, foggy corridor at all. This part suggested that she'd be a lot better off staying here. That if she left she'd be sorry. So she did stay for awhile.

What finally got her going again was a barking dog. It was an exceedingly ugly bark, bottomheavy but breaking to shrill bits in its upper registers. Each time the animal let go with it, it sounded as if it were puking up a throatful of sharp splinters. She had heard that bark before, although it might be better—quite a bit better, actually—if she managed not to remember when, or where, or what had been happening at the time.

But at least it got her moving—left foot, right foot, hayfoot, strawfoot—and suddenly it occurred to her that she could see through the fog better if she opened her eyes, so she did. It wasn't some spooky *Twilight Zone* hallway she saw but the master bedroom of their summer house on the north end of Kashwakamak Lake—the area that was known as Notch Bay. She guessed the reason she had felt cold was that she was wearing nothing but a pair of bikini panties, and her neck and shoulders hurt because she was handcuffed to the bedposts and her bottom had slid down the bed when she fainted. No tilted corridor; no foggy damp. Only the dog was real, still barking its fool head off. It now sounded quite close to the house. If Gerald heard that—

The thought of Gerald made her twitch, and the twitch sent complex spiral-sparkles of feeling through her cramped biceps and triceps. These tingles faded away to nothing at her elbows, and Jessie realized with soupy, just-waking-up dismay that her forearms were mostly without feeling and her hands might as well have been gloves stuffed with congealed mashed potatoes.

This is going to hurt, she thought, and then everything came back to her . . . especially the image of Gerald doing his header off the side of the bed. Her husband was on the floor, either dead or unconscious, and she was lying up here on the bed, thinking about what a drag it was that her lower arms and hands had gone to sleep. How selfish and self-centered could you get?

If he's dead, it's his own damned fault, the no-bullshit voice said. It tried to add a few other home truths as well, but Jessie gagged it. In her still-not-quite-conscious state she had a clearer sightline into the deeper archives of her memory banks, and she suddenly realized whose voice—slightly nasal, clipped, always on the verge of a sarcasm-tinged laugh—that was. It belonged to her college roommate, Ruth Neary. Now that Jessie knew, she found she wasn't a bit surprised. Ruth had always been extremely generous with pieces of her mind, and her advice had often scandalized her nineteen-year-old wet-behind-the-ears roommate from Falmouth Foreside . . . which had undoubtedly been the idea, or part of it; Ruth's heart had always been in the right place, and Jessie had never doubted that Ruth actually believed sixty per cent of the things she said and had actually done forty per cent of the things she claimed to have done. When it came to things sexual, the percentage was probably even higher. Ruth Neary, the first woman Jessie had ever known who absolutely refused to shave her legs and her armpits; Ruth, who had once filled an unpleasant floor-counsellor's pillowcase with strawberry-scented foam douche; Ruth, who on general principles went to every student rally and attended every experimental student play. *If all else fails, tootsie, some good-looking guy will probably take his clothes off,* she had told an amazed but fascinated Jessie after coming back from a student effort entitled "The Son of Noah's Parrot." *I mean, it doesn't* always *happen, but it* usually *does —I think that's really what student-written and -produced plays are for—so guys and girls can take off their clothes and make out in public.*

She hadn't thought of Ruth in years and now Ruth was inside her head, handing out little nuggets of wisdom just as she had in days of yore. Well, why not? Who was more qualified to advise the mentally confused and emotionally disturbed than Ruth Neary, who had gone on from the University of New Hampshire to three marriages, two suicide attempts, and four drug-and-alcohol rehabs? Good old Ruth, just another shining example of how well the erstwhile Love Generation was making the transition to middle age.

"Jesus, just what I need, Dear Abby from hell," she said, and the thick, slurry quality of her voice frightened her more than the lack of feeling in her hands and lower arms.

She tried to yank herself back up to the mostly-sitting position she had managed just before Gerald's little diving exhibition (Had that horrible egg-cracking sound been part of her dream? She prayed that it had been), and thoughts of Ruth were swallowed by a sudden burst of panic when she did not move at all. Those tingling spirals of sensation spun through her muscles again, but nothing else happened. Her arms just went on hanging above and slightly behind her, as moveless and feelingless as stovelengths of rock maple. The muzzy feeling in her head disappeared—panic beat the hell out of smelling salts, she was discovering—and her heart kicked into a higher gear, but that was all. A vivid image culled from some long-ago history text flickered behind her eyes for a moment: a circle of laughing, pointing people standing around a young woman with her head and hands in stocks. The woman was bent over like a hag in a fairy-tale and her hair hung in her face like a penitent's shroud.

Her name is Goodwife Burlingame and she's being punished for hurting her husband, she thought. *They're punishing the Goodwife because they can't get hold of the one who's really responsible for hurting him . . . the one who sounds like my old college roommate.*

But was *hurting* the right word? Was it not likely that she was now sharing this bedroom with a dead man? Was it not also likely that, dog or no dog, the Notch Bay end of the lake was entirely deserted? That if she started to scream, she would be answered only by the loon? Only that and nothing more?

It was mostly that thought, with its strange echo of Poe's "The Raven," that brought her to a sudden realization of just what was

24

going on here, what she had gotten herself into, and full-fledged, mindless terror suddenly fell on her. For twenty seconds or so (if asked how long that panic-attack lasted, she would have guessed at least three minutes and probably closer to five) she was totally in its grip. A thin rod of rational consciousness remained deep inside her, but it was helpless—only a dismayed spectator watching the woman writhe on the bed with her hair flying as she whipped her head from side to side in a gesture of negation, hearing her hoarse, frightened screams.

A deep, glassy pain at the base of her neck, just above the place where her left shoulder started, put a stop to it. It was a muscle-cramp, a bad one. Moaning, Jessie let her head fall back against the separated mahogany slats which formed the headboard of the bed. The muscle she had strained was frozen in a strenuous flexed position, and it felt as hard as a rock. The fact that her exertion had forced pins and needles of feeling all the way down her forearms to the palms of her hands meant little next to that terrible pain, and she found that leaning back against the headboard was only putting more pressure on the overstrained muscle.

Moving instinctively, without any thought at all, Jessie planted her heels against the coverlet, raised her buttocks, and shoved with her feet. Her elbows bent and the pressure on her shoulders and upper arms eased. A moment later the Charley horse in her deltoid muscle began to let go. She let out her breath in a long, harsh sigh of relief.

The wind—it had progressed quite a bit beyond the breeze stage, she noticed—gusted outside, sighing through the pines on the slope between the house and the lake. Just off the kitchen (which was in another universe as far as Jessie was concerned), the door she and Gerald had neglected to pull shut banged against the swollen jamb: one time, two time, three time, four. These were the only sounds; only these and nothing more. The dog had quit barking, at least for the time being, and the chainsaw had quit roaring. Even the loon seemed to be on its coffee-break.

The image of a lake-loon taking a coffee-break, maybe floating in the water-cooler and chatting up a few of the lady loons, caused a dusty croaking sound in her throat. Under less unpleasant circumstances, that sound might have been termed a chuckle. It dissolved the last of her panic, leaving her still afraid but at least in charge of her thoughts and actions once more. It also left her with an unpleasant metallic taste on her tongue.

That's adrenaline, toots, or whatever glandular secretion your body dumps when you sprout claws and start climbing the walls. If anyone ever asks you what panic is, now you can tell them: an emotional blank spot that leaves you feeling as if you've been sucking on a mouthful of pennies.

Her forearms were buzzing, and the tingles of sensation had at last spread into her fingers as well. Jessie rolled her hands open and closed several times, wincing as she did so. She could hear the faint sound of the handcuff chains rattling against the bedposts and took a moment to wonder if she and Gerald had been mad—it certainly seemed so now, although she had no doubt that thousands of people all over the world played similar games each and every day. She had read that there were even sexual free spirits who hanged themselves in their closets and then beat off as the blood-supply to their brains slowly decreased to nothing. Such news only served to increase her belief that men were not so much gifted with penises as cursed with them.

But if it *had* been only a game (only that and nothing more), why had Gerald felt it necessary to buy real handcuffs? *That* was sort of an interesting question, wasn't it?

Maybe, but I don't think it's the really important question just now, Jessie, do you? Ruth Neary asked from inside her head. It was really quite amazing how many different tracks the human mind could work on at the same time. On one of these she now found herself wondering what had become of Ruth, whom she had last seen ten years ago. It had been at least three years since Jessie had heard from her. The last communication had been a postcard showing a young man in an ornate red velvet suit with a ruff at the neck. The young man's mouth was open, and his long tongue had been protruding suggestively. SOME DAY MY PRINCE WILL TONGUE, the card had said. New Age wit, Jessie remembered thinking at the time. The Victorians had Anthony Trollope; the Lost Generation had H. L. Mencken; we got stuck with dirty greeting cards and bumper-sticker witticisms like AS A MATTER OF FACT, I DO OWN THE ROAD.

The card had borne a blurry Arizona postmark and the information that Ruth had joined a lesbian commune. Jessie hadn't been terribly surprised at the news; had even mused that perhaps her old friend, who could be wildly irritating and surprisingly, wistfully sweet (sometimes in the same breath) had finally found the hole on the great gameboard of life which had been drilled to accept her own oddly shaped peg.

She had put Ruth's card in the top left drawer of her desk, the one where she kept various odd lots of correspondence which would probably never be answered, and that had been the last time she'd thought about her old roomie until now—Ruth Neary, who lusted to own a Harley-Davidson barn-burner but who had never been able to master any standard transmission, even the one on Jessie's tame old Ford Pinto; Ruth, who often got lost on the UNH campus even after three years there; Ruth, who always cried when she forgot she was cooking something on the hotplate and burned it to a crisp. She did that last so often it was really a miracle she had never set their room—or the whole dorm—on fire. How odd that the confident no-bullshit voice in her head should turn out to be Ruth's.

The dog began to bark again. It sounded no closer, but it sounded no farther away, either. Its owner wasn't hunting birds, that was for sure; no hunter would have anything to do with such a canine blabbermouth. And if dog and master were out for a simple afternoon walk, how come the barks had been coming from the same place for the last five minutes or so?

Because you were right before, her mind whispered. *There is no master.* This voice wasn't Ruth's or Goodwife Burlingame's, and it certainly wasn't what she thought of as her own voice (whatever *that* was); it was very young and very scared. And, like Ruth's voice, it was strangely familiar. *It's just a stray, out here on its own. It won't help you, Jessie. It won't help us.*

But that was maybe too gloomy an assessment. After all, she didn't *know* the dog was a stray, did she? Not for sure. And until she did, she refused to believe it. "If you don't like it, sue me," she said in a low, hoarse voice.

Meanwhile, there was the question of Gerald. In her panic and subsequent pain, he had kind of slipped her mind.

"Gerald?" Her voice still sounded dusty, not really there. She cleared her throat and tried again. "Gerald!"

Nothing. Zilch. No response at all.

That doesn't mean he's dead, though, so keep your fur on, woman— don't go off on another rip.

She *was* keeping her fur on, thank you very much, and she had no intention whatever of going off on another rip. All the same, she felt a deep, welling dismay in her vitals, a feeling that was like some awful homesickness. Gerald's lack of response didn't mean he was dead, that was true, but it *did* mean he was unconscious, at the very least.

And probably *dead,* Ruth Neary added. *I don't want to piss on your parade, Jess—really—but you don't hear him breathing, do you? I mean, you usually* can *hear unconscious people breathing; they take these big snory, blubbery snatches of air, don't they?*

"How the fuck would I know?" she said, but that was stupid. She knew because she had been an enthusiastic candystriper for most of her high school years, and it didn't take long for you to get a pretty good fix on what dead sounded like; it sounded like nothing at all. Ruth had known all about the time she had spent in Portland City Hospital—what Jessie herself had sometimes called The Bedpan Years—but this voice would have known it even if Ruth hadn't, because this voice wasn't *Ruth*; this voice was *her.* She had to keep reminding herself of that, because this voice was so weirdly its own self.

Like the voices you heard before, the young voice murmured. *The voices you heard after the dark day.*

But she didn't want to think about that. *Never* wanted to think about that. Didn't she have enough problems already?

But Ruth's voice was right: unconscious people—especially those who'd gotten unconscious as the result of a good hard rap on the noggin—usually *did* snore. Which meant . . .

"He's probably dead," she said in her dusty voice. "Okay, yeah."

She leaned to the left, moving carefully, mindful of the muscle which had cramped so painfully at the base of her neck on that side. She had not quite reached the farthest extent of the chain binding her right wrist when she saw one pink, chubby arm and half of one hand—the last two fingers, actually. It was his right hand; she knew this because there was no wedding ring on his third finger. She could see the white crescents of his nails. Gerald had always been very vain about his hands and his nails. She had never realized just *how* vain until right now. It was funny how little you saw, sometimes. How little you saw even after you thought you'd seen it all.

I suppose, but I'll tell you one thing, sweetie: right now you can pull down the shades, because I don't want to see any more. No, not one thing more. But refusing to see was a luxury in which she could not, at least for the time being, indulge.

Continuing to move with exaggerated care, babying her neck and shoulder, Jessie slid as far to the left as the chain would allow. It wasn't much—another two or three inches, tops—but it fattened the angle enough for her to see part of Gerald's upper arm, part of his right shoulder, and a tiny bit of his head. She wasn't sure, but she thought she could also see tiny beads of blood at the edges of his thinning hair. She supposed it was at least technically possible that this last was just imagination. She hoped so.

"Gerald?" she whispered. "Gerald, can you hear me? Please say you can."

No answer. No movement. She could feel that deep homesick dismay again, welling and welling, like an unstanched wound.

"Gerald?" she whispered again.

Why are you whispering? He's dead. The man who once surprised you with a weekend trip to Aruba—Aruba, of all places—and once wore your alligator shoes on his ears at a New Year's Eve party . . . that man is dead. So just why in the hell are you whispering?

"Gerald!" This time she screamed his name. "Gerald, wake up!"

The sound of her own screaming voice almost sent her into another panicky, convulsive interlude, and the scariest part wasn't Gerald's continued failure to move or respond; it was the realization that the panic was still there, still *right there*, restlessly circling her conscious mind as patiently as a predator might circle the guttering campfire of a woman who has somehow wandered away from her friends and gotten lost in the deep, dark fastnesses of the woods.

You're not lost, Goodwife Burlingame said, but Jessie did not trust that voice. Its control sounded bogus, its rationality only paint-deep. *You know just where you are.*

Yes, she did. She was at the end of a twisting, rutted camp road which split off from Bay Lane two miles south of here. The camp road had been an aisle of fallen red and yellow leaves over which she and Gerald had driven, and those leaves were mute testimony to the fact that this spur, leading to the Notch Bay end of Kashwakamak, had been used little or not at all in the three weeks since the leaves had first begun to turn and then to fall. This end of the lake was almost exclusively the domain of summer people, and for all Jessie knew, the spur might not have been used since Labor Day. It was a total of five miles, first along the spur and then along Bay Lane, before one came out on Route 117, where there were a few year-round homes.

I'm out here alone, my husband is lying dead on the floor, and I'm handcuffed to the bed. I can scream until I turn blue and it won't do me any good; no one's going to hear. The guy with the chainsaw is probably the closest, and he's at least four miles away. He might even be on the other side of the lake. The dog would probably hear me, but the dog is almost certainly a stray. Gerald's dead, and that's a shame—I never meant to kill him, if that's what I did—but at least it was relatively quick for him. It won't be quick for me; if no one in Portland starts to worry about us, and there's no real reason why anyone should, at least for awhile . . .

She shouldn't be thinking this way; it brought the panic-thing closer. If she didn't get her mind out of this rut, she would soon see the panic-thing's stupid, terrified eyes. No, she absolutely shouldn't be thinking this way. The bitch of it was, once you got started, it was very hard to stop again.

But maybe it's what you deserve—the hectoring, feverish voice of Goody Burlingame suddenly spoke up. *Maybe it is. Because you* did *kill him, Jessie. You can't kid yourself about that, because I won't let you. I'm sure he wasn't in very good shape, and I'm sure it would have happened sooner or later, anyway—a heart attack at the office, or maybe in the turnpike passing lane on his way home some night, him with a cigarette in his hand, trying to light it, and a big ten-wheeler behind him, honking for him to get the hell back over into the right-hand lane and make some room. But you couldn't wait for sooner or later, could you? Oh no, not you, not Tom Mahout's good little girl Jessie. You couldn't just lie there and let him shoot his squirt, could you? Cosmo Girl Jessie Burlingame says "No man chains me down." You had to kick him in the guts and the nuts, didn't you? And you had to do it while his thermostat was already well over the red line. Let's cut to the chase, dear: you murdered him. So maybe you deserve to be right here, handcuffed to this bed. Maybe—*

"Oh, that is such bullshit," she said. It was an inexpressible relief to hear that other voice—Ruth's voice—come out of her mouth. She sometimes (well . . . maybe *often* would be closer to the truth) hated the Goodwife voice; hated it and feared it. It was often foolish and flighty, she recognized that, but it was also so *strong*, so hard to say no to.

Goody was always eager to assure her she had bought the wrong dress, or that she had chosen the wrong caterer for the end-of-summer party Gerald threw each year for the other partners in the firm and their wives (except it was really Jessie who threw it; Gerald was just the guy who stood around and said aw shucks and took all the credit). Goody was the one who always insisted she had to lose

five pounds. That voice wouldn't let up even if her ribs were showing. *Never mind your ribs!* it screamed in tones of self-righteous
horror. *Look at your* tits, *old girl! And if they aren't enough to make
you barf a keg, look at your* thighs!

"Such *bullshit*," she said, trying to make it even stronger, but
now she heard a minute shake in her voice, and that wasn't so good.
Not so good at all. "He knew I was serious . . . he *knew* it. So
whose fault does that make it?"

But was that really true? In a way it was—she had seen him
deciding to reject what he saw in her face and heard in her voice
because it would spoil the game. But in another way—a much more
fundamental way—she knew it wasn't true at all, because Gerald
hadn't taken her seriously about much of anything during the last
ten or twelve years of their life together. He had made what almost
amounted to a second career out of not hearing what she said unless
it was about meals or where they were supposed to be at such-and-
such a time on such-and-such a night (so don't forget, Gerald). The
only other exceptions to the general Rules of Ear were unfriendly
remarks about his weight or his drinking. He heard the things she
had to say on these subjects, and didn't like them, but they were
dismissible as part of some mythic natural order: fish gotta swim,
bird gotta fly, wife gotta nag.

So what, exactly, had she expected from this man? For him to
say, Yes, dear, I will free you at once, and by the way, thanks for
raising my consciousness?

Yes; she suspected some naive part of her, some untouched and
dewy-eyed little-girl part, had expected just that.

The chainsaw, which had been snarling and ripping away again
for quite some time, suddenly fell silent. Dog, loon, and even the
wind had also fallen silent, at least temporarily, and the quiet felt
as thick and as palpable as ten years of undisturbed dust in an empty
house. She could hear no car or truck engine, not even a distant
one. And now the voice which spoke belonged to no one but herself.
Oh my God, it said. *Oh my God, I am all alone out here. I am all alone.*

3

 Jessie closed her eyes tightly. Six years ago she had spent an abortive five-month period in counselling, not telling Gerald because she knew he would be sarcastic . . . and probably worried about what beans she might be spilling. She had stated her problem as stress, and Nora Callighan, her therapist, had taught her a simple relaxation technique.

Most people associate counting to ten with Donald Duck trying to keep his temper, Nora had said, *but what a ten-count really does is give you a chance to re-set all your emotional dials . . . and anybody who doesn't need an emotional re-set at least once a day has probably got problems a lot more serious than yours or mine.*

This voice was also clear—clear enough to raise a small, wistful smile on her face.

I liked Nora. I liked her a lot.

Had she, Jessie, known that at the time? She was moderately astounded to find she couldn't exactly remember, any more than she could exactly remember why she had quit going to see Nora on Tuesday afternoons. She supposed that a bunch of stuff—Community Chest, the Court Street homeless shelter, maybe the new library fund drive—had just all come up at once. Shit Happens, as another piece of New Age vapidity passing for wisdom pointed out. Quitting had probably been for the best, anyway. If you didn't draw the line somewhere, therapy just went on and on, until you and your therapist doddered off to that great group encounter session in the sky together.

Never mind—go ahead and do the count, starting with your toes. Do it just the way she taught you.

Yes—why not?

One is for feet, ten little toes, cute little piggies, all in a row.

Except that eight were comically croggled and her great toes looked like the heads on a pair of ball-peen hammers.

Two is for legs, lovely and long.

Well, not *that* long—she was only five-seven, after all, and long-waisted—but Gerald had claimed they were still her best feature, at least in the old sex-appeal department. She had always been amused by this claim, which seemed to be perfectly sincere on his part. He had somehow missed her knees, which were as ugly as the knobs on an apple tree, and her chubby upper thighs.

Three is my sex, what's right can't be wrong.

Mildly cute—a little *too* cute, many might say—but not very illuminating. She raised her head a little, as if to look at the object in question, but her eyes remained closed. She didn't need her eyes to see it, anyway; she had been co-existing with that particular accessory for a long time. What lay between her hips was a triangle of ginger-colored, crinkly hair surrounding an unassuming slit with all the aesthetic beauty of a badly healed scar. This thing—this organ that was really little more than a deep fold of flesh cradled by crisscrossing belts of muscle—seemed to her an unlikely wellspring for myth, but it certainly held mythic status in the collective male mind; it was the magic vale, wasn't it? The corral where even the wildest unicorns were eventually penned?

"Mother Macree, what bullshit," she said, smiling a little but not opening her eyes.

Except it *wasn't* bullshit, not entirely. That slit was the object of every man's lust—the heterosexual ones, at least—but it was also frequently an object of their inexplicable scorn, distrust, and hate. You didn't hear that dark anger in all their jokes, but it was present in enough of them, and in some it was right out front, raw as a sore: *What's a woman? A life-support system for a cunt.*

Stop it, Jessie, Goodwife Burlingame ordered. Her voice was upset and disgusted. *Stop it right now.*

That, Jessie decided, was a damned good idea, and she turned her mind back to Nora's ten-count. Four was for her hips (too wide), and five her belly (too thick). Six was her breasts, which *she* thought were her best feature—Gerald, she suspected, was a bit put off by the vague tracings of blue veins beneath their smoothly sloping curves; the breasts of the gatefold girls in his magazines did not show such hints of the plumbing beneath. The magazine girls didn't have tiny hairs growing out of their areolae, either.

Seven was her too-wide shoulders, eight was her neck (which used to be good-looking but had grown decidedly chicken-y in the last few years), nine was her receding chin, and ten—

Wait a minute! Wait just one goddamned minute here! the no-bullshit voice broke in furiously. *What kind of dumb game is this?*

Jessie shut her eyes tighter, appalled by the depth of anger in that voice and frightened by its *separateness*. In its anger it didn't seem like a voice coming from the central taproot of her mind at all, but like a real interloper—an alien spirit that wanted to possess her the way the spirit of Pazuzu had possessed the little girl in *The Exorcist*.

Don't want to answer that? Ruth Neary—alias Pazuzu—asked. *Okay, maybe that one's too complicated. Let me make it really simple for you, Jess: who turned Nora Callighan's badly rhymed little relaxation litany into a mantra of self-hate?*

No one, she thought back meekly, and knew at once that the no-bullshit voice would never accept that, so she added: *The Goodwife. It was her.*

No, it wasn't, Ruth's voice returned at once. She sounded disgusted at this half-assed effort to shift the blame. *Goody's a little stupid and right now she's a lot scared, but she's a sweet enough thing at the bottom, and her intentions have always been good. The intentions of whoever re-edited Nora's list were actively evil, Jessie. Don't you see that? Don't you—*

"I don't see *anything*, because my *eyes* are closed," she said in a trembling, childish voice. She almost opened them, but something told her that was apt to make the situation worse instead of better.

Who was the one, Jessie? Who taught you that you were ugly and worthless? Who picked out Gerald Burlingame as your soulmate and Prince Charming, probably years before you actually met him at that Republican Party mixer? Who decided he wasn't only what you needed but exactly what you deserved?

With a tremendous effort, Jessie swept this voice—*all* the voices, she fervently hoped—out of her mind. She began the mantra again, this time speaking it aloud.

"One is my toes, all in a row, two is my legs, lovely and long, three is my sex, what's right can't be wrong, four is my hips, curving and sweet, five is my stomach, where I store what I eat." She couldn't remember the rest of the rhymes (which was probably a mercy; she had a strong suspicion that Nora had whomped them up herself, probably with an eye toward publication in one of the soft and yearning self-help magazines which sat on the coffee-table in her waiting room) and so went on without them: "Six is my breasts, seven's my shoulders, eight's my neck . . ."

She paused to take a breath and was relieved to find her heartbeat had slowed from a gallop to a fast run.

". . . nine is my chin, and ten is my eyes. Eyes, open wide!"

She suited the action to the words and the bedroom jumped into bright existence around her, somehow new and—for the moment, at least—almost as delightful as it had been to her when she and Gerald had spent their first summer in this house. Back in 1979, a year which once had the ring of science fiction and now seemed impossibly antique.

Jessie looked at the gray barnboard walls, the high white ceiling with its reflected shimmers from the lake, and the two big windows, one on either side of the bed. The one to her left looked west, giving a view of the deck, the sloping land beyond it, and the heartbreaking bright blue of the lake. The one on her right provided a less romantic vista—the driveway and her gray dowager of a Mercedes, now eight years old and beginning to show the first small speckles of rust along the rocker-panels.

Directly across the room she saw the framed batik butterfly hanging on the wall over the dresser, and remembered with a superstitious lack of surprise that it had been a thirtieth-birthday present from Ruth. She couldn't see the tiny signature stitched in red thread from over here, but she knew it was there: *Neary, '83.* Another science-fiction year.

Not far from the butterfly (and clashing like mad, although she had never quite summoned enough nerve to point this out to her husband), Gerald's Alpha Gamma Rho beer-stein hung from a chrome peg. Rho wasn't a very bright star in the fraternity universe—the other frat-rats used to call it Alpha Grab A Hoe— but Gerald wore the pin with a perverse sort of pride and kept the stein on the wall and drank the first beer of the summer out of it each year when they came up here in June. It was the sort of ceremony that had sometimes made her wonder, long before today's festivities, if she had been mentally competent when she married Gerald.

Somebody should have put a stop to it, she thought drearily. *Somebody really should have, because just look how it turned out.*

In the chair on the other side of the bathroom door, she could see the saucy little culotte skirt and the sleeveless blouse she had worn on this unseasonably warm fall day; her bra hung on the bathroom doorknob. And lying across the bedspread and her legs, turning the tiny soft hairs on her upper thighs to golden wires, was a bright band of afternoon sunlight. Not the square of light that lay almost dead center on the bedspread at one o'clock and not the rectangle which lay on it at two; this was a wide band that would soon narrow to a stripe, and although a power outage had buggered the readout of the digital clock-radio on the dresser (it flashed 12:00 A.M. over and over, as relentless as a neon bar-sign), the band of light told her it was going on four o'clock. Before long, the stripe would start to slide off the bed and she would see shadows in the corners and under the little table over by the wall. And as the stripe became a string, first slipping across the floor and then climbing up the far wall, fading as it went, those shadows would begin to creep out of their places and spread across the room like inkstains, eating the light as they grew. The sun was westering; in another hour, an hour and a half at most, it would be going down; forty minutes or so after that, it would be dark.

This thought didn't cause panic—at least not yet—but it did lay a membrane of gloom over her mind and a dank atmosphere of dread over her heart. She saw herself lying here, handcuffed to the bed with Gerald dead on the floor beside and below her; saw them lying here in the dark long after the man with the chainsaw had gone back to his wife and kids and well-lighted home and the dog had wandered away and there was only that damned loon out there on the lake for company—only that and nothing more.

Mr. and Mrs. Gerald Burlingame, spending one last long night together.

Looking at the beer-stein and the batik butterfly, unlikely neighbors which could be tolerated only in a one-season-a-year house such as this one, Jessie thought that it was easy to reflect on the past and just as easy (although a lot less pleasant) to go wandering off into possible versions of the future. The really tough job seemed to be staying in the present, but she thought she'd better try her best to do it. This nasty situation was probably going to get a lot nastier if she didn't. She couldn't depend on some *deus ex machina* to get her out of the jam she was in, and that was a bummer, but if she succeeded in doing it herself, there would be a bonus: she'd be saved the embarrassment of lying here almost starkers while some sheriff's deputy unlocked her, asked what the hell had happened, and got a nice long look at the new widow's fair white body, all at the same time.

There were two other things going on as well. She would have given a lot to push them away, even temporarily, but she couldn't. She needed to go to the bathroom, and she was thirsty. Right now the need to ship was stronger than the need to receive, but it was her desire for a drink of water that worried her. It wasn't a big deal yet, but that would change if she wasn't able to shuck the cuffs and get to a faucet. It would change in ways she didn't like to think of.

It'd be funny if I died of thirst two hundred yards from the ninth-

biggest lake in Maine, she thought, and then she shook her head. This wasn't the ninth-biggest lake in Maine; what had she been thinking of? That was Dark Score Lake, the one where she and her parents and her brother and sister had gone all those years ago. Back before the voices. Back before—

She cut that off. Hard. It had been a long time since she'd thought about Dark Score Lake, and she didn't intend to start now, handcuffs or no handcuffs. Better to think about being thirsty.

What's to think about, toots? It's psychosomatic, that's all. You're thirsty because you know you can't get up and get a drink. It's as simple as that.

But it wasn't. She'd had a fight with her husband, and the two swift kicks she'd dealt him had started a chain reaction which finally resulted in his death. She herself was suffering the after-effects of a major hormone-spill. The technical term for it was shock, and one of the commonest symptoms of shock was thirst. She should probably count herself lucky that her mouth was no drier than it was, at least so far, and—

And maybe that's one thing I can do something about.

Gerald was the quintessential creature of habit, and one of his habits was keeping a glass of water on his side of the shelf above the headboard of the bed. She twisted her head up and to the right and yes, there it was, a tall glass of water with a little cluster of melting ice-cubes floating on top. The glass was no doubt sitting on a coaster so it wouldn't leave a ring on the shelf—that was Gerald, so considerate about the little things. Beads of condensation stood out on the glass like sweat.

Looking at these, Jessie felt her first pang of real thirst. It made her lick her lips. She slid to the right as far as the chain on the left handcuff would allow. This was only six inches, but it brought her onto Gerald's side of the bed. The movement also exposed several dark spots on the left side of the coverlet. She stared at these vacantly for several moments before remembering how Gerald had voided his bladder in his last agony. Then she quickly turned her eyes back to the glass of water, sitting up there on a round of cardboard which probably advertised some brand of yuppie suds, Beck's or Heineken being the most likely.

She reached out and up, doing it slowly, willing her reach to be long enough. It wasn't. The tips of her fingers stopped three inches short of the glass. The pang of thirst—a slight tightening in the throat, a slight prickle on the tongue—came and went again.

If no one comes or I can't think of a way to wiggle free by tomorrow morning, I won't even be able to look at that glass.

This idea had about it a cold reasonableness that was terrifying in and of itself. But she *wouldn't* still be here tomorrow morning, that was the thing. The idea was totally ridiculous. Insane. Loopy. Not worth thinking about. It—

Stop, the no-bullshit voice said. *Just stop.* And so she did.

The thing she had to face was that the idea *wasn't* totally ridiculous. She refused to accept or even entertain the possibility that she could *die* here—that *was* loopy, of course—but she could be in for some long, uncomfortable hours if she didn't dust away the cobwebs on the old thinking machine and get it running.

Long, uncomfortable . . . and maybe painful, the Goodwife said nervously. *But the pain would be an act of atonement, wouldn't it? After all, you brought this on yourself. I hope I'm not being tiresome, but if you'd just let him shoot his squirt—*

"You *are* being tiresome, Goody," Jessie said. She couldn't remember if she had ever spoken out loud to one of the interior voices before. She wondered if she was going mad. She decided she didn't give much of a shit one way or the other, at least for the time being.

Jessie closed her eyes again.

4

This time it wasn't her body she visualized in the darkness behind her lids but this whole room. Of course she was still the centerpiece, gosh, yes—Jessie Mahout Burlingame, still a shade under forty, still fairly trim at five-seven and a hundred and twenty-five pounds, gray eyes, brownish-red hair (she covered the gray that had begun to show up about five years ago with a glossy rinse and was fairly sure Gerald had never known). Jessie Mahout Burlingame, who had gotten herself into this mess without quite knowing how or why. Jessie Mahout Burlingame, now presumably the widow of Gerald, still mother of no one, and tethered to this goddamned bed by two sets of police handcuffs.

She made the imaging part of her mind zoom in on these last. A furrow of concentration appeared between her closed eyes.

Four cuffs in all, each pair separated by six inches of rubber-sleeved steel chain, each with M-17—a serial number, she assumed—stamped into the steel of the lock-plate. She remembered Gerald's telling her, back when the game was new, that each cuff had a notched take-up arm, which made the cuff adjustable. It was also possible to shorten the chains until a prisoner's hands were jammed painfully together, wrist to wrist, but Gerald had allowed her the maximum length of chain.

And why the hell not? she thought now. *After all, it was only a game . . . right, Gerald?* Yet now her earlier question occurred to her, and she wondered again if it had ever really been just a game for Gerald.

What's a woman? some other voice—a UFO voice—whispered

softly from a well of darkness deep inside her. *A life-support system for a cunt.*

Go away, Jessie thought. *Go away, you're not helping.*

But the UFO voice declined the order. *Why does a woman have a mouth* and *a cunt?* it asked instead. *So she can piss and moan at the same time. Any other questions, little lady?*

No. Given the unsettlingly surreal quality of the answers, she had no other questions. She rotated her hands inside the cuffs. The scant flesh of her wrists dragged against the steel, making her wince, but the pain was minor and her hands turned easily enough. Gerald might or might not have believed that a woman's only purpose was to serve as a life-support system for a cunt, but he hadn't tightened the cuffs enough to hurt; she would have balked at that even before today, of course (or so she told herself, and none of the interior voices were mean enough to dispute her on the subject). Still, they were too tight to slip out of.

Or were they?

Jessie gave them an experimental tug. The cuffs slid up her wrists as her hands came down, and then the steel bracelets wedged firmly against the junctions of bone and cartilage where the wrists made their complex and marvellous alliances with her hands.

She yanked harder. Now the pain was much more intense. She suddenly remembered the time Daddy had slammed the driver's-side door of their old Country Squire station wagon on Maddy's left hand, not knowing she was sliding out on his side for a change instead of on her own. How she had screamed! It had broken some bone—Jessie couldn't remember the name of it—but she *did* remember Maddy proudly showing off her soft cast and saying, "I also tore my posterior ligament." That had struck Jess and Will funny, because everyone knew that your posterior was the scientific name for your situpon. They had laughed, more in surprise than in scorn, but Maddy had gone storming off just the same, her face as dark as a thundercloud, to tell Mommy.

Posterior ligament, she thought, deliberately applying more pressure in spite of the escalating pain. *Posterior ligament and radio-ulnar something-or-other. Doesn't matter. If you can slip out of these cuffs, I think you better do it, toots, and let some doctor worry about putting Humpty back together again later on.*

Slowly, steadily, she increased the pressure, willing the handcuffs to slip down and off. If they would just go a *little* way—a quarter of an inch might do it, and a half was almost for sure—she would be past the bulkiest ridges of bone and would have more yielding tissue to deal with. Or so she hoped. There were bones in her thumbs, of course, but she would worry about them when and if the time came.

She pulled down harder, her lips parting to show her teeth in a grimace of pain and effort. The muscles on her upper arms now stood out in shallow white arcs. Sweat began to bead her brow, her cheeks, even the slight indentation of her philtrum below her nose. She poked out her tongue and licked off this last without even being aware of it.

There was a lot of pain, but the pain wasn't what caused her to stop. What did was the simple realization that she had gotten to the point of maximum pull her muscles would provide and it hadn't moved the cuffs a whit farther down than they were right now. Her brief hope of simply squeezing out of this flickered and died.

Are you sure you pulled as hard as you could? Or are you maybe only kidding yourself a little because it hurt so much?

"No," she said, still not opening her eyes. "I pulled as hard as I could. Really."

But that other voice remained, actually more glimpsed than heard: something like a comic-book question-mark.

There were deep white grooves in the flesh of her wrists—below the pad of the thumb, across the back of the hand, and over the delicate blue tracings of vein below—where the steel had bitten in, and her wrists continued to throb painfully even though she had taken off all the pressure of the cuffs by raising her hands until she could grip one of the headboard slats.

"Oh boy," she said, her voice shaky and uneven. "Doesn't this just suck the big one."

Had she pulled as hard as she could? Had she *really?*

Doesn't matter, she thought, looking up at the shimmers of reflection on the ceiling. *Doesn't matter and I'll tell you why—if I am capable of pulling harder, what happened to Maddy's left wrist when the car door slammed on it is going to happen to both of mine: bones are going to break, posterior ligaments are going to snap like rubber bands, and radio-ulnar whojiggies are going to explode like clay pigeons in a shooting gallery. The only thing that would change is that, instead of lying here chained and thirsty, I'd be lying here chained, thirsty, and with a pair of broken wrists thrown into the bargain. They'd swell, too. What I think is this: Gerald died before he ever had a chance to climb into the saddle, but he fucked me good and proper just the same.*

Okay; what other options were there?

None, Goodwife Burlingame said in the watery tone of a woman who is just a teardrop away from breaking down completely.

Jessie waited to see if the other voice—Ruth's voice—would weigh in with an opinion. It didn't. For all she knew, Ruth was floating around in the office water-cooler with the rest of the loons. In any case, Ruth's abdication left Jessie to fend for herself.

So, okay, fend, she thought. *What are you going to do about the handcuffs, now that you've ascertained simply slipping out of them is impossible? What can you do?*

There are two handcuffs in each set—the young voice, the one she hadn't yet found a name for, spoke up hesitantly. *You've tried to slip out of the ones with your hands inside them and it didn't work . . . but what about the others? The ones hooked to the bedposts? Have you thought about them?*

Jessie pressed the back of her head into her pillow and arched her neck so she could look at the headboard and the bedposts. The fact that she was looking at these things upside down barely registered. The bed was smaller than a king or a queen but quite a bit larger than a twin. It had some sort of fancy name—Court Jester Size, maybe, or Chief Lady-in-Waiting—but she found it harder and harder to keep track of such things as she got older; she didn't know if you called that good sense or encroaching senility. In any case, the bed on which she now found herself had been just right for screwing but a little too small for the two of them to share comfortably through the night.

For her and Gerald that hadn't been a drawback, because they had slept in separate rooms, both here and in the Portland house, for the last five years. It had been her decision, not his; she had gotten tired of his snoring, which seemed to get a little worse every year. On the rare occasions when they had overnight guests down here, she and Gerald had slept together—uncomfortably—in this room, but otherwise they had shared this bed only when they had sex. And his snoring hadn't been the real reason she had moved out; it had just been the most diplomatic one. The real reason had been olfactory. Jessie had first come to dislike and then actually loathe the aroma of her husband's night-sweat. Even if he showered just before coming to bed, the sour smell of Scotch whisky began to creep out of his pores by two the next morning.

Until this year, the pattern had been increasingly perfunctory sex followed by a period of drowsing (this had actually become her favorite part of the whole business), after which he would shower and leave her. Since March, however, there had been some changes. The scarves and the handcuffs—particularly the latter—had seemed to exhaust Gerald in a way plain old missionary-style sex never had, and he often fell deeply asleep next to her, shoulder to shoulder. She didn't mind this; most of those encounters had been matinees, and Gerald smelled like plain old sweat instead of a weak Scotch and water afterward. He didn't snore much, either, come to think of it.

But all those sessions—all those matinees with the scarves and the handcuffs—were in the Portland house, she thought. *We spent most of July and some of August down here, but on the occasions when we had sex—there weren't many, but there were some—it was the plain old pot-roast-and-mashed-potatoes kind: Tarzan on top, Jane on the bottom. We never played the game down here until today. Why was that, I wonder?*

Probably it had been the windows, which were too tall and oddly cut for drapes. They had never gotten around to replacing the clear glass with reflective sheets, although Gerald had continued to talk about doing that right up to . . . well . . .

Right up until today, Goody finished, and Jessie blessed her tact. *And you're right—it probably* was *the windows, at least mostly. He wouldn't have liked Fred Laglan or Jamie Brooks driving in to ask on the spur of the moment if he wanted to play nine holes of golf and seeing him boffing Mrs. Burlingame, who just happened to be attached to the bedposts with a pair of Kreig handcuffs. Word on something like that would probably get around. Fred and Jamie are good enough fellows, I guess—*

A couple of middle-aged pukes, if you ask me, Ruth broke in sourly.

—but they're only human, and a story like that would have been too good not to talk about. And there's something else, Jessie . . .

Jessie didn't let her finish. This wasn't a thought she wanted to hear articulated in the Goodwife's pleasant but hopelessly prissy voice.

It was possible that Gerald had never asked her to play the game down here because he had been afraid of some crazy joker popping out of the deck. What joker? *Well,* she thought, *let's just say that there might have been a part of Gerald that really did believe a woman was just a life-support system for a cunt . . . and that some other part of him, one I could call "Gerald's better nature," for want of a clearer term, knew it. That part could have been afraid that things might get out of control. After all, isn't that just what's happened?*

It was a hard idea to argue with. If this didn't fit the definition of out of control, Jessie didn't know what did.

She felt a moment of wistful sadness and had to restrain an urge to look back toward the place where Gerald lay. She didn't know if she had grief in her for her late husband or not, but she *did* know that if it was there, this wasn't the time to deal with it. Still, it was nice to remember something good about the man with whom she had spent so many years, and the memory of the way he had sometimes fallen asleep beside her after sex was a good one. She hadn't liked the scarves and had come to loathe the handcuffs, but she had liked looking at him as he drifted off; had liked the way the lines smoothed out of his large pink face.

And, in a way, he was sleeping beside her again right now . . . wasn't he?

That idea chilled even the flesh of her upper thighs, where the narrowing patch of sun lay. She turned the thought aside—or at least tried to—and went back to studying the head of the bed.

The posts were set in slightly from the sides, leaving her arms spread but not uncomfortably so, particularly with the six inches or so of free play afforded by the handcuff chains. There were four horizontal boards running between the posts. These were also mahogany, and engraved with simple but pleasing wave-shapes. Gerald had once suggested that they have their initials carved in the center board—he knew of a man in Tashmore Glen who would be happy to drive over and do it, he said—but she had poured cold water on the idea. It seemed both ostentatious and strangely childish to her, like teenybop sweethearts carving hearts on their study-hall desks.

The bed-shelf was set above the topmost board, just high enough to ensure that no one sitting up suddenly would bump his or her head. It held Gerald's glass of water, a couple of paperbacks left over from the summer, and, on her end, a little strew of cosmetics. These were also left over from the summer gone by, and she supposed they were dried out by now. A real shame, too—nothing cheered up a handcuffed woman more reliably than a little Country Morning Rose Blusher. All the women's magazines said so.

Jessie lifted her hands slowly, holding her arms out at a slight angle so her fists wouldn't fetch up on the underside of the shelf. She kept her head back, wanting to see what happened on the far end of the chains. The other cuffs were clamped to the bedposts between the second and third crossboards. As she lifted her fisted hands, looking like a woman bench-pressing an invisible barbell, the cuffs slid along the posts until they reached the next board up. If she could pull that board off, and the one above it, she would be able to simply slip the handcuffs off the ends of the bedposts. *Voilà.*

Probably too good to be true, hon—too easy to be true—but you might as well give it a shot. It's a way to pass the time, anyway.

47

She wrapped her hands around the engraved horizontal board currently barring any further upward progress for the cuffs clamped to the bedposts. She took a deep breath, held it, and yanked. One hard tug was enough to tell her that way was also blocked; it was like trying to pull a steel retaining rod out of a concrete wall. She could not feel even a millimeter's worth of give.

I could yank on that bastard for ten years and not even move it, let alone pull it off the bedposts, she thought, and let her hands fall back to their former slack, chain-supported position above the bed. A despairing little cry escaped her. To her it sounded like the caw of a thirsty crow.

"What am I going to do?" she asked the shimmers on the ceiling, and at last gave way to desperate, frightened tears. "Just what in the hell am I going to *do?*"

As if in answer, the dog began to bark again, and this time it was so close it scared her into a scream. It sounded, in fact, as if it was right outside the east window, in the driveway.

5

he dog wasn't in the driveway; it was even closer than that. The shadow stretching up the asphalt almost to the front bumper of the Mercedes meant it was on the back porch. That long, trailing shadow looked as if it belonged to some twisted and monstrous freakshow dog, and she hated it on sight.

Don't be so damned silly, she scolded herself. *The shadow only looks that way because the sun's going down. Now open your mouth and make some noise, girl—it doesn't* have *to be a stray, after all.*

True enough; there might be a master in the picture somewhere, but she didn't hold out much hope for the idea. She guessed that the dog had been drawn to the back deck by the wire-covered garbage bin just outside the door. Gerald had sometimes called this tidy little construction, with its cedar shingles on top and its double latches on the lid, their raccoon-magnet. This time it had drawn a dog instead of a coon, that was all—a stray, almost certainly. An ill-fed, down-on-its-luck mutt.

Still, she had to try.

"*Hey!*" she screamed. "*Hey! Is anyone there? I need some help if you are! Is anyone there?*"

The dog stopped barking instantly. Its spidery, distorted shadow jerked, turned, started to move . . . and then stopped again. She and Gerald had eaten sub sandwiches on the ride up from Portland, big oily salami-and-cheese combos, and the first thing she'd done when they arrived was to gather up the scraps and wrappings and dump them into the garbage bin. The rich smell of oil and meat was probably what had drawn the dog in the first place, and it was undoubtedly the smell which kept it from bolting back into the woods at the sound of her voice. That smell was stronger than the impulses of its feral heart.

"*Help!*" Jessie screamed, and part of her mind tried to warn her that screaming was probably a mistake, that she would only scrape her throat raw and make herself thirstier, but that rational, cautioning voice never had a chance. She had caught the stink of her own fear, it was as strong and compelling to her as the smell of the sandwich leftovers was to the dog, and it quickly carried her into a state that was not just panic but a kind of temporary insanity. "*HELP ME! SOMEBODY HELP ME! HELP! HELP! HELLLLLLP!*"

Her voice broke at last and she turned her head as far to the right as it would go, her hair plastered to her cheeks and forehead in sweaty licks and tangles, her eyes bulging. The fear of being found chained up naked with her husband lying dead on the floor beside her had ceased to be even a casual factor in her thinking. This new panic-attack was like some weird mental eclipse—it filtered out the bright light of reason and hope and allowed her to see the most awful possibilities of all: starvation, thirst-induced madness, convulsions, death. She was not Heather Locklear or Victoria Principal, and this was not a made-for-TV suspense movie on the USA cable network. There were no cameras, no lights, no director to call cut. This was *happening,* and if help didn't come, it might well go on happening until she ceased to exist as a life-form. Far from worrying about the circumstances of her detention, she had reached a point where she would have welcomed Maury Povich and the entire film crew of *A Current Affair* with tears of gratitude.

But no one answered her frantic cries—no caretaker, down here to check on his places by the lake, no curious local out rambling with his dog (and perhaps trying to discover which of his neighbors might be growing a little marijuana among the whispering pines), and certainly not Maury Povich. There was only that long, queerly unpleasant shadow, which made her think of some weird dog-spider balancing on four thin and febrile legs. Jessie took a deep, shuddery breath and tried to re-establish control over her skittish mind. Her throat was hot and dry, her nose uncomfortably wet and plugged with tears.

What now?

She didn't know. Disappointment throbbed in her head, temporarily too large to allow anything like constructive thought. The only thing of which she was completely sure was that the dog meant nothing; it was only going to stand out there on the back porch for awhile and then go away when it realized that what had drawn it was out of reach. Jessie made a low, unhappy cry and closed her eyes. Tears oozed out from beneath her lashes and spilled slowly down her cheeks. In the late-afternoon sun, they looked like drops of gold.

What now? she asked again. The wind gusted outside, making the pines whisper and the loose door bang. *What now, Goodwife? What now, Ruth? What now, all you assorted UFOs and hangers-on? Any of you—any of us—got any ideas? I'm thirsty, I need to pee, my husband is dead, and my only company is a woods-dog whose idea of heaven is the leftovers of a Three-Cheese Genoa Salami sub from Amato's in Gorham. Pretty soon it's going to decide that the smell is as close to heaven as it's going to get, and then it will bug out. So . . . what now?*

No answers. All the interior voices had fallen silent. That was bad—they were company, at least—but the panic had also gone, leaving only its heavy-metal aftertaste, and that was good.

I'll sleep for awhile, she thought, amazed to find she could actually do just that if she wanted to. *I'll sleep for awhile, and when I wake up, maybe I'll have an idea. At the very least, I can get away from the fear for awhile.*

The tiny strain-lines at the corners of her closed eyes and the two more noticeable ones between her brows began to smooth out. She could feel herself beginning to drift. She let herself go toward that refuge from self-regard with feelings of relief and gratitude. When the wind gusted this time, it seemed distant, and the restless sound of the door was even farther away: *bang-bang, bang-bang, bang.*

Her breathing, which had been deepening and slowing as she slipped into a doze, suddenly stopped. Her eyes sprang open. The only emotion she was aware of in that first moment of sleep-snatched-away disorientation was a kind of puzzled pique: she had almost *made* it, damn it all, and then that damned door—

What about that damned door? Just what about it?

The damned door hadn't finished its usual double bang, that was what about it. As if this thought had brought them into being, Jessie now heard the distinctive click of a dog's toenails on the floor of the entryway. The stray had come in through the unlatched door. It was in the house.

Her reaction was instant and unequivocal. *"You get out!"* she screamed at it, unaware that her overstrained voice had taken on a hoarse foghorn quality. *"Get out, motherfucker! Do you hear me? YOU GET THE HELL OUT OF MY HOUSE!"*

She stopped, breathing fast, eyes wide. Her skin seemed woven through with copper wires carrying a low electrical charge; the top two or three layers buzzed and crawled. She was distantly aware that the hairs on the nape of her neck were standing as erect as porcupine quills. The idea of sleep had disappeared right off the map.

She heard the initial startled scrabble of the dog's nails on the entry floor . . . then nothing. *I must have scared it away. It probably scatted right out the door again. I mean, it's got to be afraid of people and houses, a stray like that.*

I dunno, toots, Ruth's voice said. It sounded uncharacteristically doubtful. *I don't see its shadow in the driveway.*

Of course you don't. It probably went right around the other side of the house and back into the woods. Or down by the lake. Scared to death and running like hell. Doesn't that make sense?

Ruth's voice didn't answer. Neither did Goody's, although at this point Jessie would have welcomed either one of them.

"I *did* scare it away," she said. "I'm sure I did."

But still she lay there, listening as hard as she could, hearing nothing but the hush-thump of blood in her ears. At least, not yet.

6

 She hadn't scared it away.

It *was* afraid of people and houses, Jessie had been right about that, but she had underestimated its desperate condition. Its former name—Prince—was hideously ironic now. It had encountered a great many garbage bins just like the Burlingames' in its long, starving circuit of Kashwakamak Lake this fall, and it had quickly dismissed the smell of salami, cheese, and olive oil coming from this one. The aroma was tantalizing, but bitter experience had taught the former Prince that the source of it was beyond its reach.

There were other smells, however; the dog got a whiff of them each time the wind lazed the back door open. These smells were fainter than the ones coming from the box, and their source was inside the house, but they were too good to ignore. The dog knew it would probably be driven off by shouting masters who chased and kicked with their strange, hard feet, but the smells were stronger than its fear. One thing might have countered its terrible hunger, but it as yet knew nothing of guns. That would change if it lived until deer-season, but that was still two weeks away and the shouting masters with their hard, hurtful feet were the worst things it could imagine for now.

It slipped through the door when the wind opened it and trotted into the entryway . . . but not too far. It was ready to beat a hasty retreat the instant danger threatened.

Its ears told it that the inhabitant of this house was a bitchmaster, and she was clearly aware of the dog because she had shouted at it, but what the stray heard in the bitchmaster's raised voice was fear, not anger. After its initial backward jerk of fright, the dog stood its ground. It waited for some other master to join its cries to those of the bitchmaster or to come running, and when this didn't happen, the dog stretched its neck forward, sniffing at the slightly stale air of the house.

At first it turned to the right, in the direction of the kitchen. It was from this direction that the puffs of scent dispersed by the flapping door had come. The smells were dry but pleasant: peanut butter, Ry-Krisp crackers, raisins, cereal (this latter smell was drifting from a box of Special K in one of the cupboards—a hungry fieldmouse had gnawed a hole in the bottom of the box).

The dog took a step in that direction, then swung its head back the other way to make sure no master was creeping up on it— masters most frequently shouted, but they could be sly, too. There was no one in the hallway leading down to the left, but the dog caught a much stronger scent coming from that direction, one that caused its stomach to cramp with terrible longing.

The dog stared down the hall, its eyes sparkling with a mad mixture of fear and desire, its snout wrinkled backward like a rumpled throw-rug, its long upper lip rising and falling in a nervous, spasmodic sneer that revealed its teeth in small white winks. A stream of anxious urine squirted from it and pattered on the floor, marking the front hall—and thus the whole house—as the dog's territory. This sound was too small and too brief for even Jessie's straining ears to catch.

What it smelled was blood. The scent was both strong and wrong. In the end, the dog's extreme hunger tipped the scales; it must eat soon or die. The former Prince began to walk slowly down the hall toward the bedroom. The smell grew stronger as it went. It was blood, all right, but it was the wrong blood. It was the blood of a master. Nevertheless, that smell, one far too rich and compelling to deny, had gotten into its small, desperate brain. The dog kept walking, and as it neared the bedroom door, it began to growl.

7

 Jessie heard the click of the dog's nails and understood it was indeed still in the house, and coming this way. She began to scream. She knew this was probably the worst thing a person could do—it went against all the advice she'd ever heard about never showing a potentially dangerous animal that you were afraid—but she couldn't help it. She had too good an idea of what was drawing the stray toward the bedroom.

She pulled her legs up, using the handcuffs to yank herself back against the headboard at the same time. Her eyes never left the door to the hallway as she did this. Now she could hear the dog growling. The sound made her bowels feel loose and hot and liquid.

It halted in the doorway. Here the shadows had already begun to gather, and to Jessie the dog was only a vague shape low to the floor—not a big one, but no toy poodle or Chihuahua, either. Two orange-yellow crescents of reflected sunlight marked its eyes.

"*Go away!*" Jessie screamed at it. "*Go away! Get out! You're . . . you're not welcome here!*" *That* was a ridiculous thing to say . . . but under the circumstances, what wasn't? *I'll be asking it to fetch me the keys from the top of the dresser before you know it,* she thought.

There was movement from the hindquarters of the shadowy shape in the doorway: it had begun to wag its tail. In some sentimental girl's novel, this probably would have meant the stray had confused the voice of the woman on the bed with the voice of some beloved but long-lost master. Jessie knew better. Dogs didn't just wag their tails when they were happy; they—like cats—also wagged them when they were indecisive, still trying to evaluate a situation. The dog had barely flinched at the sound of her voice, but it didn't quite trust the dim room, either. Not yet, at least.

The former Prince had yet to learn about guns, but it had learned a good many other hard lessons in the six weeks or so since the last day of August. That was when Mr. Charles Sutlin, a lawyer from Braintree, Massachusetts, had turned it out in the woods to die rather than take it back home and pay a combined state and town dog-tax of seventy dollars. Seventy dollars for a pooch which was nothing but a Heinz Fifty-seven was a pretty tall set of tickets, in Charles Sutlin's opinion. A little *too* tall. He had bought a motor-sailer for himself only that June, granted, a purchase that was well up in the five-figure range, and you could claim there was some fucked-up thinking going on if you compared the price of the boat and the price of the dog-tax—of course you could, *anybody* could, but that wasn't really the point. The point was that the motor-sailer had been a *planned* purchase. That particular acquisition had been on the old Sutlin drawing-board for two years or more. The dog, on the other hand, was just a spur-of-the-moment buy at a roadside vegetable stand in Harlow. He never would have bought it if his daughter hadn't been with him and fallen in love with the pup.

"That one, Daddy!" she'd said, pointing. "The one with the white spot on his nose—the one that's standing all by himself like a little prince." So he'd bought her the pup—no one ever said he didn't know how to make his little girl happy—but seventy bucks (maybe as much as a hundred if Prince was classified as a Class B, Larger Dog) was serious dough when you were talking about a mutt that had come without a single piece of paperwork. Too much dough, Mr. Charles Sutlin had decided as the time to close up the cottage on the lake for another year began to approach. Taking it back to Braintree in the back seat of the Saab would also be a pain in the ass—it would shed everywhere, might even puke or take a shit on the carpeting. He could buy it a Vari Kennel, he supposed, but those little beauts started at $29.95 and worked up from there. A dog like Prince wouldn't be happy in a kennel, anyway. He would be happier running wild, with the whole north woods for his kingdom. Yes, Sutlin had told himself on that last day of August as he parked on a deserted stretch of Bay Lane and then coaxed the dog out of the back seat. Old Prince had the heart of a happy wanderer—you only had to take a good close look at him to see that. Sutlin wasn't a stupid man and part of him knew this was self-serving bullshit, but part of him was also exalted by the *idea* of it, and as he got back into his car and drove off, leaving Prince standing at the side of the road and looking after him, he was whistling the theme from *Born Free*, occasionally bursting into a snatch of the lyrics: "Booorn freeee . . . to follow your *heaaaart*!" He had slept well that night, not sparing a thought for Prince (soon to be the former Prince), who spent the same night curled up beneath a fallen tree, shivering and wakeful and hungry, whining with fear each time an owl hooted or an animal moved in the woods.

Now the dog Charles Sutlin had turned out to the theme of *Born Free* stood in the doorway of the master bedroom of the Burlingame summer home (the Sutlin cottage was on the far side of the lake and the two families had never met, although they had exchanged casual nods at the town boat-dock over the last three or four summers). Its head was down, its eyes were wide, and its hackles were up. It was unaware of its own steady growl; all of its concentration was focused on the room. It understood in some deep, instinctual way that the blood-smell would soon overwhelm all caution. Before that happened, it must assure itself as completely as it could that this was not a trap. It didn't want to be caught by masters with hard, hurtful feet, or by those who picked up hard pieces of the ground and threw them.

"Go away!" Jessie tried to shout, but her voice came out sounding weak and trembly. She wasn't going to make the dog go away by shouting at it; the bastard somehow knew she couldn't get up off the bed and hurt it.

This can't be happening, she thought. *How could it be, when just three hours ago I was in the passenger seat of the Mercedes with my seatbelt around me, listening to the Rainmakers on the tape player and reminding myself to see what was playing at the Mountain Valley Cinemas, just in case we did decide to spend the night? How can my husband be dead when we were singing along with Bob Walkenhorst? "One more summer," we sang, "one more chance, one more stab at romance." We both know all the words to that one, because it's a great one, and that being the case, how can Gerald possibly be dead? How can things have possibly gotten from there to here? Sorry, folks, but this just has to be a dream. It's much too absurd for reality.*

The stray began to advance slowly into the room, legs stiff with caution, tail drooping, eyes wide and black, lips peeled back to reveal a full complement of teeth. About such concepts as absurdity it knew from nothing.

The former Prince, with whom the eight-year-old Catherine Sutlin had once romped joyfully (at least until she'd gotten a Cabbage Patch doll named Marnie for her birthday and temporarily lost some of her interest), was part Lab and part collie . . . a mixed breed, but a long way from being a mongrel. When Sutlin had turned it out on Bay Lane at the end of August, it had weighed eighty pounds and its coat had been glossy and sleek with health, a not unattractive mixture of brown and black (with a distinctive white collie bib on the chest and undersnout). It now weighed a bare forty pounds, and a hand passed down its side would have felt each straining rib, not to mention the rapid, feverish beat of its heart. One ear had been badly gashed. Its coat was dull and bedraggled and full of burdocks. A half-healed pink scar, souvenir of a panicky scramble under a barbed wire fence, zig-zagged down one haunch, and a few porcupine quills stuck out of its muzzle like crooked whiskers. It had found the porker lying dead under a log about ten days ago, but had given up on it after the first noseful of quills. It had been hungry but not yet desperate.

Now it was both. Its last meal had been a few maggoty scraps nosed out of a discarded garbage bag in a ditch running beside Route 117, and that had been two days ago. The dog which had quickly learned to bring Catherine Sutlin a red rubber ball when she rolled it across the living-room floor or into the hall was now quite literally starving on its feet.

Yes, but here—right here, on the floor, *within sight!*—were pounds and pounds of fresh meat, and fat, and bones filled with sweet marrow. It was like a gift from the God of Strays.

The onetime darling of Catherine Sutlin continued to advance on the corpse of Gerald Burlingame.

8

This isn't going to happen, Jessie told herself. *No way it can, so just relax.*

She went on telling herself this right up to the moment when the upper half of the stray's body was cut off from her view by the left side of the bed. Its tail began to wag harder than ever, and then there was a sound she recognized —the sound of a dog drinking from a puddle on a hot summer day.

Except it wasn't *quite* like that. This sound was rougher, somehow, not so much the sound of lapping as of *licking.* Jessie stared at the rapidly wagging tail, and her mind suddenly showed her what was hidden from her eyes by the angle of the bed. This homeless stray with its burdock-tangled fur and its weary, wary eyes was licking the blood out of her husband's thinning hair.

"*NO!*" She lifted her buttocks off the bed and swung her legs around to the left. "*GET AWAY FROM HIM! JUST GET AWAY!*" She kicked out, and one of her heels brushed across the raised knobs of the dog's spine.

It pulled back instantly and raised its muzzle, its eyes so wide they showed delicate rings of white. Its teeth parted, and in the fading afternoon light the cobweb-thin strands of saliva stretched between its upper and lower incisors looked like threads of spun gold. It lunged forward at her bare foot. Jessie yanked it back with a scream, feeling the hot mist of the dog's breath on her skin but saving her toes. She curled her legs under her again without being aware that she was doing it, without hearing the cries of outrage from the muscles in her overstrained shoulders, without feeling her joints roll reluctantly in their bony beds.

The dog looked at her a moment longer, continuing to snarl, threatening her with its eyes. *Let's have an understanding, lady,* the eyes said. *You do your thing and I'll do mine. That's the understanding. Sound okay to you? It better, because if you get in my way, I'm going to fuck you up. Besides, he's dead—you know it as well as I do, and why should he go to waste when I'm starving? You'd do the same. I doubt if you see that now, but I believe you may come around to my way of thinking on the subject, and sooner than you think.*

"*GET OUT!*" she screamed. Now she sat on her heels with her arms stretched out to either side, looking more like Fay Wray on the sacrificial jungle altar than ever. Her posture—head up, breasts thrust outward, shoulders thrown so far back they were white with strain at their farthest points, deep triangular hollows of shadow at the base of her neck—was that of an exceptionally hot pin-up in a girlie magazine. The obligatory pout of sultry invitation was missing, however; the expression on her face was that of a woman who stands very near the borderline between the country of the sane and that of the mad. *"GET OUT OF HERE!"*

The dog continued to look up at her and snarl for a few moments. Then, when it had apparently assured itself that the kick wouldn't be repeated, it dismissed her and lowered its head again. There was no lapping or licking this time. Jessie heard a loud smacking sound instead. It reminded her of the enthusiastic kisses her brother Will used to place on Gramma Joan's cheek when they went to visit.

The growling continued for a few seconds, but it was now oddly muffled, as if someone had slipped a pillowcase over the stray's head. From her new sitting position, with her hair almost brushing the bottom of the shelf over her head, Jessie could see one of Gerald's plump feet as well as his right arm and hand. The foot was shaking back and forth, as if Gerald were bopping a little to some jivey piece of music—"One More Summer" by the Rainmakers, for instance.

She could see the dog better from her new vantage point; its body was now visible all the way up to the place where its neck started. She would have been able to see its head, too, if it had been up. It wasn't, though. The stray's head was down, and its rear legs were stiffly braced. Suddenly there was a thick ripping sound —a *snotty* sound, like someone with a bad cold trying to clear his throat. She moaned.

"Stop . . . oh please, can't you stop?"

The dog paid no attention. Once it had sat up and begged for table scraps, its eyes appearing to laugh, its mouth appearing to grin, but those days, like its former name, were long gone and hard to find. This was now, and things were what they were. Survival was not a matter for politeness or apology. It hadn't eaten for two days, there was food here, and although there was also a master here who didn't want it to take the food (the days when there had been masters who laughed and patted its head and called it GOOD DOG and gave it scraps for doing its small repertoire of tricks were all gone), this master's feet were small and soft instead of hard and hurtful, and its voice said it was powerless.

The former Prince's growls changed to muffled pants of effort, and as Jessie watched, the rest of Gerald's body began to bop along with his foot, first just jiving back and forth and then actually starting to *slide*, as if he had gotten all the way into the groove, dead or not.

Get down, Disco Gerald! Jessie thought wildly. *Never mind the Chicken or the Shag—do the Dog!*

The stray couldn't have moved him if the rug had still been down, but Jessie had made arrangements to have the floor waxed the week after Labor Day. Bill Dunn, their caretaker, had let the men from Skip's Floors 'n More in and they had done a hell of a job. They had wanted the missus to fully appreciate their work the next time she happened to stop down, so they had left the bedroom rug rolled up in the entry closet, and once the stray got Disco Gerald moving on the glossy floor, he moved almost as easily as John Travolta in *Saturday Night Fever*. The only real problem the dog had was keeping its own traction. Its long, dirty claws helped in this regard, digging in and inscribing short, jagged marks into the glossy wax as it backed up with its teeth buried to the gumlines in Gerald's flabby upper arm.

I'm not seeing this, you know. None of this is really happening. Just a little while ago we were listening to the Rainmakers, and Gerald turned down the volume long enough to tell me that he was thinking about going up to Orono for the football game this Saturday. U. of M. against B.U. I remember him scratching the lobe of his right ear while he talked. So how can he be dead with a dog dragging him across our bedroom floor by the arm?

Gerald's widow's peak was in disarray—probably as a result of the dog's licking the blood out of it—but his glasses were still firmly in place. She could see his eyes, half-open and glazed, glaring up from their puffy sockets at the fading sunripples on the ceiling. His face was still a mask of ugly red and purple blotches, as if even death had not been able to assuage his anger at her sudden capricious (Had he seen it as capricious? Of course he had) change of mind.

"Let go of him," she told the dog, but her voice was now meek and sad and strengthless. The dog barely twitched its ears at the sound of it and didn't pause at all. It merely went on pulling the thing with the disarrayed widow's peak and the blotchy complexion. This thing no longer looked like Disco Gerald—not a bit. Now it was only Dead Gerald, sliding across the bedroom floor with a dog's teeth buried in its flabby biceps.

A frayed flap of skin hung over the dog's snout. Jessie tried to tell herself it looked like wallpaper, but wallpaper did not—at least as far as she knew—come with moles and a vaccination scar. Now she could see Gerald's pink, fleshy belly, marked only by the small-caliber bullet-hole that was his navel. His penis flopped and dangled in its nest of black pubic hair. His buttocks whispered along the hardwood boards with ghastly, frictionless ease.

Abruptly the suffocating atmosphere of her terror was pierced by a shaft of anger so bright it was like a stroke of heat-lightning inside her head. She did more than accept this new emotion; she welcomed it. Rage might not help her get out of this nightmarish situation, but she sensed that it would serve as an antidote to her growing sense of shocked unreality.

"You bastard," she said in a low, trembling voice. "You cowardly, slinking *bastard*."

Although she couldn't reach anything on Gerald's side of the bed-shelf, Jessie found that, by rotating her left wrist inside the handcuff so that her hand was pointing back over her shoulder, she could walk her fingers over a short stretch of the shelf on her own side. She couldn't turn her head enough to see the things she was touching—they were just beyond that hazy spot people call the corner of their eye—but it didn't really matter. She had a pretty good idea of what was up there. She pattered her fingers back and forth, running their tips lightly over tubes of make-up, pushing a few farther back on the shelf and knocking others off it. Some of these latter landed on the coverlet; others bounced off the bed or her left thigh and landed on the floor. None of them were even close to the sort of thing she was looking for. Her fingers closed on a jar of Nivea face cream, and for a moment she allowed herself to think it might do the trick, but it was only a sample-sized jar, too small and light to hurt the dog even if it had been made of glass instead of plastic. She dropped it back onto the shelf and resumed her blind search.

At their farthest stretch, her exploring fingers encountered the rounded edge of a glass object that was by far the biggest thing she had touched. For a moment she couldn't place it, and then it came to her. The stein hanging on the wall was only one souvenir of Gerald's Alpha Grab A Hoe days; she was touching another one. It was an ashtray, and the only reason she hadn't placed it immediately was because it belonged on Gerald's end of the shelf, next to his glass of icewater. Someone—possibly Mrs. Dahl, the cleaning lady, possibly Gerald himself—had moved it over to her side of the bed, maybe in the course of dusting the shelf, or maybe to make room for something else. The reason didn't matter, anyway. It was there, and right now that was enough.

Jessie closed her fingers over its rounded edge, feeling two notches in it—cigarette parking-spaces. She gripped the ashtray, drew her hand back as far as she could, then brought it forward again. Her luck was in and she snapped her wrist down at the instant the handcuff chain snubbed tight, like a big-league pitcher breaking off a curve. All of this was an act of pure impulse, the missile sought for, found, and thrown before she had time to ensure the failure of the shot by reflecting on how unlikely it was that a woman who had gotten a D in the archery mod of her two-year college phys ed requirement could possibly hit a dog with an ashtray, especially when the dog was fifteen feet away and the hand she was throwing with happened to be handcuffed to a bedpost.

Nevertheless, she *did* hit it. The ashtray flipped over once in its flight, briefly revealing the Alpha Gamma Rho motto. She couldn't read it from where she lay and didn't have to; the Latin words for service, growth, and courage were inscribed around a torch. The ashtray started to flip again but crashed into the dog's straining, bony shoulders before it could roll all the way over.

The stray gave a yip of surprise and pain, and Jessie felt a moment of violent, primitive triumph. Her mouth pulled wide in an expression that felt like a grin and looked like a screech. She howled deliriously, arching her back and straightening her legs as she did. She was once again unaware of the pain in her shoulders as cartilage stretched and joints which had long since forgotten the limberness of twenty-one were pressed almost to the point of dislocation. She would feel it all later—every move, jerk, and twist she had made —but for now she was transported with savage delight at the success of her shot, and felt that if she did not somehow express her triumphant delirium she might explode. She drummed her feet on the coverlet and rocked her body from side to side, her sweaty hair flailing her cheeks and temples, the tendons in her throat standing out like fat wires.

"*HAH!*" she cried. "*I . . . GOT . . . YOUUUU! HAH!*"

The dog jerked backward when the ashtray struck it, and jerked again when it bounced away and shattered on the floor. Its ears flattened at the change in the bitchmaster's voice. What it heard now was not fear but triumph. Soon it would get off the bed and begin to deal out kicks with its strange feet, which would not be soft but hard after all. The dog knew it would be hurt again as it had been hurt before if it stayed here; it must run.

It turned its head to make sure its path of retreat was still open, and the entrancing smell of fresh blood and meat struck it once more as it did so. The dog's stomach cramped, sour and imperative with hunger, and it whined uneasily. It was caught, perfectly balanced between two opposing directives, and it squirted out a fresh trickle of anxious urine. The smell of its own water—an odor that spoke of sickness and weakness instead of strength and confidence—added to its frustration and confusion, and it began to bark again.

Jessie winced back from that splintery, unpleasant sound—she would have covered her ears if she could—and the dog sensed another change in the room. Something in the bitchmaster's scent had changed. Her alpha-smell was fading while it was still new and fresh, and the dog began to sense that perhaps the blow it had taken across its shoulders did not mean that other blows were coming, after all. The first blow had been more startling than painful, anyway. The dog took a tentative step toward the trailing arm it had dropped . . . toward the entrancingly thick reek of mingled blood and meat. It watched the bitchmaster carefully as it moved. Its initial assessment of the bitchmaster as either harmless, helpless, or both might have been wrong. It would have to be very careful.

Jessie lay on the bed, now faintly aware of the throbbing in her own shoulders, more aware that her throat really hurt now, most aware of all that, ashtray or no ashtray, the dog was still here. In the first hot rush of her triumph it had seemed a foregone conclusion to her that it must flee, but it had somehow stood its ground. Worse, it was advancing again. Cautiously and warily, true, but advancing. She felt a swollen green sac of poison pulsing somewhere inside her—bitter stuff, hateful as hemlock. She was afraid that if that sac burst, she would choke on her own frustrated rage.

"Get out, shithead," she told the dog in a hoarse voice that had begun to crumble about the edges. "Get out or I'll kill you. I don't know how, but I promise to God I will."

The dog stopped again, looking at her with a deeply uneasy eye.

"That's right, you better pay attention to me," Jessie said. "You just better, because I mean it. I mean every word." Then her voice rose to a shout again, although it bled off into whispers in places as her overstrained voice began to short out. *"I'll kill you, I will, I swear I will, SO GET OUT!"*

The dog which had once been little Catherine Sutlin's Prince looked from the bitchmaster to the meat; from the meat to the bitchmaster; from the bitchmaster to the meat once more. It came to the sort of decision Catherine's father would have called a compromise. It leaned forward, eyes rolling up to watch Jessie carefully at the same time, and seized the torn flap of tendon, fat, and gristle that had once been Gerald Burlingame's right bicep. Growling, it yanked backward. Gerald's arm came up; his limp fingers seemed to point through the east window at the Mercedes in the driveway.

"Stop it!" Jessie shrieked. Her wounded voice now broke more frequently into that upper register where shrieks become gaspy

falsetto whispers. *"Haven't you done enough? Just leave him alone!"*

The stray paid no heed. It shook its head rapidly from side to side, as it had often done when it and Cathy Sutlin played tug-o'-war with one of its rubber toys. This, however, was no game. Curds of foam flew from the stray's jaws as it worked, shaking the meat off the bone. Gerald's carefully manicured hand swooped wildly back and forth in the air. Now he looked like a band-conductor urging his musicians to pick up their tempo.

Jessie heard that thick throat-clearing sound again and suddenly realized she had to vomit.

No, Jessie! It was Ruth's voice, and it was full of alarm. *No, you can't do that! The smell might bring it to you . . . bring it on you!*

Jessie's face knotted into a stressful grimace as she struggled to bring her gorge under control. The ripping sound came again and she caught just a glimpse of the dog—its forepaws were once again stiff and braced, and it seemed to stand at the end of a thick dark strip of elastic the color of a Ball jar gasket—before she closed her eyes. She tried to put her hands over her face, temporarily forgetting in her distress that she was cuffed. Her hands stopped still at least two feet apart from each other and the chains jingled. Jessie moaned. It was a sound that went beyond desperation and into despair. It sounded like giving up.

She heard that wet, snotty ripping sound once more. It ended with another big-happy-kiss smack. Jessie did not open her eyes.

The stray began to back toward the hall door, its eyes never leaving the bitchmaster on the bed. In its jaws was a large, glistening chunk of Gerald Burlingame. If the master on the bed meant to try and take it back, it would make its move now. The dog could not think—at least not as human beings understand that word—but its complex network of instincts provided a very effective alternative to thought, and it knew that what it had done—and what it was about to do—constituted a kind of damnation. But it had been hungry for a long time. It had been left in the woods by a man who had gone back home whistling the theme from *Born Free*, and now it was starving. If the bitchmaster tried to take away its meal now, it would fight.

It shot one final glance at her, saw she was making no move to get off her bed, and turned away. It carried the meat into the entry and settled down with it caught firmly between its paws. The wind gusted briefly, first breezing the door open and then banging it shut. The stray glanced briefly in that direction and ascertained in its doggy, not-quite-thinking way that it could push the door open with its muzzle and escape quickly if the need arose. With this last piece of business taken care of, it began to eat.

9

The urge to vomit passed slowly, but it did pass. Jessie lay on her back with her eyes pressed tightly shut, now beginning to really feel the painful throbbing in her shoulders. It came in slow, peristaltic waves, and she had a dismaying idea that this was only the beginning.

I want to go to sleep, she thought. It was the child's voice again. Now it sounded shocked and frightened. It had no interest in logic, no patience for cans and can'ts. *I was almost asleep when the bad dog came, and that's what I want now—to go to sleep.*

She sympathized wholeheartedly. The problem was, she didn't really feel sleepy anymore. She had just seen a dog tear a chunk out of her husband, and she didn't feel sleepy at all.

What she felt was *thirsty.*

Jessie opened her eyes and the first thing she saw was Gerald, lying on his own reflection in the highly polished bedroom floor like some grotesque human atoll. His eyes were still open, still staring furiously up at the ceiling, but his glasses now hung askew with one bow sticking into his ear instead of going over it. His head was cocked at such an extreme angle that his plump left cheek lay almost against his left shoulder. Between his right shoulder and right elbow there was nothing but a dark red smile with ragged white edges.

"Dear Jesus," Jessie muttered. She looked quickly away, out the west window. Golden light—it was almost sunset light now—dazzled her, and she shut her eyes again, watching the ebb and flow of red and black as her heart pushed membranes of blood through her closed lids. After a few moments of this, she noticed that the same darting patterns repeated themselves over and over again. It was almost like looking at protozoa under a microscope, protozoa on a slide which had been tinted with a red stain. She found this repeating pattern both interesting and soothing. She supposed you didn't have to be a genius to understand the appeal such simple repeating shapes held, given the circumstances. When all the normal patterns and routines of a person's life fell apart—and with such shocking suddenness—you had to find something you could hold onto, something that was both sane and predictable. If the organized swirl of blood in the thin sheaths of skin between your eyeballs and the last sunlight of an October day was all you could find, then you took it and said thank you very much. Because if you couldn't find *something* to hold onto, something that made at least some sort of sense, the alien elements of the new world order were apt to drive you quite mad.

Elements like the sounds now coming from the entry, for instance. The sounds that were a filthy, starving stray eating part of the man who had taken you to see your first Bergman film, the man who had taken you to the amusement park at Old Orchard Beach, coaxed you aboard that big Viking ship that swung back and forth in the air like a pendulum, then laughed until tears squirted out of his eyes when you said you wanted to go again. The man who had once made love to you in the bathtub until you were literally screaming with pleasure. The man who was now sliding down that dog's gullet in gobs and chunks.

Alien elements like that.

"Strange days, pretty mamma," she said. "Strange days indeed." Her speaking voice had become a dusty, painful croak. She supposed she would do well to just shut up and give it a rest, but when it was quiet in the bedroom she could hear the panic, still there, still creeping around on the big soft pads of its feet, looking for an opening, waiting for her to let down her guard. Besides, there *was* no real quiet. The chainsaw guy had packed it in for the day, but the loon still voiced its occasional cry and the wind was rising as night approached, banging the door more loudly—and more frequently—than ever.

Plus, of course, the sound of the dog dining on her husband. While Gerald had been waiting to collect and pay for their sub sandwiches in Amato's, Jessie had stepped next door to Michaud's Market. The fish at Michaud's was always good—almost fresh enough to flop, as her grandmother would have said. She had bought some lovely fillet of sole, thinking she would pan-broil it if they decided to stay overnight. Sole was good because Gerald, who would live on a diet of nothing but roast beef and fried chicken if left to his own devices (with the occasional order of deep-fried mushrooms thrown in for nutritional purposes), actually claimed to like sole. She had bought it without the slightest premonition that he would be eaten before he could eat.

"It's a jungle out there, baby," Jessie said in her dusty, croaky voice, and realized she was now doing more than just *thinking* in Ruth Neary's voice; she actually *sounded* like Ruth, who in their college days would have lived on a diet of nothing but Dewar's and Marlboros, if left to *her* own devices.

That tough no-bullshit voice spoke up then, as if Jessie had rubbed a magic lamp. *Remember that Nick Lowe song you heard on WBLM when you were coming home from your pottery class one day last winter? The one that made you laugh?*

She did. She didn't want to, but she did. It had been a Nick Lowe tune she believed had been titled "She Used to Be a Winner (Now She's Just the Doggy's Dinner)," a cynically amusing pop meditation on loneliness set to an incongruously sunny beat. Amusing as hell last winter, yes, Ruth was right about that, but not so amusing now.

"Stop it, Ruth," she croaked. "If you're going to freeload in my head, at least have the decency to quit teasing me."

Teasing you? Jesus, tootsie, I'm not teasing you; I'm trying to wake you up!

"I *am* awake!" she said querulously. On the lake the loon cried out again, as if to back her up on that. "Partly thanks to you!"

No, you're not. You haven't been awake—really awake—for a long time. When something bad happens, Jess, do you know what you do? You tell yourself, "Oh, this is nothing to worry about, this is just a bad dream. I get them every now and then, they're no big deal, and as soon as I roll over on my back again I'll be fine." And that's what you do, you poor sap. That's just what you do.

Jessie opened her mouth to reply—such canards should not go unanswered, dry mouth and sore throat or not—but Goodwife Burlingame had mounted the ramparts before Jessie herself could do more than begin to organize her thoughts.

How can you say such awful things? You're horrible! Go away!

Ruth's no-bullshit voice uttered its cynical bark of laughter again, and Jessie thought how disquieting—how *horribly* disquieting—it was to hear part of your mind laughing in the make-believe voice of an old acquaintance who was long gone to God knew where.

Go away? You'd like that, wouldn't you? Tootsie-Wootsie, Puddin' 'n Pie, Daddy's little girl. Any time the truth gets too close, any time you start to suspect the dream is maybe not just a dream, you run away.

That's ridiculous.

Is it? Then what happened to Nora Callighan?

For a moment that shocked Goody's voice—and her own, the one that usually spoke both aloud and in her mind as "I"—to silence, but in that silence a strange, familiar image formed: a circle of laughing, pointing people—mostly women—standing around a young girl with her head and hands in stocks. She was hard to see because it was very dark—it should still have been full daylight but was for some reason very dark, just the same—but the girl's face would have been hidden even if the day had been bright. Her hair hung over it like a penitent's shroud, although it was hard to believe

70

she could have done anything *too* horrible; she was clearly no more than twelve or so. Whatever it was she was being punished for, it couldn't be for hurting her husband. This particular daughter of Eve was too young to have even begun her monthly courses, let alone have a husband.

No, that's not true, a voice from the deeper ranges of her mind suddenly spoke up. This voice was both musical yet frighteningly powerful, like the cry of a whale. *She started when she was only ten and a half. Maybe that was the problem. Maybe he smelled blood, just like that dog out in the entry. Maybe it made him frantic.*

Shut up! Jessie cried. She felt suddenly frantic herself. *Shut up, we don't talk about that!*

And speaking of smells, what's that other one? Ruth asked. Now the mental voice was harsh and eager . . . the voice of a prospector who has finally stumbled onto a vein of ore he has long suspected but has never been able to find. *That mineral smell, like salt and old pennies—*

We don't talk about that, I said!

She lay on the coverlet, her muscles tense beneath her cold skin, both her captivity and her husband's death forgotten—at least for the time being—in the face of this new threat. She could feel Ruth, or some cut-off part of her for which Ruth spoke, debating whether or not to pursue the matter. When it decided not to (not directly, at least), both Jessie and Goodwife Burlingame breathed a sigh of relief.

All right—let's talk about Nora instead, Ruth said. *Nora, your* therapist? *Nora, your* counsellor? *The one you started to go see around the time you stopped painting because some of the paintings were scaring you? Which was also the time, coincidentally or not, when Gerald's sexual interest in you seemed to evaporate and you started sniffing the collars of his shirts for perfume? You remember Nora, don't you?*

Nora Callighan was a prying bitch! the Goodwife snarled.

"No," Jessie muttered. "She was well-intentioned, I don't doubt that a bit, she just always wanted to go one step too far. Ask one question too many."

You said you liked her a lot. Didn't I hear you say that?

"I want to stop thinking," Jessie said. Her voice was wavery and uncertain. "I especially want to stop hearing voices, and talking back to them, too. It's nuts."

Well, you better listen just the same, Ruth said grimly, *because you can't run away from this the way you ran away from Nora . . . the way you ran away from* me, *for that matter.*

I never ran away from you, Ruth! Shocked denial, and not very convincing. She had done just that, of course. Had simply packed her bags and moved out of the cheesy but cheerful dorm suite she and Ruth shared. She hadn't done it because Ruth had started asking her too many of the wrong questions—questions about Jessie's childhood, questions about Dark Score Lake, questions about what might have happened there during the summer just after Jessie started to menstruate. No, only a bad friend would have moved out for such reasons. Jessie hadn't moved out because Ruth *started* asking questions; she moved out because Ruth wouldn't *stop* asking them when Jessie asked her to do so. That, in Jessie's opinion, made *Ruth* a bad friend. Ruth had seen the lines Jessie had drawn in the dust . . . and had then deliberately stepped over them anyway. As Nora Callighan had done, years later.

Besides, the idea of running away under these conditions was pretty ludicrous, wasn't it? She was, after all, handcuffed to the bed.

Don't insult my intelligence, cutie-pie, Ruth said. *Your* mind *isn't handcuffed to the bed, and we both know it. You can still run if you want to, but my advice—my* strong *advice—is don't you do it, because I'm the only chance you've got. If you just lie there pretending this is a bad dream you got from sleeping on your left side, you're going to die in handcuffs. Is that what you want? Is that your prize for living your whole life in handcuffs, ever since—*

"I will not think about that!" Jessie screamed at the empty room.

For a moment Ruth was silent, but before Jessie could do more than begin to hope that she'd gone away, Ruth was back . . . and back *at* her, worrying her like a terrier worrying a rag.

Come on, Jess—you'd probably like to believe you're crazy rather than

dig around in that old grave, but you're really not, you know. I'm you,
the Goodwife's you . . . we're all you, as a matter of fact. I have a pretty
good idea of what happened that day at Dark Score when the rest of the
family was gone, and the thing I'm really curious about doesn't have a
lot to do with the events per se. *What I'm really curious about is this:*
is there a part of you—one I don't know about—that wants *to be sharing*
space with Gerald in that dog's guts come this time tomorrow? I only
ask because that doesn't sound like loyalty to me; it sounds like lunacy.

Tears were trickling down her cheeks again, but she didn't know
if she was crying because of the possibility—finally articulated—
that she actually *could* die here or because for the first time in at
least four years she had come close to thinking about that other
summer place, the one on Dark Score Lake, and about what happened there on the day when the sun went out.

Once upon a time she had almost spilled that secret at a women's
consciousness group . . . back in the early seventies that had been,
and of course attending that meeting had been her roomie's idea,
but Jessie had gone along willingly, at least to begin with; it had
seemed harmless enough, just another act in the amazing tie-dyed
carnival that was college back then. For Jessie, those first two years
of college—particularly with someone like Ruth Neary to tour her
through the games, rides, and exhibits—had been for the most part
quite wonderful, a time when fearlessness seemed usual and
achievement inevitable. Those were the days when no dorm room
was complete without a Peter Max poster and if you were tired of
the Beatles—not that anybody was—you could slap on a little Hot
Tuna or MC5. It had all been a little too bright to be real, like
things seen through a fever which is not quite high enough to be
life-threatening. In fact, those first two years had been a blast.

The blast had ended with that first meeting of the women's consciousness group. In there, Jessie had discovered a ghastly gray
world which seemed simultaneously to preview the adult future
that lay ahead for her in the eighties and to whisper of gloomy
childhood secrets that had been buried alive in the sixties . . . but
did not lie quiet there. There had been twenty women in the living

73

room of the cottage attached to the Neuworth Interdenominational Chapel, some perched on the old sofa, others peering out of the shadows thrown by the wings of the vast and lumpy parsonage chairs, most sitting cross-legged on the floor in a rough circle— twenty women between the ages of eighteen and fortysomething. They had joined hands and shared a moment of silence at the beginning of the session. When that was over, Jessie had been assaulted by ghastly stories of rape, of incest, of physical torture. If she lived to be a hundred she would never forget the calm, pretty blonde girl who had pulled up her sweater to show the old scars of cigarette burns on the undersides of her breasts.

That was when the carnival ended for Jessie Mahout. Ended? No, that wasn't right. It was as if she had been afforded a momentary glimpse *behind* the carnival; had been allowed to see the gray and empty fields of autumn that were the real truth: nothing but empty cigarette wrappers and used condoms and a few cheap broken prizes caught in the tall grass, waiting to either blow away or be covered by the winter snows. She saw that silent stupid sterile world waiting beyond the thin layer of patched canvas which was all that separated it from the razzle-dazzle brightness of the midway, the patter of the hucksters, and the glimmer-glamour of the rides, and it terrified her. To think that only this lay ahead for her, only this and nothing more, was awful; to think that it lay *behind* her as well, imperfectly hidden by the patched and tawdry canvas of her own doctored memories, was insupportable.

After showing them the bottoms of her breasts, the pretty blonde girl had pulled her sweater back down and explained that she could say nothing to her parents about what her brother's friends had done to her on the weekend her parents had gone to Montreal because it might mean that what her *brother* had been doing to her off and on all during the last year would come out, and her parents would never have believed *that*.

The blonde girl's voice was as calm as her face, her tone perfectly rational. When she finished there was a thunderstruck pause—a moment during which Jessie had felt something tearing loose inside her and had heard a hundred ghostly interior voices screaming in mingled hope and terror—and then Ruth had spoken.

"Why *wouldn't* they believe you?" she'd demanded. "Jesus, Liv —they burned you with *live cigarettes*! I mean, you had the burns as *evidence*! Why *wouldn't* they believe you? Didn't they love you?"

Yes, Jessie thought. *Yes, they loved her. But*—

"Yes," the blonde girl said. "They loved me. They still do. But they *idolized* my brother Barry."

Sitting beside Ruth, the heel of one not-quite-steady hand resting against her forehead, Jessie remembered whispering, "Besides, it would have killed her."

Ruth turned to her, began, "What—?" and the blonde girl, still not crying, still eerily calm, said: "Besides, finding out something like that would have killed my mother."

And then Jessie had known she was going to explode if she didn't get out of there. So she had gotten up, springing out of her chair so fast she had almost knocked the ugly, bulky thing over. She had sprinted from the room, knowing they were all looking at her, not caring. What they thought didn't matter. What mattered was that the sun had gone out, *the very sun itself*, and if she told, her story would be disbelieved only if God was good. If God was in a bad mood, Jessie *would* be believed . . . and even if it didn't kill her mother, it would blow the family apart like a stick of dynamite in a rotten pumpkin.

So she had run out of the room and through the kitchen and would have belted right on through the back door, except the back door was locked. Ruth chased after her, calling for her to stop, Jessie, stop. She had, but only because that damned locked door made her. She'd put her face against the cold dark glass, actually considering—yes, for just a moment she had—slamming her head right through it and cutting her throat, anything to blot out that awful gray vision of the future ahead and the past behind, but in the end she had simply turned around and slid down to the floor, clasping her bare legs below the hem of the short skirt she'd been wearing and putting her forehead against her upraised knees and closing her eyes. Ruth sat down beside her and put an arm around her, rocking her back and forth, crooning to her, stroking her hair, encouraging her to give it up, get rid of it, sick it up, let it go.

Now, lying here in the house on the shore of Kashwakamak Lake, she wondered what had happened to the tearless, eerily calm blonde girl who had told them about her brother Barry and Barry's friends—young men who had clearly felt a woman was just a life-support system for a cunt and that branding was a perfectly just punishment for a young woman who felt more or less okay about fucking her brother but not her brother's goodbuddies. More to the point, Jessie wondered what she had said to Ruth as they sat with their backs against the locked kitchen door and their arms around each other. The only thing she could remember for sure was something like "He never burned me, he never burned me, he never hurt me at all." But there must have been more to it than that, because the questions Ruth had refused to stop asking had all pointed clearly in just one direction: toward Dark Score Lake and the day the sun had gone out.

She had finally left Ruth rather than tell . . . just as she had left Nora rather than tell. She had run just as fast as her legs could carry her—Jessie Mahout Burlingame, also known as The Amazing Gingerbread Girl, the last wonder of a dubious age, survivor of the day the sun had gone out, now handcuffed to the bed and able to run no more.

"Help me," she said to the empty bedroom. Now that she had remembered the blonde girl with the eerily calm face and voice and the stipple of old circular scars on her otherwise lovely breasts, Jessie could not get her out of her mind, nor the knowledge that it hadn't been calmness, not at all, but some fundamental disconnection from the terrible thing that had happened to her. Somehow the blonde girl's face became *her* face, and when Jessie spoke, she did so in the shaking, humbled voice of an atheist who has been stripped of everything but one final longshot prayer. "Please help me."

It wasn't God who answered but the part of her which apparently could speak only while masquerading as Ruth Neary. The voice now sounded gentle . . . but not very hopeful. *I'll try, but you have to help me. I know you're willing to do painful things, but you may have to think painful thoughts, too. Are you ready for that?*

"This isn't about *thinking*," Jessie said shakily, and thought: *So that's what Goodwife Burlingame sounds like out loud.* "It's about . . . well . . . *escaping*."

And you may have to muzzle her, Ruth said. *She's a valid part of you, Jessie—of us—and not really a bad person, but she's been left to run the whole show for far too long, and in a situation like this, her way of dealing with the world is not much good. Do you want to argue the point?*

Jessie didn't want to argue that point or any other. She was too tired. The light falling through the west window was growing steadily hotter and redder as sunset approached. The wind gusted, sending leaves rattling along the lakeside deck, which was empty now; all the deck furniture had been stacked in the living room. The pines soughed; the back door banged; the dog paused, then resumed its noisome smacking and ripping and chewing.

"I'm so thirsty," she said mournfully.

Okay, then—that's where we ought to start.

She turned her head the other way until she felt the last warmth of the sun on the left side of her neck and the damp hair stuck to her cheek, and then she opened her eyes again. She found herself staring directly at Gerald's glass of water, and her throat immediately sent out a parched, imperative cry.

Let's begin this phase of operations by forgetting about the dog, Ruth said. *The dog is just doing what it has to do to get along, and you've got to do the same.*

"I don't know if I *can* forget it," Jessie said.

I think you can, toots—I really do. If you could sweep what happened on the day the sun went out under the rug, I guess you can sweep anything under the rug.

For a moment she almost had it all, and understood she *could* have it all, if she really wanted to. The secret of that day had never been completely sunk in her subconscious, as such secrets were in the TV soap-operas and the movie melodramas; it had been buried in a shallow grave, at best. There had been some selective amnesia, but of a completely voluntary sort. If she wanted to remember what had happened on the day the sun had gone out, she thought she probably could.

As if this idea had been an invitation, her mind's eye suddenly saw a vision of heartbreaking clarity: a pane of glass held in a pair of barbecue tongs. A hand wearing an oven-mitt was turning it this way and that in the smoke of a small sod fire.

Jessie stiffened on the bed and willed the image away.

Let's get one thing straight, she thought. She supposed it was the Ruth-voice she was speaking to, but wasn't completely sure; she wasn't really sure of anything anymore. *I* don't *want* to remember. *Got it? The events of that day have nothing to do with the events of this one. They're apples and oranges. It's easy enough to understand the connections—two lakes, two summer houses, two cases of*

(*secrets silence hurt harm*)

sexual hanky-panky—but remembering what happened in 1963 can't do a thing for me now except add to my general misery. So let's just drop that whole subject, okay? Let's forget Dark Score Lake.

"What do you say, Ruth?" she asked in a low voice, and her gaze shifted to the batik butterfly across the room. For just a moment there was another image—a little girl, somebody's sweet little Punkin, smelling the sweet aroma of aftershave and looking up into the sky through a piece of smoked glass—and then it was mercifully gone.

She looked at the butterfly for a few moments longer, wanting to make sure those old memories were going to *stay* gone, and then she looked back at Gerald's glass of water. Incredibly, there were still a few slivers of ice floating on top, although the darkening room continued to hold the heat of the afternoon sun and would for awhile longer.

Jessie let her gaze drift down the glass, let it embrace those chilly bubbles of condensation standing on it. She couldn't actually see the coaster on which the glass stood—the shelf cut it off—but she didn't have to see it to visualize the dark, spreading ring of moisture forming on it as those cool beads of condensate continued to trickle down the sides of the glass and pool around it at the bottom.

Jessie's tongue slipped out and swiped across her upper lip, not imparting much moisture.

I want a drink! the scared, demanding voice of the child—of somebody's sweet little Punkin—yelled. *I want it and I want it right . . . NOW!*

But she couldn't reach the glass. It was a clear-cut case of so near and yet so far.

Ruth: *Don't give up so easy—if you could hit the goddam dog with an ashtray, tootsie, maybe you can get the glass. Maybe you can.*

Jessie raised her right hand again, straining as hard as her throbbing shoulder would allow, and still came up at least two and a half inches short. She swallowed, grimacing at the sandpapery jerk and clench of her throat.

"See?" she asked. "Are you happy now?"

Ruth didn't reply, but Goody did. She spoke up softly, almost apologetically, inside Jessie's head. *She said* get *it, not* reach *it. They . . . they might not be the same thing.* Goody laughed in an embarrassed who-am-I-to-stick-my-oar-in way, and Jessie had a moment to think again how surpassingly odd it was to feel a part of yourself laughing like that, as if it really were an entirely separate entity. *If I had a few more voices,* Jessie thought, *we could have a goddam bridge tournament in here.*

She looked at the glass a moment longer, then let herself flop back down on the pillows so she could study the underside of the shelf. It wasn't attached to the wall, she saw; it lay on four steel brackets that looked like upside-down capital L's. And the shelf wasn't attached to *them*, either—she was sure of it. She remembered once when Gerald had been talking on the phone, and had absentmindedly attempted to lean on the shelf. Her end had started to come up, levitating like the end of a seesaw, and if Gerald hadn't snatched his hand away immediately, he would have flipped the shelf like a tiddlywink.

The thought of the telephone distracted her for a moment, but *only* a moment. It sat on the low table in front of the east window, the one with its scenic view of the driveway and the Mercedes, and it might as well have been on another planet, for all the good it could do in her current situation. Her eyes returned to the underside of the shelf, first studying the plank itself and then scanning the L-shaped brackets again.

When Gerald leaned on his end, *her* end had tilted. If she exerted enough pressure on her end to tilt *his*, the glass of water . . .

"It might slide down," she said in a hoarse, musing voice. "It might slide down to my end." Of course it might also go sliding gaily right past her to shatter on the floor, and it might bang into some unseen obstacle up there and overturn before it ever got to her, but it was worth trying, wasn't it?

Sure, I guess so, she thought. *I mean, I was planning to fly to New York in my Learjet—eat at Four Seasons, dance the night away at Birdland—but with Gerald dead I guess that would be a little tacky. And with all the good books currently out of reach—all the bad ones, too, as far as that goes—I guess I might as well try for the consolation prize.*

All right; how was she supposed to go about it?

"Very carefully," she said. *"That's* how."

She used the handcuffs to pull herself up again and studied the glass some more. Not being able to actually see the surface of the shelf now struck her as a drawback. She had a pretty good idea of what was on her end, but was less sure about Gerald's and the no-man's-land in the middle. Of course it wasn't surprising; who but someone with an eidetic memory could reel off a complete inventory of the items on a bedroom shelf? Who would have ever thought such things could matter?

Well, they matter now. I'm living in a world where all the perspectives have changed.

Yes indeed. In this world a stray dog could be scarier than Freddy Krueger, the phone was in the Twilight Zone, the sought-for desert oasis, goal of a thousand grizzled Foreign Legionnaires in a hundred desert romances, was a glass of water with a few last slivers of ice floating on top. In this new world order, the bedroom shelf had become a shipping lane as vital as the Panama Canal and an old paperback western or mystery in the wrong place could become a lethal roadblock.

Don't you think you're exaggerating a little? she asked herself uneasily, but in truth she did not. This would be a long-odds operation under the best of circumstances, but if there was junk on the runway, forget it. A single skinny Hercule Poirot—or one of the *Star Trek* novels Gerald read and then dropped like used napkins— wouldn't show above the angle of the shelf, but it would be more than enough to stop or overturn the water-glass. No, she wasn't exaggerating. The perspectives of this world really *had* changed, and enough to make her think of that science fiction movie where the hero started to shrink and went on getting smaller until he was living in his daughter's dollhouse and going in fear of the family cat. She was going to learn the new rules in a hurry . . . learn them and live by them.

Don't lose your courage, Jessie, Ruth's voice whispered.

"Don't worry," she said. "I'm going to try—I really am. But sometimes it's good to know what you're up against. I think sometimes that makes a difference."

She rotated her right wrist outward from her body as far as it would go, then raised her arm. In this position she looked like a woman-shape in a line of Egyptian hieroglyphs. She began to patter her fingers on the shelf again, feeling for obstructions along the stretch where she hoped the glass would finish up.

She touched a piece of fairly heavy-gauge paper and thumbed it for a moment, trying to think what it might be. Her first guess was a sheet from the note-pad that usually hid in the clutter on the telephone table, but it wasn't thin enough for that. Her eye happened on a magazine—either *Time* or *Newsweek*, Gerald had brought both along—lying face-down beside the phone. She remembered him thumbing rapidly through one of the magazines while he took off his socks and unbuttoned his shirt. The piece of paper on the shelf was probably one of those annoying blow-in subscription cards with which the newsstand copies of magazines are always loaded. Gerald often laid such cards aside for later use as bookmarks. It might be something else, but Jessie decided it didn't matter to her plans in any case. It wasn't solid enough to stop the glass or overturn it. There was nothing else up there, at least within reach of her stretching, wriggling fingers.

"Okay," Jessie said. Her heart had started to pound hard. Some sadistic pirate broadcaster in her mind tried to transmit a picture of the glass tumbling off the shelf and she immediately blocked the image out. "Easy; easy does it. Slow and easy wins the race. I hope."

Holding her right hand where it was, although bending it away from her body in that direction didn't work very well and hurt like the devil, Jessie raised her left hand (*My ashtray-throwing hand,* she thought with a grim glint of humor) and gripped the shelf with it well beyond the last supporting bracket on her side of the bed.

Here we go, she thought, and began to exert downward pressure with her left hand. Nothing happened.

I'm probably pulling too close to that last bracket to get enough leverage. The problem is the goddam handcuff chain. I don't have enough slack to get as far out on the shelf as I need to be.

Probably true, but the insight didn't change the fact that she wasn't doing a thing to the shelf with her left hand where it was. She would have to spider her fingers out a little farther—if she could, that was—and hope it would be enough. It was funnybook physics, simple but deadly. The irony was that she could reach *under* the shelf and push it *up* any time she liked. There was one small problem with that, however—it would tip the glass the wrong way, off Gerald's end and onto the floor. When you considered it closely, you saw that the situation really did have its amusing side; it was like an *America's Funniest Home Videos* segment sent in from hell.

Suddenly the wind dropped and the sounds from the entry seemed very loud. "*Are you enjoying him, shithead?*" Jessie screamed. Pain ripped at her throat, but she didn't—couldn't—stop. "*I hope so, because the first thing I'm going to do when I get out of these cuffs is blow your head off!*"

Big talk, she thought. *Very big talk for a woman who no longer even remembers if Gerald's old shotgun—the one that belonged to his dad— is here or in the attic of the Portland house.*

Nevertheless, there was a gratifying moment of silence from the shadowy world beyond the bedroom door. It was almost as if the dog were giving this threat its soberest, most thoughtful consideration.

Then the smackings and chewings began again.

Jessie's right wrist twanged warningly, threatening to cramp up, warning her that she had better get on with her business right away . . . if she actually had any business to do, that was.

She leaned to the left and stretched her hand as far as the chain would allow. Then she began to put the pressure on the shelf again. At first there was nothing. She pulled harder, eyes slitted almost shut, the corners of her mouth turned down. It was the face of a child who expects a dose of bad medicine. And, just before she reached the maximum downward pressure her aching arm muscles could exert, she felt a tiny shift in the board, a change in the uniform drag of gravity so minute that it was more intuited than actually sensed.

Wishful thinking, Jess—that's all you felt. Only that and nothing more.

No. It was the input of senses which had been jacked into the stratosphere by terror, perhaps, but it wasn't wishful thinking.

She let go of the shelf and just lay there for a few moments, taking long slow breaths and letting her muscles recover. She didn't want them spasming or cramping up at the critical moment; she had quite enough problems without that, thanks. When she thought she felt as ready as she *could* feel, she curled her left fist loosely around the bedpost and slid it up and down until the sweat on her palm dried and the mahogany squeaked. Then she stretched out her arm and gripped the shelf again. It was time.

Got to be careful, though. The shelf moved, no question about that, and it'll move more, but it's going to take all my strength to get that glass in motion . . . if I can do it at all, that is. And when a person gets near the end of their strength, control gets spotty.

That was true, but it wasn't the kicker. The kicker was this: she had no feel for the shelf's tip-point. Absolutely none at all.

Jessie remembered seesawing with her sister Maddy on the playground behind Falmouth Grammar School—they had come back early from the lake one summer and it seemed to her she had spent that whole August going up and down on those paint-peeling teeterboards with Maddy as her partner—and how they had been able to balance perfectly whenever they felt like it. All it took was for Maddy, who weighed a little more, to move a butt's length in toward the middle. Long hot afternoons of practice, singing jump-rope songs to each other as they went up and down, had enabled them to find each seesaw's tip-point with an almost scientific exactitude; those half a dozen warped green boards standing in a row on the sizzling hot-top had seemed almost like living things to them. She felt none of that eager liveliness under her fingers now. She would simply have to try her best and hope it was good enough.

And whatever the Bible may say to the contrary, don't let your left hand forget what your right hand is supposed to be doing. Your left may be your ashtray-throwing hand, but your right had better be your glass-catching hand, Jessie. There's only a few inches of shelf where you'll have a chance to get hold of it. If it slides past that area, it won't matter if it stays up—it'll be as out of reach as it is right now.

Jessie didn't think she *could* forget what her right hand was doing—it hurt too much. Whether or not it would be able to do what she needed it to do was another question entirely, though. She increased the pressure on the left side of the shelf as steadily and as gradually as she could. A stinging drop of sweat ran into the corner of one eye and she blinked it away. Somewhere the back door was banging again, but it had joined the telephone in that other universe. Here there was only the glass, the shelf, and Jessie. Part of her expected the shelf to come up all at once like a brutal Jack-in-the-box, catapulting everything off, and she tried to steel herself against the possible disappointment.

Worry about that if it happens, toots. In the meantime, don't lose your concentration. I think something's happening.

Something was. She could feel that minute shift again—that feel of the shelf starting to come unanchored at some point along Gerald's side. This time Jessie didn't let up her pressure but increased it, the muscles in her upper left arm standing out in hard little arcs that trembled with strain. She voiced a series of small explosive grunts. That sense of the shelf coming unanchored grew steadily stronger.

And suddenly the flat circular surface of the water in Gerald's glass was a tilted plane and she heard the last slivers of ice chatter faintly as the right end of the board actually did come up. The glass itself did not move, however, and a horrible thought occurred to her: what if some of the water trickling down the sides of the glass had seeped beneath the cardboard coaster on which it sat? What if it had formed a seal, bonding it to the shelf?

"No that can't happen." The words came out in a single whispered blurt, like a tired child's rote prayer. She pulled down harder on the left end of the shelf, using all her strength. Every last horse was now running in harness; the stable was empty. "Please don't *let* it happen. *Please.*"

Gerald's end of the shelf continued to rise, its end wavering wildly. A tube of Max Factor blush spilled off Jessie's end and landed on the floor near the place where Gerald's head had lain before the dog had come along and dragged him away from the bed. And now a new possibility—more of a probability, actually—occurred to her. If she increased the angle of the shelf much more, it would simply slide down the line of L-brackets, glass and all, like a toboggan going down a snowy hill. Thinking of the shelf as a seesaw could get her into trouble. It *wasn't* a seesaw; there was no central pivot-point to which it was attached.

"Slide, you bastard!" she screamed at the glass in a high, breathy voice. She had forgotten Gerald; had forgotten she was thirsty; had forgotten everything but the glass, now tilted at an angle so acute that water was almost slopping over the rim and she couldn't un-

derstand why it didn't simply fall over. It didn't, though; it just went on standing where it had stood all along, as if it had been glued to the spot. *"Slide!"*

Suddenly it did.

Its movement ran so counter to her black imaginings that she was almost unable to understand what was happening. Later it would occur to her that the adventure of the sliding glass suggested something less than admirable about her own mindset: she had in some fashion or other been prepared for failure. It was success which left her shocked and gaping.

The short, smooth journey of the glass down the shelf toward her right hand so stunned her that Jessie almost pulled harder with her left, a move that almost certainly would have overbalanced the precariously tilted shelf and sent it crashing to the floor. Then her fingers were actually touching the glass, and she screamed again. It was the wordless, delighted shriek of a woman who has just won the lottery.

The shelf wavered, began to slip, then paused, as if it had a rudimentary mind of its own and was considering whether or not it really wanted to do this.

Not much time, toots, Ruth warned. *Grab the goddam thing while the grabbing's good.*

Jessie tried, but the pads of her fingers only slid along the slick wet surface of the glass. There was nothing to grab, it seemed, and she couldn't get quite enough finger-surface on the thrice-damned thing to grip. Water sloshed onto her hand, and now she sensed that even if the shelf held, the glass would soon tip over.

Imagination, toots—just the old idea that a sad little Punkin like you can never do anything right.

That wasn't far from the mark—it was certainly too close for comfort—but it wasn't *on* the mark, not this time. The glass *was* getting ready to tip over, it really was, and she didn't have the slightest idea of what she could do to prevent that from happening. Why did she have to have such short, stubby, ugly fingers? *Why?* If only she could get them a little farther around the glass . . .

A nightmare image from some old TV commercial occurred to

her: a smiling woman in a fifties hairdo with a pair of blue rubber gloves on her hands. *So flexible you can pick up a dime!* the woman was screaming through her smile. *Too bad you don't have a pair, little Punkin or Goodwife or whoever the hell you are! Maybe you could get that fucking glass before everything on the goddam shelf takes the express elevator!*

Jessie suddenly realized the smiling, screaming woman in the Playtex rubber gloves was her mother, and a dry sob escaped her.

Don't give up, Jessie! Ruth yelled. *Not yet! You're close! I swear you are!*

She exerted the last tiny scrap of her strength on the left side of the shelf, praying incoherently that it wouldn't slide—not yet, *Oh please God or whoever You are, please don't let it slide, not now, not yet.*

The board *did* slide . . . but only a little. Then it held again, perhaps temporarily snagged on a splinter or balked by a warp in the wood. The glass slid a little farther into her hand, and now—crazier and crazier—*it* seemed to be talking, too, the goddam *glass.* It sounded like one of those grizzled big-city cab-drivers who have a perpetual hard-on against the world: *Jesus, lady, what else ya want me to do? Grow myself a goddam handle and turn into a fuckin pitcher forya?* A fresh trickle of water fell on Jessie's straining right hand. Now the glass would fall; now it was inevitable. In her mind she could already feel the freeze as icewater doused the back of her neck.

"*No!*"

She twisted her right shoulder a little farther, opened her fingers a little wider, let the glass slide a tiny bit deeper into the straining pocket of her hand. The cuff was digging into the back of that hand, sending jabs of pain all the way up to her elbow, but Jessie ignored them. The muscles of her left arm were twanging wildly now, and the shakes were communicating themselves to the tilted, unstable shelf. Another tube of makeup tumbled to the floor. The last few slivers of ice chimed faintly. Above the shelf, she could see the shadow of the glass on the wall. In the long sunset light it looked like a grain silo blown atilt by a strong prairie wind.

More . . . just a little bit more . . .

There IS no more!

There better be. There's got to be.

She stretched her right hand to its absolute tendon-creaking limit and felt the glass slide a tiny bit farther down the shelf. Then she closed her fingers again, praying it would finally be enough, because now there really was no more—she had pushed her resources to their absolute limit. It almost wasn't; she could still feel the wet glass trying to squirm away. It had begun to seem like a live thing to her, a sentient being with a mean streak as wide as a turnpike passing lane. Its goal was to keep flirting toward her and then squirming away until her sanity broke and she lay here in the shadows of twilight, handcuffed and raving.

Don't let it get away Jessie don't you dare DON'T YOU DARE LET THAT FUCKING GLASS GET AWAY—

And although there was no more, not a single foot-pound of pressure, not a single quarter-inch of stretch, she managed a little more anyway, turning her right wrist one final bit in toward the board. And this time when she curved her fingers around the glass, it remained motionless.

I think maybe I've got it. Not for sure, but maybe. Maybe.

Or maybe it was just that she had finally gotten to the wishful-thinking part. She didn't care. Maybe this and maybe that and none of the maybes mattered anymore and that was actually a relief. The certainty was this—she couldn't hold the shelf any longer. She had only tilted it three or four inches anyway, five at the most, but it felt as if she had bent down and picked up the whole house by one corner. *That* was the certainty.

She thought, *Everything is perspective . . . and the voices that describe the world to you, I suppose.* They *matter. The voices inside your head.*

With an incoherent prayer that the glass would remain in her hand when the shelf was no longer there to support it, she let go with her left hand. The shelf banged back onto its brackets, only slightly askew and shifted only an inch or two down to the left. The glass *did* stay in her hand, and now she could see the coaster. It clung to the bottom of the glass like a flying saucer.

Please God don't let me drop it now. Don't let me dr—

A cramp knotted her left arm, making her jerk back against the headboard. Her face knotted as well, pinching inward until the lips were a white scar and the eyes were agonized slits.

Wait, it will pass . . . it will pass . . .

Yes, of course it would. She'd had enough muscle cramps in her life to know that, but in the meantime oh *God* it hurt. If she had been able to touch the biceps of her left arm with her right hand, she knew, the skin there would have felt as if it had been stretched over a number of small smooth stones and then sewn up again with cunning invisible thread. It didn't feel like a Charley horse; it felt like rigor-fucking-mortis.

No, just a Charley horse, Jessie. Like the one you had earlier. Wait it out, that's all. Wait it out and for Christ's sweet sake don't drop that glass of water.

She waited, and after an eternity or two, the muscles in her arm began to relax and the pain began to ease. Jessie breathed out a long harsh sigh of relief, then prepared to drink her reward. *Drink, yes,* Goody thought, *but I think you owe yourself a little more than just a nice cool drink, my dear.* Enjoy *your reward . . . but enjoy it with dignity. No piggy gulping!*

Goody, you never change, she thought, but when she raised the glass, she did so with the stately calm of a guest at a court dinner, ignoring the alkali dryness along the roof of her mouth and the bitter pulse of thirst in her throat. Because you could put Goody down all you wanted—she practically begged for it sometimes—but behaving with a little dignity under these circumstances (*especially* under these circumstances) wasn't such a bad idea. She had worked for the water; why not take the time to honor herself by enjoying it? That first cold sip sliding over her lips and coiling across the hot rug of her tongue was going to taste like victory . . . and after the run of lousy luck she'd just been through, that would indeed be a taste to savor.

Jessie brought the glass toward her mouth, concentrating on the wet sweetness just ahead, the drenching downpour. Her tastebuds cramped with anticipation, her toes curled, and she could feel a furious pulse beating beneath the angle of her jaw. She realized her nipples had hardened, as they sometimes did when she was turned on. *Secrets of female sexuality you never dreamed of, Gerald,* she thought. *Handcuff me to the bedposts and nothing happens. Show me a glass of water, though, and I turn into a raving nympho.*

The thought made her smile and when the glass came to an abrupt halt still a foot away from her face, slopping water onto her bare thigh and making it ripple with gooseflesh, the smile stayed on at first. She felt nothing in those first few seconds but a species of stupid amazement and

(*?huh?*)

incomprehension. What was wrong? What *could* be wrong?

You know what, one of the UFO voices said. It spoke with a calm certainty Jessie found dreadful. Yes, she supposed she *did* know, somewhere inside, but she didn't want to let that knowledge step into the spotlight which was her conscious mind. Some truths were simply too harsh to be acknowledged. Too unfair.

Unfortunately, some truths were also self-evident. As Jessie gazed at the glass, her bloodshot, puffy eyes began to fill with horrified comprehension. The *chain* was the reason she wasn't getting her drink. The handcuff chain was just too fucking short. The fact had been so obvious that she had missed it completely.

Jessie suddenly found herself remembering the night George Bush had been elected President. She and Gerald had been invited to a posh celebration party in the Hotel Sonesta's rooftop restaurant. Senator William Cohen was the guest of honor, and the President-elect, Lonesome George himself, was expected to make a closed-circuit "television call" shortly before midnight. Gerald had hired a fog-colored limo for the occasion and it had pulled into their driveway at seven o'clock, dead on time, but at ten past the hour she had still been sitting on the bed in her best black dress, rummaging through her jewelry box and cursing as she hunted for a special pair of gold earrings. Gerald had poked his head impatiently into the room to see what was holding her up, listened with that "Why are you girls always so darned silly?" expression that she absolutely *hated* on his face, then said he wasn't sure, but he thought she was wearing the ones she was looking for. She had been. It had made her feel small and stupid, a perfect justification for his patronizing expression. It had also made her feel like flying at him and knocking out his beautifully capped teeth with one of the sexy but exquisitely uncomfortable high-heeled shoes she was wearing. What she had felt then was mild compared to what she was feeling now, however, and if anyone deserved getting their teeth knocked out, it was her.

She thrust her head as far forward as she could, pooching her lips out like the heroine of some corny old black-and-white romance movie. She got so close to the glass that she could see tiny sprays of air-bubbles caught in the last few slivers of ice, close enough to actually smell the minerals in the well-water (or to imagine she did), but she did not get quite close enough to drink from it. When she reached the point where she could simply stretch no farther, her puckered kiss-me lips were still a good four inches from the glass. It was almost enough, but almost, as Gerald (and her father as well, now that she thought about it) had been fond of saying, only counted in horseshoes.

"I don't believe it," she heard herself saying in her new hoarse Scotch-and-Marlboros voice. "I just don't believe it."

Anger suddenly woke inside her and screamed at her in Ruth Neary's voice to throw the glass across the room; if she could not drink from it, Ruth's voice proclaimed harshly, she would punish it; if she could not satisfy her thirst with what was in it, she could at least satisfy her mind with the sound of it shattering to a thousand bits against the wall.

Her grip on the glass tightened and the steel chain softened to a lax arc as she drew her hand back to do just that. Unfair! It was just so unfair!

The voice which stopped her was the soft, tentative voice of Goodwife Burlingame.

Maybe there's a way, Jessie. Don't give up yet—maybe there's still a way.

Ruth made no verbal reply to this, but there was no mistaking her sneer of disbelief; it was as heavy as iron and as bitter as a squirt of lemon-juice. Ruth still wanted her to throw the glass. Nora Callighan would undoubtedly have said that Ruth was heavily invested in the concept of payback.

Don't pay any attention to her, the Goodwife said. Her voice had lost its unusual tentative quality; it sounded almost excited now. *Put it back on the shelf, Jessie.*

And what then? Ruth asked. *What then, O Great White Guru, O Goddess of Tupperware and Patron Saint of the Church of Shop-by-Mail?*

Goody told her, and Ruth's voice fell silent as Jessie and all the other voices inside her listened.

10

She put the glass back on the shelf carefully, taking care to make sure she didn't leave it hanging over the edge. Her tongue now felt like a piece of #5 sandpaper and her throat actually seemed *infected* with thirst. It reminded her of the way she had felt in the autumn of her tenth year, when a combined case of the flu and bronchitis had kept her out of school for a month and a half. There had been long nights during that siege when she had awakened from confused, jangling nightmares she couldn't remember

(*except you can Jessie you dreamed about the smoked glass; you dreamed about how the sun went out; you dreamed about the flat and tearful smell that was like minerals in well-water; you dreamed about his hands*)

and she was drenched with sweat but felt too weak to reach for the pitcher of water on the bed-table. She remembered lying there, wet and sticky and fever-smelling on the outside, parched and full of phantoms on the inside; lying there and thinking that her real disease was not bronchitis but thirst. Now, all these years later, she felt exactly the same way.

Her mind kept trying to return to the horrible moment when she had realized she wasn't going to be able to bridge the last sliver of distance between the glass and her mouth. She kept seeing the tiny sprays of air-bubbles in the melting ice, kept smelling the faint aroma of minerals trapped in the aquifer far beneath the lake. These images taunted her like an unreachable itch between the shoulder-blades.

Nevertheless, she made herself wait. The part of her that was Goody Burlingame said she needed to take some time in spite of the taunting images and her throbbing throat. She needed to wait for her heart to slow down, for her muscles to stop trembling, for her emotions to settle a bit.

Outside, the last color was fading from the air; the world was going a solemn and melancholy gray. On the lake, the loon lifted its piercing cry into the evening gloom.

"Shut your yap, Mr. Loon," Jessie said, and chuckled. It sounded like a rusty hinge.

All right, dear, the Goodwife said. *I think it's time to try. Before it gets dark. Better dry your hands again first, though.*

She cupped both hands around the bedposts this time, rubbing them up and down until they produced squeaks. She held up her right hand and wiggled it in front of her eyes. *They laughed when I sat down at the piano,* she thought. Then, carefully, she reached just beyond the place where the glass stood on the edge of the shelf. She began to patter her fingers along the wood again. The handcuff chinked against the side of the glass once and she froze, waiting for it to overturn. When it didn't, she resumed her cautious exploration.

She had almost decided that what she was looking for had slid down the shelf—or entirely off it—when she finally touched the corner of the blow-in card. She tweezed it between the first and second fingers of her right hand and brought it carefully up and away from the shelf and the glass. Jessie steadied her grip on the card with her thumb and looked at it curiously.

It was bright purple, with noisemakers dancing tipsily along the upper edge. Confetti and streamers drifted down between the words. *Newsweek* was celebrating BIG BIG SAVINGS, the card announced, and it wanted her to join the party. *Newsweek*'s writers would keep her up to date on world events, take her behind the scenes with world leaders, and offer her in-depth coverage of arts, politics, and the sporting life. Although it did not come right out and say so, the card pretty much implied that *Newsweek* could help Jessie make sense of the entire cosmos. Best of all, those lovable lunatics in *Newsweek*'s subscription department were offering a deal so amazing it could make your urine steam and your head explode: if she used THIS VERY CARD to subscribe to *Newsweek* for three years, she would get each issue AT LESS THAN HALF THE NEWSSTAND PRICE! And was money a problem? Absolutely not! She would be billed later.

I wonder if they have Direct Bed Service for handcuffed ladies, Jessie thought. *Maybe with George Will or Jane Bryant Quinn or one of those other pompous old poops to turn the pages for me—handcuffs make doing that so dreadfully difficult, you know.*

Yet below the sarcasm, she felt a species of odd nervous wonder, and she couldn't seem to stop studying the purple card with its let's-have-a-party motif, its blanks for her name and address, and its little squares marked DiCl, MC, Visa, and AMEX. *I've been cursing these cards all my life—especially when I have to bend over and pick one of the damned things up or see myself as just another litterbug—without ever guessing that my sanity, maybe even my* life, *might depend on one someday.*

Her life? Was that really possible? Did she actually have to admit such a horrid idea into her calculations after all? Jessie was reluctantly coming to believe that she did. She might be here for quite awhile before someone discovered her, and yes, she supposed it was just barely possible that the difference between life and death could come down to a single drink of water. The idea was surreal but it no longer seemed patently ridiculous.

Same thing as before, dear—slow and easy wins the race.

Yes . . . but who would ever have believed the finish-line would turn out to be situated in such weird countryside?

She did move slowly and carefully, however, and was relieved to discover that manipulating the blow-in card one-handed was not as difficult as she had feared it might be. This was partly because it was about six inches by four—almost the size of two playing cards laid side by side—but mostly because she wasn't trying to do anything very tricky with it.

She held the card lengthwise between her first and second fingers, then used her thumb to bend the last half-inch of the long side all the way down. The fold wasn't even, but she thought it would serve. Besides, nobody was going to come along and judge her work; Brownie Crafts Hour on Thursday nights at the First Methodist Church of Falmouth was long behind her now.

She pinched the purple card firmly between her first two fingers again and folded over another half-inch. It took her almost three minutes and seven fold-overs to get to the end of the card. When she finally did, she had something that looked like a bomber joint clumsily rolled in jaunty purple paper.

Or, if you stretched your imagination a little, a straw.

Jessie stuck it in her mouth, trying to hold the crooked folds together with her teeth. When she had it as firmly as she thought she was going to get it, she began feeling around for the glass again.

Stay careful, Jessie. Don't spoil it all with impatience now!

Thanks for the advice. Also for the idea. It was great—I really mean that. Now, however, I'd like you to shut up long enough for me to take my shot. Okay?

When her fingertips touched the smooth surface of the glass, she slid them around it with the gentleness and caution of a young lover slipping her hand into her boyfriend's fly for the first time.

Gripping the glass in its new position was a relatively simple matter. She brought it around and lifted it as far as the chain would allow. The last slivers of ice had melted, she saw; *tempus* had gone *fugiting* merrily along despite her feeling that it had stopped dead in its tracks around the time the dog had put in its first appearance.

But she wouldn't think about the dog. In fact, she was going to work hard at believing that no dog had ever been here.

You're good at unhappening things, aren't you, tootsie-wootsie?

Hey, Ruth—I'm trying to keep a grip on myself as well as on the damned glass, in case you didn't notice. If playing a few mind-games helps me do that, I don't see what the big deal is. Just shut up for awhile, okay? Give it a rest and let me get on with my business.

Ruth apparently had no intention of giving it a rest, however. *Shut up!* she marvelled. *Boy, how that takes me back—it's better than a Beach Boys oldie on the radio. You always* did *give good shut up, Jessie—remember that night in the dorm after we came back from your first and last consciousness-raising session at Neuworth?*

I don't want *to remember, Ruth.*

I'm sure you don't, so I'll remember for both of us, how's that for a deal? You kept saying it was the girl with the scars on her breasts that had upset you, only her and nothing more, and when I tried to tell you what you'd said in the kitchen—about how you and your father had been alone at your place on Dark Score Lake when the sun went out in 1963, and how he'd done something to you—you told me to shut up. When I wouldn't, you tried to slap me. When I still *wouldn't, you grabbed your coat, ran out, and spent the night somewhere else—probably in Susie Timmel's little fleabag cabin down by the river, the one we used to call Susie's Lez Hotel. By the end of the week, you'd found some girls who had an apartment downtown and needed another roomie. Boom, as fast as that . . . but then, you* always *moved fast when you'd made up your mind, Jess, I'll give you that. And like I said, you always gave good shut up.*

Shu—

There! What'd I tell you?

Leave me alone!

I'm pretty familiar with that one, too. You know what hurt me the most, Jessie? It wasn't the trust thing—I knew even then that it was nothing personal, that you felt you couldn't trust anyone with the story of what happened that day, including yourself. What hurt was knowing how close you came to spilling it all, there in the kitchen of the Neuworth

Parsonage. We were sitting with our backs against the door and our arms around each other and you started to talk. You said, "I could never tell, it would have killed my Mom, and even if it didn't, she would have left him and I loved him. We all loved him, we all needed him, they would have blamed me, and he didn't do anything, not really." I asked you who didn't do anything and it came out of you so fast it was like you'd spent the last nine years waiting for someone to pop the question. "My father," you said. "We were at Dark Score Lake on the day the sun went out." You would have told me the rest—I know you would—but that was when that dumb bitch came in and asked, "Is she all right?" As if you looked all right, you know what I mean? Jesus, sometimes I can't believe how dumb people can be. They ought to make it a law that you have to get a license, or at least a learner's permit, before you're allowed to talk. Until you pass your Talker's Test, you should have to be a mute. It would solve a lot of problems. But that's not the way things are, and as soon as Hart Hall's answer to Florence Nightingale came in, you closed up like a clam. There was nothing I could do to make you open up again, although God knows I tried.

You should have just left me alone! Jessie returned. The glass of water was starting to shake in her hand, and the makeshift purple straw was trembling between her lips. *You should have stopped meddling! It didn't concern you!*

Sometimes friends can't help their concern, Jessie, the voice inside said, and it was so full of kindness that Jessie was silenced. *I looked it up, you know. I figured out what you must have been talking about and I looked it up. I didn't remember anything at all about an eclipse back in the early sixties, but of course I was in Florida at the time, and a lot more interested in snorkeling and the Delray lifeguard—I had the most incredible crush on him—than I was in astronomical phenomena. I guess I wanted to make sure the whole thing wasn't some kind of crazy fantasy or something—maybe brought on by that girl with the horrible burns on her bazooms. It was no fantasy. There was a total solar eclipse in Maine, and your summer house on Dark Score Lake would have been right in the path of totality. July of 1963. Just a girl and her Dad, watching the eclipse. You wouldn't tell me what good old Dad did to you, but I knew two things, Jessie: that he was your father, which was bad, and that you were ten-going-on-eleven, on the childhood rim of puberty . . . and that was worse.*

Ruth, please stop. You couldn't have picked a worse time to start raking up all that old—

But Ruth would not be stopped. The Ruth who had once been Jessie's roommate had always been determined to have her say—every single word of it—and the Ruth who was now Jessie's head-mate apparently hadn't changed a bit.

The next thing I knew, you were living off-campus with three little Sorority Susies—princesses in A-line jumpers and Ship 'n Shore blouses, each undoubtedly owning a set of those underpants with the days of the week sewn on them. I think you made a conscious decision to go into training for the Olympic Dusting and Floor-Waxing Team right around then. You unhappened that night at the Neuworth Parsonage, you unhappened the tears and the hurt and the anger, you unhappened me. Oh, we still saw each other once in awhile—split the occasional pizza and pitcher of Molson's down at Pat's—but our friendship was really over, wasn't it? When it came down to a choice between me and what happened to you in July of 1963, you chose the eclipse.

The glass of water was trembling harder.

"Why now, Ruth?" she asked, unaware that she was actually mouthing the words in the darkening bedroom. *Why now, that's what I want to know—given that in this incarnation you're really a part of me, why now? Why at the exact time when I can least afford being upset and distracted?*

The most obvious answer to that question was also the most unappetizing: because there was an enemy inside, a sad, bad bitch who liked her just the way she was—handcuffed, aching, thirsty, scared, and miserable—just fine. Who didn't want to see that condition alleviated in the slightest. Who would stoop to any dirty trick to see that it wasn't.

The total solar eclipse lasted just over a minute that day, Jessie . . . except in your mind. In there, it's still going on, isn't it?

She closed her eyes and focused all her thought and will on

steadying the glass in her hand. Now she spoke mentally to Ruth's voice without self-consciousness, as if she really were speaking to another person instead of to a part of her brain that had suddenly decided this was the right time to do a little work on herself, as Nora Callighan would have put it.

Let me alone, Ruth. If you still want to discuss these things after I've taken a stab at getting a drink, okay. But for now, will you please just—

"—shut the fuck *up*," she finished in a low whisper.

Yes, Ruth replied at once. *I know there's something or someone inside you, trying to throw dirt in the works, and I know it sometimes uses my voice—it's a great ventriloquist, no doubt about that—but it's not me. I loved you then, and I love you now. That was why I kept trying to stay in touch as long as I did . . . because I loved you. And, I suppose, because us high-riding bitches have to stick together.*

Jessie smiled a little, or tried to, around the makeshift straw.

Now go for it, Jessie, and go hard.

Jessie waited for a moment, but there was nothing else. Ruth was gone, at least for the time being. She opened her eyes again, then slowly bent her head forward, the rolled-up card jutting out of her mouth like FDR's cigarette holder.

Please God, I'm begging you . . . let this work.

Her makeshift straw slid into the water. Jessie closed her eyes and sucked. For a moment there was nothing, and clear despair rose up in her mind. Then water filled her mouth, cool and sweet and *there*, surprising her into a kind of ecstasy. She would have sobbed with gratitude if her mouth hadn't been so strenuously puckered around the end of the rolled-up subscription card; as it was, she could make only a foggy hooting sound through her nose.

She swallowed the water, feeling it coating her throat like liquid satin, and then began to suck again. She did this as ardently and as mindlessly as a hungry calf working at its mother's teat. Her straw was a long way from perfect, delivering only sips and slurps and rills instead of a steady stream, and most of what she was sucking into the tube was spilling out again from the imperfect seals and crooked folds. On some level she knew this, could hear water pattering to the coverlet like raindrops, but her grateful mind still fervently believed that her straw was one of the greatest inventions ever created by the mind of woman, and that this moment, this drink from her dead husband's water-glass, was the apogee of her life.

Don't drink it all, Jess—save some for later.

She didn't know which of her phantom companions had spoken this time, and it didn't matter. It was great advice, but so was telling an eighteen-year-old boy half-mad with six months of heavy petting that it didn't matter if the girl was finally willing; if he didn't have a rubber, he should wait. Sometimes, she was discovering, it was impossible to take the mind's advice, no matter how good it was. Sometimes the body simply rose up and slapped all that good advice aside. She was discovering something else, as well—giving in to those simple physical needs could be an inexpressible relief.

Jessie went on sucking through the rolled-up card, tilting the glass to keep the surface of the water brimming over the far end of the soggy, misshapen purple thing, aware in some part of her mind that the card was leaking worse than ever and she was insane not to stop and wait for it to dry out again, but going on anyway.

What finally stopped her was the realization that she was sucking nothing but air, and had been for several seconds. There was water left in Gerald's glass, but the tip of her makeshift straw could no longer quite touch it. The coverlet beneath the rolled-up blow-in card was dark with moisture.

I could get what's left, though. I could. If I could turn my hand a little farther in that unnatural backward direction when I needed to get hold of the miserable glass in the first place, I think I can stick my neck a little farther forward to get those last few sips of water. Think *I can?* I know *I can.*

She *did* know it, and later on she would test the idea, but for now the white-collar guys on the top floor—the ones with all the good views—had once again wrested control away from the day-laborers and shop stewards who ran the machinery; the mutiny was over. Her thirst was a long way from being entirely slaked, but her throat had quit throbbing and she felt a lot better . . . mentally as well as physically. Sharper in her thoughts and marginally brighter in her outlook.

She found she was glad she'd left that last little bit in the glass. Two sips of water through a leaky straw probably wouldn't spell the difference between remaining handcuffed to the bed and finding a way to wiggle out of this mess on her own—let alone between life and death—but getting those last couple of sips might occupy her mind when and if it tried to turn to its own morbid devices again. After all, night was coming, her husband was lying dead nearby, and it looked like she was camping out.

Not a pretty picture, especially when you added the hungry stray who was camping out with her, but Jessie found she was growing sleepy again just the same. She tried to think of reasons to fight her growing drowsiness and couldn't come up with any good ones. Even the thought of waking up with her arms numb to the elbows didn't seem like a particularly big deal. She would simply move them around until the blood was flowing briskly again. It wouldn't be pleasant, but she had no doubt about her ability to do it.

Also, you might have an idea while you're asleep, dear, Goodwife Burlingame said. *That always happens in books.*

"Maybe *you* will," Jessie said. "After all, you've had the best one so far."

She let herself lie down, using her shoulder-blades to scrunch the pillow as far up against the head of the bed as she could. Her shoulders ached, her arms (especially the left one) throbbed, and her stomach muscles were still fluttering with the strain of holding her upper body far enough forward to drink through the straw . . . but she felt strangely content, just the same. At peace with herself.

Content? How can you feel content? Your husband is dead, after all, and you played a part in that, Jessie. And suppose you are found? Suppose you are rescued? Have you thought about how this situation is going to look to whoever finds you? How do you suppose it's going to look to Constable Teagarden, as far as that goes? How long do you think it will take him to decide to call the State Police? Thirty seconds? Maybe forty? They think a little slower out here in the country, though, don't they—it might take him all of two minutes.

She couldn't argue with any of that. It was true.

Then how can you feel content, Jessie? How can you possibly feel content with things like that hanging over you?

She didn't know, but she did. Her sense of tranquility was as deep as a featherbed on the night a March gale filled with sleet roars out of the northwest, and as warm as the goosedown comforter on that bed. She suspected that most of this feeling stemmed from causes which were purely physical: if you were thirsty enough, it was apparently possible to get stoned on half a glass of water.

But there was a mental side, as well. Ten years ago she had reluctantly given up her job as a substitute teacher, finally giving in to the pressure of Gerald's persistent (or maybe "relentless" was the word she was actually looking for) logic. He was making almost a hundred thousand dollars a year by then; next to that, her five to seven grand looked pretty paltry. It was, in fact, an actual annoyance at tax time, when the IRS took most of it and then went sniffing over their financial records, wondering where the rest of it was.

When she complained about their suspicious behavior, Gerald had looked at her with a mixture of love and exasperation. It wasn't quite his "Why are you girls always so silly?" expression—that one didn't start to show up regularly for another five or six years—but it was close. *They see what I'm making,* he told her, *they see two large German cars in the garage, they look at the pictures of the place on the lake, and then they look at your tax forms and see you're working for what they think of as chump change. They can't believe it—it looks phony to them, a cover for something else—and so they go snooping around, looking for whatever that something else might be. They don't know you like I do, that's all.*

She had been unable to explain to Gerald what the substitute contract meant to her . . . or maybe it was that he had been unwilling to listen. Either way, it came to the same: teaching, even on a part-time basis, filled her up in some important way, and Gerald didn't get that. Nor had he been able to get the fact that subbing formed a bridge to the life she had lived before she'd met Gerald at that Republican mixer, when she'd been a full-time English teacher at Waterville High, a woman on her own who was working for a living, who was well-liked and respected by her colleagues, and who was beholden to no one. She had been unable to explain (or he had been unwilling to listen) how quitting teaching—even on that final part-time, piecework basis—made her feel mournful and lost and somehow useless.

That rudderless feeling—probably caused as much by her inability to catch pregnant as by her decision to return her contract unsigned—had departed from the surface of her mind after a year or so, but it had never entirely left the deeper ranges of her heart. She had sometimes felt like a cliché to herself—young teacher-lady weds successful lawyer whose name goes up on the door at the tender (professionally speaking, that is) age of thirty. This young (well, *relatively* young) woman eventually steps into the foyer of that puzzle palace known as middle age, looks around, and finds she is suddenly all alone—no job, no kids, and a husband who is almost completely focused (one wouldn't want to say fixated; that might be accurate, but it would also be unkind) on climbing that fabled ladder of success.

This woman, suddenly faced with forty just beyond the next bend in the road, is exactly the sort of woman most likely to get in trouble with drugs, booze, or another man. A younger man, usually. None of that happened to *this* young (well . . . *previously* young) woman, but Jessie still found herself with a scary amount of time on her hands—time to garden, time to go malling, time to take classes (the painting, the pottery, the poetry . . . and she could have had an affair with the man who taught the poetry if she'd wanted to, and she had almost wanted to). There had also been time to do a little work on herself, which was how she had happened to meet Nora. Yet not one of those things had left her feeling the way she felt now, as though her weariness and aches were badges of valor and her sleepiness a justly won reward . . . the handcuffed ladies' version of Miller Time, you might say.

Hey, Jess—the way you got that water really was *pretty great.*

It was another UFO, but this time Jessie didn't mind. Just as long as Ruth didn't show up for awhile. Ruth was interesting, but she was also exhausting.

A lot of people never would have even gotten the glass, her UFO fan continued, *and using the blow-in card for a straw . . . that was a master-stroke. So go ahead and feel good. It's allowed. A little nap is allowed, too.*

But the dog, Goody said doubtfully.

That dog isn't going to bother you one damned bit . . . and you know why.

Yes. The reason the dog wasn't going to bother her was lying nearby on the bedroom floor. Gerald was now nothing but a shadow among shadows, for which Jessie was grateful. Outside, the wind gusted again. The sound of it hissing through the pines was comforting, lulling. Jessie closed her eyes.

But be careful what you dream! Goody called after her in sudden alarm, but her voice was distant and not terribly compelling. Still, it tried again: *Be careful what you dream, Jessie! I'm serious!*

Yes, of course she was. The Goodwife was always serious, which meant she was also often tiresome.

Whatever I dream, Jessie thought, *it won't be that I'm thirsty. I haven't had many clear victories over the last ten years—mostly one murky guerrilla engagement after another—but getting that drink of water was a clear win. Wasn't it?*

Yes, the UFO voice agreed. It was a vaguely masculine voice, and she found herself wondering in a sleepy way if perhaps it was the voice of her brother, Will . . . Will as he'd been as a child, back in the sixties. *You bet it was. It was great.*

Five minutes later Jessie was sleeping deeply, arms up and splayed in a limp V-shape, wrists held loosely to the bedposts by the handcuffs, head lolling against her right shoulder (the less painful one), long, slow snores drifting from her mouth. And at some point—long after dark had fallen and a white rind of moon had risen in the east—the dog appeared in the doorway again.

Like Jessie, it was calmer now that its most immediate need had been met and the clamor in its stomach had been stilled to some extent. It gazed at her for a long time with its good ear cocked and its muzzle up, trying to decide if she was really asleep or only pretending. It decided (mostly on the basis of smell—the sweat which was now drying, the total absence of the crackling ozone stink of adrenaline) that she was asleep. There would be no kicks or shouts this time—not if it was careful not to wake her up.

The dog padded softly to the heap of meat in the middle of the floor. Although its hunger was now less, the meat actually smelled better. This was because its first meal had gone a long way toward breaking down the ancient, inbred taboo against this sort of meat, although the dog did not know this and wouldn't have cared if it did.

It lowered its head, first sniffing the now-attractive aroma of dead lawyer with all the delicacy of a gourmet, then closing its teeth gently on Gerald's lower lip. It pulled, applying pressure slowly, stretching the flesh further and further. Gerald began to look as if he were deep in some monstrous pout. The lip finally tore off, revealing his bottom teeth in a big dead grin. The dog swallowed this small delicacy in a single gulp, then licked its chops. Its tail began to wag again, this time moving in slow, contented sweeps. Two tiny spots of light danced on the ceiling high above; moonlight reflected from the fillings in two of Gerald's lower molars. These fillings had been done only the week before, and they were still as fresh and shiny as newly minted quarters.

The dog licked its chops a second time, looking lovingly at Gerald as it did so. Then it stretched its neck forward, almost exactly as Jessie had stretched hers in order to finally plop her straw into the glass. The dog sniffed Gerald's face, but it did not *just* sniff; it allowed its nose to go on a kind of olfactory vacation there, first sampling the faint floor-polishy aroma of brown wax buried deep in the dead master's left ear, then the intermingled odors of sweat and Prell at the hairline, then the sharp, entrancingly bitter smell of clotted blood on the crown of Gerald's head. It lingered especially long at Gerald's nose, conducting a delicate investigation into those now tideless channels with its scratched, dirty, but oh-so-sensitive muzzle. Again there was that sense of gourmandizing, a feeling that the dog was choosing among many treasures. At last it sank its sharp teeth deeply into Gerald's left cheek, clamped them together, and began to pull.

On the bed, Jessie's eyes had begun to move rapidly back and forth behind her lids and now she moaned—a high, wavering sound, full of terror and recognition.

The dog looked up at once, its body dropping into an instinctive cringe of guilt and fear. It didn't last long; already it had begun to see this pile of meat as its private larder, for which it would fight —and perhaps die—if challenged. Besides, it was only the bitch-master making that sound, and the dog was now quite sure that the bitchmaster was powerless.

It dipped its head down, seized Gerald Burlingame's cheek once more, and yanked backward, shaking its head briskly from side to side as it did so. A long strip of the dead man's cheek came free with a sound like strapping tape being pulled briskly off the dispenser roll. Gerald now wore the ferocious, predatory smile of a man who has just filled a straight-flush in a high-stakes poker game.

Jessie moaned again. The sound was followed by a string of guttural, unintelligible sleeptalk. The dog glanced up at her once more. It was sure she couldn't get off the bed and bother it, but those sounds made it uneasy, just the same. The old taboo had faded, but it hadn't disappeared. Besides, its hunger was sated; what it was doing now wasn't eating but snacking. It turned and trotted out of the room again. Most of Gerald's left cheek dangled from its mouth like the scalp of an infant.

11

It is August 14th, 1965—a little over two years since the day the sun went out. It is Will's birthday; he has gone around all day solemnly telling people that he has now lived a year for each inning in a baseball game. Jessie is unable to understand why this seems like a big deal to her brother, but it clearly does, and she decides that if Will wants to compare his life to a baseball game, that's perfectly okay.

For quite awhile *everything* that happens at her little brother's birthday party is perfectly okay. Marvin Gaye is on the record-player, true, but it is not the bad song, the dangerous song. "I wouldn't be doggone," Marvin sings, mock-threatening, "I'd be long gone . . . bay-bee." Actually sort of a cute song, and the truth is that the day has been a lot better than okay, at least so far; it has been, in the words of Jessie's great-aunt Katherine, "finer than fiddle-music." Even her Dad thinks so, although he wasn't very keen on coming back to Falmouth for Will's birthday when the idea was first suggested. Jessie has heard him say *I guess it was a pretty good idea, after all* to her Mom, and that makes *her* feel good, because it was she—Jessie Mahout, daughter of Tom and Sally, sister of Will and Maddy, wife of nobody—who put the idea over. She's the reason they're here instead of inland, at Sunset Trails.

Sunset Trails is the family camp (although after three generations of haphazard family expansion, it is really big enough to be called a compound) on the north end of Dark Score Lake. This year they have broken their customary nine weeks of seclusion there because Will wants—just once, he has told his mother and father, speaking in the tones of a nobly suffering old grandee who knows he cannot cheat the reaper much longer—to have a birthday party with his rest-of-the-year friends as well as his family.

Tom Mahout vetoes the idea at first. He is a stock broker who divides his time between Portland and Boston, and for years he has told his family not to believe all that propaganda about how guys who go to work wearing ties and shirts with white collars spend their days goofing off—either hanging around the water-cooler or dictating lunch invitations to pretty blondes from the steno pool. "No hardscrabble spud-farmer in Aroostook County works any harder than I do," he frequently tells them. "Keeping up with the market isn't easy, and it isn't particularly glamorous, either, no matter what you may have heard to the contrary." The truth is none of them have heard *anything* to the contrary, all of them (his wife included, most likely, although Sally would never say so) think his job sounds duller than donkeyshit, and only Maddy has the vaguest idea of what it is he does.

Tom insists that he *needs* that time on the lake to recover from the stresses of his job, and that his son will have *plenty* of birthdays with his friends later on. Will is turning nine, after all, not ninety. "Plus," Tom adds, "birthday parties with your pals really aren't much fun until you're old enough to have a keg or two."

So Will's request to have his birthday at the family's year-round home on the coast would probably have been denied if not for Jessie's sudden, surprising support of the plan (and to Will it's *plenty* surprising; Jessie is three years older and lots of times he's not sure she remembers she even *has* a brother). Following her initial soft-voiced suggestion that maybe it would be fun to come home—just for two or three days, of course—and have a lawn-party, with cro-quet and badminton and a barbecue and Japanese lanterns that would come on at dusk, Tom begins to warm to the idea. He is the sort of man who thinks of himself as a "strong-willed son of a bitch" and is often thought of as a "stubborn old goat" by others; whichever way you saw it, he has always been a tough man to move once he has set his feet . . . and his jaw.

When it comes to moving him—to changing his mind—his younger daughter has more luck than the rest of them put together. Jessie often finds a way into her father's mind by means of some loophole or secret passage denied to the rest of the family. Sally believes—with some justification—that their middle child has always been Tom's favorite and Tom has fooled himself into believing none of the others know. Maddy and Will see it in simpler terms: they believe that Jessie sucks up to their father and that he in turn spoils her rotten. "If Daddy caught *Jessie* smoking," Will told his older sister the year before, after Maddy had been grounded for that very offense, "he'd probably buy her a lighter." Maddy laughed, agreed, and hugged her brother. Neither they nor their mother has the slightest idea of the secret which lies between Tom Mahout and his younger daughter like a heap of rotting meat.

Jessie herself believes she is just going along with her baby brother's request—that she's sticking up for him. She has no idea, not on the surface of her mind, anyway, how much she has come to hate Sunset Trails and how eager she is to get away. She has also come to hate the lake she once passionately loved—especially its faint, flat mineral smell. By 1965 she can hardly bear to go swimming there, even on the hottest of days. She knows her mother thinks it's her shape—Jessie began to bud early, as Sally did herself, and at the age of twelve she has most of her woman's figure—but it's not her shape. She's gotten used to that, and knows that she's a long way from being a *Playboy* pin-up in either of her old, faded Jantzen tank suits. No, it's not her breasts, not her hips, not her can. It's that *smell.*

Whatever reasons and motives may be swirling around beneath, Will Mahout's request is finally approved by the Mahout family's head honcho. They made the trip back to the coast yesterday, leaving early enough for Sally (eagerly assisted by both daughters) to prepare for the party. And now it's August 14th, and August 14th is surely the apotheosis of summer in Maine, a day of faded-blue-denim skies and fat white clouds, all of it freshened by a salt-tangy breeze.

Inland—and that includes the Lakes District, where Sunset Trails has stood on the shore of Dark Score Lake since Tom Mahout's grandfather built the original cabin in 1923—the woods and lakes and ponds and bogs lie sweltering under temperatures in the mid-nineties and humidity just below the saturation point, but here on the seacoast it's only eighty. The seabreeze is an extra bonus, rendering the humidity negligible and sweeping away the mosquitoes and sandflies. The lawn is filled with children, mostly Will's friends but girls who chum with Maddy and Jessie as well, and for once, *mirabile dictu,* they all seem to be getting along. There hasn't been a single argument, and around five o'clock, as Tom raises the first martini of the day to his lips, he glances at Jessie, who is standing nearby with her croquet mallet propped on her shoulder like a sentry's rifle (and who is clearly within earshot of what sounds like a casual husband-and-wife conversation but which may actually be a shrewd bank-shot compliment aimed at his daughter), then back at his wife. "I guess it was actually a pretty good idea, after all," he says.

Better than good, Jessie thinks. *Absolutely great and totally monster, if you want to know the truth.* Even that isn't what she really means, really thinks, but it would be dangerous to say the rest out loud; it would tempt the gods. What she really thinks is that the day is flawless—a sweet and perfect peach of a day. Even the song blasting out of Maddy's portable record player (which Jessie's big sister has cheerfully carted out to the patio for this occasion, although it is ordinarily the Great Untouchable Icon) is okay. Jessie is never really going to *like* Marvin Gaye—no more than she is ever going to like that faint mineral smell which rises from the lake on hot summer afternoons—but *this* song is okay. I'll be doggone if you ain't a pretty thing . . . bay-bee: silly, but not dangerous.

It is August 14th, 1965, a day that was, a day that still *is* in the mind of a dreaming woman handcuffed to a bed in a house on the shore of a lake forty miles south of Dark Score (but with the same mineral smell, that nasty, evocative smell, on hot, still summer days), and although the twelve-year-old girl she was doesn't see Will creeping up behind her as she bends over to address her croquet ball, turning her bottom into a target simply too tempting for a boy who has only lived one year for each inning in a baseball game to ignore, part of her mind knows he is there, and that this is the seam where the dream has been basted to the nightmare.

She lines up her shot, concentrating on the wicket six feet away. A hard shot but not an *impossible* one, and if she drives the ball through, she may well catch Caroline after all. That would be nice, because Caroline almost *always* wins at croquet. Then, just as she draws her mallet back, the music coming from the record-player changes.

"*Oww, listen everybody,*" Marvin Gaye sings, sounding a lot more than just *mock*-threatening to Jessie this time, "*especially you girls . . .*"

Chills of gooseflesh run up Jessie's tanned arms.

"*. . . is it right to be left alone when the one you love is never home? . . . I love too hard, my friends sometimes say . . .*"

Her fingers go numb and she loses any sense of the mallet in her hands. Her wrists are tingling, as if bound by

(*stocks Goody's in the stocks come and see Goody in the stocks come and laugh at Goody in the stocks*)

unseen clamps, and her heart is suddenly full of dismay. It is the other song, the wrong song, the *bad* song.

"*. . . but I believe . . . I believe . . . that a woman should be loved that way . . .*"

She looks up at the little group of girls waiting for her to make her shot and sees that Caroline is gone. Standing there in her place is Nora Callighan. Her hair is in braids, there's a dab of white zinc on the tip of her nose, she's wearing Caroline's yellow sneakers and Caroline's locket—the one with the tiny picture of Paul McCartney inside it—but those are Nora's green eyes, and they are looking at her with a deep adult compassion. Jessie suddenly remembers that Will—undoubtedly egged on by his buddies, who are as jazzed up on Cokes and German chocolate cake as Will himself—is creeping up behind her, that he is preparing to goose her. She will overreact wildly when he does, swinging around and punching him in the mouth, perhaps not spoiling the party completely but certainly putting a ding in its sweet perfection. She tries to let go of the mallet, wanting to straighten and turn around before any of this can happen. She wants to change the past, but the past is heavy—trying to do that, she discovers, is like trying to pick up the house by one corner so you can look under it for things that have been lost, or forgotten, or hidden.

Behind her, someone has cranked the volume on Maddy's little record-player and that terrible song blares louder than ever, triumphant and glittery and sadistic: "*IT HURTS ME SO INSIDE . . . TO BE TREATED SO UNKIND . . . SOMEBODY, SOMEWHERE . . . TELL HER IT AIN'T FAIR . . .*"

She tries again to get rid of the mallet—to throw it away—but she can't do it; it's as if someone has handcuffed her to it.

Nora! she cries. *Nora, you have to help me! Stop him!*

(It was at this point in the dream that Jessie moaned for the first time, momentarily startling the dog back from Gerald's body.)

Nora shakes her head, slowly and gravely. *I can't help you, Jessie. You're on your own—we all are. I generally don't tell my patients that, but I think in your case it's best to be honest.*

You don't understand! I can't go through this again! I CAN'T!

Oh, don't be so silly, Nora says, suddenly impatient. She begins to turn away, as if she can no longer bear the sight of Jessie's upturned, frantic face. *You will not die; it's not poison.*

Jessie looks around wildly (although she remains unable to straighten up, to stop presenting that tempting target to her impending brother) and sees that her friend Tammy Hough is gone; standing there in Tammy's white shorts and yellow halter is Ruth Neary. She's holding Tammy's red-striped croquet mallet in one hand and a Marlboro in the other. Her mouth is hooked up at the corners in her usual sardonic grin, but her eyes are grave and full of sorrow.

Ruth, help me! Jessie shouts. *You have to* help *me!*

Ruth takes a big drag on her cigarette, then grinds it into the grass with one of Tammy Hough's cork-soled sandals. *Jeepers-*

*creepers, tootsie—he's going to goose you, not stick a cattle-prod up your
ass. You know that as well as I do; you've been through all this before.
So what's the big deal?*

It isn't *just a goose! It* isn't, *and you know it!*

The old hooty-owl hooty-hoos to the goose, Ruth says.

What? What does that m—

It means how can I know anything about ANYTHING? Ruth
shoots back. There is anger on the surface of her voice, deep hurt
beneath. *You wouldn't tell me—you wouldn't tell anybody. You ran
away. You ran like a rabbit that sees the shadow of some old hooty-owl
on the grass.*

I COULDN'T *tell!* Jessie shrieks. Now she can see a shadow on
the grass beside her, as if Ruth's words have conjured it up. It is
not the shadow of an owl, however; it is the shadow of her brother.
She can hear the stifled giggles of his friends, knows he is reaching
out to do it, and still she cannot even straighten up, let alone move
away. She is helpless to change what is going to happen, and she
understands that this is the very essence of both nightmare and
tragedy.

I COULDN'T! *she shrieks at Ruth again. I couldn't, not ever! It
would have killed my Mom . . . or destroyed the family . . . or both!
He said! Daddy said!*

*I hate to be the one to send you this particular newsflash, tootsie-
wootsie, but your dear old Dad will have been dead twelve years come
December. Also, can't we dispense with at least a little of this melodrama? It's not as if he hung you from the clothesline by the nipples
and then set you on fire, you know.*

But she doesn't want to hear this, doesn't want to consider—
even in a dream—any reappraisal of her buried past; once the
dominos start to fall, who knows where it will all end? So she
blocks her ears to what Ruth is saying and continues to fix her old
college roommate with that deep, pleading stare that so often
caused Ruth (whose tough-cookie veneer was never more than
frosting-deep, anyway) to laugh and give in, to do whatever it was
Jessie wanted her to do.

Ruth, you have to help me! You have to!

But this time the pleading stare doesn't work. *I don't think so, toots. The Sorority Susies are all gone, the time for shutting up is over, running away is out of the question, and waking up is not an option. This is the mystery train, Jessie. You're the pussycat; I'm the owl. Here we go—all aboard. Fasten your seatbelt, and fasten it tight. This is an E-ticket ride.*

No!

But now, to Jessie's horror, the day begins to darken. It could just be the sun going behind a cloud, but she knows it isn't. The sun is going out. Soon the stars will shine in a summer afternoon sky and the old hooty-owl will hooty-hoo to the dove. The time of the eclipse has come.

No! she screams again. *That was two years ago!*

You're wrong on that one, toots, Ruth Neary says. *For you it never ended. For you the sun never came back out.*

She opens her mouth to deny that, to tell Ruth she's as guilty of wild overdramatization as Nora, who kept shoving her toward doors she didn't want to open, who kept assuring her that the present can be improved by examining the past—as if one could improve the taste of today's dinner by slathering it with the maggoty remains of yesterday's. She wants to tell Ruth, as she told Nora on the day she walked out of Nora's office for good, that there is a big difference between living with something and being kept prisoner by it. *Don't you two goofs understand that the Cult of Self is just another cult?* she wants to say, but before she can do more than open her mouth, the invasion comes: a hand between her slightly spread legs, the thumb shoving rudely at the cleft of her buttocks, the fingers pressed against the material of her shorts just above her vagina, and it is not her brother's innocent little hand this time; the hand between her legs is much bigger than Will's and not a bit innocent. The bad song is on the radio, the stars are out at three o'clock in the afternoon, and this

(you will not die it's not poison)

is how the big people goose each other.

She whirls, expecting to see her father. He did something like this to her during the eclipse, a thing she supposes the whining Cult-of-Selfers, the Live-in-the-Pasters like Ruth and Nora, would call child abuse. Whatever it was, it will be him—she's sure of that much—and she is afraid she will exact a terrible punishment for the thing he did, no matter how serious or trivial that thing was: she will raise the croquet mallet and drive it into his face, smashing his nose and knocking out his teeth, and when he falls down on the grass the dogs will come and eat him up.

Except it isn't Tom Mahout standing there; it's Gerald. He's naked. The Penis of an Attorney pokes out at her from below the soft pink bowl of his belly. He has a set of Kreig police handcuffs in each hand. He holds them out to her in the weird afternoon darkness. Unnatural starlight gleams on the cocked jaws which are stamped M-17 because his source could not provide him with any F-23s.

Come on, Jess, he says, grinning. *It isn't as though you don't know the score. Besides, you liked it. That first time you came so hard you almost blew up. I don't mind telling you that was the best piece of ass I ever had in my life, so good I sometimes dream about it. And do you know why it was so good? Because you didn't have to take any of the responsibility. Almost all women like it better when the man takes over completely—it's a proven fact of female psychology. Did you come when your father molested you, Jessie? I bet you did. I bet you came so hard you almost blew up. The Cult-of-Selfers may want to argue about these things, but we know the truth, don't we? Some women can say they want it, but some need a man to* tell *them they want it. You're one of the latter. But that's okay, Jessie; that's what the cuffs are for. Only they were never really handcuffs at all. They're bracelets of love. So put them on, sweetheart. Put them on.*

She backs up, shaking her head, not knowing if she wants to laugh or cry. The subject itself is new, but the rhetoric is all too familiar. *The lawyer's tricks don't work on me, Gerald—I've been married to one too long. What we both know is that the business with the handcuffs was never about me at all. It was about you . . . about waking up your*

*old booze-stunned John Thomas a little, to be blunt. So you can just save
your fucked-up version of female psychology, okay?*

Gerald is smiling in a knowing, disconcerting way. *Good try, babe.
It doesn't wash, but it was still a damned good shot. The best defense is
a good offense, right? I think I taught you that. Never mind, though.
Right now you've got a choice to make. Either put the bracelets on or
swing that mallet and kill me again.*

She looks around and realizes with dawning panic and dismay
that everyone at Will's party is watching her confrontation with this
naked (except for his glasses, that is), overweight, sexually aroused
man . . . and it's not just her family and her childhood friends,
either. Mrs. Henderson, who will be her Freshman Advisor at college, is standing by the punch-bowl; Bobby Hagen, who will take
her to the Senior Prom—and fuck her afterward in the back seat
of his father's Oldsmobile 88—is standing on the patio next to the
blonde girl from the Neuworth Parsonage, the one whose parents
loved her but idolized her brother.

Barry, Jessie thinks. *She's Olivia and her brother's Barry.*

The blonde girl is listening to Bobby Hagen but looking at Jessie,
her face calm but somehow haggard. She is wearing a sweatshirt
which shows R. Crumb's Mr. Natural hurrying down a city street.
The words in the balloon coming out of Mr. Natural's mouth say,
"Vice is nice, but incest is best." Behind Olivia, Kendall Wilson,
who will hire Jessie for her first teaching job, is cutting a piece of
chocolate birthday cake for Mrs. Paige, her childhood piano teacher.
Mrs. Paige is looking remarkably lively for a woman who died of
a stroke two years ago while picking apples at Corrit's Orchards in
Alfred.

Jessie thinks, *This isn't like dreaming; it's like drowning. Everyone
I've ever known seems to be standing here under this weird starlit afternoon sky, watching my naked husband try to put me in handcuffs while
Marvin Gaye sings "Can I Get a Witness." If there's any comfort to be
had, it's this: things can't possibly get any worse.*

Then they do. Mrs. Wertz, her first-grade teacher, starts to laugh.
Old Mr. Cobb, their gardener until he retired in 1964, laughs with

her. Maddy joins in, and Ruth, and Olivia of the scarred breasts. Kendall Wilson and Bobby Hagen are bent almost double, and they are clapping each other on the back like men who have heard the granddaddy of all dirty jokes in the local barber-shop. Perhaps the one whose punchline is *A life-support system for a cunt.*

Jessie looks down at herself and sees that now she is naked, too. Written across her breasts in a shade of lipstick known as Peppermint Yum-Yum are three damning words: DADDY'S LITTLE GIRL.

I have to wake up, she thinks. *I'll die of shame if I don't.*

But she doesn't, at least not right away. She looks up and sees that Gerald's knowing, disconcerting smile has turned into a gaping wound. Suddenly the stray dog's blood-soaked snout pokes out between his teeth. The dog is also grinning, and the head that comes shoving out between *its* fangs like the onset of some obscene birth belongs to her father. His eyes, always a bright blue, are now gray and haggard above his grin. They are Olivia's eyes, she realizes, and then she realizes something else, as well: the flat mineral smell of lakewater, so bland and yet so horrible, is everywhere.

"I love too hard, my friends sometimes say," her father sings from inside the mouth of the dog which is inside the mouth of the husband, *"But I believe, I believe, that a woman should be loved that way . . ."*

She casts the mallet aside and runs, screaming. As she passes the horrible creature with its bizarre chain of nested heads, Gerald snaps one of the handcuffs around her wrist.

Got you! he yells triumphantly. *Got you, me proud beauty!*

At first she thinks the eclipse must not have been total yet after all, because the day has begun to grow still darker. Then it occurs to her that she is probably fainting. This thought is accompanied by feelings of deep relief and gratitude.

Don't be silly, Jess—you can't faint in a dream.

But she thinks she may be doing just that, and in the end it doesn't matter much whether it is a faint or only a deeper cave of sleep toward which she is fleeing like the survivor of some cataclysm. What matters is that she is finally escaping the dream which has assaulted her in a much more fundamental way than her father's act on the deck that day, she is finally escaping, and gratitude seems like a beautifully normal response to these circumstances.

She has almost made it into that comforting cave of darkness when a sound intrudes: a splintery, ugly sound like a loud spasm of coughing. She tries to flee the sound and finds she cannot. It has her like a hook, and like a hook it begins to pull her up toward the vast but fragile silver sky that separates sleep from consciousness.

12

The former Prince, who had once been the pride and joy of young Catherine Sutlin, sat in the kitchen entryway for about ten minutes after its latest foray into the bedroom. It sat with its head up, its eyes wide and unblinking. It had been existing on very short commons over the last two months, it had fed well this evening—gorged, in fact—and it should have been feeling logy and sleepy. It had been both for awhile, but now all sleepiness had departed. What replaced it was a feeling of nervousness which grew steadily worse. Something had snapped several of the hair-thin tripwires posted in that mystical zone where the dog's senses and its intuition overlapped. The bitchmaster continued to moan in the other room, and to make occasional talking noises, but her sounds were not the source of the stray's jitters; they were not what had caused it to sit up when it had been on the verge of drifting placidly off to sleep, and not the reason why its good ear was now cocked alertly forward and its muzzle had wrinkled back far enough to show the tips of its teeth.

It was something else . . . something not right . . . something which was possibly dangerous.

As Jessie's dream peaked and then began to spiral down into darkness, the dog suddenly scrambled to its feet, unable to bear the steady sizzle in its nerves any longer. It turned, pushed open the loose back door with its snout, and jumped out into the windy dark. As it did, some strange and unidentifiable scent came to it. There was danger in that scent . . . almost certainly danger.

The dog raced for the woods as fast as its swollen, overloaded belly would allow. When it had gained the safety of the undergrowth, it turned and squirmed a little way back toward the house. It had retreated, true enough, but a great many more alarm-bells would have to go off inside before it would consider completely abandoning the wonderful supply of food it had found.

Safely hidden, its thin, weary, intelligent face crisscrossed with overlapping ideograms of moonshadow, the stray began to bark, and it was this sound which eventually drew Jessie back to consciousness.

13

During their summers on the lake in the early sixties, before William was able to do much more than paddle in the shallows with a pair of bright orange water-wings attached to his back, Maddy and Jessie, always good friends despite the difference in their ages, often went down to swim at the Neidermeyers'. The Neidermeyers had a float equipped with a diving platform, and it was there that Jessie began to develop the form which won her a place first on her high school swim-team and then on the All-State team in 1971. What she remembered second-best about diving from the board on the Neidermeyers' float (first—for then and for always—was the swoop through the hot summer air toward the blue glitter of the waiting

water) was how it felt to come up from the depths, through con-flicting layers of warm and cold.

Coming up from her troubled sleep was like that.

First there was a black, roaring confusion that was like being inside a thundercloud. She bumped and yawed her way through it, not having the slightest idea of who she was or *when* she was, let alone where she was. Then a warmer, calmer layer: she had been caught in the most awful nightmare in all of recorded history (at least in *her* recorded history), but a nightmare was *all* it had been, and now it was over. As the surface neared, however, she encoun-tered another chilly layer: an idea that the reality waiting ahead was almost as bad as the nightmare. Maybe worse.

What is it? she asked herself. *What could possibly be worse than what I've just been through?*

She refused to think about that. The answer was within reach, but if it occurred to her, she might decide to flip over and start finning her way back down into the depths again. To do that would be to drown, and while drowning might not be the worst way to step out—not as bad as running your Harley into a rock wall or parachuting into a cat's cradle of high-voltage wires, for instance—the idea of opening her body to that flat mineral smell, which reminded her simultaneously of copper and oysters, was insup-portable. Jessie kept stroking grimly upward, telling herself that she would worry about reality when and if she actually broke the surface.

The last layer she passed through was as warm and fearful as freshly spilled blood: her arms were probably going to be deader than stumps. She just hoped she would be able to command enough movement in them to get the blood flowing again.

Jessie gasped, jerked, and opened her eyes. She hadn't the slight-est idea of how long she had been asleep, and the clock-radio on the dresser, stuck in its own hell of obsessive repetition (twelve-twelve-twelve, it flashed into the darkness, as if time had stopped forever at midnight), was no help. All she knew for sure was that it was full dark and the moon was now shining through the skylight instead of the east window.

Her arms were jumping with a nervous jitter-jive of pins and needles. She usually disliked that feeling intensely, but not now; it was a thousand times better than the muscle cramps she had expected as the price of waking her dead extremities back up. A moment or two later she noticed a spreading dampness beneath her legs and bottom and realized that her previous need to urinate was gone. Her body had taken care of the problem while she slept.

She doubled her fists and cautiously pulled herself up a little, wincing at the pain in her wrists and the deep, sobbing ache the movement caused in the backs of her hands. *Most of that pain's a result of trying to slip out of the cuffs,* she thought. *You got nobody to blame but yourself, sweetheart.*

The dog had begun to bark again. Each shrill cry was like a splinter pounded into her eardrum, and she realized that sound was what had pulled her up and out of her sleep just as she had been about to dive below the nightmare. The location of the sounds told her the dog was back outside. She was glad it had left the house, but a little puzzled, as well. Maybe it just hadn't been comfortable under a roof after spending such a long time outside. That idea made a certain amount of sense . . . as much as anything else in this situation, anyway.

"Get it together, Jess," she advised herself in a solemn, sleep-foggy voice, and maybe—just maybe—she was doing that. The panic and the unreasoning shame she'd felt in the dream were departing. The dream itself seemed to be drying out, taking on the curiously desiccated quality of an overexposed photograph. Soon, she realized, it would be gone entirely. Dreams on waking were like the empty cocoons of moths or the split-open husks of milk-weed pods, dead shells where life had briefly swirled in furious but fragile storm-systems. There had been times when this amnesia—if that was what it was—had struck her as sad. Not now. She had never in her life equated forgetting with mercy so quickly and completely.

And it doesn't matter, she thought. *It was just a dream after all. I mean, all those heads sticking out of heads? Dreams are supposed to be symbolic, of course—yes, I know—and I suppose there might have been some symbolism in this one . . . maybe even some truth. If nothing else, I think that now I understand why I hit Will when he goosed me that day. Nora Callighan would undoubtedly be thrilled—she'd call it a breakthrough. Probably it is. It doesn't do a thing about getting me out of this fucking jailhouse jewelry, though, and that's still my top priority. Does anyone disagree with that?*

Neither Ruth nor Goody replied; the UFO voices were likewise silent. The only response, in fact, came from her stomach, which was sorry as hell all this had happened but still felt compelled to protest the cancellation of supper with a long, low rumble. Funny, in a way . . . but apt to be less so come tomorrow. By then her thirst would have come raging back, too, and she was under no illusions about how long those last two sips of water would stave it off.

I've got to center my concentration—I've just got to. The problem isn't food, and it isn't water, either. Right now those things matter as little as why I punched Will in the mouth at his ninth-birthday party. The problem is how I'm—

Her thoughts broke off with the clean snap of a knot exploding in a hot fire. Her eyes, which had been wandering aimlessly across the darkened room, locked on the far corner, where the wind-driven shadows of the pines danced wildly in the nacreous light falling through the skylight.

There was a man standing there.

Terror greater than any she had ever known crept over her. Her bladder, which had in fact relieved only the worst of its discomfort, now voided itself in a painless gush of heat. Jessie hadn't the slightest idea of that or anything else. Her terror had blown her mind temporarily clean from wall to wall and ceiling to floor. No sound escaped her, not even the smallest squeak; she was as incapable of sound as she was of thought. The muscles of her neck, shoulders, and arms turned to something that felt like warm water and she slid down the headboard until she hung from the handcuffs in a kind of slack swoon. She didn't black out—didn't even come close to it—but that mental emptiness and the total physical incapacity which accompanied it were worse than a blackout. When thought did attempt to return, it was at first blocked by a dark, featureless wall of fear.

A man. A man in the corner.

She could see his dark eyes gazing at her with fixed, idiotic attention. She could see the waxy whiteness of his narrow cheeks and high forehead, although the intruder's actual features were blurred by the diorama of shadows which went flying across them. She could see slumped shoulders and dangling apelike arms which ended in long hands; she sensed feet somewhere in the black triangle of shadow thrown by the bureau, but that was all.

She had no idea how long she lay in that horrible semi-swoon, paralyzed but aware, like a beetle stung by a trapdoor spider. It seemed like a very long time. The seconds dripped by, and she found herself unable to even close her eyes, let alone avert them from her strange guest. Her first terror of him began to abate a little, but what replaced it was somehow worse: horror and an unreasoning, atavistic revulsion. Jessie later thought that the wellspring of these feelings—the most powerful negative emotions she had ever experienced in her life, including those which had swept her only a short time before, as she had watched the stray dog preparing to dine on Gerald—was the creature's utter stillness. It had crept in here while she slept and now merely stood in the corner, camouflaged by the ceaseless ebb and flow of shadows over its face and body, staring at her with its strangely avid black eyes, eyes so large and rapt they reminded her of the sockets in a skull.

Her visitor only stood there in the corner; merely that and nothing more.

She lay in the handcuffs with her arms stretched above her, feeling like a woman at the bottom of a deep well. Time passed, marked only by the idiot blink of the clock proclaiming it was twelve, twelve, twelve, and at last a coherent thought stole back into her brain, one which seemed both dangerous and vastly comforting.

There's no one here but you, Jessie. The man you see in the corner is a combination of shadows and imagination—no more than that.

She fought her way back to a sitting position, pulling with her arms, grimacing at the pain in her overtaxed shoulders, pushing with her feet, trying to dig her bare heels into the coverlet, breathing in harsh little blurts of effort . . . and while doing these things, her eyes never left the hideously elongated shape in the corner.

It's too tall and too thin to be a real man, Jess—you see that, don't you? It's nothing but wind, shadows, a soupçon of moonlight . . . and a few leftovers from your nightmare, I imagine. Okay?

It almost was. She started to relax. Then, from outside, the dog voiced another hysterical volley of barks. And didn't the figure in the corner—the figure that was nothing but wind, shadows, and a soupçon of moonlight—didn't that nonexistent figure turn its head slightly in that direction?

No, surely not. Surely that was just another trick of the wind and the dark and the shadows.

That might well be; in fact she was almost sure that part—the head-turning part—had been an illusion. But the rest of it? The figure itself? She could not quite convince herself that it was *all* imagination. Surely no figure which looked *that much* like a man could be just an illusion . . . could it?

Goodwife Burlingame spoke up suddenly, and although her voice was fearful, there was no hysteria in it, at least not yet; oddly, it was the Ruth part of her which had suffered the most extreme horror at the idea she might not be alone in the room, and it was the Ruth part that was still close to gibbering.

If that thing's not real, Goody said, *why did the dog leave in the first place? I don't think it would have done that without a very good reason, do you?*

Yet she understood that Goody was deeply frightened just the same, and yearning for some explanation of the dog's departure that didn't include the shape Jessie either saw or thought she saw standing in the corner. Goody was begging her to say that her original idea, that the dog had left simply because it no longer felt comfortable in the house, was much more likely. Or maybe, she thought, it had left for the oldest reason of all: it had smelled another stray, this one a bitch in heat. She supposed it was even possible that the dog had been spooked by some noise—a branch knocking against an upstairs window, say. She liked that one the best, because it suggested a kind of rough justice: that the dog had also been spooked by some imaginary intruder, and its barks were intended to frighten this nonexistent newcomer away from its pariah's supper.

Yes, say any of those things, Goody suddenly begged her, *and even if you can't believe any of them yourself, make* me *believe them.*

But she didn't think she could do that, and the reason was standing in the corner beside the bureau. There *was* someone there. It wasn't a hallucination, it wasn't a combination of wind-driven shadows and her own imagination, it wasn't a holdover from her dream, a momentary phantom glimpsed in the perceptual no-man's-land between sleeping and waking. It was a

(*monster it's a monster a boogeymonster come to eat me up*)

man, not a monster but a *man,* standing there motionlessly and watching her while the wind gusted, making the house creak and the shadows dance across its strange, half-glimpsed face.

This time the thought—*Monster! Boogeymonster!*—rose from the lower levels of her mind to the more brightly lit stage of her consciousness. She denied it again, but she could feel her terror returning, just the same. The creature on the far side of the room might be a man, but even if it was, she was becoming more and more sure that there was something very wrong with its face. If only she could see it better!

You wouldn't want to, a whispery, ominous UFO voice advised her.

But I have to talk to it—have to establish contact, Jessie thought, and immediately responded to herself in a nervous, scolding voice that felt like Ruth and Goody mixed together: *Don't think of it as an it, Jessie—think of it as a he. Think of it as a man, someone who's maybe been lost in the woods, someone who's as scared as you are.*

Good advice, perhaps, but Jessie found she *couldn't* think of the figure in the corner as a he, any more than she was able to think of the stray as a he. Nor did she think the creature in the shadows was either lost or frightened. What she felt coming from the corner were long, slow waves of malevolence.

That's stupid! Talk to it, Jessie! Talk to him*!*

She tried to clear her throat and discovered there was nothing to clear—it was as dry as a desert and as smooth as a soapstone. Now she could feel her heart pounding in her chest, its beat very light, very fast, very irregular.

The wind gusted. The shadows blew white-and-black patterns across the walls and the ceiling, making her feel like a woman trapped inside a kaleidoscope for the colorblind. For just a moment she thought she saw a nose—thin and long and white—below those black, motionless eyes.

"Who—"

At first she could manage only that one tiny whisper which couldn't have been heard on the far side of the bed, let alone across the room. She stopped, licked her lips, and tried again. She was aware that her hands were clamped into painfully tight balls, and she forced her fingers to loosen.

"Who are you?" Still a whisper, but a little better than before.

The figure didn't answer, only stood there with its narrow white hands dangling by its knees, and Jessie thought: *Its knees? Knees? Not possible, Jess—when a person's hands are hanging at his sides, they stop at the upper thighs.*

Ruth responded, her voice so hushed and fearful Jessie almost didn't recognize it. *A normal person's hands stop at the upper thighs, isn't that what you mean? But do you think a normal person would creep into someone's house in the middle of the night, then just stand in the corner, watching, when he finds the lady of the manor chained to the bed? Just stand there and nothing more?*

Then it *did* move one leg . . . or perhaps it was only the distracting motion of the shadows again, this time picked up by the lower quadrant of her vision. The combination of shadows and moonlight and wind lent a terrible ambiguity to this entire episode, and again Jessie found herself doubting the visitor's reality. The possibility that she was still sleeping occurred to her, that her dream of Will's birthday party had simply veered off in some strange new direction . . . but she didn't really believe it. She was awake, all right.

Whether or not the leg actually did move (or even if there *was* a leg), Jessie's gaze was momentarily drawn downward. She thought she saw some black object sitting on the floor between the creature's feet. It was impossible to tell what it might be because the bureau's shadow rendered that the darkest part of the room, but her mind suddenly returned to that afternoon, when she had been trying to persuade Gerald that she really meant what she was saying. The only sounds had been the wind, the banging door, the barking dog, the loon, and . . .

The thing sitting on the floor between her visitor's feet was a chainsaw.

Jessie was instantly sure of this. Her visitor had been using it earlier, but not to cut firewood. It was *people* he had been cutting up, and the dog had run because it had smelled the approach of this madman, who had come up the lake path swinging his blood-spattered Stihl saw in one gloved hand—

Stop it! Goody shouted angrily. *Stop this foolishness right this minute and get a grip on yourself!*

But she discovered she *couldn't* stop it, because this was no dream and also because she had become increasingly sure that the figure standing in the corner, as silent as Frankenstein's monster before the lightning-bolts, was real. But even if it was, it hadn't spent the afternoon turning people into pork-chops with a chainsaw. Of course not—that was nothing but a movie-inspired variation of the simple, gruesome summer-camp tales that seemed so funny when you were gathered around the fire, roasting marshmallows with the rest of the girls, and so awful later on, when you lay shivering in your sleeping-bag, believing that each snapping twig signalled the approach of the Lakeview Man, that legendary brain-blasted survivor of the Korean War.

The thing standing in the corner wasn't the Lakeview Man, and it wasn't a chainsaw murderer, either. There *was* something on the floor (at least she was pretty sure there was), and Jessie supposed it *could* be a chainsaw, but it could also be a suitcase . . . a back-pack . . . a salesman's sample case . . .

Or my imagination.

Yes. Even though she was looking right at it, whatever it was, she knew she couldn't rule out the possibility of imagination. Yet in some perverse way this only reinforced the idea that the creature *itself* was real, and it was becoming harder and harder to dismiss the feeling of malevolence which came crawling out of the tangle of black shadows and powdery moonlight like a constant low snarl.

It hates me, she thought. *Whatever it is, it hates me. It must. Why else would it just stand there and not help me?*

She looked back up at that half-seen face, at the eyes which seemed to glitter with such feverish avidity in their round black sockets, and she began to weep.

"Please, is someone there?" Her voice was humble, choked with tears. "If there is, won't you please help me? Do you see these handcuffs? The keys are right there beside you, on top of the bureau . . ."

Nothing. No movement. No response. It only stood there—if it was there at all, that was—looking out at her from behind its feral mask of shadows.

"If you didn't want me to tell anyone I saw you, I wouldn't," she tried again. Her voice wavered, blurred, swooped and slid. "I sure wouldn't! And I'd be so . . . so grateful . . ."

It watched her.

Only that and nothing more.

Jessie felt the tears rolling slowly down her cheeks. "You're scaring me, you know," she said. "Won't you say something? Can't you talk? *If you're really there, can't you please talk to me?*"

A thin, terrible hysteria seized her then and flew away with some valuable, irreplaceable part of her caught firmly in its scrawny talons. She wept and pleaded with the fearful figure standing motionless in the corner of the bedroom; she remained conscious throughout but sometimes wavered into that curious blank place reserved for those whose terror has become so great it approaches rapture. She would hear herself asking the figure in a hoarse, weepy voice to *please* let her out of the handcuffs, to please oh please oh *please* let her out of the handcuffs, and then she would drop back into that weird blank spot. She knew her mouth was still moving because she could feel it. She could also hear the sounds that were coming out of it, but while she was in the blank place, these sounds were not words but only loose blabbering torrents of sound. She could also hear the wind blowing and the dog barking, aware but not knowing, hearing but not understanding, losing everything in her horror of the half-seen shape, the awful visitor, the uninvited guest. She could not cease her contemplation of its narrow, misshapen head, its white cheeks, its slumped shoulders . . . but more and more it was the creature's hands to which her eyes were drawn: those dangling, long-fingered hands that ended much farther down on the legs than normal hands had any right to do. Some unknown length of time would pass in this blank fashion (*twelve-twelve-twelve*, the clock on the dresser reported; no help there) and then she would come back a little, would start thinking thoughts instead of experiencing only an endless rush of incoherent images, would start hearing her lips speaking words instead of just babbling sounds. But she had moved on while she was in that blank space; her words now had nothing to do with the handcuffs or the keys on the dresser. What she heard instead was the thin, screamy whisper of a woman reduced to begging for an answer . . . any answer.

"What are you?" she sobbed. "A man? A devil? *What in God's name are you?*"

The wind gusted.

The door banged.

Before her, the figure's face seemed to change . . . seemed to wrinkle upward in a grin. There was something horribly familiar about that grin, and Jessie felt the core of her sanity, which had borne this assault with remarkable strength until now, at last begin to waver.

"Daddy?" she whispered. "Daddy, is that you?"

Don't be silly! the Goodwife cried, but Jessie could now feel even that sustaining voice wavering toward hysteria. *Don't be a goose, Jessie! Your father has been dead since 1980!*

Instead of helping, it made things worse. *Much* worse. Tom Mahout had been interred in the family crypt in Falmouth, and that was less than a hundred miles from here. Jessie's burning, terrified mind insisted upon showing her a hunched figure, its clothes and rotted shoes caked with blue-green mold, slinking across moon-drenched fields and hurrying through tracts of scruffy woods between suburban housing developments; she saw gravity working on the decayed muscles of its arms as it came, gradually stretching them until the hands were swinging beside the knees. It was her father. It was the man who had delighted her with rides on his shoulders at three, who had comforted her at the age of six when a capering circus clown frightened her into tears, who had told her bedtime stories until she was eight—old enough, he said, to read them on her own. Her father, who had cobbled together home-made filters on the afternoon of the eclipse and held her on his lap as the moment of totality approached, her father who had said, *Don't worry about anything . . . don't worry, and don't look around.* But she had thought maybe *he* was worried, because his voice had been all thick and shaky, hardly like his usual voice at all.

In the corner, the thing's grin seemed to widen and suddenly the room was filled with that smell, that flat smell that was half-metallic and half-organic; a smell that reminded her of oysters in cream, and how your hand smelled after you'd been clutching a fistful of pennies, and the way the air smelled just before a thunderstorm.

"Daddy, is it you?" she asked the shadowy thing in the corner, and from somewhere came the distant cry of the loon. Jessie could feel the tears trickling slowly down her cheeks. And now something exceedingly odd was happening, something she never would have expected in a thousand years. As she became increasingly sure that it *was* her father, that it was Tom Mahout standing in the corner, twelve years gone in death or not, her terror began to leave her. She had drawn her legs up, but now she let them slip back down and fall open. As she did, a fragment of her dream recurred—

DADDY'S LITTLE GIRL printed across her breasts in Peppermint Yum-Yum lipstick.

"All right, go ahead," she told the shape. Her voice was a little hoarse but otherwise steady. "It's why you came back, isn't it? So go ahead. How could I stop you, anyway? *Just promise you'll unlock me afterward. That you'll unlock me and let me go.*"

The figure made no response of any kind. It only stood within its surreal jackstraws of moonlight and shadow, grinning at her. And as the seconds passed (*twelve-twelve-twelve,* the clock on the dresser said, seeming to suggest that the whole idea of time passing was an illusion, that time had in fact frozen solid), Jessie thought that perhaps she had been right in the first place, that there was really no one in here with her at all. She had begun to feel like a weathervane in the grip of those prankish, contradictory gusts of wind that sometimes blow just before a severe thunderstorm or a tornado.

Your father cannot come back from the dead, Goodwife Burlingame said in a voice that strove to be firm and failed miserably. Still, Jessie saluted her effort. Come hell or high water, the Goodwife stayed right in there and kept pitching. *This isn't a horror movie or an episode of* The Twilight Zone, *Jess; this is real life.*

But another part of her—a part which was perhaps the home of those few voices inside which were the *real* UFOs, not just the wiretaps her subconscious had patched into her conscious mind at some point—insisted that there was a darker truth here, something that trailed from the heels of logic like an irrational (and perhaps supernatural) shadow. This voice insisted that things *changed* in the dark. Things *especially* changed in the dark, it said, when a person was alone. When that happened, the locks fell off the cage which held the imagination, and anything—any *things*—might be set free.

It can *be your Daddy,* this essentially alien part of her whispered, and with a chill of fear Jessie recognized it as the voice of madness and reason mingled together. *It* can *be, never doubt it. People are almost always safe from ghosts and ghouls and the living dead in daylight, and they're usually safe from them at night if they're with others, but when a person is alone in the dark, all bets are off. Men and women alone in the dark are like open doors, Jessie, and if they call out or scream for help, who knows what dread things may answer? Who knows what some men and women have seen in the hour of their solitary deaths? Is it so hard to believe that some of them may have died of fear, no matter what the words on the death certificates say?*

"I don't believe that," she said in a blurry, wavering voice. She spoke louder, striving for a firmness she didn't feel. "You're not my father! I don't think you're *anyone*! I think you're only made of moonlight!"

As if in answer, the figure bent forward in a kind of mocking bow, and for one moment its face—a face which seemed too real to doubt—slipped out of the shadows. Jessie uttered a rusty shriek as the pallid rays falling through the skylight painted its features with tawdry carnival gilt. It wasn't her father; compared with the evil and the lunacy she saw in the face of her visitor, she would have welcomed her father, even after twelve years in a cold coffin. Red-rimmed, hideously sparkling eyes regarded her from deep eye-sockets wrapped in wrinkles. Thin lips twitched upward in a dry grin, revealing discolored molars and jagged canines which seemed almost as long as the stray dog's fangs.

One of its white hands lifted the object she had half-seen and half-intuited sitting by its feet in the darkness. At first she thought it had taken Gerald's briefcase from the little room he used as a study down here, but when the creature lifted the box-shaped thing into the light, she saw it was a lot bigger than Gerald's briefcase and much older. It looked like the sort of old-fashioned sample case travelling salesmen had once carried.

"Please," she whispered in a strengthless, wheezing little voice. "Whatever you are, please don't hurt me. You don't have to let me go if you don't want to, that's all right, but please don't hurt me."

Its grin grew, and she saw tiny twinkles far back in its mouth— her visitor apparently had gold teeth or gold fillings in there, just like Gerald. It seemed to laugh soundlessly, as if gratified by her terror. Then its long fingers were unsnapping the catches of its bag

(*I am dreaming, I think, now it does feel like a dream, oh thank God it does*)

and holding it open to her. The case was full of bones and jewelry. She saw finger-bones and rings and teeth and bracelets and ulnae and pendants; she saw a diamond big enough to choke a rhino glittering milky trapezoids of moonlight from within the stiff, delicate curves of an infant's ribcage. She saw these things and wanted them to be a dream, yes, *wanted* them to be, but if it was, it was like no dream she'd ever had before. It was the *situation*—handcuffed to the bed while a half-seen maniac silently showed off his treasures—that was dreamlike. The feeling, however . . .

The feeling was reality. There was no getting around it. *The feeling was reality.*

The thing standing in the corner held the open case out for her inspection, one hand supporting the bottom. It plunged its other hand into the tangle of bones and jewelry and stirred it, producing a tenebrous click and rustle that sounded like dirt-clogged castanets. It stared at her as it did this, the somehow unformed features of its strange face wrinkled upward in amusement, its mouth gawping in that silent grin, its slumped shoulders rising and falling in strangled chuffs of laughter.

No! Jessie screamed, but no sound came out.

Suddenly she felt someone—most likely the Goodwife, and boy, had she ever underestimated the intestinal fortitude of *that* lady—running for the switches which governed the circuit-breakers in her head. Goody had seen tendrils of smoke starting to seep out through the cracks in the closed doors of those panels, had understood what they meant, and was making a final, desperate effort to shut down the machinery before the motors overheated and the bearings froze.

The grinning figure across the room reached deeper into the case and held out a handful of bones and gold to Jessie in the moonlight.

There was an intolerably bright flash inside her head and then the lights went out. She did not faint prettily, like the heroine in a florid stage play, but was snapped brutally backward like a condemned murderer who has been strapped into the hotseat and has just gotten his first jolt of the juice. All the same it was an end to the horror, and for the time being that was enough. Jessie Burlingame went into the darkness without a murmur of protest.

14

She struggled briefly back to consciousness some time later, aware of only two things: the moon had made it around to the west windows, and she was terribly afraid . . . of what she at first didn't know. Then it came to her: Daddy had been here, was perhaps here still. The creature hadn't looked like him, that was true, but that was only because Daddy had been wearing his eclipse face.

Jessie struggled up, pushing with her feet so hard she shoved the coverlet down beneath her. She wasn't able to do much with her arms, however. The jittering pins and needles had stolen away while she'd been unconscious, and they had no more feeling than a couple of chair-legs. She stared into the corner by the bureau with wide, moon-silvered eyes. The wind had died and the shadows were, at least for the time being, still. There was nothing in the corner. Her dark visitor had gone.

Maybe not, Jess—maybe he's just changed location. Maybe he's hiding under the bed, how's that for a thought? If he is, he could reach up at any second and put one of his hands on your hip.

The wind stirred—only a puff, not a gust—and the back door banged weakly. Those were the only sounds. The dog had fallen silent, and it was this more than anything else which convinced her that the stranger was gone. She had the house to herself.

Jessie's gaze dropped to the large dark blob on the floor.

Correction, she thought. *There's Gerald. Can't forget about him.*

She put her head back and closed her eyes, aware of a steady low pulse in her throat, not wanting to wake up enough for that pulse to transform itself into what it really was: thirst. She didn't know if she could go from black unconsciousness to ordinary sleep or not, but she knew that was what she wanted; more than anything else—except perhaps for someone to drive down here and rescue her—she wanted to sleep.

There was no one here, Jessie—you know that, don't you? It was, absurdity of absurdities, Ruth's voice. Tough-talking Ruth, whose stated motto, cribbed from a Nancy Sinatra song, was "One of these days these boots are gonna walk all over you." Ruth, who had been reduced to a pile of quivering jelly by the shape in the moonlight.

Go ahead, toots, Ruth said. *Make fun of me all you want—maybe I even deserve it—but don't kid yourself. There was no one here. Your imagination put on a little slide-show, that's all. That's all there was to it.*

You're wrong, Ruth, Goody responded calmly. *Someone was here, all right, and Jessie and I both know who it was. It didn't exactly* look *like Daddy, but that was only because he had his eclipse face on. The face wasn't the important part, though, or how tall he looked—he might have had on boots with special high heels, or maybe he was wearing shoes with lifts in them. For all I know, he could have been on stilts.*

Stilts! Ruth cried, amazed. *Oh dear God, now I've heard* evvvery*thing! Never mind the fact that the man died before Reagan's Inauguration Day tux got back from the cleaners; Tom Mahout was so clumsy he should have had walking-downstairs insurance.* Stilts? *Oh babe, you* have *got to be putting me on!*

That part doesn't matter, Goody said with a kind of serene stubbornness. *It was him. I'd know that smell anywhere—that thick, blood-warm smell. Not the smell of oysters or pennies. Not even the smell of blood. The smell of . . .*

The thought broke up and drifted away.

Jessie slept.

15

She ended up alone with her father at Sunset Trails on the afternoon of July 20th, 1963, for two reasons. One was a cover for the other. The cover was her claim that she was still a little frightened of Mrs. Gilette, even though it had been at least five years (and probably closer to six) since the incident of the cookie and the slapped hand. The real reason was simple and uncomplicated: it was her Daddy she wanted to be with during such a special, once-in-a-lifetime event.

Her mother had suspected as much, and being moved around like a chesspiece by her husband and her ten-year-old daughter hadn't pleased her, but by then the matter was practically a *fait accompli*. Jessie had gone to her Daddy first. She was still four months away from her eleventh birthday, but that didn't make her a fool. What Sally Mahout suspected was true: Jessie had launched a conscious, carefully thought-out campaign which would allow her to spend the day of the eclipse with her father. Much later Jessie would think that this was yet another reason to keep her mouth shut about what had happened on that day; there might be those —her mother, for instance—who would say that she had no right to complain; that she had in fact gotten about what she deserved.

On the day before the eclipse, Jessie had found her father sitting on the deck outside his den and reading a paperback copy of *Profiles in Courage* while his wife, son, and elder daughter laughed and swam in the lake below. He smiled at her when she took the seat next to him, and Jessie smiled back. She had brightened her mouth with lipstick for this interview—Peppermint Yum-Yum, in fact, a birthday present from Maddy. Jessie hadn't liked it when she first tried it on—she thought it a baby shade, and that it tasted like Pepsodent—but Daddy had said he thought it was pretty, and that had transformed it into the most valuable of her few cosmetic resources, something to be treasured and used only on special occasions like this one.

He listened carefully and respectfully as she spoke, but he made no particular attempt to disguise the glint of amused skepticism in his eyes. *Do you* really *mean to tell me you're still afraid of Adrienne Gilette?* he asked when she had finished rehashing the oft-told tale of how Mrs. Gilette had slapped her hand when she had reached for the last cookie on the plate. *That must have been back in . . . I don't know, but I was still working for Dunninger, so it must have been before 1959. And you're still spooked all these years later? How absolutely Freudian, my dear!*

Well-lll . . . you know . . . just a little. She widened her eyes, trying to communicate the idea that she was *saying* a little but *meaning* a lot. In truth she didn't know if she was still scared of old Pooh-Pooh Breath or not, but she *did* know she considered Mrs. Gilette a boring old blue-haired booger, and she had no intention of spending the only total eclipse of the sun she'd probably ever see in her company if she could possibly work things around so she could watch it with her Daddy, whom she adored beyond the power of words to tell.

She evaluated his skepticism and concluded with relief that it was friendly, perhaps even conspiratorial. She smiled and added: *But I also want to stay with you.*

He raised her hand to his mouth and kissed her fingers like a French monsieur. He hadn't shaved that day—he often didn't when he was at camp—and the rough scrape of his whiskers sent a pleasurable shiver of goosebumps up her arms and back.

Comme tu es douce, he said. *Ma jolie mademoiselle. Je t'aime.*

She giggled, not understanding his clumsy French but suddenly sure it was all going to work out just the way she had hoped it would.

It would be fun, she said happily. *Just the two of us. I could make an early supper and we could eat it right here, on the deck.*

He grinned. *Eclipse Burgers* à deux?

She laughed, nodding and clapping her hands with delight.

Then he had said something that struck her as a little odd even at the time, because he was not a man who cared much about clothes and fashions: *You could wear your pretty new sundress.*

Sure, if you want, she said, although she had already made a mental note to ask her mother to try and exchange the sundress. It *was* pretty enough—if you weren't offended by red and yellow stripes almost bright enough to shout, that was—but it was also too small and too tight. Her mother had ordered it from Sears, going mostly by guess and by gosh, filling in a single size larger than that which had fit Jessie the year before. As it happened, she had grown a little faster than that, in a number of ways. Still, if Daddy liked it . . . and if he would come over to her side of this eclipse business and help her push . . .

He *did* come over to her side, and pushed like Hercules himself. He began that night, suggesting to his wife after dinner (and two or three mellowing glasses of *vin rouge*) that Jessie be excused from tomorrow's "eclipse-watch" outing to the top of Mount Washington. Most of their summer neighbors were going; just after Memorial Day they'd begun having informal meetings on the subject of how and where to watch the upcoming solar phenomenon (to Jessie these meetings had seemed like ordinary run-of-the-mill summer cocktail parties), and had even given themselves a name—The Dark Score Sun Worshippers. The Sun Worshippers had rented one of the school district's mini-buses for the occasion and were planning to voyage to the top of New Hampshire's tallest mountain equipped with box lunches, Polaroid sunglasses, specially constructed reflector-boxes, specially filtered cameras . . . and champagne, of course. Lots and lots of champagne. To Jessie's mother and older sister, all this had seemed to be the very definition of frothy, sophisticated fun. To Jessie it had seemed the essence of all that was boring . . . and that was *before* you added Pooh-Pooh Breath into the equation.

She had gone out on the deck after supper on the evening of the 19th, presumably to read twenty or thirty pages of Mr. C. S. Lewis's *Out of the Silent Planet* before the sun went down. Her actual purpose was a good deal less intellectual: she wanted to listen as her father made his—*their*—pitch, and to silently root him on. She and Maddy had been aware for years that the combination living room/ dining room of the summer house had peculiar acoustical qualities, probably caused by its high, steeply angled ceiling; Jessie had an idea that even Will knew about the way sound carried from in there to out here on the deck. Only their parents seemed unaware that the room might as well have been bugged, and that most of the important decisions they had made in that room as they sipped after-dinner cognac or cups of coffee were known (to their daughters, at least) long before the marching orders were handed down from staff headquarters.

Jessie noticed she was holding the Lewis novel upside down and made haste to rectify that situation before Maddy happened by and gave her a big, silent horselaugh. She felt a little guilty about what she was doing—it was a lot closer to eavesdropping than to rooting, when you got right down to it—but not quite guilty enough to stop. And in fact she considered herself still to be on the right side of a thin moral line. After all, it wasn't as if she were hiding in the closet, or anything; she was sitting right out here in full view, bathed in the bright light of the westering sun. She was sitting out here with her book, and wondering if there were ever eclipses on Mars, and if there were Martians up there to watch them if there were. If her parents thought no one could hear what they were saying just because they were sitting at the table in there, was that *her* fault? Was she supposed to go in and *tell* them?

"I don't *theenk* so, my *deah*," Jessie whispered in her snottiest Elizabeth Taylor *Cat on a Hot Tin Roof* voice, and then cupped her hands over a big, goofy grin. And she guessed she was also safe from her big sister's interference, at least for the time being; she could hear Maddy and Will below her in the rumpus room, squabbling good-naturedly over a game of Cootie or Parcheesi or something like that.

I really don't think it would hurt *her to stay here with me tomorrow, do you?* her father was asking in his most winning, good-humored voice.

No, of course not, Jessie's mother replied, *but it wouldn't exactly kill her to go someplace with the rest of us this summer, either. She's turned into a* complete *Daddy's girl.*

She went down to the puppet show in Bethel with you and Will last week. In fact, didn't you tell me that she stayed with Will—even bought him an ice cream out of her own allowance—while you went into that auction barn?

That was no sacrifice for our Jessie, Sally replied. She sounded almost grim.

What do you mean?

I mean she went to the puppet show because she wanted to, and she took care of Will because she wanted to. Grimness had given way to a more familiar tone: exasperation. *How can you understand what I mean?* that tone asked. *How can you* possibly, *when you're a man?*

This was a tone Jessie had heard more and more frequently in her mother's voice these last few years. She knew that was partly because she herself heard more and saw more as she grew up, but she was pretty sure it was also because her mother *used* that tone more frequently than she once had. Jessie couldn't understand why her father's brand of logic always made her mother so crazy.

All of a sudden the fact that she did something because she wanted to is a cause for concern? Tom was now asking. *Maybe even a mark against her? What do we do if she develops a social conscience as well as a family one, Sal? Put her in a home for wayward girls?*

Don't patronize me, Tom. You know perfectly well what I mean.

Nope; this time you've lost me in the dust, sweet one. This is supposed to be our summer vacation, remember? And I've always sort of had the idea that when people are on vacation, they're supposed to do what they want to do, and be with who they want to be with. In fact, I thought that was the whole idea.

Jessie smiled, knowing it was all over but the shouting. When the eclipse started tomorrow afternoon, she was going to be here with her Daddy instead of on top of Mount Washington with Pooh-Pooh Breath and the rest of The Dark Score Sun Worshippers. Her father was like some world-class chessmaster who had given a talented amateur a run for her money and was now polishing her off.

You could come, too, Tom—Jessie would come if you did.

That was a tricky one. Jessie held her breath.

Can't, my love—I'm expecting a call from David Adams on the Brookings Pharmaceuticals portfolio. Very important stuff . . . also very risky stuff. At this stage, handling Brookings is like handling blasting caps. But let me be honest with you: even if I could, I'm not really sure I would. I'm not nuts about the Gilette woman, but I can get along with her. That asshole Sleefort, on the other hand—

Hush, Tom!

Don't worry—Maddy and Will are downstairs and Jessie's way out on the front deck . . . see her?

At that moment, Jessie suddenly became sure that her father knew *exactly* what the acoustics of the living room/dining room were like; he knew that his daughter was hearing every word of this discussion. *Wanted* her to hear every word. A warm little shiver traced its way up her back and down her legs.

I should have known it came down to Dick Sleefort! Her mother sounded angrily amused, a combination that made Jessie's head spin. It seemed to her that only adults could combine emotions in so many daffy ways—if feelings were food, adult feelings would be things like chocolate-covered steak, mashed potatoes with pineapple bits, Special K with chili powder sprinkled on it instead of sugar. Jessie thought that being an adult seemed more like a punishment than a reward.

This is really exasperating, Tom—the man made a pass at me six years ago. He was drunk. Back in those days he was always *drunk, but he's cleaned up his act. Polly Bergeron told me he goes to A.A., and—*

Bully for him, her father said dryly. *Do we send him a get-well card or a merit-badge, Sally?*

Don't be flip. You almost broke the man's nose—

Yes, indeed. When a fellow comes into the kitchen to freshen his drink and finds the rumdum from up the road with one hand on his wife's behind and the other down the front of her—

Never mind, she said primly, but Jessie thought that for some reason her mother sounded almost *pleased.* Curiouser and curiouser. *The point is, it's time you discovered that Dick Sleefort isn't a demon from the deeps and it's time Jessie discovered Adrienne Gilette is just a lonely old woman who once slapped her hand at a lawn-party as a little joke. Now please don't get all crazy on me, Tom; I'm not claiming it was a good joke; it wasn't. I'm just saying that Adrienne didn't know that. There was no bad intent.*

Jessie looked down and saw her paperback novel was bent almost double in her right hand. How could her mother, a woman who'd graduated *cum laude* (whatever that meant) from Vassar, possibly be so stupid? The answer seemed clear enough to Jessie: she couldn't be. Either she knew better or she refused to see the truth, and you arrived at the same conclusion no matter which answer you decided was the right one: when forced to choose between believing the ugly old woman who lived up the road from them in the summertime and her own daughter, Sally Mahout had chosen Pooh-Pooh Breath. Good deal, huh?

If I'm a Daddy's girl, that's why. That and all the other stuff she says that's like that. That's why, but I could never tell her and she'll never see it on her own. Never in a billion years.

Jessie forced herself to relax her grip on the paperback. Mrs. Gilette *had* meant it, there *had* been bad intent, but her father's suspicion that she had ceased being afraid of the old crow had probably been more right than wrong, just the same. Also, she was going to get her way about staying with her father, so none of her mother's ess-aitch-eye-tee really mattered, did it? She was going to be here with her Daddy, she wouldn't have to deal with old Pooh-Pooh Breath, and these good things were going to happen because . . .

"Because he sticks up for me," she murmured.

Yes; that was the bottom line. Her father stuck up *for* her, and her mother stuck it *to* her.

Jessie saw the evening star glowing mildly in the darkening sky and suddenly realized she had been out on the deck, listening to them circle the subject of the eclipse—and the subject of *her*—for almost three-quarters of an hour. She discovered a minor but interesting fact of life that night: time speeds by fastest when you are eavesdropping on conversations about yourself.

With hardly a thought, she raised her hand and curled it into a tube, simultaneously catching the star and sending it the old formula: wish I may, wish I might. *Her* wish, already well on the way to being granted, was that she be allowed to stay here tomorrow with her Daddy. To stay with him no matter what. Just two folks who knew how to stick up for each other, sitting out on the deck and eating Eclipse Burgers *à deux* . . . like an old married couple.

As for Dick Sleefort, he apologized to me later, Tom. I don't remember if I ever told you that or not—

You did, but I don't remember him ever apologizing to me.

He was probably afraid you'd knock his block off, or at least try to, Sally replied, speaking again in that tone of voice Jessie found so peculiar—it seemed to be an uneasy mixture of happiness, good humor, and anger. Jessie wondered for just a moment if it was possible to sound that way and be completely sane, and then she squashed the thought quickly and completely. *Also, I want to say one more thing about Adrienne Gilette before we leave the subject entirely . . .*

Be my guest.

She told me—in 1959, this was, two whole summers later—that she went through the change that year. She never specifically mentioned Jessie and the cookie incident, but I think she was trying to apologize.

Oh. It was her father's coolest, most lawyerly "Oh." *And did either of you ladies think to pass that information on to Jessie . . . and explain to her what it meant?*

Silence from her mother. Jessie, who still had only the vaguest notion of what "going through the change" meant, looked down and saw she had once again gripped the book tight enough to bend it and once again forced herself to relax her hands.

Or to apologize? His tone was gentle . . . caressing . . . deadly.

Stop cross-examining me! Sally burst out after another long, considering silence. *This is your home, not Part Two of Superior Court, in case you hadn't noticed!*

You brought the subject up, not me, he said. *I just asked—*

Oh, I get so tired *of the way you twist everything around,* Sally said. Jessie knew from her tone of voice that she was either crying or getting ready to. For the first time that she could remember, the sound of her mother's tears called up no sympathy in her own heart, no urge to run and comfort (probably bursting into tears herself in the process). Instead she felt a queer, stony satisfaction.

Sally, you're upset. Why don't we just—

You're damned tooting I am. Arguments with my husband have a way of doing that, isn't that strange? Isn't that just the weirdest thing you ever heard*? And do you know* what *we're arguing about? I'll give you a hint, Tom—it's not Adrienne Gilette and it's not Dick Sleefort and it's not the eclipse tomorrow. We're arguing about* Jessie, *about our* daughter, *and what else is new?*

She laughed through her tears. There was a dry hiss as she scratched a match and lit a cigarette.

Don't they say it's the squeaky wheel that always gets the grease? And that's our Jessie, isn't it? The squeaky wheel. Never quite satisfied with the arrangements until she gets a chance to put on the finishing touches. Never quite happy with someone else's plans. Never able to let well enough alone.

Jessie was appalled to hear something very close to hate in her mother's voice.

Sally—

Never mind, Tom. She wants to stay here with you? Fine. She wouldn't be pleasant to have along, anyway; all she'd do is pick fights with her sister and whine about having to watch out for Will. All she'd do is squeak, in other words.

Sally, Jessie hardly ever whines, and she's very good about—

Oh, you don't see *her!* Sally Mahout cried, and the spite in her voice made Jessie cringe back in her chair. *I swear to God, sometimes you behave as if she were your girlfriend instead of your daughter!*

This time the long pause belonged to her father, and when he spoke, his voice was soft and cold. *That's a lousy, underhanded, unfair thing to say,* he finally replied.

Jessie sat on the deck, looking at the evening star and feeling dismay deepening toward something like horror. She felt a sudden urge to cup her hand and catch the star again—this time to wish everything away, beginning with her request to her Daddy that he fix things so she could stay at Sunset Trails with him tomorrow.

Then the sound of her mother's chair being pushed back came. *I apologize,* Sally said, and although she still sounded angry, Jessie thought she now sounded a little afraid, as well. *Keep her tomorrow, if that's what you want! Fine! Good! You're welcome to her!*

Then the sound of her heels, tapping rapidly away, and a moment later the *snick* of her father's Zippo as he lit his own cigarette.

On the deck, Jessie felt warm tears spring to her eyes—tears of shame, hurt, and relief that the argument had ended before it could get any worse . . . for hadn't both she and Maddy noticed that their parents' arguments had gotten both louder and hotter just lately? That the coolness between them afterward was slower to warm up again? It wasn't possible, was it, that they—

No, she interrupted herself before the thought could be completed. *No, it's not. It's not possible at all, so just shut up.*

Perhaps a change of scene would induce a change of thought. Jessie got up, trotted down the deck steps, then walked down the path to the lakefront. There she sat, throwing pebbles into the water, until her father came out to find her, half an hour later.

"Eclipse Burgers for two on the deck tomorrow," he said, and kissed the side of her neck. He had shaved and his chin was smooth, but that small, delicious shiver went up her back again just the same. "It's all fixed."

"Was she mad?"

"Nope," her father said cheerfully. "Said it was fine by her either way, since you'd done all your chores this week and—"

She had forgotten her earlier intuition that he knew a lot more about the acoustics of the living room/dining room than he had ever let on, and the generosity of his lie moved her so deeply that she almost burst into tears. She turned to him, threw her arms around his neck, and covered his cheeks and lips with fierce little kisses. His initial reaction was surprise. His hands jerked backward, and for just a moment they were cupping the tiny nubs of her breasts. That shivery feeling passed through her again, but this time it was much stronger—almost strong enough to be painful, like a shock—and with it, like some weird *déjà vu,* came that recurring sense of adulthood's strange contradictions: a world where you could order blackberry meatloaf or eggs fried in lemon-juice whenever you wanted to . . . and where some people actually *did.* Then his hands slipped all the way around her, they were pressed safely against her shoulder-blades, hugging her warmly against him, and if they had stayed where they shouldn't have been a moment longer than they should have done, she barely noticed.

I love you, Daddy.

Love you, too, Punkin. A hundred million bunches.

16

The day of the eclipse dawned hot and muggy but relatively clear—the weather forecasters' warnings that low-hanging clouds might obscure the phenomenon were going to prove groundless, it seemed, at least in western Maine.

Sally, Maddy, and Will left to catch The Dark Score Sun Worshippers' bus at around ten o'clock (Sally gave Jessie a stiff, silent peck on the cheek before leaving, and Jessie responded in kind), leaving Tom Mahout with the girl his wife had called "the squeaky wheel" the night before.

Jessie changed out of her shorts and Camp Ossippee tee-shirt and into her new sundress, the one which was pretty (if you weren't offended by red and yellow stripes almost bright enough to shout, that was) but too tight. She put on a dab of Maddy's My Sin perfume, a little of her mother's Yodora deodorant, and a fresh application of Peppermint Yum-Yum lipstick. And although she had never been one to linger before the mirror, fussing with herself (that was her mother's term, as in "Maddy, stop fussing with yourself and come out of there!"), she took time to put her hair up that day because her father had once complimented her on that particular style.

When she had put the last pin into place, she reached for the bathroom light-switch, then paused. The girl looking back at her from the mirror didn't seem like a girl at all, but a teenager. It wasn't the way the sundress accentuated the tiny swellings that wouldn't really be breasts for another year or two, and it wasn't the lipstick, and it wasn't her hair, held up in a clumsy but oddly fetching chignon; it was all of these things together, a sum greater than its parts because of . . . what? She didn't know. Something in the way the upsweep of her hair accented the shape of her cheekbones, perhaps. Or the bare curve of her neck, so much sexier than either the mosquito-bumps on her chest or her hipless tomboy's body. Or maybe it was just the look in her eyes—some sparkle that either had been hidden before today or had never been there at all.

Whatever it was, it made her linger a moment longer, looking at her reflection, and suddenly she heard her mother saying: *I swear to God, sometimes you behave as if she were your girlfriend instead of your daughter!*

She bit her pink lower lip, brow furrowing a little, remembering the night before—the shiver that had gone through her at his touch, the feel of his hands on her breasts. She could feel that shiver trying to happen again, and she refused to let it. There was no sense shivering over stupid stuff you couldn't understand. Or even thinking about it.

Good advice, she thought, and turned off the bathroom light.

She found herself growing more and more excited as noon passed and the afternoon drew along toward the actual time of the eclipse. She turned the portable radio to WNCH, the rock-and-roll station in North Conway. Her mother abhorred 'NCH, and after thirty minutes of Del Shannon and Dee Dee Sharp and Gary "U.S." Bonds, would make whoever had tuned it in (usually Jessie or Maddy, but sometimes Will) change to the classical music station which broadcast from the top of Mount Washington, but her father actually seemed to enjoy the music today, snapping his fingers and humming along. Once, during The Duprees' version of "You Belong to Me," he swept Jessie briefly into his arms and danced her along the deck. Jessie got the barbecue going around three-thirty, with the onset of the eclipse still an hour away, and went to ask her father if he wanted two burgers or just one.

She found him on the south side of the house, below the deck on which she stood. He was wearing only a pair of cotton shorts (YALE PHYS ED was printed on one leg) and a quilted oven-mitt. He had tied a bandanna around his forehead to keep the sweat out of his eyes. He was crouched over a small, smoky sod fire. The combination of the shorts and the bandanna gave him an odd but pleasant look of youth; Jessie could for the first time in her life see the man with whom her mother had fallen in love during her senior summer.

Several squares of glass—panes cut carefully out of the crumbling putty in an old shed window—were piled up beside him. He was holding one in the smoke rising from the fire, using the barbecue tongs to turn the glass square this way and that like some sort of weird camp delicacy. Jessie burst out laughing—it was mostly the oven-mitt that struck her funny—and he turned around, also grinning. The thought that the angle made it possible for him to look up her dress crossed her mind, but only fleetingly. He was her *father*, after all, not some cute boy like Duane Corson from down at the marina.

What are you doing? she giggled. *I thought we were having hamburgers for lunch, not glass sandwiches!*

Eclipse-viewers, not sandwiches, Punkin, he said. *If you put two or three of these together, you can look at the eclipse for the whole period of totality without damaging your eyes. You have to be really careful, I've read; you can burn your retinas and not even know you've done it until later.*

Ag! Jessie said, shivering a little. The idea of burning yourself without knowing you were doing it struck her as incredibly gross. *How long will it be total, Daddy?*

Not long. A minute or so.

Well, make some more of those glass whatchamacallums—I don't want to burn my *eyes. One Eclipse Burger or two?*

One will be fine. If it's a big one.

Okay.

She turned to go.

Punkin?

She looked back at him, a small, compact man with fine beads of sweat standing out on his forehead, a man with as little body hair as the man she would later marry, but without either Gerald's thick glasses or his paunch, and for a moment the fact that this man was her father seemed the least important thing about him. She was struck again by how handsome he was, and how young he looked. As she watched, a bead of sweat rolled slowly down his stomach, tracked just east of his navel, and made a small dark spot on the elastic waistband of his Yale shorts. She looked back at his face and was suddenly, exquisitely aware of his eyes on her. Even narrowed against the smoke as they were now, those eyes were absolutely gorgeous, the brilliant gray of daybreak on winter water. Jessie found she had to swallow before she could answer; her throat was dry. Possibly it was the acrid smoke from his sod fire. Or possibly not.

Yes, Daddy?

For a long moment he said nothing, only went on looking up at her with sweat running slowly down his cheeks and forehead and chest and belly, and Jessie was suddenly frightened. Then he smiled again and all was well.

You look very pretty today, Punkin. In fact, if it doesn't sound too yucky, you look beautiful.

Thank you—it doesn't sound yucky at all.

His comment pleased her so much (especially after her mother's angry editorial comments of the night before, or perhaps because of them) that a lump rose in her throat and she felt like crying for a moment. She smiled instead, and sketched a curtsey in his direction, and then hurried back to the barbecue with her heart pounding a steady drumroll in her chest. One of the things her mother had said, the most awful thing, tried to rise into her mind

(*you behave as if she were your*)

and Jessie squashed it as ruthlessly as she would have squashed a bad-tempered wasp. Still, she felt gripped by one of those crazy adult mixes of emotion—ice cream and gravy, roast chicken stuffed with sourballs—and could not seem to entirely escape it. Nor was she sure she even *wanted* to. In her mind she kept seeing that single drop of sweat tracking lazily down his stomach, being absorbed by the soft cotton of his shorts, leaving that tiny dark place. It was from that image that the emotional turmoil seemed chiefly to arise. She kept seeing it and seeing it and seeing it. It was crazy.

Well, so what? It was a crazy day, that was all. Even the sun was going to do something crazy. Why not leave it at that?

Yes, the voice that would one day masquerade as Ruth Neary agreed. *Why not?*

The Eclipse Burgers, garnished with sautéed mushrooms and mild red onion, were nothing short of fabulous. *They certainly eclipse the last batch your mother made,* her father told her, and Jessie giggled wildly. They ate on the deck outside Tom Mahout's den, balancing metal trays on their laps. A round deck-table, littered with condiments, paper plates, and eclipse-watching paraphernalia, stood between them. The observation gear included Polaroid sunglasses, two home-made cardboard reflector-boxes of the sort which the rest of the family had taken with them to Mount Washington, panes of smoked glass, and a stack of hotpads from the drawer beside the kitchen stove. The panes of smoked glass weren't hot anymore,

Tom told his daughter, but he wasn't terribly competent with the glass-cutter, and he was afraid there still might be nicks and jagged spots along the edges of some of the panes.

The last thing I need, he told her, *is for your mother to come home and find a note saying I've taken you to the Emergency Room at Oxford Hills Hospital so they can try to sew a couple of your fingers back on.*

Mom really wasn't exactly crazy about this idea, was she? Jessie asked.

Her Daddy gave her a brief hug. *No,* he said, *but I was. I was crazy enough about it for both of us.* And he gave her a smile so bright she just had to smile back.

It was the reflector-boxes they used first as the onset of the eclipse—4:29 P.M., EDT—neared. The sun lying in the center of Jessie's reflector-box was no bigger than a bottlecap, but it was so fiercely bright that she groped a pair of the sunglasses from the table and put them on. According to her Timex, the eclipse should have already started—it said 4:30.

I guess my watch is fast, she said nervously. *Either that or there's a bunch of astronomers all over the world with egg on their faces.*

Check again, Tom said, smiling.

When she looked back into the reflector-box, she saw that the brilliant circle was no longer a *perfect* circle; a crescent of darkness now dented the right-hand side. A shiver slipped down her neck. Tom, who had been watching her instead of the image inside his own reflector-box, saw it.

Punkin? All right?

Yes, but . . . it's a little scary, isn't it?

Yes, he said. She glanced at him and was deeply relieved to see he meant it. He looked almost as scared as she felt, and this only added to his winning boyishness. The idea that they might be afraid of different things never entered her mind. *Want to sit on my lap, Jess?*

Can I?

You bet.

She slipped onto his lap, still holding her own reflector-box in her hands. She wiggled around to get comfortable against him, liking the smell of his faintly sweaty, sunwarmed skin and a faint trace of some aftershave—Redwood, she thought it was called. The sundress rode up on her thighs (it could hardly do anything else, as short as it was), and she barely noticed when he put his hand on one of her legs. This was her father, after all—*Daddy*—not Duane Corson from down at the marina, or Richie Ashlocke, the boy she and her friends moaned and giggled over at school.

The minutes passed slowly. Every now and then she squirmed around, trying to get comfortable—his lap seemed strangely full of angles this afternoon—and at one point she must have dozed off for three or four minutes. It might have been even longer, because the puff of breeze that came strolling down the deck and woke her up was surprisingly cold against her sweaty arms, and the afternoon had changed somehow; colors which had seemed bright before she leaned back against his shoulder and closed her eyes were now pale pastels, and the light itself had weakened somehow. It was as if, she thought, the day had been strained through cheesecloth. She looked into her reflector-box and was surprised—almost stunned, actually—to see that only half the sun was there now. She looked at her watch and saw it was nine minutes past five.

It's happening, Daddy! The sun's going out!

Yes, he agreed. His voice was odd, somehow—deliberate and thoughtful on top, somehow blurry down below. *Right on schedule.*

She noticed in a vague sort of way that his hand had slipped higher—quite a bit higher, actually—on her leg while she had been dozing.

Can I look through the smoked glass yet, Dad?

Not yet, he said, and his hand slid higher still along her thigh. It was warm and sweaty but not unpleasant. She put her own hand over it, turned to him, and grinned.

It's exciting, isn't it?

Yes, he said in that same odd blurry tone. *Yes it is, Punkin. Quite a bit more than I thought it would be, actually.*

More time passed. In the reflector-box, the moon continued to nibble away at the sun as five-twenty-five passed, and then five-thirty. Almost all of her attention was now focused on the diminishing image in the reflector-box, but some faint part of her became aware once again of how oddly hard his lap was this afternoon. Something was pressing against her bottom. It wasn't painful, but it was insistent. To Jessie, it felt like the handle of some tool—a screwdriver, or maybe her mother's tackhammer.

Jessie wriggled again, wanting to find a more comfortable spot on his lap, and Tom drew in a quick hissing mouthful of air over his bottom lip.

Daddy? Am I too heavy? Did I hurt you?

No. You're fine.

She glanced at her watch. Five-thirty-seven now; four minutes to totality, maybe a little more if her watch was running fast.

Can I look at it through the glass yet?

Not yet, Punkin. But very soon.

She could hear Debbie Reynolds singing something from the Dark Ages, courtesy of WNCH: *"The old hooty-owl . . . hooty-hoos to the dove . . . Tammy . . . Tammy . . . Tammy's in love."* It finally drowned in a sticky swirl of violins and was replaced by the disc jockey, who told them it was getting dark in Ski Town, U.S.A. (this was the way the 'NCH deejays almost always referred to North Conway), but that the skies were too cloudy over on the New Hampshire side of the border to actually see the eclipse. The deejay told them there were a lot of disappointed folks wearing sunglasses across the street on the town common.

We're not disappointed folks, are we, Daddy?

Not a bit, he agreed, and shifted beneath her again. *We're about the most happy folks in the universe, I guess.*

Jessie peered into the reflector-box again, forgetting everything except the tiny image which she could now look at without narrowing her eyes down to protective slits behind the heavily tinted Polaroid sunglasses. The dark crescent on the right which had signalled the onset of the eclipse had now become a blazing crescent of sunlight on the left. It was so bright it almost seemed to float over the surface of the reflector-box.

Look out on the lake, Jessie!

She did, and behind the sunglasses her eyes widened. In her rapt examination of the shrinking image in the reflector-box, she had missed what was going on all around her. Pastels had now faded to ancient watercolors. A premature twilight, both entrancing and horrifying to the ten-year-old girl, was slipping across Dark Score Lake. Somewhere in the woods, an old hooty-owl cried out softly, and Jessie felt a sudden hard shudder bend its way through her body. On the radio, an Aamco Transmission ad ended and Marvin Gaye began to sing: "*Oww, listen everybody, especially you girls, is it right to be left alone when the one you love is never home?*"

The owl hooted again in the woods to the north of them. It was a scary sound, Jessie suddenly realized—a *very* scary sound. This time when she shivered, Tom slipped an arm around her. Jessie leaned gratefully back against his chest.

It's creepy, Dad.

It won't last long, honey, and you'll probably never see another one. Try not to be too scared to enjoy it.

She looked into her reflector-box. There was nothing there.

"*I love too hard, my friends sometimes say . . .*"

Dad? Daddy? It's gone. Can I—

Yes. Now it's okay. But when I say you have to stop, you have to stop. No arguments, understand?

She understood, all right. She found the idea of retinal burns—burns you apparently didn't even know you were getting until it was too late to do anything about them—a lot scarier than the hooty-owl off in the woods. But there was no *way* she wasn't going to at least have a peek, now that it was actually here, actually *happening*. No *way*.

"*But I believe,*" Marvin sang with the fervor of the converted, "*Yes I believe . . . that a woman should be loved that way . . .*"

Tom Mahout gave her one of the oven potholders, then three panes of smoked glass in a stack. He was breathing fast, and Jessie suddenly felt sorry for him. The eclipse had probably given him the creeps, too, but of course he was an adult and wasn't supposed to let on. In a lot of ways adults were sad creatures. She thought about turning around to comfort him, then decided that would probably make him feel even worse. Make him feel stupid. Jessie could sympathize. She hated to feel stupid worse than anything. Instead, she held the smoked panes of glass up in front of her, then slowly raised her head from her reflector-box to look through them.

"Now you chicks should all agree," Marvin sang, *"this ain't the way it's s'posed to be, So lemme* hear *ya! Lemme hearya say YEAH YEAH!"*

What Jessie saw when she looked through the makeshift viewer—

17

At this point the Jessie handcuffed to the bed in the summer house on the north shore of Kashwakamak Lake, the Jessie who was not ten but thirty-nine and a widow of almost twelve hours, suddenly realized two things: that she was asleep, and that she was not so much *dreaming* about the day of the eclipse as *reliving* it. She had gone on awhile thinking it *was* a dream, only a dream, like her dream of Will's birthday party, where most of the guests had either been dead or people she wouldn't actually meet for years. This new mind-movie had the surreal-but-sensible quality of the earlier one, but that was an untrustworthy yardstick because that whole *day* had been surreal and dreamlike. First the eclipse, and then her father—

No more, Jessie decided. *No more, I'm getting out of this.*

She made a convulsive effort to rise out of the dream or recollection or whatever it was. Her mental effort translated into a whole-body twitch, and the handcuff chains jingled mutedly as she twisted violently from side to side. She almost made it; for a moment she was almost out. And she *could* have made it, *would* have made it, if she hadn't thought better of it at the last moment. What stopped her was an inarticulate but overwhelming terror of a shape—some waiting shape that might make what had happened that day on the deck seem insignificant by comparison . . . if she had to face it, that was.

But maybe I don't have to. Not yet.

And perhaps the urge to hide in sleep wasn't all—there might have been something else, as well. Some part of her that intended to have this out in the open once and for all, no matter what the cost.

She sank back down on the pillow, eyes closed, arms held up and sacrificially spread, her face pale and tight with strain.

"Especially you girls," she whispered into the darkness. "Especially all you girls."

She sank back on the pillow, and the day of the eclipse claimed her again.

18

hat Jessie saw through her sunglasses and her home-made filter was so strange and so awesome that at first her mind refused to grasp it. There seemed to be a vast round beauty mark, like the one below the corner of Anne Francis's mouth, hanging there in the afternoon sky.

"If I talk in my sleep . . . 'cause I haven't seen my baby all week . . ."

It was at this point that she first felt her father's hand on the nub of her right breast. It squeezed gently for a moment, drifted across to the left one, then returned to the right again, as if he were making a size comparison. He was breathing very fast now; the respiration in her ear was like a steam engine, and she was again aware of that hard thing pressing against her bottom.

"*Can I get a witness?*" Marvin Gaye, that auctioneer of soul, was shouting. "*Witness, witness?*"

Daddy? Are you all right?

She felt a delicate tingle in her breasts again—pleasure and pain, roast turkey with a Nehi glaze and chocolate gravy—but this time she also felt alarm and a kind of startled confusion.

Yes, he said, but his voice sounded almost like the voice of a stranger. *Yes, fine, but don't look around.* He shifted. The hand which had been on her breasts went somewhere else; the one on her thigh moved up farther, pushing the hem of the sundress ahead of it.

Daddy, what are you doing?

Her question was not exactly fearful; mostly it was curious. Still, there was an undertone of fear there, something like a length of fine red thread. Above her, a furnace of strange light glowed fiercely around the dark circle hanging in the indigo sky.

Do you love me, Punkin?

Yes, sure—

Then don't worry about anything. I'd never hurt you. I want to be sweet to you. Just watch the eclipse and let me be sweet to you.

I'm not sure I want to, Daddy. That sense of confusion was growing deeper, the red thread was fattening. *I'm afraid of burning my eyes. Burning my watchamacallums.*

"*But I believe,*" Marvin sang, "*a woman's a man's best friend . . . and I'm gonna stick by her . . . to the very end.*"

Don't worry. He was panting now. *You have another twenty seconds. At least that. So don't worry. And don't look around.*

She heard the snap of elastic, but it was his, not hers; her underpants were where they were supposed to be, although she realized that if she looked down she would be able to see them—that was how far up he had pushed her dress.

Do you love me? he asked again, and although she was gripped by a terrible premonition that the right answer to this question had become the wrong one, she was ten years old and it was still the only answer she had to give. She told him that she did.

"Witness, witness," Marvin pleaded, fading out now.

Her father shifted, pressing the hard thing more firmly against her bottom. Jessie suddenly realized what it was—not the handle of a screwdriver or the tackhammer from the toolbox in the pantry, that was for sure—and the alarm she felt was matched by a momentary spiteful pleasure which had more to do with her mother than with her father.

This is what you get for not sticking up for me, she thought, looking at the dark circle in the sky through the layers of smoked glass, and then: *I guess this is what we both get.* Her vision suddenly blurred, and the pleasure was gone. Only the mounting sense of alarm was left. *Oh jeez,* she thought. *It's my retinas . . . it must be my retinas starting to burn.*

The hand on her thigh now moved between her legs, slid up until it was stopped by her crotch, and cupped her firmly there. He shouldn't be doing that, she thought. It was the wrong place for his hand. Unless—

He's goosing you, a voice inside suddenly spoke up.

In later years that voice, which she eventually came to think of as that of the Goodwife, frequently filled her with exasperation; it was sometimes the voice of caution, often the voice of blame, and almost always the voice of denial. Unpleasant things, demeaning things, painful things . . . they would all go away eventually if you ignored them enthusiastically enough, that was the Goodwife's view. It was a voice apt to stubbornly insist that even the most obvious wrongs were actually rights, parts of a benign plan too large and complex for mere mortals to grasp. There would be times (mostly during her eleventh and twelfth years, when she called that voice Miss Petrie, after her second-grade teacher) when she would actually raise her hands to her ears to try and blot out that quacking, reasonable voice—useless, of course, since it originated on the side of her ears she couldn't get to—but in that moment of dawning dismay while the eclipse darkened the skies over western Maine and reflected stars burned in the depths of Dark Score Lake, that moment when she realized (sort of) what the hand between her legs was up to, she heard only kindness and practicality, and she seized upon what the voice was saying with panicky relief.

It's just a goose, that's all it is, Jessie.

Are you sure? she cried back.

Yes, the voice replied firmly—as the years went by, Jessie would discover that this voice was almost *always* sure, wrong or right. *He means it as a joke, that's all. He doesn't know he's scaring you, so don't open your mouth and spoil a lovely afternoon. This is no big deal.*

Don't you believe it, toots! the other voice—the tough voice—responded. *Sometimes he behaves as if you're his goddamned* girlfriend *instead of his daughter, and that's what he's doing* right now*! He's not* goosing *you, Jessie! He's* fucking *you!*

She was almost positive that was a lie, almost positive that strange and forbidden schoolyard word referred to an act that could not be accomplished with just a hand, but doubts remained. With sudden dismay she remembered Karen Aucoin telling her not to ever let a boy put his tongue in her mouth, because it could start a baby in her throat. Karen said it sometimes happened that way, but that a woman who had to vomit her baby to get it out almost always died, and usually the baby died, too. *I ain't ever going to let a boy French-kiss me,* Karen said. *I might let one feel me on top, if I really loved him, but I don't ever want a baby in my throat. How would you* EAT?

At the time, Jessie had found this concept of pregnancy so crazy it was almost charming—and who but Karen Aucoin, who worried about whether or not the light stayed on when you shut the refrigerator door, could have come up with such a thing? Now, however, the idea shimmered with its own weird logic. Suppose—just *suppose*—it was true? If you could get a baby from a boy's tongue, if *that* could happen, then—

And there was that hard thing pressing into her bottom. That thing that wasn't the handle of a screwdriver or her mother's tackhammer.

Jessie tried to squeeze her legs together, a gesture that was ambivalent to her but apparently not to him. He gasped—a painful, scary sound—and pressed his fingers harder against the sensitive mound just beneath the crotch of her underpants. It hurt a little. She stiffened against him and moaned.

It occurred to her much later that her father very likely misinterpreted that sound as passion, and it was probably just as well that he did. Whatever his interpretation, it signalled the climax of this strange interlude. He arched suddenly beneath her, sending her smoothly upward. The movement was both terrifying and strangely pleasurable . . . that he should be so strong, that she should be so moved. For one moment she almost understood the nature of the chemicals at work here, dangerous yet compelling, and that control of them might lie within her grasp—if she *wanted* to control them, that was.

I don't, she thought. *I don't want anything to do with it. Whatever it is, it's nasty and horrible and scary.*

Then the hard thing pressed against her buttock, the thing that wasn't the handle of a screwdriver or her mother's tackhammer, was spasming, and some liquid was spreading there, soaking a hot spot through her pants.

It's sweat, the voice which would one day belong to the Goodwife said promptly. *That's what it is. He sensed you were afraid of him, afraid to be on his lap, and that made him nervous. You ought to be sorry.*

Sweat, my eye! the other voice, the one which would one day belong to Ruth, returned. It spoke quietly, forcefully, fearfully. *You know what it is, Jessie—it's the stuff you heard Maddy and those other girls talking about the night Maddy had her slumber party, after they thought you were finally asleep. Cindy Lessard called it spunk. She said it was white and that it squirts out of a guy's thing like toothpaste. That's the stuff that makes babies, not French kissing.*

For a moment she balanced up there on the stiff lift of his wave, confused and afraid and somehow excited, listening to him snatch one harsh breath after another out of the humid air. Then his hips and thighs slowly relaxed and he lowered her back down.

Don't look at it any longer, Punkin, he said, and although he was still panting, his voice was almost normal again. That scary excitement had gone out of it, and there was no ambivalence about what she felt now: deep simple relief. Whatever had happened—if anything really had—it was over.

Daddy—

Nope, don't argue. Your time is up.

He took the stack of smoked glass panes gently from her hand. At the same time he kissed her neck, even more gently. Jessie stared out at the weird darkness cloaking the lake as he did it. She was faintly aware that the owl was still calling, and that the crickets had been fooled into beginning their evensongs two or three hours early. An afterimage floated in front of her eyes like a round black tattoo surrounded by an irregular halo of green fire and she thought: *If I looked at it too long, if I burned my retinas, I'll probably have to look at that for the rest of my life, like what you see after someone shoots off a flashbulb in your eyes.*

Why don't you go inside and change into jeans, Punkin? I guess maybe the sundress wasn't such a good idea, after all.

He spoke in a dull, emotionless voice that seemed to suggest that wearing the sundress had been all her idea (*Even if it wasn't, you should have known better,* the Miss Petrie voice said instantly), and a new idea suddenly occurred to her: What if he decided he had to tell Mom about what had happened? The possibility was so horrifying that Jessie burst into tears.

I'm sorry, Daddy, she wept, throwing her arms around him and pressing her face into the hollow of his neck, smelling the vague and ghostly aroma of his aftershave or cologne or whatever it was. *If I did something wrong, I'm really, really, really sorry.*

God, no, he said, but he still spoke in that dull, preoccupied voice, as if trying to decide if he should tell Sally what Jessie had done, or if it could perhaps be swept under the rug. *You didn't do anything wrong, Punkin.*

Do you still love me? she persisted. It occurred to her that she was mad to ask, mad to risk an answer which might devastate her, but she *had* to ask. *Had* to.

Of course, he replied at once. A little more animation came into his voice as he said it, enough to make her understand that he was telling the truth (and oh what a relief that was), but she still suspected things had changed, and all because of something she barely understood. She knew the

(*goose it was a goose just a kind of goose*)

had had something to do with sex, but she had no idea just how much or how serious it might have been. It probably wasn't what the girls at the slumber party had called "going all the way" (except for the strangely knowledgeable Cindy Lessard; she had called it "deep-sea diving with the long white pole," a term which had struck Jessie as both horrible and hilarious), but the fact that he hadn't put his thing in her thing still might not mean she was safe from being what some of the girls, even at her school, called "pee-gee." What Karen Aucoin had told her last year when they were walking home from school recurred to her, and Jessie tried to shut it out. It almost certainly wasn't true, and he hadn't stuck his tongue in her mouth even if it was.

In her mind she heard her mother's voice, loud and angry: *Don't they say it's the squeaky wheel that always gets the grease?*

She felt the hot wet spot against her buttocks. It was still spreading. Yes, she thought. I guess that's right. I guess the squeaky wheel *does* get the grease.

Daddy—

He raised his hand, a gesture he often made at the dinner table when her mother or Maddy (usually her mother) started getting hot under the collar about something. Jessie couldn't remember Daddy ever making this gesture to her, and it reinforced her feeling that something had gone horribly awry here, and that there were apt to be fundamental, unappealable changes as the result of some terrible error (probably agreeing to wear the sundress) she had made. This idea caused a feeling of sorrow so deep that it felt like invisible fingers working ruthlessly inside her, sifting and winnowing her guts.

In the corner of her eye, she noticed that her father's gym shorts were askew. Something was poking out, something pink, and it sure as hell wasn't the handle of a screwdriver.

Before she could look away, Tom Mahout caught the direction of her glance and quickly adjusted his shorts, causing the pink thing to disappear. His face contracted in a momentary *moue* of disgust, and Jessie cringed inside again. He had caught her looking, and had mistaken her random glance for unseemly curiosity.

What just happened, he began, then cleared his throat. *We need to talk about what just happened, Punkin, but not right this minute. Dash inside and change your clothes, maybe take a quick shower while you're at it. Hurry up so you don't miss the end of the eclipse.*

She had lost all interest in the eclipse, although she would never tell him that in a million years. She nodded instead, then turned back. *Daddy, am I all right?*

He looked surprised, unsure, wary—a combination which increased the feeling that angry hands were at work inside her, kneading her guts . . . and she suddenly understood that he felt as bad as she did. Perhaps worse. And in an instant of clarity untouched by any voice save her own, she thought: *You ought to! Jeepers, you started it!*

Yes, he said . . . but his tone did not entirely convince her. *Right as rain, Jess. Now go on inside and fix yourself up.*

All right.

She tried to smile—tried hard—and actually succeeded a little. Her father looked startled for a moment, and then he returned her smile. That relieved her somewhat, and the hands which had been working inside her temporarily loosened their grip. By the time she had reached the big upstairs bedroom she shared with Maddy, however, the feelings had begun to return. The worst by far was the fear that he would feel he had to tell her mother about what had happened. And what would her mother think?

That's our Jessie, isn't it? The squeaky wheel.

The bedroom had been divided off girls-at-camp-style with a clothesline strung down the middle. She and Maddy had hung some old sheets on this line, and then colored bright designs on them with Will's Crayolas. Coloring the sheets and dividing the room had been great fun at the time, but it seemed stupid and kiddish to her now, and the way her overblown shadow danced on the center sheet was actually scary; it looked like the shadow of a monster. Even the fragrant smell of pine resin, which she usually liked, seemed heavy and cloying to her, like an air-freshener you sprayed around heavily to cover up some unpleasant stink.

That's our Jessie, never quite satisfied with the arrangements until she gets a chance to put on the finishing touches. Never quite happy with someone else's plans. Never able to let well enough alone.

She hurried into the bathroom, wanting to outrun that voice, rightly guessing she wouldn't be able to. She turned on the light and pulled the sundress over her head in one quick jerk. She threw it into the laundry hamper, glad to be rid of it. She looked at herself in the mirror, wide-eyed, and saw a little girl's face surrounded by a big girl's hairdo . . . one which was now coming loose from the pins in strands and puffs and locks. It was a little girl's body, too —flat-chested and slim-hipped—but it wouldn't be that way for long. It had already started to change, and it had done something to her father it had no business doing.

I never want boobs and curvy hips, she thought dully. If they make things like this happen, who would?

The thought made her aware of that wet spot on the seat of her underpants again. She slipped out of them—cotton pants from Sears, once green, now so faded they were closer to gray—and held them up curiously, her hands inside the waistband. There was something on the back of them, all right, and it wasn't sweat. Nor did it look like any kind of toothpaste she had ever seen. What it looked like was pearly-gray dish detergent. Jessie lowered her head and sniffed cautiously. She smelled a faint odor which she associated with the lake after a run of hot, still weather, and with their well-water all the time. She once took her father a glass of water which smelled particularly strong to her and asked if *he* could smell it.

He had shaken his head. *Nope,* he'd said cheerfully, *but that doesn't mean it isn't there. It just means I smoke too damn much. My guess is that it's the smell of the aquifer, Punkin. Trace minerals, that's all. A little smelly, and it means your mother has to spend a fortune on fabric softener, but it won't hurt you. Swear to God.*

Trace minerals, she thought now, and sniffed that bland aroma again. She was unable to think why it fascinated her, but it did. *The smell of the aquifer, that's all. The smell of—*

Then the more assertive voice spoke up. On the afternoon of the eclipse it sounded a bit like her mother's voice (it called her tootsie, for one thing, as Sally sometimes did when she was irritated with Jessie for shirking some chore or forgetting some responsibility), but Jessie had an idea it was really the voice of her own adult self. If its combative bray was a little distressing, that was only because it was too early for that voice, strictly speaking. It was here just the same, though. It was here, and it was doing the best it could to put her back together again. She found its brassy loudness oddly comforting.

It's the stuff Cindy Lessard was talking about, that's what it is— it's his spunk, tootsie. I suppose you ought to be grateful it ended up on your underwear instead of someplace else, but don't go telling yourself any fairy-tales about how it's the lake you smell, or trace minerals from deep down in the aquifer, or anything else. Karen Aucoin is a dipshit, there was never a woman in the history of the world *who grew a baby in her throat and you know it, but Cindy Lessard is no dipshit. I think she's seen this stuff, and now you've seen it, too. Man's-stuff. Spunk.*

Suddenly revolted—not so much by what it was as from whom it had originated—Jessie threw the underpants into the hamper on top of the sundress. Then she had a vision of her mother, who emptied the hampers and did the wash in the dank basement laundry room, fishing this particular pair of panties out of this particular hamper and finding this particular deposit. And what would she think? Why, that the family's troublesome squeaky wheel had gotten the grease, of course . . . what else?

Her revulsion turned to guilty horror, and Jessie quickly fished the underpants back out. All at once the flat odor seemed to fill her nose, thick and bland and sickening. *Oysters and copper,* she thought, and that was all it took. She fell on her knees in front of the toilet, the underpants wadded up in one clenched hand, and vomited. She flushed quickly, before the smell of partly digested hamburger could get into the air, then turned on the cold sink-tap and rinsed her mouth out. Her fear that she was going to spend the next hour or so in here, kneeling in front of the toilet and puking, began to subside. Her stomach seemed to be settling. If she could just keep from getting another whiff of that bland copper-creamy smell . . .

Holding her breath, she thrust the panties under the cold tap, rinsed them, wrung them out, and flung them back in the hamper. Then she took a deep breath, pushing her hair away from her temples with the backs of her damp hands at the same time. If her mother asked her what a damp pair of panties was doing in the dirty clothes—

Already you're thinking like a criminal, the voice that would one day belong to the Goodwife mourned. *Do you see what being a bad girl gets you, Jessie? Do you? I certainly hope you d—*

Be quiet, you little creep, the other voice snarled back. *You can nag all you want later on, but right now we're trying to take care of a little business here, if you don't mind. Okay?*

No answer. That was good. Jessie brushed nervously at her hair again, although very little of it had fallen back down against her temples. If her mother asked what the damp panties were doing in the dirty-clothes hamper, Jessie would simply say it was so hot she went for a dip without changing out of her shorts. All three of them had done that on several occasions this summer.

Then you better remember to run your shorts and shirt under the tap, too. Right, toots?

Right, she agreed. *Good point.*

She slipped into the robe hanging on the back of the bathroom door and returned to the bedroom to get the shorts and the tee-shirt she'd been wearing when her mother, brother, and older sister left that morning . . . a thousand years ago, it now seemed. She didn't see them at first, and got down on her knees to look under the bed.

The other woman is on her knees, too, a voice remarked, *and she smells that same smell. That smell that's like copper and cream.*

166

Jessie heard but didn't hear. Her mind was on her shorts and tee-shirt—on her cover story. As she had suspected, they were under the bed. She reached for them.

It's coming out of the well, the voice remarked further. *The smell from the well.*

Yes, yes, Jessie thought, grabbing the clothes and starting back to the bathroom. The smell from the well, very good, you're a poet and you don't know it.

She made him fall down the well, the voice said, and that finally got through. Jessie came to a dead stop in the bathroom doorway, her eyes widening. She was suddenly afraid in some new and deadly way. Now that she was actually listening to it, she realized that this voice was not like any of the others; this one was like a voice you might pick up on the radio late at night, when conditions were exactly right—a voice that might come from far, far away.

Not that *far, Jessie; she is in the path of the eclipse, too.*

For one moment, the upper hallway of the house on Dark Score Lake seemed to be gone. What replaced it was a tangle of blackberry bushes, shadowless under the eclipse-darkened sky, and a clear smell of sea-salt. Jessie saw a skinny woman in a housedress with her salt-and-pepper hair put up in a bun. She was kneeling by a splintered square of boards. There was a puddle of white fabric beside her. Jessie was quite sure it was the skinny woman's slip. Who are you? Jessie asked the woman, but she was already gone . . . if she had ever been there in the first place, that was.

Jessie actually glanced over her shoulder to see if perhaps that spooky skinny woman had gotten behind her. But the upstairs hallway was deserted; she was alone.

She looked down at her arms and saw they were rippled with gooseflesh.

You're losing your mind, the voice that would one day be Goodwife Burlingame mourned. *Oh Jessie, you've been bad, you've been very bad, and now you're going to have to pay by losing your mind.*

"I'm *not,*" she said. She looked at her pale, strained face in the bathroom mirror. "I'm *not!*"

She waited for a moment in a kind of horrified suspension to see if any of the voices—or the image of the woman kneeling by the splintered boards with her slip puddled on the ground beside her —would come back, but she neither heard nor saw anything. That creepy *other* who had told Jessie some she had pushed some he down some well was apparently gone.

Strain, toots, the voice that would one day be Ruth advised, and Jessie had a clear idea that while the voice didn't exactly believe that, it had decided Jessie had better get moving again, and right away. *You thought about a woman with a slip beside her because you've got underwear on the brain this afternoon, that's all. I'd forget the whole thing, if I were you.*

That was great advice. Jessie quickly dampened her shorts and shirt under the tap, wrung them out, and then stepped into the shower. She soaped, rinsed, dried, hurried back to the bedroom. She ordinarily wouldn't have bothered with the robe again for the quick dash across the hall, but this time she did, only holding it shut instead of taking time to belt it closed.

She paused in the bedroom again, biting her lip, praying that the weird other voice wouldn't come back, praying that she wouldn't have another of those crazy hallucinations or illusions or whatever they were. Nothing came. She dropped the robe on her bed, hurried across to her bureau, pulled on fresh underwear and shorts.

She smells that same smell, she thought. *Whoever that woman is, she smells the same smell coming out of the well she made the man fall into, and it's happening now, during the eclipse. I'm sure—*

She turned, a fresh blouse in one hand, and then froze. Her father was standing in the doorway, watching her.

19

Jessie awoke in the mild, milky light of dawn with the perplexing and ominous memory of the woman still filling her mind—the woman with her graying hair pulled back in that tight countrywoman's bun, the woman who had been kneeling in the blackberry tangles with her slip puddled beside her, the woman who had been looking down through broken boards and smelling that awful bland smell. Jessie hadn't thought of that woman in years, and now, fresh from her dream of 1963 that hadn't been a dream but a recollection, it seemed to her that she had been granted some sort of supernatural vision on that day, a vision that had perhaps been caused by stress and then lost again for the same reason.

But it didn't matter—not that, not what had happened with her father out on the deck, not what had happened later, when she had turned around to see him standing in the bedroom door. All that had happened a long time ago, and as for what was happening right now—

I'm in trouble. I think I'm in very serious trouble.

She lay back against the pillows and looked up at her suspended arms. She felt as dazed and helpless as a poisoned insect in a spider's web, wanting no more than to be asleep again—dreamlessly this time, if possible—with her dead arms and dry throat in another universe.

No such luck.

There was a slow, somnolent buzzing sound somewhere close by. Her first thought was *alarm clock.* Her second, after two or three minutes of dozing with her eyes open, was *smoke detector.* That idea caused a brief, groundless burst of hope which brought her a little closer to real waking. She realized that what she was hearing didn't really sound very much like a smoke detector at all. It sounded like . . . well . . . like . . .

It's flies, toots, okay? The no-bullshit voice now sounded tired and wan. *You've heard about the Boys of Summer, haven't you? Well, these are the Flies of Autumn, and their version of the World Series is currently being played on Gerald Burlingame, the noted attorney and handcuff-fetishist.*

"Jesus, I gotta get up," she said in a croaking, husky voice she barely recognized as her own.

What the hell does that *mean?* she thought, and it was the answer—Not a goddam thing, thanks very much—that finished the job of bringing her back to full wakefulness. She didn't *want* to be awake, but she had an idea that she had better accept the fact that she was and do as much with it as she could, while she could.

And you probably better start by waking up your hands and arms. If they will *wake up, that is.*

She looked at her right arm, then turned her head on the rusty armature of her neck (which was only partially asleep) and looked at her left. Jessie realized with sudden shock that she was looking at them in a completely new way—looking at them as she might have looked at pieces of furniture in a showroom window. They seemed to have no business with Jessie Burlingame at all, and she supposed there was nothing so odd about that, not really; they were, after all, utterly without feeling. Sensation only started a little below her armpits.

She tried to pull herself up and was dismayed to find the mutiny in her arms had gone further than she had suspected. Not only did they refuse to move *her*; they refused to move *themselves*. Her brain's order was totally ignored. She looked up at them again, and they no longer looked like furniture to her. Now they looked like pallid cuts of meat hanging from butchers' hooks, and she let out a hoarse cry of fear and anger.

Never mind, though. The arms weren't happening, at least for the time being, and being mad or afraid or both wasn't going to change that a bit. How about the fingers? If she could curl them around the bedposts, then maybe . . .

. . . or maybe not. Her fingers seemed as useless as her arms. After nearly a full minute of effort, Jessie was rewarded only by a single numb twitch from her right thumb.

"Dear God," she said in her grating dust-in-the-cracks voice. There was no anger in it now, only fear.

People died in accidents, of course—she supposed she had seen hundreds, perhaps even thousands, of "death-clips" on the TV news during her lifetime. Body-bags carried away from wrecked cars or winched out of the jungle in Medi-Vac slings, feet sticking out from beneath hastily spread blankets while buildings burned in the background, white-faced, stumble-voiced witnesses pointing to pools of sticky dark stuff in alleys or on barroom floors. She had seen the white-shrouded shape that had been John Belushi toted out of the Chateau Marmont Hotel in Los Angeles; she had seen aerialist Karl Wallenda lose his balance, fall heavily to the cable he had been trying to cross (it had been strung between two resort hotels, she seemed to remember), clutch it briefly, and then plunge to his death below. The news programs had played that one over and over as if obsessed with it. So she knew people died in accidents, of *course* she knew it, but until now she had somehow never realized there were people *inside* those people, people just like her, people who hadn't had the slightest idea they would never eat another cheeseburger, watch another round of Final Jeopardy (and please make sure your answer is in the form of a question), or call their best friends to say that penny poker on Thursday night or shopping on Saturday afternoon seemed like a *great* idea. No more beer, no more kisses, and your fantasy of making love in a hammock during a thunderstorm was never going to be fulfilled, because you were going to be too busy being dead. Any morning you rolled out of bed might be your last.

It's a lot more than a case of might this morning, Jessie thought. *I think now it's a case of probably. The house—our nice quiet lakeside house—may very well be on the news Friday or Saturday night. It'll be Doug Rowe wearing that white trenchcoat of his I hate so much and talking into his microphone and calling it "the house where prominent Portland lawyer Gerald Burlingame and his wife Jessie died." Then he'll send it back to the studio and Bill Green will do the sports, and that isn't being morbid, Jessie; that isn't the Goodwife moaning or Ruth ranting. It's—*

But Jessie knew. It was the truth. It was just a silly little accident, the kind of thing you shook your head over when you saw it reported in the paper at breakfast; you said "Listen to this, honey," and read the item to your husband while he ate his grapefruit. Just a silly little accident, only this time it was happening to her. Her mind's constant insistence that it was a mistake was understandable but irrelevant. There was no Complaint Department where she could explain that the handcuffs had been Gerald's idea and so it was only fair that she should be let off. If the mistake was going to be rectified, she would have to be the one to do it.

Jessie cleared her throat, closed her eyes, and spoke to the ceiling. "God? Listen a minute, would You? I need some help here, I really do. I'm in a mess and I'm terrified. Please help me get out of this, okay? I . . . um . . . I pray in the name of Jesus Christ." She struggled to amplify this prayer and could only come up with something Nora Callighan had taught her, a prayer which now seemed to be on the lips of every self-help huckster and dipshit guru in the world: "God grant me the serenity to accept the things I cannot change, the courage to change the things I can, and the wisdom to know the difference. Amen."

Nothing changed. She felt no serenity, no courage, most certainly no wisdom. She was still only a woman with dead arms and a dead husband, cuffed to the posts of this bed like a cur-dog chained to a ringbolt and left to die unremarked and unlamented in a dusty back yard while his tosspot master serves thirty days in the county clink for driving without a license and under the influence.

"Oh please don't let it hurt," she said in a low, trembling voice. "If I'm going to die, God, please don't let it hurt. I'm such a baby about pain."

Thinking about dying at this point is probably a really bad idea, toots. Ruth's voice paused, then added: *On second thought, strike the probably.*

Okay, no argument—thinking about dying was a bad idea. So what did that leave?

Living. Ruth and Goodwife Burlingame said it at the same time.

All right, living. Which brought her around full circle to her arms again.

They're asleep because I've been hanging on them all night. I'm still *hanging on them. Getting the weight off is step one.*

She tried to push herself backward and upward with her feet again, and felt a sudden weight of black panic when they at first also refused to move. She lost herself for a few moments then, and when she came back she was pistoning her legs rapidly up and down, pushing the coverlet, the sheets, and the mattress-pad down to the foot of the bed. She was gasping for breath like a bicycle-racer topping the last steep hill in a marathon race. Her butt, which had also gone to sleep, sang and zipped with wake-up needles.

Fear had gotten her fully awake, but it took the half-assed aerobics which accompanied her panic to kick her heart all the way up into passing gear. At last she began to feel tingles of sensation—bone-deep and as ominous as distant thunder—in her arms.

If nothing else works, toots, keep your mind on those last two or three sips of water. Keep reminding yourself that you're never going to get hold of that glass again unless your hands and arms are in good working order, let alone drink from it.

Jessie continued to push with her feet as the morning brightened. Sweat plastered her hair against her temples and streamed down her cheeks. She was aware—vaguely—that she was deepening her water-debt every moment she persisted in this strenuous activity, but she saw no choice.

Because there is *none, toots—none at all.*

Toots this and toots that, she thought distractedly. *Would you please put a sock in it, you mouthy bitch?*

At last her bottom began to slide up toward the head of the bed. Each time it moved, Jessie tensed her stomach muscles and did a mini sit-up. The angle made by her upper and lower body slowly began to approach ninety degrees. Her elbows began to bend, and as the drag of her weight began to leave her arms and shoulders, the tingles racing through her flesh increased. She didn't stop moving her legs when she was finally sitting up but continued to pedal, wanting to keep her heart-rate up.

A drop of stinging sweat ran into her left eye. She flicked it away with an impatient shake of her head and went on pedaling. The tingles continued to increase, darting upward and downward from her elbows, and about five minutes after she'd reached her current slumped position (she looked like a gawky teenager draped over a movie theater seat), the first cramp struck. It felt like a blow from the dull side of a meat-cleaver.

Jessie threw her head back, sending a fine mist of perspiration flying from her head and hair, and shrieked. As she was drawing breath to repeat the cry, the second cramp struck. This one was much worse. It felt as if someone had dropped a glass-encrusted noose of cable around her left shoulder and then yanked it tight. She howled, her hands snapping shut into fists with such sudden savagery that two of her fingernails splintered away from the quick and began to bleed. Her eyes, sunk into brown hollows of puffy flesh, were squeezed tightly shut, but tears escaped nevertheless and went trickling down her cheeks, mixing with the runnels of sweat from her hairline.

Keep pedaling, toots—don't stop now.

"*Don't you call me* toots!" Jessie screamed.

The stray dog had crept back to the rear stoop just before first light, and at the sound of her voice, its head jerked up. There was an almost comical expression of surprise on its face.

"*Don't you call me that, you bitch! You hateful bi—*"

Another cramp, this one as sharp and sudden as a thunderbolt coronary, punched through her left triceps all the way to the armpit, and her words dissolved into a long, wavering scream of agony. Yet she kept on pedaling.

Somehow she kept on pedaling.

174

20

When the worst of the cramps had passed—at least she *hoped* the worst of them had—she took a breather, leaning back against the slatted mahogany crossboards which formed the head of the bed, her eyes closed and her breath gradually slowing down—first to a lope, then a trot, and finally to a walk. Thirst or no thirst, she felt surprisingly good. She supposed part of the reason lay in that old joke, the one with the punchline that went "It feels so good when I stop." But she had been an athletic girl and an athletic woman until five years ago (well, all right, maybe it was closer to ten), and she could still recognize an endorphin rush when she was having one. Absurd, given the circumstances, but also very nice.

Maybe not so absurd, Jess. Maybe useful. Those endorphins clear the mind, which is one reason why people work better after they've taken some exercise.

And her mind *was* clear. The worst of her panic had blown away like industrial smogs before a strong wind, and she felt more than rational; she felt wholly sane again. She never would have believed it possible, and she found this evidence of the mind's tireless adaptability and almost insectile determination to survive a little spooky. *All of this and I haven't even had my morning coffee,* she thought.

The image of coffee—black, and in her favorite cup with the blue flowers around its middle—made her lick her lips. It also made her think of the *Today* program. If her interior clock was right, *Today* would be coming on just about now. Men and women all over America—unhandcuffed, for the most part—were sitting at kitchen tables, drinking juice and coffee, eating bagels and scrambled eggs (or maybe one of those cereals that are supposed to simultaneously soothe your heart and excite your bowels). They were watching Bryant Gumbel and Katie Couric yuck it up with Joe Garagiola. A little later they would watch Willard Scott wish a couple of centenarians a happy day. There would be guests—one who would talk about something called the prime rate and something else called the Fed, one who would show viewers how they could keep their pet Chows from chewing up their slippers, and one who would plug his latest movie—and none of them would realize that over in western Maine there was an accident in progress; that one of their more-or-less-loyal viewers was unable to tune in this morning because she was handcuffed to a bed less than twenty feet from her naked, dogchewed, flyblown husband.

She turned her head to the right and looked up at the glass Gerald had set down carelessly on his side of the shelf shortly before the festivities had commenced. Five years ago, she reflected, that glass probably wouldn't have been there, but as Gerald's nightly Scotch consumption increased, so had his daily intake of all other liquids —mostly water, but he also drank tons of diet soda and iced tea. For Gerald, at least, the phrase "drinking problem" seemed to have been no euphemism but the literal truth.

Well, she thought drearily, *if he did have a drinking problem, it's certainly cured now, isn't it?*

The glass was exactly where she had left it, of course; if her visitor of the previous night had not been a dream (*Don't be silly, of course it was a dream,* the Goodwife said nervously), it must not have been thirsty.

I'm going to get that glass, Jessie thought. *I'm also going to be extremely careful, in case there are more muscle-cramps. Any questions?*

There weren't, and this time getting the glass turned out to be a cakewalk, because it was a lot easier to reach; there was no need for the balancing act. She discovered an added bonus when she picked up her makeshift straw. As it dried, the blow-in card had curled up along the folds she had made. This strange geometrical construct looked like free-form origami and worked much more efficiently than it had the previous night. Getting the last of the water was even easier than getting the glass, and as Jessie listened to the Malt Shoppe crackle from the bottom of the glass as her weird straw tried to suck up the last couple of drops, it occurred to her that she would have lost a lot less water to the coverlet if she had known she could "cure" the straw. Too late now, though, and no use crying over spilled water.

The few sips did little more than wake up her thirst, but she would have to live with that. She put the glass back on the shelf, then laughed at herself. Habit was a tough little beast. Even under bizarre circumstances such as these, it was a tough little beast. She had risked cramping up all over again to return the empty glass to the shelf instead of just bombing it over the side of the bed to shatter on the floor. And why? Because Neatness Counts, that was why. That was one of the things Sally Mahout had taught her tootsie, her little squeaky wheel who never got quite enough grease and who was never able to let well enough alone—her little tootsie who had been willing to go to any lengths, including seducing her own father, to make sure that things would continue to go the way she wanted them to go.

In the eye of her memory, Jessie saw the Sally Mahout she had seen so often back then: cheeks flushed with exasperation, lips pressed tightly together, hands rolled into fists and planted on her hips.

"And you would have believed it, too," Jessie said softly. "Wouldn't you, you bitch?"

Not fair, part of her mind responded uneasily. *Not fair, Jessie!*

Except it *was* fair, and she knew it. Sally had been a long way from the ideal mother, especially during those years when her marriage to Tom had been laboring along like an old car with dirt in the transmission. Her behavior during those years had often been paranoid, and sometimes irrational. Will had for some reason been almost completely spared her tirades and suspicions, but she had sometimes frightened both of her daughters badly.

That dark side was gone now. The letters Jessie got from Arizona were the banal, boring notes of an old lady who lived for Thursday Night Bingo and saw her child-rearing years as a peaceful, happy time. She apparently did not remember screaming at the top of her lungs that the next time Maddy forgot to wrap her used tampons in toilet paper before throwing them in the trash she would kill her, or the Sunday morning when she had—for no reason Jessie had ever been able to understand—stormed into Jessie's bedroom, thrown a pair of high-heeled shoes at her, and then stormed out again.

Sometimes when she got her mother's notes and postcards—*All well here, sweetheart, heard from Maddy, she writes so faithfully, my appetite's a little better since it cooled off*—Jessie felt an urge to snatch up the telephone and call her mother and scream: *Did you forget everything, Mom? Did you forget the day you threw the shoes at me and broke my favorite vase and I cried because I thought you must know, that he must have finally broken down and told you, even though it had been three years since the day of the eclipse by then? Did you forget how often you scared us with your screams and your tears?*

That's unfair, Jessie. Unfair and disloyal.

Unfair it might be, but that did not make it untrue.

If she had known what happened that day—

The image of the woman in stocks recurred to Jessie again, there and gone almost too fast to be recognized, like subliminal advertising: the pinned hands, the hair covering the face like a penitent's shroud, the little knot of pointing, contemptuous people. Mostly women.

Her mother might not have come right out and said so, but yes—she *would* have believed it was Jessie's fault, and she really might have thought it was a conscious seduction. It wasn't that much of a stretch from squeaky wheel to Lolita, was it? And the knowledge that something sexual had happened between her husband and her daughter very likely would have caused her to stop thinking about leaving and actually do it.

Believed it? You *bet* she would have believed it.

This time the voice of propriety didn't bother with even a token protest, and a sudden insight came to Jessie: her father had grasped instantly what it had taken her almost thirty years to figure out. He had known the true facts just as he had known about the odd acoustics of the living room/dining room in the lake house.

Her father had used her in more ways than one on that day.

Jessie expected a flood of negative emotions at this sorry realization; she had, after all, been played for a sucker by the man whose primary jobs had been to love and protect her. No such flood came. Perhaps this was partly because she was still flying on endorphins, but she had an idea it had more to do with relief: no matter how rotten that business had been, she had finally been able to get outside it. Her chief emotions were amazement that she had held onto the secret for as long as she had, and a kind of uneasy perplexity. How many of the choices she had made since that day had been directly or indirectly influenced by what had happened during the final minute or so she had spent on her Daddy's lap, looking at a vast round mole in the sky through two or three pieces of smoked glass? And was her current situation a result of what had happened during the eclipse?

Oh, that's too much, she thought. *If he'd raped me, maybe it would be different. But what happened on the deck that day was really just another accident, and not a very serious one, at that—if you want to know what a* serious *accident is, Jess, look at the situation you're in here. I might as well blame old Mrs. Gilette for slapping my hand at that lawn-party, the summer I was four. Or a thought I had coming down the birth-canal. Or sins from some past life that still needed expiation. Besides, what he did to me on the deck wasn't anything compared to what he did to me in the bedroom.*

And there was no need to dream that part of it; it was right there, perfectly clear and perfectly accessible.

21

When she looked up and saw her father standing in the bedroom doorway, her first, instinctive gesture had been to cross her arms over her breasts. Then she saw the sad and guilty look on his face and dropped them again, although she felt heat rising in her cheeks and knew that her own face was turning the unlovely, patchy red that was her version of a maidenly blush. She had nothing to show up there (well, *almost* nothing), but she still felt more naked than naked, and so embarrassed she could almost swear she felt her skin sizzling. She thought: *Suppose the others come back early? Suppose* she *walked in right now and saw me like this, with my shirt off?*

Embarrassment became shame, shame became terror, and still, as she shrugged into the blouse and began to button it, she felt another emotion underlying these. That feeling was anger, and it was not much different from the drilling anger she would feel years later when she realized that Gerald knew she meant what she was saying but was pretending he didn't. She was angry because she didn't *deserve* to feel ashamed and terrified. After all, *he* was the grownup, *he* was the one who had left that funny-smelling crud on the back of her underpants, *he* was the one who was supposed to be ashamed, and that wasn't the way it was working. That wasn't the way it was working at *all*.

By the time her blouse was buttoned and tucked into her shorts, the anger was gone, or—same difference—banished back to its cave. And what she kept seeing in her mind was her mother coming back early. It wouldn't matter that she was fully dressed again. The fact that something bad had happened was on their faces, just hanging out there, big as life and twice as ugly. She could see it on his face and feel it on her own.

"Are you all right, Jessie?" he asked quietly. "Not feeling faint, or anything?"

"No." She tried to smile, but this time she couldn't quite manage it. She felt a tear slip down one cheek and wiped it away quickly, guiltily, with the heel of her hand.

"I'm sorry." His voice was trembling, and she was horrified to see tears standing in *his* eyes—oh, this just got worse and worse and worse. "I'm so sorry." He turned abruptly, ducked into the bathroom, grabbed a towel off the rack, and wiped his face with it. While he did this, Jessie thought fast and hard.

"Daddy?"

He looked at her over the towel. The tears in his eyes were gone. If she hadn't known better, she would have sworn they had never been there at all.

The question almost stuck in her throat, but it had to be asked. *Had* to be.

"Do we . . . do we have to tell Mom about it?"

He took a long, sighing, trembling breath. She waited, her heart in her mouth, and when he said "I think we have to, don't you?" it sank all the way to her feet.

She crossed the room to him, staggering a little—her legs seemed to have no feeling in them at all—and wrapped her arms around him. "Please, Daddy. Don't. Please don't tell. *Please* don't. Please . . ." Her voice blurred, collapsed into sobs, and she pressed her face against his bare chest.

After a moment he slipped his arms around her, this time in his old, fatherly way.

"I hate to," he said, "because things have been pretty tense be-tween the two of us just lately, hon. I'd be surprised if you didn't know that, actually. A thing like this could make them a lot worse. She hasn't been very . . . well, very affectionate lately, and that was most of the problem today. A man has . . . certain needs. You'll understand about that somed—"

"But if she finds out, she'll say it was *my* fault!"

"Oh, no—I don't think so," Tom said, but his tone was surprised, considering . . . and, to Jessie, as dreadful as a death-sentence. "No-ooo . . . I'm sure—well, *fairly* sure—that she . . ."

She looked up at him, her eyes streaming and red. "*Please* don't tell her, Daddy! Please don't! Please don't!"

He kissed her brow. "But Jessie . . . I *have* to. *We* have to."

"Why? *Why*, Daddy?"

"Because—"

22

Jessie shifted a little. The chains jingled; the cuffs themselves rattled on the bedposts. The light was now streaming in through the east windows.

" 'Because you couldn't keep it a secret,' " she said dully. " 'Because if it's going to come out, Jessie, it's better for both of us that it should come out now, rather than a week from now, or a month from now, or a year from now. Even *ten* years from now.' "

How well he had manipulated her—first the apology, then the tears, and finally the hat-trick: turning *his* problem into *her* problem. *Br'er Fox, Br'er Fox, whatever else y'all do, don't th'ow me in dat briar patch!* Until, finally, she had been swearing to him that she would keep the secret forever, that torturers couldn't drag it out of her with tongs and hot coals.

She could in fact remember promising him something just like that through a rain of hot, frightened tears. Finally he had stopped shaking his head and had only looked across the room with his eyes narrowed and his lips pressed tightly together—this she saw in the mirror, as he almost surely knew she would.

"You could never tell anyone," he'd said at last, and Jessie remembered the swooning relief she'd felt at those words. What he was saying was less important than the tone in which he was saying it. Jessie had heard that tone a good many times before, and knew it drove her mother crazy that she, Jessie, could cause him to speak that way more often than Sally herself. *I'm changing my mind,* it said. *I'm doing it against my better judgment, but I* am *changing it; I'm swinging around to your side.*

"No," she had agreed. Her voice was wavery, and she had to keep gulping back tears. "I wouldn't tell, Daddy—not ever."

"Not just your mother," he said, "but *anyone. Ever.* That's a big responsibility for a little girl, Punkin. You might be tempted. For instance, if you were studying with Caroline Cline or Tammy Hough after school, and one of them told you a secret of hers, you might want to tell—"

"Them? *Never-Never-Never!*"

And he must have seen the truth of it on her face: the thought of either Caroline or Tammy finding out that her father had touched her had filled Jessie with horror. Satisfied on that score, he had pushed on to what she now guessed must have been his chief concern.

"Or your sister." He pushed her back from him and looked sternly down into her face for a long moment. "There could come a time, you see, when you wanted to tell her—"

"Daddy, no, I'd never—"

He gave her a gentle shake. "Keep quiet and let me finish, Punkin. You two are close, I know that, and I know that girls sometimes feel an urge to share things they ordinarily wouldn't tell. If you felt that way with Maddy, could you still manage to keep quiet?"

"*Yes!*" In her desperate need to convince him, she had begun to cry once more. Of course it was more likely that she would tell Maddy—if there was anyone in the world to whom she might one day confide such a desperate secret, it would be her big sister . . . except for one thing. Maddy and Sally shared the same sort of closeness Jessie and Tom had shared, and if Jessie ever told her sister about what had happened on the deck, the chances that their mother would know before the day was out were very good. Given that insight, Jessie thought she could quite easily withstand the temptation to tell Maddy.

"Are you really sure?" he had asked doubtfully.

"Yes! Really!"

He'd begun to shake his head again in a regretful way that terrified her all over again. "I just think, Punkin, that it might be better to get it out in the open right away. Take our medicine. I mean, she can't *kill* us—"

Jessie, however, had heard her anger when Daddy had asked that she be excused from the trip to Mount Washington . . . and anger wasn't all. She didn't like to think of it, but at this point she could not afford the luxury of denial. There had been jealousy and something very close to hatred in her mother's voice, as well. A vision, momentary but of paralyzing clarity, had come to Jessie as she stood with her father in the bedroom doorway, trying to persuade him to hold his peace: the two of them cast out on the road like Hansel and Gretel, homeless, tramping back and forth across America . . .

. . . and sleeping together, of course. Sleeping together at night.

She had broken down utterly then, weeping hysterically, begging him not to tell, promising him she would be a good girl forever and ever if he just wouldn't tell. He had let her cry until he must have felt the moment was exactly right, and then he had said gravely: "You know, you've got an awful lot of power for a little girl, Punkin."

She had looked up at him, cheeks wet and eyes full of fresh hope.

He nodded slowly, then began to dry her tears with the towel he had used on his own face. "I've never been able to refuse you anything that you really wanted, and I can't this time, either. We'll try it your way."

She threw herself into his arms and began covering his face with kisses. Somewhere far back in her mind she had been afraid this might

(*get him going*)

start trouble again, but her gratitude had completely overwhelmed such caution, and there had been no trouble.

"Thank you! Thank you, Daddy! Thank you!"

He had taken her by the shoulders and held her at arm's length again, smiling instead of grave this time. But that sadness had still been on his face, and now, almost thirty years later, Jessie didn't think that expression had been part of the show. The sadness had been real, and that somehow made the terrible thing he had done worse instead of better.

"I guess we have a bargain," he said. "I say nothing, you say nothing. Right?"

"Right!"

"Not to anyone else, not even to each other. Forever and ever, amen. When we walk out of this room, Jess, it never happened. Okay?"

She had agreed at once, but at the same time the memory of that smell had recurred to her, and she had known there was at least one question she had to ask him before it never happened.

"And there's something I need to say once more. I need to say I'm sorry, Jess. I did a shabby, shameful thing."

He had looked away when he said that, she remembered. All the time he had been deliberately driving her into hysterics of guilt and fear and impending doom, all the time he had been making sure she would never say anything by threatening to tell everything, he had looked right at her. When he offered that last apology, however, his gaze had shifted to the crayon designs on the sheets which divided the room. This memory filled her with something that felt simultaneously like grief and rage. He had been able to face her with his lies; it was the truth which had finally caused him to look away.

She remembered opening her mouth to tell him he didn't have to say that, then closing it again—partly because she was afraid anything she said might cause him to change his mind back again, but mostly because, even at ten, she had realized she had a right to an apology.

"Sally's been cold—it's the truth, but as an excuse it's pretty sad shit. I don't have the slightest idea what came over me." He had laughed a little, still not looking at her. "Maybe it was the eclipse.

185

If it was, thank God we'll never see another one." Then, as if speaking to himself: "Christ, if we keep our mouths shut and she finds out anyway, later on—"

Jessie had put her head against his chest and said, "She won't. I'll never tell, Daddy." She paused, then added, "What *could* I tell, anyway?"

"That's right." He smiled. "Because nothing happened."

"And I'm not . . . I mean, I couldn't be . . ."

She had looked up, hoping he might tell her what she needed to know without her asking, but he only looked back at her, eyebrows raised in a silent interrogative. The smile had been replaced by a wary, waiting expression.

"I couldn't be pregnant, then?" she blurted.

He winced, and then his face had tensed as he worked to suppress some strong emotion. Horror or grief, she'd thought then; it was only all these years later that it occurred to her that what he might actually have been trying to control was a burst of wild, relieved laughter. At last he had gotten himself under control and kissed the tip of her nose.

"No, honey, of course not. The thing that makes women pregnant didn't happen. *Nothing* like that happened. I was wrestling with you a little, that's all—"

"And you goosed me." She remembered saying that very clearly now. "You goosed me, that's what you did."

He had smiled. "Yep. That's close enough. You're just as fine as ever, Punkin. Now, what do you think? Does that close the subject?"

She had nodded.

"Nothing like this is ever going to happen again—you know that, don't you?"

She nodded again, but her own smile had faltered. What he was saying should have relieved her, and it did, a little, but something in the gravity of his words and the sorrow on his face had almost sparked her panic again. She remembered taking his hands and squeezing them as hard as she could. "You love me, though, don't you, Daddy? You still love me, right?"

He had nodded and told her he loved her more than ever.

"Then hug me! Hug me hard!"

And he did, but now Jessie could remember something else: his lower body had not touched hers.

Not then and never again, Jessie thought. *Not that I remember, anyway. Even when I graduated from college, the only other time I saw him cry over me, he gave me one of those funny old-maid hugs, the kind you do with your ass pooching out so there isn't even a chance you can bump crotches with the person you're hugging. Poor, poor man. I wonder if any of the people he did business with over the years ever saw him as rattled as I saw him on the day of the eclipse. All that pain, and over what? A sexual accident about as serious as a stubbed toe. Jesus, what a life it is. What a fucking life.*

She began to pump her arms slowly up and down again almost without being aware of it, only wanting to keep the blood flowing into her hands, wrists, and forearms. She guessed it was probably eight o'clock by now, or almost. She had been chained to this bed for eighteen hours. Incredible but true.

Ruth Neary's voice spoke up so suddenly that it made her jump. It was filled with disgusted wonder.

You're still making excuses for him, aren't you? Still letting him off the hook and blaming yourself, after all these years. Even now. Amazing.

"Quit it," she said hoarsely. "None of that has the slightest goddam thing to do with the mess I'm in now—"

What a piece of work you are, Jessie!

"—and even if it did," she went on, raising her voice slightly, "*even if it did,* it doesn't have the slightest goddam thing to do with getting *out* of the mess I'm in now, *so just give it a rest!*"

You weren't Lolita, Jessie, no matter what he might have made you think. You were about nine country miles from Lolita.

Jessie refused to reply. Ruth went one better; she refused to shut up.

If you still think your dear old Daddy was a parfit gentle knight who spent most of his time shielding you from the fire-breathing mommy-dragon, you better think again.

"Shut up." Jessie began to pump her arms up and down faster.

The chains jingled; the cuffs rattled. "Shut up, you're horrible."

He planned it, Jessie. Don't you understand? It wasn't just some spur-of-the-moment thing, a sex-starved father copping a quick feel; he planned *it.*

"You lie," Jessie snarled. Sweat rolled down from her temples in large clear droplets.

Do I? Well, ask yourself this—whose idea was it for you to wear the sundress? The one that was both too small and too tight? Who knew you'd be listening—and admiring—while he maneuvered around your mother? Who had his hands on your tits the night before, and who was wearing gym-shorts and nothing else on the day of?

Suddenly she imagined Bryant Gumbel in the room with her, natty in a three-piece suit and gold wrist-chain, standing here by the bed while a guy with a Mini-cam stood beside him, panning slowly up her almost naked body before focusing on her sweaty, blotchy face. Bryant Gumbel doing a live remote with The Incredible Handcuffed Woman, leaning forward with a microphone to ask her, *When did you first realize your father might have had the hots for you, Jessie?*

Jessie stopped pumping her arms and closed her eyes. There was a closed, stubborn look on her face. *No more,* she thought. *I guess I can live with the voices of Ruth and the Goodwife if I have to . . . even with the assorted UFOs who chip in their two cents' worth every once in awhile . . . but I draw the line at doing a live interview with Bryant Gumbel while dressed in nothing but a pair of pee-stained panties. Even in my imagination I draw the line at that.*

Just tell me one thing, Jessie, another voice said. No UFO here; it was the voice of Nora Callighan. *One thing and we'll consider the subject closed, at least for now and probably forever. Okay?*

Jessie was silent, waiting, wary.

When you finally lost your temper yesterday afternoon—when you finally kicked out—who were you kicking at? *Was it Gerald?*

"Of *course* it was Ger—" she began, and then broke off as a single image, perfectly clear, filled her mind. It was the white string of drool which had been hanging from Gerald's chin. She saw it elongate, saw it fall to her midriff just above the navel. Only a little spit, that was all, no big deal after all the years and all the passionate kisses with their mouths open and their tongues duelling; she and Gerald had swapped a fair amount of lubrication, and the only price they'd ever paid was a few shared colds.

No big deal, that was, until yesterday, when he'd refused to let her go when she wanted, needed, to be let go. No big deal until she'd smelled that flat sad mineral smell, the one she associated with the well-water at Dark Score, and with the lake itself on hot summer days . . . days like July 20th, 1963, for instance.

She had *seen* spit; she had *thought* spunk.

No, that's not true, she thought, but she didn't need to summon Ruth to play devil's advocate this time; she knew it *was* true. *It's his goddam spunk*—that had been her exact thought, and after that she had ceased thinking altogether, at least for awhile. Instead of thinking she had launched that reflexive countering movement, driving one foot into his stomach and the other into his balls. Not spit but spunk; not some new revulsion at Gerald's game but that old stinking horror suddenly surfacing like a sea-monster.

Jessie glanced at the huddled, mutilated body of her husband. Tears pricked her eyes for a moment, and then the sensation passed. She had an idea that the Survival Department had decided tears were a luxury she could not afford, at least for the time being. Still, she was sorry—sorry Gerald was dead, yes, of course, but even sorrier she was here, in this situation.

Her eyes shifted to thin air a little above Gerald, and Jessie produced a shabby, pained smile.

"I guess that's all I've got to say right now, Bryant. Give my best to Willard and Katie, and by the way—would you mind unlocking these handcuffs before you go? I'd really appreciate it."

Bryant didn't answer. Jessie wasn't all that surprised.

23

If you're going to live through this experience, Jess, I suggest you stop rehashing the past and start deciding what you're going to do with the future . . . starting with the next ten minutes or so. I don't think that dying of thirst on this bed would be very pleasant, do you?

No, not very pleasant . . . and she thought that thirst would be far from the worst of it. Crucifixion had been in the back of her mind almost since she'd awakened, floating up and down like some nasty drowned thing which is just a little too waterlogged to come all the way to the surface. She had read an article about this charming old method of torture and execution for a college history class, and had been surprised to learn that the old nails-through-the-hands-and-feet trick was only the beginning. Like magazine subscriptions and pocket calculators, crucifixion was the gift that kept on giving.

The real hardships began with cramps and muscle-spasms. Jessie reluctantly recognized that the pains she had suffered so far, even the paralyzing Charley horse which had put an end to her first panic-attack, were only tweaks compared to the ones which were waiting. They would rack her arms, diaphragm, and abdomen, growing steadily worse, more frequent, and more widespread as the day passed. Numbness would eventually begin to creep into her extremities no matter how hard she worked to keep the blood flowing, but numbness would bring no relief; by then she would almost certainly have begun suffering excruciating chest and stomach cramps. There were no nails in her hands and feet and she was lying down instead of hanging from a cross at the side of the road like one of the defeated gladiators in *Spartacus*, but those variations might only draw out her agony.

So what are you going to do right now, while you're still pretty much free of pain and able to think?

"Whatever I can," she croaked, "so why don't you just shut up and let me think about it for a minute?"

Go ahead—be my guest.

She would start with the most obvious solution and work her way down from there . . . if she had to. And what *was* the most obvious solution? The keys, of course. They were still lying on top of the bureau, where he had left them. Two keys, but both exactly the same. Gerald, who could be almost endearingly corny, had often referred to them as the Primary and the Backup (Jessie had clearly heard those capital letters in her husband's voice).

Suppose, just for the sake of argument, she could somehow slide the bed across the room to the bureau. Would she be able to actually get hold of one of those keys and put it to use? Jessie reluctantly realized that there were two questions there, not one. She supposed she might be able to pick up one of the keys in her teeth, but then what? She still wouldn't be able to get it into the lock; her experience with the water-glass suggested there was going to be a gap no matter how much she stretched.

Okay; scratch the keys. Descend to the next rung on the ladder of probability. What might that be?

She thought about it for almost five minutes without success, turning it around and around in her mind like the sides of a Rubik's Cube, pumping her arms up and down as she did so. At some point during her ruminations, her eyes wandered to the phone sitting on the low table by the east window. She had dismissed it earlier as being in another universe, but perhaps she had been too hasty. The table, after all, was closer than the bureau, and the phone was a lot bigger than a handcuff key.

If she could move the bed over to the telephone table, might she not be able to lift the receiver off the cradle with her foot? And if she could do that, maybe she could use her big toe to push the Operator button at the bottom, between the keys marked * and #. It sounded like some crazy sort of vaudeville act, but—

Push the button, wait, then start screaming my head off.

Yes, and half an hour later either the big blue Medcu van from Norway or the big orange one marked Castle County Rescue would turn up and trundle her off to safety. A crazy idea, all right, but so was turning a magazine subscription card into a straw. It could work, crazy or not—that was the point. It certainly had more potential than somehow pushing the bed all the way across the room and then trying to find a way to get one of the keys into one of the handcuff locks. There was one big problem with the idea, however: she would somehow have to find a way to move the bed to the right, and that was a heavy proposition. She guessed that, with its mahogany head- and footboards, it had to weigh at least three hundred pounds, and that estimate might be conservative.

But you can at least try it, babe, and you might get a big surprise— the floor's been waxed since Labor Day, remember. If a stray dog with its ribs sticking out can move your husband, maybe you can move this bed. You haven't got anything to lose by trying, do you?

A good point.

Jessie worked her legs toward the left side of the bed, shifting her back and shoulders patiently to the right as she did so. When she got as far as she was going to using that method, she pivoted on her left hip. Her feet went over the side . . . and suddenly her legs and torso were not just *moving* to the left but *sliding* to the left, like an avalanche trying to happen. A horrible cramp jig-jagged up her left side as her body stretched in ways it hadn't been meant to even under the best of conditions. It felt as if someone had given her a fast, harsh scrape with a hot poker.

The short chain between the right-hand set of cuffs yanked taut, and for a moment the news from her left side was blotted out by fresh agony pulsing out of her right arm and shoulder. It felt as if someone were trying to twist that arm completely off. *Now I know what a turkey drumstick feels like,* she thought.

Her left heel thumped onto the floor; her right hung three inches above it. Her body was twisted unnaturally to the left with her right arm cast strenuously back behind her in a kind of frozen wave. The taut chain gleamed heartlessly above its rubber sleeve in the early-morning sun.

Jessie was suddenly sure she was going to die in this position, with her left side and right arm screaming. She would have to lie here, gradually growing numb as her flagging heart lost the battle to pump blood to all parts of her stretched and twisted body. Panic overtook her again and she howled for help, forgetting there was no one in the neighborhood but one raggedy-ass stray with a bellyful of lawyer. She flailed frantically for the bedpost with her right hand, but she had slid just a little too far; the dark-stained mahogany was half an inch beyond the tips of her straining fingers.

"Help! Please! Help! Help!"

No answer. The only sounds in this silent sunny bedroom were her sounds: hoarse, screaming voice, rasping breath, pounding heart. No one here but her, and unless she was able to get back onto the bed, she was going to die like a woman hung on a meat-hook. Nor was the situation done getting worse: her butt was still sliding toward the edge of the bed, pulling her right arm steadily backward at an angle which was becoming more and more extreme.

Without thinking about it or planning it (unless the body, goaded by pain, sometimes thinks for itself), Jessie braced her bare left heel on the floor and shoved backward with all her might. It was the only brace-point remaining to her painfully slued body, and the maneuver worked. Her lower body arched, the chain between the cuffs binding her right hand grew slack, and she seized the bedpost with the panicky zeal of a drowning woman seizing a life-ring. She used it to yank herself backward, ignoring the scream of her back and biceps. When her feet were up again, she paddled frantically back from the edge, as if she had dipped into a swimming pool filled with baby sharks and had noticed just in time to save her toes.

At last she regained her former slumped sitting position against the crossboards, arms outstretched, the small of her back resting on the sweat-soaked pillow in its badly wrinkled cotton case. She let her head loll back against the mahogany slats, breathing rapidly, her bare breasts oiled with sweat she couldn't afford to lose. She closed her eyes and laughed weakly.

Say, that was pretty exciting, wasn't it, Jessie? I think it's the fastest and hardest your heart has beat since 1985, when you came within a

Christmas party kiss or so of going to bed with Tommy Delguidace. Nothing to lose by trying, isn't that what you thought? Well now you know better.

Yes. And she knew something else, as well.

Oh? And what's that, toots?

"I know that fucking phone is out of reach," she said.

Yes indeed. When she had pushed off with her left heel just now, she had shoved with all the enthusiasm of total, ass-freezing panic. The bed hadn't moved an iota, and now that she had a chance to think about it, she was glad it hadn't. If it had jigged to the right, she would still be hanging off it. And even if she had been able to push it all the way across to the telephone table that way, why . . .

"I'd've been hanging over the wrong fucking side," she said, half-laughing and half-sobbing. "Jesus, somebody shoot me."

Doesn't look good, one of the UFO voices—one she definitely could have done without—told her. *In fact, it sort of looks like the Jessie Burlingame Show just got its cancellation notice.*

"Pick another choice," she said huskily. "I don't like that one."

There aren't *any others. There weren't that many to begin with, and you've researched them all.*

She closed her eyes again and for the second time since this nightmare began, she saw the playground behind the old Falmouth Grammar School on Central Avenue. Only this time it wasn't the image of two little girls balancing on a seesaw that filled her mind; instead she saw one little boy—her brother Will—skinning the cat on the monkey-bars.

She opened her eyes, slumped down, and bent her head to look more closely at the headboard. Skinning the cat meant hanging from a bar, then curling your legs up and over your own shoulders. You finished with a quick little pivot which enabled you to land on your feet again. Will had been so adept at this neat and economical movement that it had looked to Jessie as if he were turning somersaults inside his own hands.

Suppose I could do that? Just skin the cat right over the top of this goddam headboard. Swing over the top and . . .

"And land on my feet," she whispered.

For several moments this seemed dangerous but feasible. She would have to move the bed out from the wall, of course—you couldn't skin the cat if you didn't have a place to land—but she had an idea she could manage that. Once the bed-shelf was removed (and it would be easy to knock it off its support brackets, unanchored as it was), she would do a backover roll and plant her bare feet against the wall above the top of the headboard. She hadn't been able to move the bed sideways, but with the wall to push against—

"Same weight, ten times the leverage," she muttered. "Modern physics at its finest."

She was reaching for the shelf with her left hand, meaning to tip it up and off the L-brackets, when she took another good look at Gerald's goddam police handcuffs with their suicidally short chains. If he had clipped them onto the bedposts a little higher—between the first and second crossboards, say—she might have chanced it; the maneuver would probably have resulted in a pair of broken wrists, but she had reached a point where a pair of broken wrists seemed an entirely acceptable price to pay for escape . . . after all, they would heal, wouldn't they? Instead of between the first and second crossboards, however, the cuffs were attached between the second and third, and that was just a little too far down. Any attempt to skin the cat over the headboard would do more than break her wrists; it would result in a pair of shoulders not just dislocated but actually ripped out of their sockets by her descending weight.

And try moving this goddam bed anywhere with a pair of broken wrists and two dislocated shoulders. Sound like fun?

"No," she said huskily. "Not too much."

Let's cut through it, Jess—you're stuck here. You can call me the voice of despair if it makes you feel better, or if it helps you to hold onto your sanity for a little while longer—God knows I'm all for sanity—but what I really am is the voice of truth, and the truth of this situation is that you're stuck here.

Jessie turned her head sharply to one side, not wanting to hear this self-styled voice of truth, and found she was no more able to shut it out than she had been able to shut out the other ones.

Those are real handcuffs you're wearing, not the cute little bondage numbers with the padding inside the wristlets and a hidden escape-lever you can push if someone gets carried away and starts going a little too far. You're for-real locked up, and you don't happen to be either a fakir from the Mysterious East, capable of twisting your body up like a pretzel, or an escape artist like Harry Houdini or David Copperfield. I'm just telling it the way I see it, okay? And the way I see it, you're toast.

She suddenly remembered what had happened after her father had left her bedroom on the day of the eclipse—how she had thrown herself on her bed and cried until it had seemed her heart would either break or melt or maybe just seize up for good. And now, as her mouth began to tremble, she looked remarkably as she had then: tired, confused, frightened, and lost. That last most of all.

Jessie began to cry, but after the first few tears, her eyes would produce no more; stricter rationing measures had apparently gone into effect. She cried anyway, tearlessly, her sobs as dry as sandpaper in her throat.

24

In New York City, the regulars of the *Today* program had signed off for another day. On the NBC affiliate which served southern and western Maine, they were replaced first by a local chat-show (a large, motherly woman in a gingham apron showed how easy it was to slow-cook beans in your Crock-pot), then by a game-show where celebrities cracked jokes and contestants uttered loud, orgasmic screams when they won cars and boats and bright red Dirt Devil vacuum cleaners. In the Burlingame home on scenic Kashwakamak Lake, the new widow dozed uneasily in her restraints, and then began to dream once more. It was a nightmare, one made more vivid and somehow more persuasive by the very shallowness of the dreamer's sleep.

In it Jessie was lying in the dark again, and a man—or a manlike thing—was once more standing across from her in the corner of the room. The man wasn't her father; the man wasn't her husband; the man was a stranger, *the* stranger, the one who haunts all our sickest, most paranoid imaginings and deepest fears. It was the face of a creature Nora Callighan, with her good advice and sweet, practical nature, had never taken into account. This black being could not be conjured away by anything with an ology suffix. It was a cosmic wildcard.

But you do *know me,* the stranger with the long white face said. It bent down and grasped the handle of its bag. Jessie noted, with no surprise at all, that the handle was a jawbone and the bag itself was made of human skin. The stranger picked it up, flicked the clasps, and opened the lid. Again she saw the bones and the jewels; again it reached its hand into the tangle and began to move it in slow circles, producing those ghastly clickings and clackings and rappings and tappings.

No I don't, she said. *I don't know who you are, I don't, I don't, I* don't*!*

I'm Death, of course, and I'll be back tonight. Only tonight I think I'll do a little more than just stand in the corner; tonight I think I'll jump out at you, just . . . like . . . this!

It leaped forward, dropping the case (bones and pendants and rings and necklaces spilled out toward where Gerald lay sprawled with his mutilated arm pointing toward the hallway door) and shooting out its hands. She saw its fingers ended in dark filthy nails so long they were really claws, and then she shook herself awake with a gasp and a jerk, the handcuff chains swinging and jingling as she made warding-off gestures with her hands. She was whispering the word "No" over and over again in a slurry monotone.

197

It was a dream! Stop it, Jessie, it was just a dream!

She slowly lowered her hands, letting them dangle limply inside the cuffs once more. Of course it had been—just a variation of the bad dream she'd had last night. It had been realistic, though—Jesus, yes. Far worse, when you got right down to it, than the one of the croquet party, or even the one in which she had recalled the furtive and unhappy interlude with her father during the eclipse. It was passing strange that she had spent so much time this morning thinking about those dreams and so little thinking about the far scarier one. In fact, she really hadn't thought of the creature with the weirdly long arms and the gruesome souvenir case at all until she'd dozed off and dreamed of him just now.

A snatch of song occurred to her, something from the Latter Psychedelic Age: *"Some people call me the space cowboy . . . yeah . . . some call me the gangster of love . . ."*

Jessie shuddered. The space cowboy. That was somehow just right. An outsider, someone who had nothing to do with anything, a wildcard, a—

"A stranger," Jessie whispered, and suddenly remembered the way its cheeks had wrinkled when it began to grin. And once *that* detail had fallen into place, others began falling into place around it. The gold teeth twinkling far back in the grinning mouth. The pouty, poochy lips. The livid brow and the blade of nose. And there was the case, of course, like something you might expect to see banging against a travelling salesman's leg as he ran to catch his train—

Stop it, Jessie—stop giving yourself the horrors. Don't you have enough problems without worrying about the boogeyman?

She most certainly did, but she found that, now that she had begun thinking about the dream, she couldn't seem to stop. Worse than that was the fact that the more she thought about it, the less dreamlike it became.

What if I was awake? she thought suddenly, and once the idea was articulated, she was horrified to discover some part of her had believed just that all along. It had only been waiting for the rest of her to catch up.

No, oh no, it was just a dream, that's all—

But what if it wasn't? What if it wasn't?

Death, the white-faced stranger agreed. *It was Death you saw. I'll be back tonight, Jessie. And tomorrow night I'll have your rings in my case with the rest of my pretty things . . . my souvenirs.*

Jessie realized she was shivering violently, as if she had caught a chill. Her wide eyes looked helplessly into the empty corner where the

(*space cowboy   gangster of love*)

had stood, the corner which was now bright with morning sunshine but would be dark with tangles of shadow tonight. Knots of gooseflesh had begun to pop up on her skin. The inescapable truth came again: she was probably going to die here.

Eventually someone will find you, Jessie, but it might take a long time. The first assumption will be that the two of you are off on some wild romantic fling. Why not? Didn't you and Gerald give every outward appearance of second-decade wedded bliss? It was only the two of you who knew that, at the end, Gerald could get it up with any reliability only if you were handcuffed to the bed. Sort of makes you wonder if someone played a few little games with him *on the day of the eclipse, doesn't it?*

"Stop talking," she muttered. "All of you, stop talking."

But sooner or later people will *get nervous and start hunting for you. It'll probably be Gerald's colleagues who actually get the wheels turning, don't you think? I mean, there are a couple of women in Portland you call friends, but you've never really let them inside your life, have you? Acquaintances is really all they are, ladies to have tea with and swap catalogues with. None of them are going to worry much if you drop out of sight for a week or ten days. But Gerald will have appointments, and when he doesn't show up by Friday noon, I think some of his bullpen buddies will start making phone calls and asking questions. Yes, that's the way it will probably start, but I think it'll probably be the caretaker who actually discovers the bodies, don't you? I bet he'll turn his face away while he's throwing the spare blanket from the closet shelf over you, Jessie. He won't want to see the way your fingers stick out of the handcuffs, as stiff as pencils and as white as candles. He won't want to look at your frozen mouth, or the foam long since dried to scales on your lips. Most of all he won't want to look at the expression of horror in your eyes, so he'll shift his own eyes to the side while he covers you up.*

Jessie moved her head from side to side in a slow, hopeless gesture of negation.

Bill will call the police and they'll show up with the forensics unit and the County Coroner. They'll all stand around the bed smoking cigars (Doug Rowe, undoubtedly wearing his awful white trenchcoat, will be standing outside with his film-crew, of course), and when the coroner pulls off the blanket, they'll wince. Yes—I think even the most hardened of them are going to wince a little, and some of them may actually leave the room. Their buddies will razz them about it later. And the ones who stay will nod and tell each other that the person on the bed died hard. "You only have to look at her to see that," they'll say. But they won't know the half of it. They won't know that the real reason your eyes are staring and your mouth is frozen in a scream is because of what you saw at the end. What you saw coming out of the dark. Your father may have been your first lover, Jessie, but your last is going to be the stranger with the long white face and the travelling bag made out of human skin.

"Oh please, can't you *quit?*" Jessie moaned. "No more voices, please, no more *voices.*"

But this voice wouldn't stop; wouldn't even acknowledge her. It just went on and on, whispering directly into her mind from some-place far down on her brain-stem. Listening to it was like having a mud-slimed piece of silk drawn lightly back and forth across her face.

They'll take you to Augusta and the State Medical Examiner will cut you open so he can inventory your guts. That's the rule in cases of unattended or questionable death, and yours is going to be both. He'll have a peek at what's left of your last meal—the salami-and-cheese sub from Amato's in Gorham—and take a little section of brain to look at under his microscope, and in the end he'll call it death by misadventure. "The lady and gentleman were playing an ordinarily harmless game," he'll say, "only the gentleman had the bad taste to have a heart attack at a critical moment and the woman was left to . . . well, it's best not to go into it. Best not to even think about it any more than is strictly necessary. Suffice it to say that the lady died hard—you only have to look at her to see that." That's how it's going to shake out, Jess. Maybe someone will notice your wedding ring is gone, but they won't hunt for it long, if at all. Nor will the ME notice that one of your bones—an unimportant one, the third phalange in your right foot, let's say—is gone. But we'll know, won't we, Jessie? In fact, we know already. We'll know that it took them. The cosmic stranger; the space cowboy. We'll know—

Jessie drove her head back against the headboard hard enough to send a school of big white fish exploding across her field of vision. It hurt—it hurt a lot—but the mind-voice cut out like a radio in a power-failure, and that made it worth it.

"There," she said. "And if you start up again, I'll do *that* again. I'm not kidding, either. I'm tired of listening to—"

Now it was her own voice, speaking unselfconsciously aloud in the empty room, that cut out like a radio in a power-failure. As the spots before her eyes began to fade, she saw the morning sunlight glinting off something which lay about eighteen inches beyond Gerald's outstretched hand. It was a small white object with a narrow thread of gold twisting up through the center, making it look like the yin-yang symbol. At first Jessie thought it was a finger-ring, but it was really too small for that. Not a finger-ring but a pearl earring. It had dropped to the floor while her visitor had been stirring the contents of its case around, showing them off to her.

"No," she whispered. "No, not possible."

But it was *there*, glinting in the morning sunshine and every bit as real as the dead man who seemed almost to be pointing at it: a pearl earring spliced with a delicate glint of gold.

It's one of mine! It spilled out of my jewelry box, it's been there since the summer, and I'm just noticing it now!

Except that she only owned one set of pearl earrings, they had no gold highlights, and they were back in Portland, anyway.

Except that the men from Skip's had been in to wax the floors the week after Labor Day, and if there *had* been an earring left on the floor, one of them would have picked it up and put it either on the dresser or in his own pocket.

Except there was something else, too.

No there's not. There's not, and don't you dare say there is.

It was just beyond the orphan earring.

Even if there was, I wouldn't look at it.

Except she couldn't *not* look at it. Her eyes moved past the earring of their own accord and fixed on the floor just inside the door to the front hall. There was a little spot of dried blood there, but it wasn't the blood which had caught her attention. The blood belonged to Gerald. The blood was all right. It was the footprint beside it that worried her.

If there was a track there, it was there before!

Much as Jessie wished she could believe that, the track had *not* been there before. Yesterday there hadn't been a single scuff on this floor, let alone a foot-track. Nor had she or Gerald left the one she was looking at. That was a shoe-shaped ring of dried mud, probably from the overgrown path that meandered along the shore of the lake for a mile or so before cutting back into the woods and heading south, toward Motton.

Someone had been in the bedroom with her last night after all, it seemed.

As this thought settled inexorably into Jessie's overstrained mind, she began to scream. Outside, on the back stoop, the stray lifted its scuffed, scratched muzzle from its paws for a moment. It cocked its good ear. Then it lost interest and lowered its head again. It wasn't as if the noise were being made by anything dangerous, after all; it was only the bitchmaster. Besides, the smell of the dark thing which had come in the night was on her now. It was one the stray was very familiar with. It was the smell of death.

The former Prince closed its eyes and went back to sleep.

25

At last she began to get herself under some kind of control again. She did this, absurdly enough, by reciting Nora Callighan's little mantra.

"One is for feet," she said, her dry voice cracking and wavering in the empty bedroom, "ten little toes, cute little piggies, all in a row. Two is for legs, lovely and long, three is my sex, where everything's wrong."

She pushed steadily on, reciting the couplets she could remember, skipping the ones she couldn't, keeping her eyes closed. She went through the whole thing half a dozen times. She was aware that her heartbeat was slowing down and the worst of her terror was once more draining away, but she had no conscious awareness of the radical change she had made in at least one of Nora's jangly little couplets.

After the sixth repetition she opened her eyes and looked about the room like a woman who has just awakened from a short, restful nap. She avoided the corner by the bureau, however. She didn't want to look at the earring again, and she most certainly didn't want to look at the footprint.

Jessie? The voice was very soft, very tentative. Jessie thought it was the voice of the Goodwife, now drained of both its shrill ardor and its feverish denial. *Jessie, can I say something?*

"No," she responded immediately in her harsh dust-in-the-cracks voice. "Take a hike. I want to be done with all you bitches."

Please, Jessie. Please listen to me.

She closed her eyes and found she could actually see that part of her personality she had come to call Goody Burlingame. Goody was still in the stocks, but now she raised her head—an act that couldn't have been easy with the cruel wooden restraint pressing into the back of her neck. Her hair fell away from her face momentarily, and Jessie was surprised to see not the Goodwife but a young girl.

Yeah, but she's still me, Jessie thought, and almost laughed. If this wasn't a case of comic-book psychology, she didn't know what was. She had just been thinking about Nora, and one of Nora's favorite hobbyhorses was about how people had to care for "the child inside." Nora claimed that the most common reason for unhappiness was failure to feed and nurture that interior child.

Jessie had nodded solemnly at all this, keeping her belief that the idea was mostly sentimental Aquarian/New Age slop to herself. She had liked Nora, after all, and although she thought Nora had held onto a few too many sets of mental love-beads from the late sixties and early seventies, she was clearly seeing Nora's "child inside" now, and that seemed perfectly all right. Jessie supposed that the concept might even have some symbolic validity, and under the circumstances, the stocks made a hell of an apt image, didn't they? The person in them was the Goodwife-in-waiting, the Ruth-in-waiting, the Jessie-in-waiting. She was the little girl her father had called Punkin.

"So talk," Jessie said. Her eyes were still closed, and a combination of stress, hunger, and thirst had combined to make the vision of the girl in the stocks almost exquisitely real. Now she could see the words FOR SEXUAL ENTICEMENT written on a sheet of vellum nailed above the girl's head. The words were written in candy-pink Peppermint Yum-Yum lipstick, of course.

Nor was her imagination done yet. Next to Punkin was another set of stocks, with another girl in them. This one was perhaps seventeen, and fat. Her complexion was blotched with pimples. Behind the prisoners, a town common appeared, and after a moment Jessie could see a few cows grazing on it. Someone was ringing a bell—over the next hill, it sounded like—with monotonous regularity, as if the ringer intended to keep it up all day . . . or at least until the cows came home.

You're losing your mind, Jess, she thought faintly, and she supposed this was true but unimportant. She might even count it among her blessings before much longer. She pushed the thought away and turned her attention back to the girl in the stocks. As she did, she found her exasperation had been replaced by tenderness and anger. This version of Jessie Mahout was older than the one who had been molested during the eclipse, but not *much* older—twelve, perhaps, fourteen at the outside. At her age she had no business being in stocks on the town common for *any* crime, but sexual enticement? Sexual *enticement,* for heaven's sake? What kind of bad joke was that? How could people be so cruel? So willfully blind?

What do you want to tell me, Punkin?

Only that it's real, the girl in the stocks said. Her face was pale with pain, but her eyes were grave and concerned and lucid. *It's real, you know it is, and it will be back tonight. I think that this time it will do more than just look. You have to get out of the handcuffs before the sun goes down, Jessie. You have to be out of this house before it comes back.*

Once again she wanted to cry, but there were no tears; there was nothing but that dry, sandpapery sting.

I can't! she cried. *I've tried everything! I* can't *get out on my own!*

You forgot one thing, the girl in the stocks told her. *I don't know if it's important or not, but it might be.*

What?

The girl turned her hands over inside the holes which held them, exposing her clean pink palms. *He said there were two kinds, remember? M-17 and F-23. You almost remembered yesterday, I think. He wanted F-23s, but they don't make many and they're hard to get, so he had to settle for two pairs of M-17s. You* do *remember, don't you? He told you all about it on the day he brought the handcuffs home.*

She opened her eyes and looked at the cuff which enclosed her right wrist. Yes, he certainly had told her all about it; had, in fact, babbled like a coke addict on a two-pipe high, beginning with a late-morning call from the office. He'd wanted to know if the house was empty—he could never remember which days the housekeeper had off—and when she assured him it was, he had asked her to slip into something comfortable. "Something that's almost there" was the way he'd put it. She remembered being intrigued. Even over the phone, Gerald had sounded ready to blow a fuse, and she had suspected he was thinking kinky. That was all right with her; they were closing in on their forties, and if Gerald wanted to experiment a little, she was willing enough to accommodate him.

He had arrived in record time (he must have left all three miles of the 295 city bypass smoking behind him, she thought), and what Jessie remembered best about that day was how he had gone bustling about the bedroom, cheeks flushed and eyes sparkling. Sex wasn't the first thing that came to her mind when she thought of Gerald (in a word-association test, *security* would probably have popped out first), but that day the two things had been all but interchangeable. Certainly sex had been the only thing on his mind; Jessie believed his usually polite attorney's pecker would have ripped the fly out of his natty pinstripe trousers if he'd been any slower getting them off.

Once they and the shorts beneath had been discarded, he had slowed down a little, ceremoniously opening the Adidas sneaker box he'd brought upstairs with him. He brought out the two sets of handcuffs which had been inside and held them up for her inspection. A pulse had been fluttering in his throat, a flickery little movement almost as fast as a hummingbird's wing. She remembered that, too. Even then his heart must have been under a strain.

You would have done me a big favor, Gerald, if you'd popped your cork right then and there.

She wanted to be horrified at this unkind thought about the man with whom she had shared so much of her life, and found the most she could manage was an almost clinical self-disgust. And when her thoughts returned to how he'd looked that day—those flushed cheeks and sparkling eyes—her hands curled quietly into hard little fists.

"Why couldn't you leave me alone?" she asked him now. "Why did you have to be such a prick about it? Such a *bully?*"

Never mind. Don't think about Gerald; think about the cuffs. Two sets of Kreig Security Hand Restraints, size M-17. The M designation for Male; the 17 for the number of notches on the latch-locks.

A sensation of bright heat bloomed in her stomach and chest. *Don't feel that,* she told herself, *and if you absolutely* have *to feel it, pretend it's indigestion.*

That was impossible, however. It was hope she felt, and it wouldn't be denied. The best she could do was balance it with reality, keep reminding herself of her first failed attempt to squeeze out of the cuffs. Yet in spite of her efforts to remember the pain and the failure, what she found herself thinking about was how close—how fucking *close*—she had come to escape. Another quarter of an inch might have been enough to turn the trick, she had thought then, and a half would have done it for sure. The bony outcrops below her thumbs were a problem, yes, but was she actually going to die on this bed because she was unable to bridge a gap not much wider than her upper lip? Surely not.

Jessie made a strong effort to set these thoughts aside and return her mind to the day Gerald had brought the cuffs home. To how he had held them up with the wordless awe of a jeweler displaying the finest diamond necklace to ever pass through his hands. She had been fairly impressed with them herself, come to that. She remembered how shiny they had been, and how the light from the window had pricked gleams of light off the blued steel of the cuffs and the notched curves of the latch-locks which allowed one to adjust the handcuffs to wrists of various sizes.

She'd wanted to know where he had gotten them—it was a matter of simple curiosity, not accusation—but all he would tell her was that one of the courthouse sharpies had helped him out. He dropped her a hazy little half-wink when he said it, as if there were dozens of these shifty fellows drifting through the various halls and ante-chambers of the Cumberland County Courthouse, and he knew them all. In fact, he'd behaved that afternoon as if it had been a couple of Scud missiles he'd scored instead of two pairs of handcuffs.

She had been lying on the bed, dressed in a white lace teddy and matching silk hose, an ensemble which was most definitely almost there, watching him with a mixture of amusement, curiosity, and excitement . . . but amusement had held the pole position that day, hadn't it? Yes. Seeing Gerald, who always tried so hard to be Mr. Cool, go striding around the room like a horse in heat had struck her as very amusing indeed. His hair had been frizzed up in the wild corkscrews Jessie's kid brother used to call "chickens," and he'd still been wearing his black nylon dress-for-success socks. She remembered biting the insides of her cheeks—and quite hard, too—to keep her smile from showing.

Mr. Cool had been talking faster than an auctioneer at a bankruptcy sale that afternoon. Then, all at once, he had stopped in mid-spiel. An expression of comic surprise had overspread his face.

"Gerald, what's wrong?" she had asked.

"I just realized that I don't know if you even want to *consider* this," he had replied. "I've been prattling on and on, I'm just about frothing at the you-know-what, as you can plainly see, and I never once asked you if—"

She had smiled then, partially because she'd gotten very bored with the scarves and hadn't known how to tell him, but mostly just because it was good to see him excited about sex again. All right, it was maybe a little weird to get turned on by the idea of locking your wife up in handcuffs before going deep-sea diving with the long white pole. So what? It was just between the two of them, wasn't it, and it was all in fun—really no more than an X-rated comic opera. Gilbert and Sullivan Do Bondage, I'm just a hand-cuffed lay-dee in the King's Nay-vee. Besides, there were weirder kinks; Frieda Soames from across the street had once confessed to Jessie (after two drinks before lunch and half a bottle of wine during) that her ex-husband had enjoyed being powdered and diapered.

Biting the insides of her cheeks hadn't worked the second time, and she had burst out laughing. Gerald had looked at her with his head cocked slightly to the right and a little smile tilting up the left corner of his mouth. It was an expression she had come to know well over the last seventeen years—it meant he was either preparing to be angry or to laugh along with her. It was usually impossible to tell which way he would tip.

"Want to share?" he'd asked.

She hadn't replied immediately. She stopped laughing instead and fixed him with what she hoped was an expression worthy of the meanest Nazi bitch-goddess ever to grace the cover of a *Man's Adventure* magazine. When she felt she had achieved the right degree of icy hauteur, she raised her arms and said five uncalculated words which had brought him leaping across to the bed, obviously dizzy with excitement:

"Get over here, you bastard."

In no time at all he had been fumbling the cuffs onto her wrists and then attaching them to the bedposts. There were no slats on the headboard in the master bedroom of the Portland house; if he *had* suffered his heart attack there, she could have slipped the cuffs right off the tops of the posts. As he panted and fussed over the cuffs, one knee rubbing delightfully against her down below while he did it, he talked. And one of the things he had told her was about M and F, and how the latch-locks worked. He had wanted Fs, he told her, because the female cuffs had latch-locks with twenty-three notches instead of seventeen, the number most male cuffs had. More notches meant the female cuffs would close smaller. They were hard to come by, though, and when his courthouse friend had told Gerald he could get him two sets of men's hand restraints at a very reasonable price, Gerald had jumped at the chance.

"Some women can pull right out of men's cuffs," he'd told her, "but you're fairly big-boned. Besides, I didn't want to wait. Now . . . let's just see . . ."

He had snapped the cuff on her right wrist, pushing the latch-lock in fast at first but slowing down as he approached the end, asking her if he was hurting her as each notch clicked past. It was fine all the way to the last notch, but when he had asked her to try and get out, she hadn't been able to do so. Her wrist had slipped most of the way through the cuff, all right, and Gerald had told her later that not even that was supposed to happen, but when it bound up along the back of her hand and at the base of her thumb, his comical expression of anxiety had faded.

"I think they're going to do just fine," he had said. She remembered that very well, and she remembered what he'd said next even more clearly: "We're going to have a lot of fun with these."

With the memory of that day still vivid in the front of her mind, Jessie once again began to apply downward pressure, trying to somehow shrink her hands enough so she could yank them through the cuffs. The pain struck sooner this time, starting not in her hands but in the overtaxed muscles of her shoulders and arms. Jessie squeezed her eyes shut, bore down harder, and tried to shut out the hurt.

Now her hands joined the chorus of outrage, and as she once more approached the outer limit of her muscular leverage and the cuffs began to dig into the scant flesh which covered the backs of her hands, they began to scream. *Posterior ligament,* she thought, head cocked, lips drawn back in a wide, spitless grin of pain. *Posterior ligament, posterior ligament, motherfucking posterior ligament!*

Nothing. No give. And she began to suspect—to *strongly* suspect—that there was more involved than ligaments. There were *bones* there as well, a couple of pukey little bones running along the outsides of her hands below the lower thumb-joint, a couple of pukey little bones that were probably going to get her killed.

With a final shriek of mingled pain and disappointment, Jessie let her hands go limp once more. Her shoulders and upper arms quivered with exhaustion. So much for sliding out of the cuffs because they were M-17s instead of F-23s. The disappointment was almost worse than the physical pain; it stung like poisoned nettles.

"*Shit and fuck!*" she cried at the empty room. "*Shit and fuck, shit-and-fuck, shittenfuck!*"

Somewhere along the lake—farther off today, by the sound—the chainsaw started up, and that made her even angrier. The guy from yesterday, back for more. Just some swinging dick in a red-and-black-checked flannel shirt from L. L. Bean's, out there playing Paul Kiss-My-Ass Bunyan, roaring away with his Stihl and dreaming about crawling into bed with his little honey at the end of the day . . . or maybe it was football he was dreaming of, or just a few frosty cold ones down at the marina bar. Jessie saw the dork in the checked flannel shirt as clearly as she had seen the young girl in the stocks, and if thoughts alone could have killed him, his head would have exploded out through his asshole at that very moment.

"*It's not fair!*" she screamed. "*It's just not f—*"

A kind of dry cramp seized her throat and she fell silent, grimacing and afraid. She had felt the hard splinters of bone which barred her escape—oh God, had she—but she had been close, just the same. That was the real wellspring of her bitterness—not the pain, and certainly not the unseen woodcutter with his blatting chainsaw. It was knowing that she had gotten close, but nowhere near close enough. She could continue to grit her teeth and endure the pain, but she no longer believed it would do her the slightest bit of good. That last quarter to half an inch was going to remain mockingly out of her reach. The only thing she would manage to do if she kept on pulling was to cause edema and swelling in her wrists, worsening her situation instead of bettering it.

"And don't you tell me I'm toast, don't you *dare*," she said in a whispery, scolding voice. "I don't want to hear that."

You have to get out of them somehow, the young girl's voice whispered back. *Because he—it—really is going to come again. Tonight. After the sun goes down.*

"I don't believe it," she croaked. "I don't believe that man was real. I don't care about the footprint and the earring. I just don't believe it."

Yes, you do.

No, I don't!

Yes, you do.

Jessie let her head droop to one side, hair hanging almost down to the mattress, mouth quivering abjectly.

Yes, she did.

26

She started to doze off again in spite of her worsening thirst and throbbing arms. She knew it was dangerous to sleep—that her strength would continue to ebb while she was out of it—but what difference did it really make? She had explored all her options and she was still America's Handcuffed Sweetheart. Besides, she wanted that lovely oblivion—craved it, in fact, the way a hophead craves his drug. Then, just before she drifted off, a thought which was both simple and shockingly direct lit up her confused, drifting mind like a flare.

The face cream. The jar of face cream on the shelf above the bed.

Don't get your hopes up, Jessie—that would be a bad mistake. If it didn't fall right off onto the floor when you tipped the shelf up, it probably slid to a place where you haven't got a snowball's chance in hell of getting hold of it. So don't get your hopes up.

The thing was, she couldn't *not* get them up, because if the face cream was still there and still in a place where she could get hold of it, it might provide just enough slip to free one hand. Maybe both, although she didn't think that would be necessary. If she could pull out of one cuff, she would be able to get off the bed, and if she could get off the bed, she thought she would have it made.

It was just one of those small plastic sample jars they send through the mail, Jessie. It must *have slid off onto the floor.*

It hadn't, though. When Jessie had turned her head as far to the left as it would go without popping her neck out of joint, she was able to see a dark blue blob at the farthest edge of her vision.

It's not really there, the hateful, doom-mongering part of her whispered. *You* think *it's there, perfectly understandable, but it's really not. It's just a hallucination, Jessie, just you seeing what most of your mind wants you to see, orders you to see. Not me, though; I'm a realist.*

She looked again, straining a tiny bit farther to the left in spite of the pain. Instead of disappearing, the blue blob grew momentarily clearer. It was the sample jar, all right. There was a reading-lamp on Jessie's side of the bed, and this hadn't slid off onto the floor when she tilted the shelf because the base was fastened to the wood. A paperback copy of *The Valley of Horses* which had been lying on the shelf since mid-July had slid against the base of the lamp, and the jar of Nivea cream had slid against the book. Jessie realized it was possible that her life was going to be saved by a reading-lamp and a bunch of fictional cave-people with names like Ayla and Oda and Uba and Thonolan. It was more than amazing; it was surreal.

Even if it's there, you'll never be able to reach it, the doom-monger told her, but Jessie barely heard it. The thing was, she thought she *could* reach the jar. She was almost sure of it.

She turned her left hand within its restraint and reached slowly up to the shelf, moving with infinite care. It would not do to make a mistake now, to nudge the jar of Nivea cream out of reach along the shelf, or knock it backward against the wall. For all she knew, there might now be a gap between the shelf and the wall, a gap a small sample-sized jar could easily drop through. And if that happened, she was quite sure her mind would break. Yes. She would hear the jar hit the floor down there, landing among the mouse-turds and dust bunnies, and then her mind would just . . . well, break. So she had to be careful. And if she was, everything might yet be all right. Because . . .

Because maybe there is a God, she thought, *and He doesn't want me to die here on this bed like an animal in a leg-hold trap. It makes sense, when you stop to think about it. I picked that jar up off the shelf when the dog started chewing on Gerald, and then I saw it was too small and too light to do any damage even if I managed to hit the dog with it. Under those circumstances—revolted, confused, and scared out of my mind—the most natural thing in the world would have been to drop it before feeling around on the shelf for something heavier. Instead of doing that, I put it back on the shelf. Why would I or anyone else do such an illogical thing? God, that's why. That's the only answer I can think of, the only one that fits. God saved it for me because He knew I'd need it.*

She whispered her cuffed hand gently along the wood, trying to turn her splayed fingers into a radar dish. There must be no slip-ups. She understood that, questions of God or fate or providence aside, this was almost certainly going to be both her best chance and her last one. And as her fingers touched the smooth, curved surface of the jar, a snatch of talking blues occurred to her, a little dustbowl ditty probably composed by Woody Guthrie. She had first heard it sung by Tom Rush, back in her college days:

> *If you want to go to heaven*
> *Let me tell you how to do it,*
> *You gotta grease your feet*
> *With a little mutton suet.*
> *You just slide out of the devil's hand*
> *And ooze on over to the Promised Land;*
> *Take it easy,*
> *Go greasy.*

She slipped her fingers around the jar, ignoring the rusty pull of her shoulder muscles, moving with a slow, caressing care, and hooked the jar gently toward her. Now she knew how safecrackers felt when they were using nitro. *Take it easy,* she thought, *go greasy.* Had truer words ever been spoken in the whole history of the world?

"I don't *theeenk* so, my deah," she said in her snottiest Elizabeth Taylor *Cat on a Hot Tin Roof* voice. She did not hear herself do this, did not even realize she had spoken.

Already she could feel the blessed balm of relief stealing over her; it was as sweet as that first drink of fresh, cool water was going to be when she poured it over the rusty razorwire embedded in her throat. She was going to slide out of the devil's hand and ooze on over to the Promised Land; absolutely no doubt about it. As long as she oozed *carefully*, that was. She had been tested; she had been tempered in the fire; now she would reap her reward. She had been a fool to ever doubt.

I think you better stop thinking that way, the Goodwife said in a worried tone. *It will make you careless, and I have an idea that very few careless people ever manage to slide out of the devil's hand.*

Probably true, but she hadn't the slightest *intention* of being careless. She had spent the last twenty-one hours in hell, and no one knew any better than she did how much was riding on this one. No one *could* know, not ever.

"I'll be careful," Jessie crooned. "I'll think out every step. I promise I will. And then I . . . I'll . . ."

She would what?

Why, she would go greasy, of course. Not just until she got out of the handcuffs, but from now on. Jessie suddenly heard herself talking to God again, and this time she did it with an easy fluency.

I want to make You a promise, she told God. *I promise to go right on oozing. I'm going to start by having a big spring cleaning inside my head and throwing out all the broken stuff and the toys I outgrew a long time ago—all the stuff that isn't doing anything but taking up space and contributing to the fire-hazard, in other words. I might call Nora Callighan and ask her if she wants to help. I think I might call Carol Symonds, too . . . Carol Rittenhouse these days, of course. If there's anyone in our old bunch who still knows where Ruth Neary is, it'll be Carol. Listen to me, Lord—I don't know if anyone ever gets to the Promised Land or not, but I promise to stay greasy and keep trying. Okay?*

And she saw (almost as though it were an approving answer to her prayer) exactly how it was supposed to go. Getting the top off the jar would be the toughest part; it would require patience and great care, but she would be helped by its unusually small size. Plant the jar's base on the palm of her left hand; brace the top with her fingers; use her thumb to do the actual unscrewing. It would help if the cap was loose, but she was pretty sure she would be able to get it off in any case.

You're damn right I'll get it off, toots, Jessie thought grimly.

The most dangerous moment would probably come when the cap actually started to turn. If it happened all at once and she wasn't ready for it, the jar might shoot right out of her hand. Jessie voiced a croaky little laugh. "Fat chance," she told the empty room. "Fat fucking chance, my deah."

Jessie held the jar up, looking at it fixedly. It was hard to see through the translucent blue plastic, but the container appeared to be at least half full, maybe a little more. Once the cap was off, she would simply turn the jar over in her hand and let the goo seep out onto her palm. When she'd gotten as much as she could, she would tilt her hand up to the vertical, letting the cream slide down to her wrist. Most of it would pool between her flesh and the cuff. She would spread it by rotating her hand back and forth. She already knew where the vital spot was, anyway: the area just below the thumb. And when she was as greasy as she could get, she'd give one last pull, hard and steady. She would block out all pain and keep pulling until her hand slid through the cuff and she was free at last, free at last, Great God Almighty, free at last. She could do it. She knew she could.

"But carefully," she murmured, letting the base of the jar settle onto her palm and spacing the pads of her fingers and her thumb at intervals around the cap. And—

"It's *loose!*" she cried in a hoarse, trembling voice. "Oh my and pumpkin pie, it really *is!*"

She could hardly believe it—and the doom-monger buried somewhere deep inside refused to—but it was true. She could feel the cap rock a little on its spiral groove when she pressed the tips of her fingers gently up and down against it.

Carefully, Jess—oh so carefully. Just the way you saw it.

Yes. In her mind she now saw something else—saw herself, sitting at her desk in Portland, wearing her best black dress, the fashionably short one she had bought herself last spring as a present for sticking to her diet and losing ten pounds. Her hair, freshly washed and smelling of some sweet herbal shampoo instead of old sour sweat, was held in a simple gold clip. The top of the desk was flooded with friendly afternoon sunshine from the bow windows. She saw herself writing to The Nivea Corporation of America, or whoever it was that made Nivea face cream. *Dear Sirs,* she would write, *I just had to let you know what a lifesaver your product really is . . .*

When she applied pressure to the jar's cap with her thumb, it began to turn smoothly, without a single jerk. All according to plan. *Like a dream,* she thought. *Thank You, God. Thank You. Thank You so very, very, very m—*

Sudden movement snagged the corner of her eye and her first thought was not that someone had found her and she was saved but that the space cowboy had come back to take her for itself before she could get away. Jessie voiced a shrill, startled cry. Her gaze leaped up from its intent focus-point on the jar. Her fingers clutched it in an involuntary spasm of fright and surprise.

It was the dog. The dog had returned for a late-morning snack and was standing in the doorway, checking out the bedroom before coming in. At the same instant Jessie realized this, she also realized that she had squeezed the small blue jar much too hard. It was squirting through her fingers like a freshly peeled grape.

"*No!*"

She clutched for it and almost reinstated her grip. Then it tumbled out of her hand, struck her hip, and bounced off the bed. There was a mild and stupid clacking sound as the jar struck the wooden floor. This was the very sound which she had believed, less than three minutes ago, would drive her mad. It did not, and now she discovered a newer, deeper terror: in spite of everything which had happened to her, she was still a very long way from insanity. It seemed to her that, no matter what horrors might lie ahead for her now that this last door to escape had been barred, she must face them sane.

"Why do you have to come in now, you bastard?" she asked the former Prince, and something in her grating, deadly voice made it pause and look at her with a caution all her screams and threats had not been able to inspire. "Why now, God damn you? Why *now?*"

The stray decided the bitchmaster was probably still harmless in spite of the sharp edges which now glinted in her voice, but it still kept a wary eye on her as it trotted over to its supply of meat. It was better to be safe. It had suffered greatly in the course of learning that simple lesson, and it wasn't one it would forget easily, or soon—it was always better to be safe.

It gave her one final look with its bright and desperate eyes before dipping its head, seizing one of Gerald's love-handles, and tearing a large portion of it away. Seeing this was bad, but for Jessie it was not the worst. The worst was the cloud of flies which rose from their feeding- and nesting-ground when the stray locked its teeth and yanked. Their somnolent buzz finished the job of demolishing some vital, survival-oriented part of her, some part that had to do with both hope and heart.

The dog stepped back as delicately as a dancer in a movie musical, its good ear cocked, the meat dangling from its jaws. Then it turned and trotted quickly from the room. The flies were beginning re-settlement operations even before it was out of sight. Jessie leaned her head back against the mahogany crossboards and closed her eyes. She began praying again, but this time it was not escape she prayed for. This time she prayed that God would take her quickly and mercifully, before the sun went down and the white-faced stranger came back.

27

The next four hours were the worst of Jessie Burlingame's life. The cramps in her muscles grew steadily more frequent and more intense, but it wasn't intramuscular pain that made the hours between eleven and three so terrible; it was her mind's stubborn, gruesome refusal to relinquish its hold on lucidity and go into the dark. She had read Poe's "The Tell-Tale Heart" in junior high school, but not until now had she grasped the real horror of its opening lines: *Nervous! True, very nervous I am and have been, but why will you say I am mad?*

Madness would be a relief, but madness would not come. Neither would sleep. Death might beat them both, and dark certainly would. She could only lie on the bed, existing in a dull olive-drab reality shot through with occasional gaudy blasts of pain as her muscles cramped up. The cramps mattered, and so did her horrible, tiresome sanity, but little else seemed to—certainly the world outside this room had ceased to hold any real meaning for her. In fact, she came strongly to believe that there *was* no world outside this room, that all the people who had once filled it had gone back to some existential Central Casting office, and all the scenery had been packed away like stage-flats after one of Ruth's beloved college drama society productions.

Time was a cold sea through which her consciousness forged like a waddling, graceless icebreaker. Voices came and went like phantoms. Most spoke inside her head, but for awhile Nora Callighan talked to her from the bathroom, and at another point Jessie had a conversation with her mother, who seemed to be lurking in the hall. Her mother had come to tell her that Jessie never would have gotten into a mess like this if she had been better about picking up her clothes. "If I had a nickel for every slip I ever fished out of the corner and turned rightside-out," her mother said, "I could buy the Cleveland Gas Works." This had been a favorite saying of her mother's, and Jessie realized now that none of them had ever asked her why she would *want* the Cleveland Gas Works.

She continued to exercise weakly, pedaling with her feet and pumping her arms up and down as far as the handcuffs—and her own flagging strength—would allow. She no longer did this to keep her body ready for escape when the right option finally occurred to her, because she had finally come to understand, in her heart and in her head, that there were no options left. The jar of face cream had been the last. She was exercising now only because the movement seemed to alleviate the cramps a little.

In spite of the exercise, she could feel coldness creeping into her feet and hands, settling onto her skin like a skim of ice and then working its way in. This was nothing like the gone-to-sleep feeling with which she had awakened this morning; it was more like the frostbite she had suffered during a long afternoon of cross-country skiing as a teenager—sinister gray spots on the back of one hand and on the flesh of her calf where her legging hadn't quite covered, dead spots that seemed impervious to even the baking heat of the fireplace. She supposed this numbness would finally overwhelm the cramps and that, in the end, her death might turn out to be quite merciful after all—like going to sleep in a snowbank—but it was moving much too slowly.

Time passed but it wasn't time; it was just a relentless, unchanging flow of information passing from her sleepless senses to her eerily lucid mind. There was only the bedroom, the scenery outside (the last few stage-flats, yet to be packed away by the propmaster in charge of this shitty little production), the buzz of flies turning Gerald into a late-season incubator, and the slow movement of the shadows along the floor as the sun made its way across a painted autumn sky. Every now and then a cramp would stab into one of her armpits like an icepick or pound a thick steel nail into her right side. As the afternoon wore endlessly along, the first cramps began to strike into her belly, where all hunger pangs had now ceased, and into the overstressed tendons of her diaphragm. These latter were the worst, freezing the sheath of muscles in her chest and locking down her lungs. She stared up at the reflected water-ripples on the ceiling with agonized, bulging eyes as each one struck, arms and legs trembling with effort as she tried to continue breathing until the cramp eased. It was like being buried up to the neck in cold wet cement.

Hunger passed but thirst did not, and as that endless day turned about her, she came to realize that simple thirst (only that and nothing more) might accomplish what the increasing levels of pain and even the fact of her own oncoming death hadn't been able to: it might drive her mad. It wasn't just her throat and mouth now; every part of her body cried out for water. Even her eyeballs were thirsty, and the sight of the ripples dancing on the ceiling to the left of the skylight made her groan softly.

With these very real perils closing in on her, the terror she had felt of the space cowboy should have waned or disappeared entirely, but as the afternoon drew on, she found the white-faced stranger weighing more heavily on her mind rather than less. She saw its shape constantly, standing just beyond the small circle of light which enclosed her reduced consciousness, and although she could make out little more than its general shape (thin to the point of emaciation), she found she could see the sunken sickly grin that curved its mouth with greater and greater clarity as the sun dragged its harrow of hours into the west. In her ear she heard the dusty murmur of the bones and jewels as its hand stirred them in its old-fashioned case.

It would come for her. When it was dark it would come. The dead cowboy, the outsider, the specter of love.

You did see it, Jessie. It was Death, and you did see it, as people who die in the lonely places often do. Of course they do; it's stamped on their twisted faces, and you can read it in their bulging eyes. It was Old

221

Cowboy Death, and tonight when the sun goes down, he'll be back for you.

Shortly after three, the wind, which had been calm all day, began to pick up. The back door began to bang restlessly against the jamb again. Not long after, the chainsaw quit and she could hear the faint sound of wind-driven wavelets slapping against the rocks along the shore. The loon did not raise its voice; perhaps it had decided the time had come to fly south, or at least relocate to a part of the lake where the screaming lady could not be heard.

It's just me now. Until the other one gets here, at least.

She no longer made any effort to believe her dark visitor was only imagination; things had gone much too far for that.

A fresh cramp sank long, bitter teeth into her left armpit, and she pulled her cracked lips back in a grimace. It was like having your heart poked with the tines of a barbecue fork. Then the muscles just below her breasts tightened and the bundle of nerves in her solar plexus seemed to ignite like a pile of dry sticks. This pain was new, and it was enormous—far beyond anything she had experienced thus far. It bent her backward like a greenwood stick, torso twisting from side to side, knees snapping open and shut. Her hair flew in clots and clumps. She tried to scream and couldn't. For a moment she was sure this was it, the end of the line. One final convulsion, as powerful as six sticks of dynamite planted in a granite ledge, and out you go, Jessie; cashier's on your right.

But this one passed, too.

She relaxed slowly, panting, her head turned up toward the ceiling. For the moment, at least, the dancing reflections up there didn't torment her; all her concentration was focused on that fiery bundle of nerves between and just below her breasts, waiting to see if the pain was really going to go away or if it would flare up again instead. It went . . . but grudgingly, with a promise to be back soon. Jessie closed her eyes, praying for sleep. Even a short release from the long and tiresome job of dying would be welcome at this point.

Sleep didn't come, but Punkin, the girl from the stocks, did. She was free as a bird now, sexual enticement or no sexual enticement, walking barefooted across the town common of whatever Puritan village it was that she inhabited, and she was gloriously alone—there was no need to walk with her eyes decorously cast down so that some passing boy might not catch her gaze with a wink or a grin. The grass was a deep velvety green, and far away, on top of the next hill (*this has to be the world's* biggest *town common,* Jessie thought), a flock of sheep was grazing. The bell Jessie had heard before was sending its flat, monotonous peals across the darkening day.

Punkin was wearing a blue flannel nightie with a big yellow exclamation point on the front—hardly Puritan dress, although it was certainly modest enough, covering her from neck to feet. Jessie knew the garment well, and was delighted to see it again. Between the ages of ten and twelve, when she had finally been persuaded to donate it to the rag-basket, she must have worn that silly thing to two dozen slumber parties.

Punkin's hair, which had obscured her face completely while the neck-stock held her head down, was now tied back with a velvet bow of darkest midnight blue. The girl looked lovely and deeply happy, which didn't surprise Jessie at all. The girl had, after all, escaped *her* bonds; she was free. Jessie felt no jealousy of her on this account, but she did have a strong desire—almost a need—to tell her that she must do more than simply enjoy her freedom; she must treasure it and guard it and use it.

I went to sleep after all. I must have, because this has got to be a dream.

Another cramp, this one not quite as terrible as the one which had set fire to her solar plexus, froze the muscles in her right thigh and set her right foot wagging foolishly in the air. She opened her eyes and saw the bedroom, where the light had once again grown long and slanting. It was not quite what the French call *l'heure bleue,* but that time was now fast approaching. She heard the banging door, smelled her sweat and urine and sour, exhausted breath. All was exactly as it had been. Time had moved forward, but it had not *leaped* forward, as it so often seems to have done when one awakens from an unplanned doze. Her arms were a little colder, she thought, but no more or less numb than they had been. She hadn't been asleep and she hadn't been dreaming . . . but she had been doing *something*.

I can do it again, too, she thought, and closed her eyes. She was back on the improbably huge town common the moment she did. The girl with the big yellow exclamation point sprouting up between her small breasts was looking at her gravely and sweetly.

There's one thing you haven't tried, Jessie.

That's not true, she told Punkin. *I've tried everything, believe me. And you know what? I think that if I hadn't dropped that damned jar of face cream when the dog scared me, I might have been able to squeak out of the left cuff. It was bad luck, that dog coming in when it did. Or bad karma. Bad something, anyway.*

The girl drifted closer, the grass whispering beneath her bare feet.

Not the left cuff, Jessie. It's the right *one you can squeak out of. It's an outside shot, I'll grant you that, but it's possible. The real question now, I think, is whether you really* want *to live.*

Of course *I* want *to live!*

Closer still. Those eyes—a smoke color that tried to be blue and didn't quite make it—now seemed to peer right through her skin and into the heart of her.

Do you? I wonder.

What are you, crazy? Do you think I want to still be here, handcuffed to this bed, when—

Jessie's eyes—still trying to be blue after all these years and still not quite making it—slowly opened again. They gazed around the room with an expression of terrified solemnity. Saw her husband, now lying in an impossibly twisted position, glaring up at the ceiling.

"I don't want to still be handcuffed to this bed when it gets dark and the boogeyman comes back," she told the empty room.

Close your eyes, Jessie.

She closed them. Punkin stood there in her old flannel nightie, gazing at her calmly, and Jessie could now see the other girl as well—the fat one with the pimply skin. The fat girl hadn't been as lucky as Punkin; there had been no escape for her, unless death itself was an escape in certain cases—a hypothesis Jessie had become quite willing to accept. The fat girl had either choked to death or suffered some sort of seizure. Her face was the purple-black color of summer thunderheads. One eye bulged from its socket; the other had burst like a squeezed grape. Her tongue, bloody where she had bitten it repeatedly in her last extremity, protruded between her lips.

Jessie turned back to Punkin with a shudder.

I don't want to end up like that. Whatever else may be wrong with me, I don't want to end up like that. How did you get out?

Slid out, Punkin replied promptly. *Slid out of the devil's hand; oozed on over to the Promised Land.*

Jessie felt a throb of anger through her exhaustion.

Haven't you heard a single word I've said? I dropped the goddam jar of Nivea! The dog came in and startled me and I dropped *it! How can I—*

Also, I remembered the eclipse. Punkin spoke abruptly, with the air of one who has become impatient with some complex but meaningless social formula; you curtsey, I bow, we all join hands. *That's how I really got out; I remembered the eclipse and what happened on the deck while the eclipse was going on. And you'll have to remember, too. I think it's the only chance you have to get free. You can't run away anymore, Jessie. You have to turn and face the truth.*

That again? Only that? Jessie felt a deep wave of exhaustion and disappointment. For a moment or two, hope had almost returned, but there was nothing here for her. Nothing at all.

You don't understand, she told Punkin. *We've been down this path before—all the way down. Yes, I suppose that what my father did to me then might have something to do with what's happening to me now, I suppose that's at least possible, but why go through all that pain again when there's so much other pain to go through before God finally gets tired of torturing me and decides to pull down the blinds?*

There was no answer. The little girl in the blue nightie, the little

225

girl who had once been her, was gone. Now there was only darkness behind Jessie's closed lids, like the darkness of a movie screen after the show has ended, so she opened her eyes again and took a long look around the room where she was going to die. She looked from the bathroom door to the framed batik butterfly to the bureau to her husband's body, lying beneath its noxious throw-rug of sluggish autumn flies.

"Quit it, Jess. Go back to the eclipse."

Her eyes widened. That actually *did* sound real—a real voice coming not from the bathroom or the hall or from inside her own head, but seeming to seep out of the very air itself.

"Punkin?" Her voice was only a croak now. She tried to sit up a little more, but another ferocious cramp threatened her midsection and she lay back against the headboard at once, waiting for it to pass. "Punkin, is that you? Is it, dear?"

For a moment she thought she heard something, that the voice said something else, but if it did, she was unable to make out the words. And then it was entirely gone.

Go back to the eclipse, Jessie.

"No answers there," she muttered. "Nothing there but pain and stupidity and . . ." And what? What else?

The old Adam. The phrase rose naturally into her mind, lifted from some sermon she must have heard as a bored child sitting between her mother and father, kicking her feet in order to watch the light falling through the colored church windows shift and glimmer on her white patent-leather shoes. Just some phrase that had caught on sticky flypaper in her subconscious and stayed with her. *The old Adam*—and maybe that was all it was, as simple as that. A father who had half-consciously arranged to be alone with his pretty, vivacious young daughter, thinking all the while *There won't be any harm in it, no harm, not a bit of harm.* Then the eclipse had started, and she had sat on his lap in the sundress that was both too tight and too short—the sundress he himself had asked her to wear—and what had happened had happened. Just a brief, goatish interlude that had shamed and embarrassed them both. He had squirted his squirt—that was the long and short of it (and if there was some sort of pun buried in there, she didn't give a shit about it); had shot it all over the back of her underwear, in fact—definitely not approved behavior for Daddies and definitely not a situation she had ever seen explored on *The Brady Bunch*, but . . .

But let's face it, Jessie thought. *I got off with barely a scratch compared to what could have happened . . . what* does *happen every day. It doesn't just happen in places like Peyton Place and along Tobacco Road, either. My father wasn't the first college-educated, upper-middle-class man to ever get a hard-on for his daughter, and I wasn't the first daughter to ever find a wet spot on the back of her underpants. That's not to say it was right, or even excusable; it's just to say that it's over, and it could have been a lot worse.*

Yes. And right now forgetting all that seemed a much better idea than going through it yet again, no matter what Punkin had to say on the subject. Best to let it fade into the general darkness which came with any solar eclipse. She still had a lot of dying to do in this stinking, fly-filled bedroom.

She closed her eyes and immediately the scent of her father's cologne seemed to drift into her nose. That, and the smell of his light, nervous sweat. The feel of the hard thing against her bottom. His little gasp as she squirmed on his lap, trying to get comfortable. Feeling his hand as it settled lightly on her breast. Wondering if he was all right. He had begun to breathe so *fast*. Marvin Gaye on the radio: "*I love too hard, my friends sometimes say, but I believe . . . I believe . . . that a woman should be loved that way . . .*"

Do you love me, Punkin?

Yes, sure—

Then don't worry about anything. I'd never hurt you. Now his other hand was moving up her bare leg, pushing the sundress ahead of it, bunching it in her lap. *I want . . .*

" 'I want to be sweet to you,' " Jessie muttered, shifting a little against the headboard. Her face was sallow and drawn. "That's what he said. Good Christ, he actually *said* that."

"*Everybody knows . . . especially you girls . . . that a love can be sad, well my love is twice as bad . . .*"

I'm not sure I want to, Daddy . . . I'm afraid of burning my eyes.

You have another twenty seconds. At least that. So don't worry. And don't look around.

Then there had been the snap of elastic—not hers but his—as he set the old Adam free.

In defiance of her advancing dehydration, a single tear slipped from Jessie's left eye and rolled slowly down her cheek. "I'm doing it," she said in a hoarse, choked voice. "I'm remembering. I hope you're happy."

Yes, Punkin said, and although Jessie could no longer see it, she could feel that strange, sweet gaze on her. *You've gone too far, though. Back up a little. Just a little.*

An enormous sense of relief washed through Jessie as she realized the thing Punkin wanted her to remember had not happened during or after her father's sexual advances, but *before* them . . . although not long before.

Then why did I have to go through the rest of that awful old stuff?

The answer to that was pretty obvious, she supposed. It didn't matter if you wanted one sardine or twenty, you still had to open the can and look at all of them; you had to smell that horrible fish-oil stink. And besides, a little ancient history wasn't going to kill her. The handcuffs holding her to the bed might, but not these old memories, painful as they might be. It was time to quit bitching and moaning and get down to business. Time to find whatever it was Punkin said she was supposed to find.

Go back to just before he started to touch you that other way—the wrong way. Go back to the reason why the two of you were out there in the first place. Go back to the eclipse.

Jessie closed her eyes tighter and went back.

28

Punkin? All right?

Yes, but . . . it's a little scary, isn't it?

Now she doesn't have to look into the reflector-box to know something's happening; the day is beginning to darken the way it does when a cloud passes over the sun. But this is no cloud; the murk has unravelled and what clouds there are lie quite far to the east.

Yes, he says, and when she glances at him, she is enormously relieved to see he means it. *Want to sit on my lap, Jess?*

Can I?

You bet.

So she does, glad of his nearness and warmth and his sweet smell—the smell of Daddy—as the day continues to darken. Glad most of all because it *is* a little scary, scarier than she imagined it would be. What scares her the most is the way their shadows on the deck are fading. She has never seen shadows fade quite like this before, and is almost positive she never will again. That's perfectly okay with me, she thinks, and snuggles closer, glad to be (at least for the duration of this slightly spooky interlude) her father's Punkin again instead of plain old Jessie—too tall, too gawky . . . too squeaky.

Can I look through the smoked glass yet, Dad?

Not yet. His hand, heavy and warm on her leg. She puts her own hand over it, then turns to him and grins.

It's exciting, isn't it?

Yes. Yes it is, Punkin. Quite a bit more than I thought it would be, actually.

She wriggles again, wanting to find a way to coexist with the hard part of him against which her bottom is now resting. He draws in a quick hissing mouthful of air over his bottom lip.

Daddy? Am I too heavy? Did I hurt you?

No. You're fine.

Can I look at it through the glass yet?

Not yet, Punkin. But very soon.

The world no longer has the look it gets when the sun dives into a cloud; now it seems as if twilight has come in the middle of the afternoon. She hears the old hooty-owl in the woods, and the sound makes her shiver. On WNCH Debbie Reynolds is fading out, and the deejay who comes in on top of them will soon be replaced by Marvin Gaye.

Look out on the lake! Daddy tells her, and when she does, she sees a weird twilight creeping over a lackluster world from which every strong color has been subtracted, leaving nothing but subdued pastels. She shivers and tells him it's creepy; he tells her to try not to be too scared to enjoy it, a statement she will examine carefully— too carefully, perhaps—for double meanings years later. And now . . .

Dad? Daddy? It's gone. Can I—

Yes. Now it's okay. But when I say you have to stop, you have to stop. No arguments, understand?

He gives her three panes of smoked glass in a stack, but first he gives her a potholder. He gives it to her because he made the viewers from panes of glass cut from an old shed window, and he is less than confident of his abilities with the glass-cutter. And as she looks down at the potholder in this experience which is both dream and memory, her mind suddenly leaps even further back, as nimbly as an acrobat turning a flip, and she hears him say *The last thing I need . . .*

29

"... is for your mother to come home and find a note saying ..."

Jessie's eyes flashed open as she spoke these words to the empty room, and the first thing they saw was the empty glass: Gerald's water-glass, still standing on the shelf. Standing there near the cuff binding her wrist to the bedpost. Not the left wrist but the right.

... a note saying I've taken you to the Emergency Room so they can try to sew a couple of your fingers back on.

Now Jessie understood the purpose of that old, hurtful memory; understood what Punkin had been trying to tell her all along. The answer had nothing to do with the old Adam, or with the faint mineral smell of the wet spot on her old cotton underpants. It had everything to do with half a dozen panes of glass carefully cut from the crumbling putty of an old shed window. She had lost the jar of Nivea cream, but there was still at least one other source of lubrication left to her, wasn't there? One other way to ooze on over to the Promised Land. There was blood. Until it clotted, blood was almost as slippery as oil.

It's going to hurt like hell, Jessie.

Yes, of course it would hurt like hell. But she thought she had heard or read somewhere that there were fewer nerves in the wrists than at many of the body's vital checkpoints; that was why slitting one's wrists, especially in a tubful of hot water, had been a preferred method of suicide ever since the original toga-parties in Imperial Rome. Besides, she was half-numb already.

"I was half-numb to let him lock me up in these things in the first place," she croaked.

If you cut too deep, you'll bleed to death just like those old Romans.

Yes, of course she would. But if she didn't cut at all, she'd lie here until she died of seizures or dehydration . . . or until her friend with the bag of bones showed up tonight.

"Okay," she said. Her heart was pumping very hard, and she was fully awake for the first time in hours. Time restarted with a ram and a jerk, like a freight-train pulling out of a siding and back onto the main line. "Okay, that's the convincer."

Listen, a voice said urgently, and Jessie realized with amazement that it was the voice of Ruth *and* the Goodwife. They had merged, at least for the time being. *Listen carefully, Jess.*

"I'm listening," she told the empty room. She was also looking. It was the glass she was looking at. One of a set of twelve she'd gotten on sale at Sears three or four years ago. Six or eight of them broken by now. Soon there would be another. She swallowed and grimaced. It was like trying to swallow around a flannel-covered stone lodged in her throat. "I'm listening very carefully, believe me."

Good. Because once you start this, you won't be able to stop again. Everything's got to happen fast, because your system is already dehydrated. But remember this: even if things go all wrong—

"—they'll work out just fine," she finished. And it was true, wasn't it? The situation had taken on a simplicity that was, in its own ghastly way, sort of elegant. She didn't *want* to bleed to death, of course—who would?—but it would be better than the intensifying cramps and the thirst. Better than him. *It.* The hallucination. Whatever it was.

She licked her dry lips with her dry tongue and caught at her flying, confused thoughts. Tried to put them in order as she had done before going after the sample jar of face cream which was now lying uselessly on the floor beside the bed. It was getting harder to think, she discovered. She kept hearing snatches of

(*go greasy*)

that talking blues, kept smelling her father's cologne, kept feeling that hard thing against her bottom. And then there was Gerald.

Gerald seemed to be talking to her from his place on the floor. *It's going to be back, Jessie. Nothing you can do will stop it. It will teach you a lesson, me proud beauty.*

She flicked her eyes toward him, then looked hastily back at the water-glass. Gerald appeared to be grinning ferociously at her with the part of his face which the dog had left intact. She made another effort to set her wits to work, and after some effort, the thoughts began to roll.

She took ten minutes, going over the steps again and again. There wasn't much, in truth, to go over—her agenda was suicidally risky but not complicated. She mentally rehearsed each move several times just the same, looking for the minor mistake which might cost her her last chance at life. She couldn't find it. In the end there was only one major drawback—it would have to be done very fast, before the blood could start to coagulate—and there were only two possible outcomes: a quick escape, or unconsciousness and death.

She reviewed the whole thing one more time—not putting off the necessary nasty business but examining it the way she would have examined a scarf she had knitted for runs and dropped stitches—while the sun continued its steady westward run. On the back stoop the dog got up, leaving the glistening knot of gristle upon which it had been gnawing. It ambled toward the woods. It had caught a whiff of that black scent again, and with its belly full, even a whiff was too much.

30

*T*welve-twelve-twelve, the clock flashed, and whatever time it really was, it was time.

One more thing before you start. You've got yourself nerved up to the sticking point, and that's good, but keep your focus. If you start off by dropping the damn glass on the floor, you really will be fucked.

"Stay out, dog!" she called shrilly, with no idea that the dog had retreated to the stand of woods beyond the head of the driveway some minutes before. She hesitated a moment longer, considering another prayer, and then decided she had done all the praying she intended to do. Now she would depend on her voices . . . and on herself.

She reached for the glass with her right hand, moving without her former tentative care. Part of her—probably the part which had so liked and admired Ruth Neary—understood that this final job was not about care and caution but about bringing down the hammer and bringing it down hard.

Now I must be Samurai Lady, she thought, and smiled.

She closed her fingers upon the glass she had worked so hard to get in the first place, looked at it curiously for a moment—looked at it as a gardener might look at some unexpected specimen she has found growing in among her beans or peas—then gripped it. She slitted her eyes almost completely shut to protect them from flying splinters, then brought the glass down hard on the shelf, in the manner of one who cracks the shell of a hardboiled egg. The sound the glass made was absurdly familiar, absurdly *normal,* a sound no different from that made by the hundreds of glasses which had either slipped through her fingers during the washing-up or been knocked onto the floor by her elbow or straying hand in all the years since she had graduated from her plastic Dandy Duck cup at the age of five. Same old *ker-smash*; there was no special resonance to indicate the fact that she had just begun the unique job of risking her life in order to save it.

She did feel a single random chunk of glass strike low on her forehead, just above the eyebrow, but that was the only one to hit her face. Another piece—a big one, by the sound—spun off the shelf and shattered on the floor. Jessie's lips were pressed together in a tight white line, anticipating what would surely be the major source of pain, at least to begin with: her fingers. They had been gripping the glass tightly when it shattered. But there was no pain, only a sense of faint pressure and even fainter heat. Compared with the cramps which had been ripping at her for the last couple of hours, it was nothing.

The glass must have broken lucky, and why not? Isn't it time I had a little luck?

Then she raised her hand and saw the glass hadn't broken lucky after all. Dark red blisters of blood were welling up at the tips of her thumb and three of her four fingers; only her pinky had escaped being cut. Shards of glass stuck out of her thumb, second, and third fingers like weird quills. The creeping numbness in her extremities—and perhaps the keen edges on the pieces of glass which had cut her—had kept her from feeling the lacerations much, but they were there. As she watched, fat drops of blood began to patter down on the pink quilted surface of the mattress, staining it a far darker color.

Those narrow darts of glass, sticking out of her middle two fingers like pins from a pincushion, made her feel like throwing up even though there was nothing at all in her stomach.

Some Samurai Lady you turned out to be, one of the UFO voices sneered.

But they're my fingers! she cried at it. *Don't you see? They're my fingers!*

She felt panic flutter, forced it back, and returned her attention to the chunk of water-glass she was still holding. It was a curved upper section, probably a quarter of the whole, and on one side it had broken in two smooth arcs. They came to an almost perfect point which glittered cruelly in the afternoon sun. A lucky break, that . . . maybe. If she could keep her courage up. To her this curving prong of glass looked like a fantastic fairy-tale weapon—a tiny scimitar, something to be carried by a warlike pixie on its way to do battle beneath a toadstool.

Your mind is wandering, dear, Punkin said. *Can you afford that?*

The answer, of course, was no.

Jessie laid the quarter-section of drinking glass back down on the shelf, placing it carefully so she would be able to reach it without serious contortions. It lay on its smooth curved belly, the scimitar-shaped prong jutting out. A tiny spark of reflected sun glittered hotly at the tip. She thought it might do very well for the next job, if she was careful not to bear down too hard. If she did that, she would probably push the glass off the shelf or snap off the accidental blade-shape.

"Just be careful," she said. "You won't need to bear down if you're careful, Jessie. Just pretend—"

But the rest of that thought

(*you're carving roast beef*)

didn't seem very productive, so she blocked it before more than its leading edge could get through. She lifted her right arm, extending it until the handcuff chain was almost taut and her wrist hovered above the gleaming hook of glass. She wanted very much to sweep away the rest of the glass littering the shelf—she sensed it waiting for her up there like a minefield—but she didn't dare. Not after her experience with the jar of Nivea cream. If she accidentally knocked the blade-shaped piece of glass off the shelf, or broke it, she would need to sift through the leftovers for an acceptable substitute. Such precautions seemed almost surreal to her, but she did not for a single moment try to tell herself they were unnecessary. If she was going to get out of this, she was going to have to bleed a lot more than she was bleeding now.

Do it just the way you saw it, Jessie, that's all . . . and don't chicken out.

"No chickening out," Jessie agreed in her harsh dust-in-the-cracks voice. She spread her hand and then shook her wrist, hoping to get rid of the glass poking out of her fingers. She mostly succeeded; only the sliver in her thumb, buried deeply in the tender flesh beneath the nail, refused to go. She decided to leave it and get on with the rest of her business.

What you're planning to do is absolutely crazy, a nervous voice told her. No UFO here; this was a voice Jessie knew well. It was the voice of her mother. *Not that I'm surprised, you understand; it's a typical Jessie Mahout overreaction, and if I've seen it once, I've seen it a thousand times. Think about it, Jessie—why cut yourself up and maybe bleed to death? Someone will come and rescue you; anything else is simply unthinkable. Dying in one's summer house? Dying in* handcuffs? *Utterly ridiculous, take my word for it. So rise above your usual whiny nature, Jessie—just this one time. Don't cut yourself on that glass. Don't you do it!*

That was her mother, all right; the mimicry was so good it was eerie. She wanted you to believe you were hearing love and common sense masquerading as anger, and while the woman had not been entirely incapable of love, Jessie thought the real Sally Mahout was the woman who had one day marched into Jessie's room and thrown a pair of high heels at her without a single word of explanation, either then or later.

Besides, everything that voice had said was a lie. A *scared* lie.

"No," she said, "I *won't* take your word for it. No one's coming . . . except maybe the guy from last night. No chickening out."

With that, Jessie lowered her right wrist toward the gleaming blade of glass.

31

It was important that she see what she was doing, because she felt almost nothing at first; she could have cut her wrist to bleeding ribbons and felt little save those distant sensations of pressure and warmth. She was greatly relieved to find that seeing wasn't going to be a problem; she had smashed the glass at a good place on the shelf (*A break at last!* part of her mind rejoiced sarcastically), and her view was almost completely unobstructed.

Hand tilted back, Jessie sank her inner wrist—that part which bears the lines palm-readers call the Bracelets of Fortune—onto the broken curve of glass. She watched, fascinated, as the jutting point first dimpled her skin, then popped it. She kept pressing and her wrist kept eating the glass. The dimple filled up with blood and disappeared.

Jessie's first reaction was disappointment. The glass hook hadn't created the gusher she had hoped for (and half feared). Then the sharp edge severed the blue bundles of vein lying closest to the surface of her skin, and the blood began flowing out faster. It did not come in the pulsing jets she had expected but in a fast, steady flow, like water from a tap which has been spun almost all the way open. Then something bigger parted and the stream became a freshet. It coursed across the shelf and spilled down her forearm. Too late to back out now; she was for it. One way or the other, she was for it.

Pull back, at least! the mother-voice screamed. *Don't make it any worse—you've done enough! Try it now!*

A tempting idea, but Jessie thought that what she had done so far was a long way from being enough. She didn't know the word "degloving," a technical term used most commonly by doctors in connection with burn-victims, but now that she had begun this grisly operation, she understood she could not depend on blood alone to slide her free. Blood might not be enough.

She slowly and carefully twisted her wrist, splitting the tight skin of her lower hand. Now she felt a weird tingling across her palm, as if she had cut into some small but vital sheath of nerves which had been half-dead to begin with. The third and fourth fingers of her right hand swooned forward as if they had been killed. The first two, along with the thumb, began to jitter wildly back and forth. As mercifully numb as her flesh was, Jessie still found something inexpressibly horrible in these signs of the damage she was doing herself. Those two crumpled fingers, so like little corpses, were somehow worse than all the blood she had spilled thus far.

Then both this horror and the growing feeling of heat and pressure in her wounded hand were overwhelmed as a fresh cramp moved into her side like a storm-front. It dug at her mercilessly, trying to tear her out of her twisted position, and Jessie fought back with terrified fury. She *couldn't* move now. She would almost certainly knock her improvised cutting tool to the floor if she did.

"No you don't," she muttered through her clenched teeth. "No, you bastard—get out of Dodge."

She held herself rigidly in position, trying to keep from bearing down on the fragile glass blade any harder than she already was, not wanting to snap it off and have to try finishing with some less apt tool. But if the cramp spread from her side to her right arm, as it was apparently trying to—

"No," she moaned. "Go away, do you hear? Just go the fuck *away!*"

She waited, knowing she could not afford to wait, also knowing she could do nothing else; she waited and listened to the sound of her life's blood pattering to the floor from the bottom of the headboard. She watched more blood run off the shelf in little streamlets.

239

Tiny sparkles of glass gleamed in some of these. She had begun to feel like a victim in a slasher movie.

You can't wait any longer, Jessie! Ruth rapped at her. *You're all out of time!*

What I'm really out of is luck, and I never had that goddam much to start with, she told Ruth.

At that moment she either felt the cramp loosen a little or was able to kid herself that she did. Jessie revolved her hand inside the cuff, screaming with pain as the cramp pounced once more, sinking its hot claws into her midsection, trying to set it on fire again. She kept moving just the same, however, and now it was the back of her wrist that she impaled. The soft inner part was turned up and Jessie watched, fascinated, as the deep gash across her Bracelets of Fortune opened its black-red mouth wide and appeared to laugh at her. She drove the glass as deeply into the back of her hand as she dared, still fighting the cramp in her midriff and lower chest, then yanked her hand back toward her, spraying a fine mist of backspatter across her forehead, her cheeks, and the bridge of her nose. The broken chunk of glass with which she had performed this rudimentary surgery went spinning to the floor, and there the pixie-blade shattered. Jessie spared it not a single thought; its job was done. Meantime, there was one more step to be taken, one more thing to see: whether the cuff would maintain its jealous hold on her, or if flesh and blood might not at last conspire to make it let go.

The cramp in her side gave a final deep pinch and then began to loosen. Jessie noted its departure no more than she had noted the loss of her primitive glass scalpel. She could feel the force of her concentration—her mind seemed to burn with it, like a torch coated with pine resin—and all of it was fixed on her right hand. She held it up, examining it, in the golden sunlight of late afternoon. The fingers were thickly streaked with gore. Her forearm appeared to have been daubed with slobbers of bright red latex paint. The handcuff was little more than a curved shape rising out of the general flood, and Jessie knew it was as good as it was going to be. She cocked her arm and then pulled downward, as she had twice before. The handcuff slid . . . slid some more . . . and then bound up again. It had been stopped once more by the obdurate outcrop of bone below the thumb.

"*No!*" she shrieked, and yanked harder. "*I refuse to die this way! Do you hear me? I REFUSE TO DIE THIS WAY!*"

The handcuff bit in deep, and for a moment Jessie was sickeningly sure that it would not move so much as another millimeter, that the next time it moved would be when some cigar-chomping cop unlocked it and took it off her dead body. She could not move it, no power on earth could move it, and neither the princes of heaven nor the potentates of hell *would* move it.

Then there was a sensation in the back of her wrist that felt like heat-lightning, and the handcuff jerked upward a little. It stopped, then began to move again. That hot, electrical tingle began to spread as it did, quickly becoming a dark burning which first spread all the way around her hand like a bracelet and then bit in like a battalion of hungry red ants.

The cuff was moving because the skin it rested on was moving, sliding the way a heavy object on a rug will slide if someone pulls the rug. The ragged, circular cut she had inscribed about her wrist widened, pulling wet strands of tendon across the gap and creating a red bracelet. The skin on the back of her hand began to wrinkle and bunch ahead of the cuff, and now what she thought of was how the coverlet had looked when she had pushed it down to the bottom of the bed with her pedaling feet.

I'm peeling my hand, she thought. *Oh dear Jesus, I'm peeling it like an orange.*

"Let go!" she screamed at the handcuff, suddenly infuriated beyond all reason. In that moment it became a live thing to her, some hateful clinging creature with many teeth, like a lamprey eel or a rabid weasel. "*Oh, won't you ever let me go?*"

The cuff had slid much further than it had on her previous attempts to slip out of it, but still it clung, stubbornly refusing to give her that last quarter (or perhaps it was now only an eighth) of an inch. The bleary, blood-greased circle of steel now lay across a hand partially stripped of skin, baring a shiny meshwork of tendons the color of fresh plums. The back of her hand looked like a turkey drumstick from which the crispy outer skin has been removed. The steady downward pressure she was exerting had yanked the wound across her inner wrist even wider, creating a blood-caked chasm. Jessie wondered if she might not yank her hand right off in this final effort to free herself. And now the handcuff, which had still been moving a little—at least she thought it had been—stopped again. And this time it stopped cold.

Of course it has, Jessie! Punkin screamed. *Look at it! It's all crooked! If you could straighten it out again—*

Jessie pistoned her arm forward, snapping the handcuff chain back onto her wrist. Then, before her arm could even think of cramping, she pulled downward again, using every bit of strength she had left. A red mist of pain engulfed her hand as the cuff tore across the raw meat between her wrist and the middle of her hand. All the skin which had been pulled away was puddled loosely here, on a diagonal running from the base of her pinky to the base of her thumb. For a moment this loose mass of skin held the cuff back, and then it rolled under the steel with a tiny squelch. That left only that last outcrop of bone, but that was enough to stop her progress. Jessie pulled harder. Nothing happened.

That's it, she thought. *Everybody out of the pool.*

Then, just as she was about to relax her aching arm, the cuff slid over the small protrusion which had held it for so long, flew off the ends of her fingers, and clacked against the bedpost. It all happened so fast that Jessie was at first unable to grasp that it *had* happened. Her hand no longer looked like the sort of equipment normally issued to human beings, but it *was* her hand, and it was free.

Free.

Jessie looked from the empty blood-smeared cuff to her mangled hand, her face slowly filling with comprehension. *Looks like a bird that flew into a factory machine and then got spit out the other end,* she thought, *but that cuff's not on it anymore. It's really not.*

"Can't believe it," she croaked. "Can't. Fucking. Believe it."

Never mind, Jessie. You have to hurry.

She started like someone being shaken awake from a doze. Hurry? Yes indeed. She didn't know how much blood she had lost—a pint seemed a reasonable enough guess, judging from the sodden mattress and the streamlets running and dripping down the crossboards—but she knew that if she lost much more she was going to pass out, and the trip from unconsciousness to death would be a short one—just a quick ferry-ride across a narrow river.

Not going to happen, she thought. It was the tough-as-nails voice again, but this time it belonged to no one but her, and that made Jessie happy. *I didn't go through all this nasty shit just to die passed out on the floor. I haven't seen the paperwork, but I'm pretty sure that isn't in my contract.*

All right, but your legs—

It was a reminder she didn't really need. She hadn't been on her pins in over twenty-four hours, and despite her efforts to keep them waked up, it could be a bad mistake to depend on them too much, at least to begin with. They might cramp up; they might try to buckle under her; they might do both. But forewarned was forearmed . . . or so they said. Of course she had gotten a lot of advice like that in the course of her lifetime (advice most often ascribed to that mysterious, ubiquitous group known as "they"), and nothing she had ever seen on *Firing Line* or read in the *Reader's Digest* had prepared her for what she had just done. Still, she would be as careful as she could. Jessie had an idea she might not have a lot of leeway in that regard, however.

She rolled left, her right arm trailing after her like the tail of a kite or the rusty exhaust-pipe of an old car. The only part of it that felt completely alive was the back of her hand, where the exposed packets of tendon burned and raved. The pain was bad, and that sense that her right arm wanted a divorce from the rest of her body was worse, but these things were all but lost in an uprush of mingled hope and triumph. She felt an almost divine joy in her ability to roll across the bed without being stopped by the cuff around her wrist. Another cramp struck her, slamming into her lower belly like the business end of a Louisville Slugger, but she ignored it. Had she called that feeling joy? Oh, that was much too mild a word. It was ecstasy. Full, flat-out ecsta—

Jessie! The edge of the bed! Jesus, stop!

It didn't look like the edge of the bed; it looked like the edge of the world on one of those old-fashioned maps from before the time of Columbus. *Beyond here there be monsters and sarpents,* she thought. *Not to mention a fractured left wrist. Stop, Jess!*

But her body ignored the command; it kept on rolling, cramps and all, and Jessie had just enough time to rotate her left hand inside the left cuff before she thumped onto her belly at the edge of the bed, then went off it entirely. Her toes hit the floor with a jarring smash, but her scream was not entirely one of pain. Her feet were, after all, on the floor again. *They were actually on the floor.*

She finished her clumsy escape from the bed with her left arm stuck stiffly off in the direction of the post to which it was still tethered and her right arm temporarily trapped between her chest and the side of the bed. She could feel warm blood pumping onto her skin and running down her breasts.

Jessie got her face over to one side, then had to wait in this new, agonizing position as a cramp of paralyzing, glassy intensity gripped her back from the nape of her neck to the cleft of her buttocks. The sheet against which her breasts and lacerated hand were pressed was growing soggy with blood.

I have to get up, she thought. *I have to get up right away, or I'll bleed to death right here.*

The cramp in her back passed and at last she found herself able to plant her feet solidly beneath her. Her legs felt nowhere near as weak and swoony as she had been afraid they might be; in fact, they felt absolutely eager to be about their appointed business. Jessie pushed upward. The shackle clipped around the left-hand bedpost slid up as far as it could before encountering the next-highest crossboard, and Jessie suddenly found herself in a position she had strongly come to suspect she would never attain again: standing on her own two feet, beside the bed which had been her prison . . . almost her coffin.

A feeling of enormous gratitude tried to wash over her, and she pushed against it as firmly as she had pushed against the panic. There might be time for gratitude later, but the things to remember right now were that she still wasn't free of the goddamned bed, and her time to *get* free was severely limited. It was true that she hadn't felt the slightest sensation of faintness or lightheadedness yet, but she had an idea that meant nothing. When the collapse came, it would probably come all at once; shoot out the lights.

Still, had standing up—only that, and nothing more—ever been so great? So inexpressibly wonderful?

"Nope," Jessie croaked. "Don't think so."

Holding her right arm across her chest and keeping the wound in her inner wrist pressed tightly against the upper slope of her left breast, Jessie made a half-turn, placing her bottom against the wall. She was now standing next to the left side of the bed, in a position that looked almost like a soldier's parade rest. She took a long, deep breath, then asked her right arm and poor stripped right hand to go back to work.

The arm rose creakily, like the arm of an old and badly cared-for mechanical toy, and her hand settled on the bed-shelf. Her third and fourth fingers still refused to move at her command, but she was able to grip the shelf between her thumb and first two fingers well enough to tip it off its brackets. It landed on the mattress where she had lain for so many hours, the mattress where her outline still lay, a sunken, sweaty shape pressed into the pink quilting, its upper half partially traced in blood. Looking at that shape made Jessie feel sick and angry and afraid. Looking at it made her feel crazy.

She shifted her eyes from the mattress with the shelf now lying on it to her trembling right hand. She raised it to her mouth and used her teeth to grip the sliver of glass poking out from beneath the thumbnail. The glass slipped, then slid between an upper canine and incisor, slicing deeply into the tender pink meat of her gum. There was a quick, penetrating sting and Jessie felt blood spew into her mouth, its taste sweet-salty, its texture as thick as the cherry cough-syrup she'd had to swallow when she had the flu as a child. She paid no attention to this new cut—she'd made her peace with much worse in the last few minutes—but only reset her grip and drew the sliver smoothly free of her thumb. When it was out, she spat it onto the bed along with a mouthful of warm blood.

"Okay," she murmured, and began to wriggle her body in between the wall and the headboard, panting harshly as she did so.

The bed moved out from the wall more easily than she could have hoped for, but one thing she'd never questioned was that it *would* move, if she ever managed to get sufficient leverage. Now she had it, and began to herd the hateful bed across the waxed floor. Its foot slid off to the right as she went because she was only able to push on the left side, but Jessie had taken this into account and was comfortable with it. Had, in fact, made it a part of her rudimentary plan. *When your luck changes,* she thought, *it changes all the way. You may have cut your upper gum all to shit, Jess, but you haven't stepped on a single piece of broken glass. So just keep moving this bed, sweetheart, and keep counting your bl—*

Her foot thumped against something. She looked down and saw she had kicked Gerald's plump right shoulder. Blood pattered down on his chest and face. A drop fell in one staring blue eye. She felt no pity for him; she felt no hate for him; she felt no love for him. She felt a kind of horror and disgust for herself, that all the feelings with which she had occupied herself over the years—those so-called civilized feelings that were the meat of every soap-opera, talk-show, and radio phone-in program—should prove so shallow compared with the survival instinct, which had turned out (in her case, at least), to be as overbearing and brutally insistent as a bulldozer blade. But that was the case, and she had an idea that if Arsenio or Oprah ever found themselves in this situation, they would do most of the things she had done.

"Out of my way, Gerald," she said, and kicked him (denying the enormous satisfaction it gave her even as it welled up inside). Gerald refused to move. It was as if the chemical changes which were part of his decay had bonded him to the floor. The flies rose in a buzzing, disturbed cloud just above his distended midsection. That was all.

"Fuck it, then," Jessie said. She began to push the bed again. She managed to step over Gerald with her right foot, but her left came down squarely on his belly. The pressure created a ghastly buzzing sound in his throat and forced a brief but filthy breath of gas from his gaping mouth. "Excuse yourself, Gerald," she muttered, and then left him behind without another look. It was the bureau she was looking at now, the bureau with the keys resting on top of it.

As soon as she had left Gerald behind, the blanket of disturbed flies resettled and resumed their day's work. There was, after all, so much to do and so little time in which to do it.

32

Her biggest fear had been that the foot of the bed would try to hang up either in the bathroom door or the far corner of the room, making it necessary for her to back and fill like a woman trying to shoehorn a big car into a small parking space. As it turned out, the rightward-tending arc the bed described as she moved it slowly across the room was almost perfect. She only had to make a single mid-course correction, pulling her end of the bed a little farther to the left so she could be sure the other end would clear the bureau. It was while she was doing this—pulling with her head down and her butt out and both arms wrapped tightly around the bedpost— that she suffered her first bout of lightheadedness . . . only as she lay with her weight against the post, looking like a woman who is so drunk and tired that she can only stand up by pretending to dance cheek-to-cheek with her boyfriend, she thought that *dark-headedness* would probably be a better way to describe it. The dominant feeling was one of loss—not just of thought and will but of sensory input as well. For one confused moment she was convinced that time had whiplashed, flinging her to a place that was neither Dark Score nor Kashwakamak but some other place entirely, a place that was on the ocean rather than any inland lake. The smell was no longer oysters and pennies but sea-salt. It was the day of the eclipse again, that was the only thing that was the same. She had run into the blackberry tangles to get away from some other man, some other Daddy who wanted to do a lot more than shoot his squirt on the back of her panties. And now he was at the bottom of the well.

Déjà vu poured over her like strange water.

Oh Jesus, what is *this?* she thought, but there was no answer, only that puzzling image again, one she hadn't thought of since she had returned to the sheet-divided bedroom to change her clothes on the day of the eclipse: a skinny woman in a housedress, her dark hair put up in a bun, a puddle of white fabric beside her.

Whoa, Jessie thought, clutching at the bedpost with her tattered right hand and trying desperately to keep her knees from buckling. *Hold on, Jessie—just hold on. Never mind the woman, never mind the smells, never mind the darkness. Hold on and the darkness will pass.*

She did, and it did. The image of the skinny woman kneeling beside her slip and looking at the splintered hole in the old boards went first, and then the darkness began to fade. The bedroom brightened again, gradually taking on its former five o'clock autumn hue. She saw motes of dust dancing in the light slanting in through the lakeside windows, saw her own shadow-legs stretching across the floor. They broke at the knees so that the rest of her shadow could climb the wall. The darkness pulled back, but it left a high sweet buzzing in her ears. When she looked down at her feet she saw they too were coated with blood. She was walking in it, leaving tracks in it.

You're running out of time, Jessie.

She knew.

Jessie lowered her chest to the headboard again. Getting the bed started was harder this time, but she finally managed it. Two minutes later she was standing next to the bureau she had stared at so long and hopelessly from the other side of the room. A tiny dry smile quivered the corners of her lips. *I'm like a woman who's spent her whole life dreaming of the black sands of Kona and can't believe it when she's finally standing on them,* she thought. *It seems like just another dream, only maybe a little more real than most, because in this one your nose itches.*

Her nose didn't itch, but she was looking down at the crumpled snake of Gerald's tie and the knot was still in it. That last was the sort of detail even the most realistic dreams rarely supplied. Beside the red tie were two small, round-barrelled keys, clearly identical. The handcuff keys.

Jessie raised her right hand and looked at it critically. The third and fourth fingers still hung limply. She wondered briefly just how much nerve-damage she had done to her hand, then dismissed the thought. It might matter later on—as some of the other things she had dismissed for the duration of this gruelling fourth-quarter drive downfield might matter later on—but for the time being, nerve-damage to her right hand was no more important to her than the price of hogbelly futures in Omaha. The important thing was that the thumb and first two fingers on that hand were still taking messages. They shook a little, as if expressing shock at the sudden loss of their lifelong neighbors, but they still responded.

Jessie bent her head and spoke to them.

"You have to stop doing that. Later on you can shake like mad, if you want, but right now you have to help me. You *have* to." Yes. Because the thought of dropping the keys or knocking them off the bureau after getting this far . . . that was unthinkable. She stared sternly at her fingers. They didn't stop trembling, not entirely, but as she watched, their jitters quieted to a barely visible thrumming.

"Okay," she said softly. "I don't know if that's good enough or not, but we're going to find out."

At least the keys were the same, which gave her two chances. She found nothing at all strange in the fact that Gerald had brought them both; he was nothing if not methodical. Planning for contingencies, he often said, was the difference between being good and being great. The only contingencies he hadn't planned on this time were the heart attack and the kick which had provoked it. The result, of course, was that he was neither good nor great, only dead.

"The doggy's dinner," Jessie muttered, once again having no idea at all she was speaking aloud. "Gerald used to be a winner, but now he's just the doggy's dinner. Right, Ruth? Right, Punkin?"

She tweezed one of the small steel keys between the thumb and forefinger of her sizzling right hand (as she touched the metal, that pervasive feeling that all this was a dream recurred), picked it up, looked at it, then looked at the cuff which enclosed her left wrist. The lock was a small circle pressed into its side; to Jessie it looked like the sort of doorbell a rich person might have at the tradesman's entrance of the manor house. To open the lock, you simply stuck the hollow barrel of the key into the circle until you heard it click into place, then turned it.

She lowered the key toward the lock, but before she could slip the barrel in, another wave of that peculiar darkheadedness rolled through her mind. She swayed on her feet and found herself once again thinking of Karl Wallenda. Her hand began to shake again.

"Stop that!" she cried fiercely, and jammed the key desperately at the lock. "Stop th—"

The key missed the circle, struck the hard steel beside it instead, and turned in her blood-slicked fingers. She held onto it a second longer, and then it squirted out of her grasp—went greasy, one might have said—and fell to the floor. Now there was only the one key left, and if she lost that—

You won't, Punkin said. *I swear you won't. Just go for it before you lose your courage.*

She flexed her right arm once, then raised the fingers toward her face. She looked at them closely. The shakes were abating again, not enough to suit her, but she couldn't wait. She was afraid she would black out if she did.

She reached out with her faintly trembling hand, and came very close to pushing the remaining key over the edge of the bureau in her first effort to grip it. It was the numbness—the goddam numbness that simply wouldn't leave her fingers. She took a deep breath, held it, made a fist in spite of the pain and the fresh flow of blood it provoked, then let the air out of her lungs in a long, whistling sigh. She felt a little better. This time she pressed her first finger to the small head of the key and dragged it toward the edge of the bureau instead of trying to pick it up immediately. She didn't stop until it was sticking out over the edge.

If you drop it, Jessie! the Goodwife moaned. *Oh, if you drop this one, too!*

"Shut up, Goody," Jessie said, and pushed her thumb up against the bottom of the key, creating a pincers. Then, trying not to think at all about what was going to happen to her if this went wrong, she lifted the key and brought it to the cuff. There was a bad run of seconds when she was unable to align the shaking barrel of the key with the lock, and a worse one when the lock itself momentarily doubled . . . then quadrupled. Jessie squeezed her eyes shut, took another deep breath, then popped them open. Now she saw only one lock again, and she jabbed the key into it before her eyes could do any more tricks.

"Okay," she breathed. "Let's see."

She applied clockwise pressure. Nothing happened. Panic tried to jump up into her throat, and then she suddenly remembered the rusty old pickup truck Bill Dunn drove on his caretaking rounds, and the joke sticker on the back bumper: LEFTY LOOSEY, RIGHTY TIGHTY, it said. Above the words was a drawing of a large screw.

"Lefty loosey," Jessie muttered, and tried turning the key counter-clockwise. For one moment she did not understand that the cuff had popped open; she thought the loud click she heard was the sound of the key breaking off in the lock, and she shrieked, sending a spray of blood from her cut mouth to the top of the dresser. Some of it spattered Gerald's tie, red on red. Then she saw the notched latch-lock was standing open, and realized she had done it—she had actually done it.

Jessie Burlingame pulled her left hand, a little puffy around the wrist but otherwise unharmed, free of the open cuff, which fell back against the headboard as its mate had done. Then, with an expression of deep, wondering awe, she raised both hands slowly up to her face. She looked from the left to the right and back to the left again. She was unmindful of the fact that the right was covered with blood; it was not blood she was interested in, at least not yet. For the moment she only wanted to make absolutely sure she was really free.

She looked back and forth between her hands for almost thirty seconds, her eyes moving like those of a woman watching a Ping-Pong match. Then she drew in a deep breath, cocked her head back, and uttered another high-pitched, drilling shriek. She felt a fresh wave of darkness, big and smooth and vicious, thunder through her, but she ignored it and went on shrieking. It seemed to her that she had no choice; it was either shriek or die. The brittle broken-glass edge of madness in that shriek was unmistakable, but it was still a scream of utter triumph and victory. Two hundred yards away, in the woods at the head of the driveway, the former Prince lifted its head from its muzzle and looked uneasily toward the house.

She couldn't seem to take her eyes off her hands, couldn't seem to stop shrieking. She had never felt anything remotely like what she was feeling now, and some distant part of her thought: *If sex was even half this good, people would be doing it on every streetcorner— they just wouldn't be able to help themselves.*

Then she ran out of breath and swayed backward. She grabbed for the headboard, but a moment too late—she lost her balance and spilled onto the bedroom floor. As she went down, Jessie realized that part of her had been expecting the handcuff chains to snub her before she fell. Pretty funny, when you thought about it.

She struck the open wound on the inside of her wrist as she landed. Pain lit up her right arm like the lights on a Christmas tree and this time when she screamed it was *all* pain. She bit it off quickly when she felt herself drifting away from consciousness again. She opened her eyes and stared into her husband's torn face. Gerald looked back at her with an expression of endless, glazed surprise

—This wasn't supposed to happen to me, I'm a lawyer with my name on the door. Then the fly which had been washing its front legs on his upper lip disappeared up one of his nostrils and Jessie turned her head so quickly she thumped it on the floorboards and saw stars. When she opened her eyes this time, she was looking up at the headboard, with its gaudy drips and runnels of blood. Had she been standing way up there only a few seconds ago? She was pretty sure she had been, but it was hard to believe—from here, the fucking bed looked approximately as tall as the Chrysler Building.

Get moving, Jess! It was Punkin, once more yelling in that urgent, annoying voice of hers. For someone with such a sweet little face, Punkin could certainly be a bitch when she set her mind to it.

"Not a bitch," she said, letting her eyes slip closed. A small, dreamy smile touched the corners of her mouth. "A squeaky wheel."

Get moving, damn it!

Can't. Need a little rest first.

If you don't get moving right away, you can rest forever! Now shag your fat ass!

That got to her. "Nothing fat about it, Miss Smartmouth," she muttered pettishly, and tried to struggle to her feet. It took only two efforts (the second thwarted by another of those paralyzing cramps across her diaphragm) to convince her that getting up was, at least for the time being, a bad idea. And doing so would actually create more problems than it would solve, because she needed to get into the bathroom, and the foot of the bed now lay across the doorway like a roadblock.

Jessie went under the bed, moving with a gliding, swimming motion that was almost graceful, blowing a few errant dust bunnies out of her way as she went. They drifted off like small gray tumbleweeds. For some reason the dust bunnies made her think of the woman in her vision again—the woman kneeling in the blackberry tangles with her slip in a white pile beside her. She slid into the gloom of the bathroom and a new smell smote her nostrils: the dark, mossy smell of water. Water dripping from the tub faucets;

water dripping from the shower head; water dripping from the washbasin taps. She could even smell the peculiar waiting-to-be-mildew odor of a damp towel in the basket behind the door. Water, water, everywhere, and every drop to drink. Her throat shrank dryly inside her neck, seeming to cry out, and she became aware that she was actually *touching* water—a small puddle from the leaky pipe under the sink, the one the plumber never seemed to get to no matter how many times he was asked. Gasping, Jessie pulled herself over to the puddle, dropped her head, and began to lick the linoleum. The taste of the water was indescribable, the silky feel of it on her lips and tongue beyond all dreams of sweet sensuousness.

The only problem was that there wasn't enough. That enchantingly dank, enchantingly *green* smell was all around her, but the puddle below the sink was gone and her thirst wasn't slaked but only awake. That smell, the smell of shady springs and old hidden wellheads, did what even Punkin's voice hadn't been able to do: it got Jessie on her feet again.

She used the edge of the sink to haul herself up. She caught just a glimpse of an eight-hundred-year-old woman looking out of the mirror at her, and then she twisted the basin tap marked C. Fresh water—all the water in the world—came gushing out. She tried to voice that triumphant shriek again, but this time managed nothing but a harsh susurrant whisper. She bent over the basin, her mouth opening and closing like the mouth of a fish, and lunged into that mossy wellhead perfume. It was also the bland mineral smell which had so haunted her over all the years since her father had molested her during the eclipse, but now it was all right; now it was not the smell of fear and shame but of life. Jessie inhaled it, then coughed it out joyously again as she shoved her open mouth into the water jetting from the tap. She drank until a powerful but painless cramp caused her to heave it all back up again. It came still cool from its short visit in her stomach and sprayed the mirror with pink droplets. Then she gasped in several breaths and tried again.

The second time the water stayed down.

33

The water brought her back wonderfully, and when she at last turned off the tap and looked at herself in the mirror again, she felt like a reasonable facsimile of a human being—weak, hurting, and shaky on her feet . . . but alive and aware, just the same. She thought she would never again experience anything as deeply satisfying as those first few swallows of cold water from the gushing tap, and in all her previous experience, only her first orgasm came close to rivalling that moment. In both cases she had been totally commanded by the cells and tissues of her physical being for a few brief seconds, conscious thought (but not consciousness itself) wiped away, and the result had been ecstasy. *I'll never forget it,* she thought, knowing she had forgotten it already, just as she had forgotten the gorgeous honeyed sting of that first orgasm as soon as the nerves had stopped firing off. It was as if the body disdained memory . . . or refused the responsibility of it.

Never mind all that, Jessie—you have to hurry!

Can't you stop yapping at me? she responded. Her wounded wrist was no longer gushing, but it was still doing a hell of a lot more than trickling, and the bed she saw reflected in the bathroom mirror was a horror—the mattress soaked with blood and the headboard streaked with it. She had read that people could lose a great deal of blood and keep on functioning, but when they started to tip over, everything went at once. And she had to be pushing the envelope.

She opened the medicine cabinet, looked at the box of Band-Aids, and uttered a harsh caw of laughter. Her eye happened on the small box of Always maxi-pads sitting discreetly behind a clutter of perfumes and colognes and aftershaves. She knocked two or three of the bottles over dragging the box out, and the air filled with a gagging combination of scents. She stripped the paper cover from one of the pads, which she then wrapped around her wrist like a fat white bracelet. Poppies began to bloom on it almost at once.

Who would have thought the lawyer's wife had so much blood in her? she mused, and uttered another harsh caw of laughter. There was a tin wheel of Red Cross tape on the top shelf of the medicine cabinet. She took it, using her left hand. Her right now seemed capable of very little except bleeding and howling with pain. Yet she still felt a deep love for it, and why not? When she'd needed it, when there had been absolutely nothing else, it had grasped the remaining key, put it in the lock, and turned it. No, she had nothing at all against Ms. Right.

That was you, Jessie, Punkin said. *I mean . . . we're all you. You do know that, don't you?*

Yes. She knew that perfectly well.

She pushed the cover off the adhesive tape and held the roll clumsily with her right hand while she used her left thumb to lift up the end of the tape. She returned the roll to her left hand, pressed the end of the tape to her makeshift bandage, and revolved the roll around her right wrist several times, binding the already damp sanitary pad as tightly against the slash on the inside of her wrist as she could. She tore the tape off the roll with her teeth, hesitated, and then added a white, overlapping armlet of adhesive tape just below her right elbow. Jessie had no idea how much good such a makeshift tourniquet could do, but she didn't think it could do any harm.

She tore the tape a second time, and as she dropped the much-diminished roll back onto the counter, she saw a green bottle of Excedrin standing on the middle shelf of the medicine cabinet. No childproof cap, either—God be thanked. She took it down with her left hand and used her teeth to pry off the white plastic top.

The smell of the aspirin tablets was acrid, sharp, faintly vinegary.

I don't think that's a good idea at all, Goodwife Burlingame said nervously. *Aspirin thins the blood and slows clotting.*

That was probably true, but the exposed nerves on the back of her right hand were now shrieking like a fire-alarm, and if she didn't do something to damp them down a little, Jessie thought she would soon be rolling around on the floor and baying at the reflections on the ceiling. She shook two Excedrin into her mouth, hesitated, shook in two more. She turned on the tap again, swallowed them, then looked guiltily at the makeshift bandage on her wrist. The red was still sinking through the layers of paper; soon she would be able to take the pad off and wring blood out of it like hot red water. An awful image . . . and once she had it in her head, she could not seem to get rid of it.

If you made that worse— Goody began dolefully.

Oh, give me a break, the Ruth-voice responded. It spoke briskly but not unkindly. *If I die of blood-loss now, am I supposed to blame it on four aspirin after I damned near scalped my right hand in order to get off the bed in the first place? That's surreal!*

Yes indeed. *Everything* seemed surreal now. Except that wasn't exactly the right word. The right word was . . .

"*Hyper*-real," she said in a low, musing voice.

Yes, that was it. Definitely it. Jessie turned around so she was facing out the bathroom door again, then gasped in alarm. The part of her head which monitored equilibrium reported that she was *still* turning. For a moment she imagined dozens of Jessies, an overlapping chain of them, documenting the arc of her turn like frames of movie-film. Her alarm deepened as she observed that the golden bars of light slanting in through the west window had taken on an actual texture—they looked like swatches of bright yellow snake-skin. The dust motes spinning through them had become sprays of diamond grit. She could hear the fast light beat of her heart, could smell the mixed aromas of blood and well-water. It was like sniffing an ancient copper pipe.

I'm getting ready to pass out.

No, Jess, you're not. You can't afford to pass out.

That was probably true, but she was pretty sure it was going to happen, anyway. There was nothing she could do about it.

Yes, there is. And you know what.

She looked down at her skinned hand, then raised it. There would be no need to actually *do* anything except relax the muscles of her right arm. Gravity would take care of the rest. If the pain of her peeled hand striking the edge of the counter weren't enough to drag her out of this terrible bright place she suddenly found herself in, nothing would be. She held the hand beside her blood-smeared left breast for a long moment, trying to nerve herself up enough to do it. Finally she lowered it to her side again. She couldn't— simply could not. It was one thing too much. One *pain* too much.

Then get moving before you pass out.

I can't do that, either, she responded. She felt more than tired; she felt as if she had just smoked a whole bong of absolutely primo Cambodian Red by herself. All she wanted to do was stand here and watch the motes of diamond-dust spin their slow circles in the sunbeams coming in through the west window. And maybe get one more drink of that dark-green, mossy-tasting water.

"Oh Jeez," she said in a faraway, frightened voice. "Jeez, Louise."

You have to get out of the bathroom, Jessie—you have to. Just worry about that, for now. I think you better crawl over the bed this time; I'm not sure you can make it underneath again.

But . . . but there's broken glass on the bed. What if I cut myself?

That brought Ruth Neary out again, and she was raving.

You've already taken most of the skin off your right hand—do you think a few more lacerations are going to make a difference? Jesus Christ, tootsie, what if you die in this bathroom with a cunt-diaper on your wrist and a big stupid grin on your face? How's that for a what-if? Get moving, bitch!

Two careful steps took her back to the bathroom doorway. Jessie only stood there for a moment, swaying and blinking her eyes against the sundazzle like someone who has spent the whole afternoon in a movie-theater. The next step took her to the bed. When her thighs were touching the bloodstained mattress, she carefully put her left knee up, grasped one of the footposts to ensure her balance, and then got onto the bed. She was unprepared for the feelings of fear and loathing which washed over her. She could no more imagine ever sleeping in this bed again than she could imagine sleeping in her own coffin. Just kneeling on it made her feel like screaming.

You don't need to have a deep, meaningful relationship with it, Jessie—just get across the fucking thing.

Somehow she managed to do that, avoiding the shelf and the crumbles and jags of broken water-glass by crossing at the foot of the mattress. Each time her eyes caught sight of the handcuffs dangling from the posts at the head of the bed, one sprung open, the other a closed steel circle covered with blood—*her* blood—a little sound of loathing and distress escaped her. The handcuffs didn't look like inanimate things to her. They looked alive. And still hungry.

She reached the far side of the bed, gripped the footpost with her good left hand, turned herself around on her knees with all the care of a hospital convalescent, then lay on her belly and lowered her feet to the floor. She had a bad moment when she didn't think she had strength enough to stand up again; that she would just lie there until she passed out and slid off the bed. Then she pulled in a deep breath and used her left hand to shove. A moment later she was on her feet. The sway was worse now—she looked like a sailor lurching into the Sunday morning segment of a weekend binge— but she was up, by God. Another wave of darkheadedness sailed across her mind like a pirate galleon with huge black sails. Or an eclipse.

Blind, rocking back and forth on her feet, she thought: *Please, God, don't let me pass out. Please God, okay? Please.*

At last the light began to come back into the day. When Jessie thought things had gotten as bright as they were going to, she slowly crossed the room to the telephone table, holding her left arm a few inches out from her body to maintain her balance. She picked up the receiver, which seemed to weigh as much as a volume of the *Oxford English Dictionary,* and brought it to her ear. There was no sound at all; the line was smooth and dead. Somehow this didn't surprise her, but it raised a question: had Gerald unplugged the phone from the wall, as he sometimes did when they were down here, or had her night-visitor cut the wires outside someplace?

"It wasn't Gerald," she croaked. "I would have seen him."

Then she realized that wasn't necessarily so—she had headed for the bathroom as soon as they were in the house. He could have done it then. She bent down, grasped the flat white ribbon that went from the back of the phone to the connector-box on the baseboard behind the chair, and pulled. She thought she felt a little give at first, and then nothing. Even that initial give might have been just her imagination; she knew perfectly well that her senses were no longer very trustworthy. The jack might just be bound up on the chair, but—

No, Goody said. *It won't come because it's still plugged in—Gerald never disconnected it at all. The reason the phone doesn't work is because that thing that was in here with you last night cut the wire.*

Don't listen to her; underneath that loud voice of hers, she's scared of her own shadow, Ruth said. *The connector-plug's hung up on one of the chair's back legs—I practically guarantee it. Besides, it's easy enough to find out, isn't it?*

Of course it was. All she had to do was pull the chair out and take a look behind it. And if the plug was out, put it back in.

What if you do all that and the phone still *doesn't work?* Goody asked. *Then you'll know something else, won't you?*

Ruth: *Stop dithering—you need help, and you need it fast.*

It was true, but the thought of pulling out the chair filled her with weary gloom. She could probably do it—the chair was big, but it still couldn't weigh a fifth of what the bed had weighed, and she had managed to move *that* all the way across the room— but the *thought* was heavy. And pulling the chair out would only be the beginning. Once it was moved, she would have to get down on her knees . . . crawl into the dim, dusty corner behind it to find the connector-box . . .

Jesus, tootsie! Ruth cried. She sounded alarmed. *You don't have any* choice*! I thought that at long last we all agreed on at least one thing, that you need help, and you need it f—*

Jessie suddenly slammed the door on Ruth's voice, and slammed it hard. Instead of moving the chair, she bent over it, picked up the culotte skirt, and carefully pulled it up her legs. Drops of blood from the soaked bandage on her wrist splattered across the front of it at once, but she hardly saw them. She was busy ignoring the jangle of angry, perplexed voices, and wondering just who had let all these weird people into her head in the first place. It was like waking up one morning and discovering your home had become a boarding hotel overnight. All the voices were expressing horrified disbelief at what she was planning to do, but Jessie suddenly discovered she didn't give much of a shit. This was her life. *Hers.*

She picked up the blouse and slipped her head into it. To her confused, shocked mind, the fact that yesterday had been warm enough for this casual sleeveless top seemed to conclusively prove the existence of God. She didn't think she would have been able to bear sliding her stripped right hand down a long sleeve.

Never mind that, she thought, *this is nuts, and I don't need any make-believe voices to tell me so. I'm thinking about driving out of here —about trying, anyway—when the only thing I have to do is move that chair and plug the phone back in. It must be the blood-loss—it's driven me temporarily insane. This is a nutty idea. Christ, that chair can't weigh fifty pounds . . . I'm almost home and dry!*

Yes, except it wasn't the chair, and it wasn't the idea of the Rescue Services guys finding her in the same room as the naked, chewed corpse of her husband. Jessie had a pretty good idea she would be preparing to leave in the Mercedes even if the phone were in perfect working order and she had already summoned the police, the ambulance, and the Deering High School Marching Band. Because the phone wasn't the important thing—not at all. The important thing was . . . well . . .

The important thing is that I have to get the fuck out of here right away, she thought, and suddenly she shuddered. Her bare arms broke out in gooseflesh. *Because that thing is going to come back.*

Bullseye. The problem wasn't Gerald, or the chair, or what the Rescue Services guys might think when they got down here and saw the situation. It wasn't even the question of the telephone. The problem was the space cowboy; her old friend Dr. Doom. *That* was why she was putting on her clothes and splashing a little more of her blood around instead of making an effort to re-establish communications with the outside world. The stranger was some-place close by; of that she felt certain. It was only waiting for dark, and dark was close now. If she passed out while she was trying to push the chair away from the wall, or while she was crawling gaily around in the dust and the cobwebs behind it, she might still be here, all alone, when the thing with the suitcase of bones arrived. Worse, she might still be alive.

Besides, her visitor *had* cut the line. She had no way of knowing this . . . but her heart knew it just the same. If she went through all the rigamarole of moving the chair and plugging the t-connector back in, the phone would still be dead, just like the one in the kitchen and the one in the front hall.

And what's the big deal, anyway? she told her voices. *I'm planning to drive out to the main road, that's all. Compared to performing im-promptu surgery with a water-glass and pushing a double bed across the room while losing a pint of blood, it'll be a breeze. The Mercedes is a good car, and it's a straight shot up the driveway. I'll putter out to Route 117 at ten miles an hour, and if I feel too weak to drive all the way to Dakin's Store once I make the highway, I'll just pull across the road, put on the four-way flashers, and lay on the horn when I see someone coming. No reason why that shouldn't work, with the road flat and open for a mile and a half in either direction. The big thing about the car is the locks. Once I'm in it, there'll be doors I can lock. It won't be able to get in.*

It, Ruth tried to sneer, but Jessie thought she sounded scared—yes, even her.

That's right, she returned. *You were the one who always used to tell me I ought to put my head on hold more often and follow my heart, weren't you? You bet you were. And do you know what my heart says now, Ruth? It says that the Mercedes is the only chance I have. And if you want to laugh at that, go right ahead . . . but my mind is made up.*

Ruth apparently did not want to laugh. Ruth had fallen silent.

Gerald handed me the car-keys just before he got out of the car, so he could reach into the back seat and get his briefcase. He did do that, didn't he? Please God, let my memory of that be right.

Jessie slipped her hand into the left pocket of her skirt and found only a couple of Kleenex. She reached down with her right hand, pressed it gingerly against the outside of that pocket, and let out a sigh of relief as she felt the familiar bulge of the car-key and the big round joke fob Gerald had given her for her last birthday. The words on the fob read YOU SEXY THING. Jessie decided she had never felt less sexy and more like a thing in her entire life, but that was okay; she could live with it. The key was in her pocket, that was the important thing. The key was her ticket out of this awful place.

Her tennies stood side by side underneath the telephone table, but Jessie decided she was as dressed as she intended to get. She started slowly toward the hall door, moving in tiny little invalid steps. As she went, she reminded herself to try the phone in the hall before going outside—it couldn't hurt.

She had barely rounded the head of the bed when the light began to slink out of the day again. It was as if the fat bright sunbeams slanting through the west window were connected to a dimmer-circuit, and someone was turning down the rheostat. As they dimmed, the diamond-dust revolving within them disappeared.

Oh no, not now, she pleaded. *Please, you've got to be kidding.* But the light continued to fade, and Jessie suddenly realized she was swaying again, her upper body describing ever-widening circles in the air. She groped for the bedpost and instead found herself clutching the bloody handcuff from which she had so recently escaped.

July 20th, 1963, she thought incoherently. *5:42 P.M. Total eclipse. Can I get a witness?*

The mixed smell of sweat, semen, and her father's cologne filled

263

her nose. She wanted to gag on it, but she was suddenly too weak. She managed two more tottery steps, then fell forward onto the bloodstained mattress. Her eyes were open and they blinked occasionally, but otherwise she lay as limp and moveless as a woman who has been cast up, drowned, on some deserted beach.

34

Her first returning thought was that the darkness meant she was dead.

Her second was that if she was dead, her right hand wouldn't feel as if it had first been napalmed and then flayed with razor-blades. Her third was the dismayed realization that if it was dark and her eyes were open—as they seemed to be—then the sun had gone down. That jolted her up from the in-between place where she had been lying, not quite unconscious but deep in a post-shock lassitude, in a hurry. At first she couldn't remember why the idea of sundown should be so frightening, and then

(*space cowboy—monster of love*)

it all came back to her in a rush so strong it was like an electrical shock. The narrow, corpse-white cheeks; the high forehead; the rapt eyes.

The wind had come up strongly once more while she had been lying semi-conscious on the bed, and the back door was banging again. For a moment the door and the wind were the only sounds, and then a long, wavering howl rose in the air. Jessie believed it was the most awful sound she had ever heard; the sound she imagined a victim of premature burial might make after being disinterred and dragged, alive but insane, from her coffin.

The sound faded into the uneasy night (and it *was* night, no doubt about that), but a moment later it came again: an inhuman falsetto, full of idiot terror. It rushed over her like a living thing, making her shudder helplessly on the bed and grope for her ears. She covered them, but could not shut out that terrible cry when it came a third time.

"Oh, don't," she moaned. She had never felt so cold, so cold, so cold. "Oh, don't . . . don't."

The howl funneled away into the gusty night and was not immediately renewed. Jessie had a moment to catch her breath and realize it was only a dog, after all—probably *the* dog, in fact, the one who had turned her husband into its own personal McDonald's Drive-Thru. Then the cry *was* renewed, and it was impossible to believe any creature from the natural world could make such a sound; surely it was a banshee, or a vampire writhing with a stake in its heart. As the howl rose toward its crystalline peak, Jessie suddenly understood why the animal was making that sound.

It had come back, just as she had feared it would. The dog knew it, sensed it, somehow.

She was shivering all over. Her eyes feverishly scanned the corner where she had seen her visitor standing last night—the corner where it had left the pearl earring and the single footprint. It was far too dark to see either of these artifacts (always assuming they were there at all), but for a moment Jessie thought she saw the creature itself, and she felt a scream rise in her throat. She closed her eyes tight, opened them again, and saw nothing but the wind-driven shadows of the trees outside the west window. Farther on in that direction, beyond the writhing shapes of the pines, she could see a fading band of gold on the line of the horizon.

It might be seven o'clock, but if I can still see the last of the sunset, it's probably not even that late. Which means I was only out for an hour, an hour and a half, tops. Maybe it's not too late to get out of here. Maybe—

This time the dog seemed actually to *scream*. The sound made Jessie feel like screaming back. She grasped one of the footposts because she had started to sway on her feet again, and suddenly realized she couldn't remember getting off the bed in the first place. That was how much the dog had freaked her out.

Get control of yourself, girl. Take a deep breath and get control of yourself.

She *did* take a deep breath, and the smell she drew in with the air was one she knew. It was like that flat mineral smell which had haunted her all these years—the smell that meant sex, water, and father to her—but not *exactly* like that. Some other odor or odors seemed mixed into this version of it—old garlic . . . ancient onions . . . dirt . . . unwashed feet, maybe. The smell tumbled Jessie back down a well of years and filled her with the helpless, inarticulate terror children feel when they sense some faceless, nameless creature—some It—waiting patiently beneath the bed for them to stick out a foot . . . or perhaps dangle a hand . . .

The wind gusted. The door banged. And somewhere closer by, a board creaked stealthily the way boards do when someone who is trying to be quiet treads lightly upon them.

It's come back, her mind whispered. It was all the voices now; they had entwined in a braid. *That's what the dog smells, that's what you smell, and Jessie, that's what made the board creak. The thing that was here last night has come back for you.*

"Oh God, please, no," she moaned. "Oh God no. Oh God no. Oh dear God don't let that be true."

She tried to move, but her feet were frozen to the floor and her left hand was nailed to the bedpost. Her fear had immobilized her as surely as oncoming headlights immobilize a deer or rabbit caught in the middle of the road. She would stand here, moaning under her breath and trying to pray, until it came to her, came *for* her— the space cowboy, the reaper of love, just some door-to-door salesman of the dead, his sample case filled with bones and finger-rings instead of Amway or Fuller brushes.

The dog's ululating cry rose in the air, rose in her *head*, until she thought it must surely drive her mad.

I'm dreaming, she thought. *That's why I couldn't remember standing up; dreams are the mind's version of Reader's Digest Condensed Books, and you can never remember unimportant stuff like that when you're having one. I passed out, yes—that really happened, only instead of going down into a coma, I came up into natural sleep. I guess that means the bleeding must have stopped, because I don't think people who are bleeding to death have nightmares when they're going down for the count. I'm sleeping, that's all. Sleeping and having the granddaddy of all bad dreams.*

A fabulously comforting idea, and only one thing wrong with it: it wasn't true. The dancing tree-shadows on the wall by the bureau were real. So was that weird smell drifting through the house. She was awake, and she had to get out of here.

I can't move! she wailed.

Yes you can, Ruth told her grimly. *You didn't get out of those fucking handcuffs just to die of fright, tootsie. Get moving, now—I don't need to tell you how to do it, do I?*

"No," Jessie whispered, and slapped lightly at the bedpost with the back of her right hand. The result was an immediate and enormous blast of pain. The vise of panic which had been holding her shattered like glass, and when the dog voiced another of those freezing howls, Jessie barely heard it—her hand was a lot closer, and it was howling a lot louder.

And you know what to do next, toots—don't you?

Yes—the time had come to make like a hockey player and get the puck out of here, to make like a library and book. The thought of Gerald's rifle surfaced for a second, and then she dismissed it. She didn't have the slightest idea where the gun was, or even if it was here at all.

Jessie walked slowly and carefully across the room on her trembling legs, once again holding out her left hand to steady her balance. The hallway beyond the bedroom door was a carousel of moving shadows with the door to the guest bedroom standing open on the right and the small spare room Gerald used as a study standing open on the left. Farther down on the left was the archway which gave on the kitchen and living room. On the right was the unlatched back door . . . the Mercedes . . . and maybe freedom.

Fifty steps, she thought. *Can't be any more than that, and it's probably less. So get going, okay?*

But at first she just couldn't. Bizarre as it would undoubtedly seem to someone who hadn't been through what she had been through during the last twenty-eight hours or so, the bedroom represented a kind of dour safety to her. The hallway, how-ever . . . anything might be lurking out there. *Anything.* Then something which sounded like a thrown stone thudded against the west side of the house, just outside the window. Jessie uttered her own small howl of terror before realizing it was just the branch of the hoary old blue spruce out there by the deck.

Get hold of yourself, Punkin said sternly. *Get hold of yourself and get out of here.*

She tottered gamely onward, left arm still out, counting steps under her breath as she went. She passed the guest bedroom at twelve. At fifteen she reached Gerald's study, and as she did, she began to hear a low, toneless hissing sound, like steam escaping a very old radiator. At first Jessie did not associate the sound with the study; she thought she was making it herself. Then, as she was raising her right foot to make the sixteenth step, the sound inten-sified. This time it registered more clearly, and Jessie realized she *couldn't* be the one making it, because she was holding her breath.

Slowly, very slowly, she turned her head toward the study, where her husband would never again work on legal briefs while he chain-smoked Marlboros and sang old Beach Boys hits under his breath. The house was groaning around her like an old ship plowing through a moderately heavy sea, creaking in its various joints as the wind shouldered against it with cold air. Now she could hear a clapping shutter as well as the banging door, but these sounds were some-where else, in some other world where wives were not handcuffed and husbands did not refuse to listen and night-creatures did not stalk. She could hear the muscles and tendons in her neck creaking

like old bedsprings as she turned her head. Her eyes throbbed in
their sockets like chunks of hot charcoal.

I don't want to look! her mind screamed. *I don't want to look, I
don't want to see!*

But she was helpless not to look. It was as if strong invisible
hands were turning her head while the wind gusted and the back
door banged and the shutter clapped and the dog once more sent
its desolate, bone-chilling howl spiralling into the black October
sky. Her head turned until she was looking into her dead husband's
study, and yes, sure enough, there it was, a tall figure standing
beside Gerald's Eames chair and in front of the sliding glass door.
Its narrow white face hung in the darkness like a stretched skull.
The dark, squarish shadow of its souvenir case squatted between
its feet.

She drew in breath to scream with, but what came out was a
sound like a teakettle with a broken whistle: "*Huhhhh-
aaahhhhhhh.*"

Only that and nothing more.

Somewhere, in that other world, hot urine was running down
her legs; she had wet her pants for a second record-breaking day.
The wind gusted in that other world, making the house shiver on
its bones. The blue spruce knocked its branch against the west wall
again. Gerald's study was a lagoon of dancing shadows, and it was
once more very difficult to tell what she was seeing . . . or if she
was in fact seeing anything at all.

The dog raised its keen, horrified cry again and Jessie thought:
*Oh, you're seeing it, all right. Maybe not as well as the dog out there is
smelling it, but you are seeing it.*

As if to remove any lingering doubts she might have had on this
score, her visitor poked its head forward in a kind of parody of
inquisitiveness, giving Jessie a clear but mercifully brief look at it.
The face was that of an alien being that has tried to mimic human
features without much success. It was too narrow, for one thing—
narrower than any face Jessie had ever seen in her life. The nose
seemed to have no more thickness than a butter-knife. The high

forehead bulged like a grotesque garden bulb. The thing's eyes were simple black circles below the thin upside-down V's of its brows; its pudgy, liver-colored lips seemed to be simultaneously pouting and melting.

No, not melting, she thought with the bright narrow lucidity that sometimes lives, like the glowing filament in a lightbulb, within a sphere of complete terror. *Not melting,* smiling. *It's trying to smile at me.*

Then it bent over to grasp its case, and its narrow, incoherent face was mercifully lost from view again. Jessie staggered back a step, tried to scream again, and could only produce another loose, glassy whisper. The wind moaning around the eaves was louder.

Her visitor straightened up again, holding the case with one hand and unlatching it with the other. Jessie realized two things, not because she wanted to but because her mind's ability to pick and choose what it would sense had been completely demolished. The first had to do with the smell she had noted earlier. It wasn't garlic or onions or sweat or dirt. It was rotting flesh. The second had to do with the creature's arms. Now that she was closer and could see better (she wished it weren't so, but it was), they impressed her more forcibly—freakish, elongated things that seemed to waver in the wind-driven shadows like tentacles. They presented the case to her as if for her approval, and now Jessie saw it was not a travelling salesman's case but a wicker box that looked like an oversized fisherman's creel.

I've seen a box like that before, she thought. *I don't know if it was on some old TV show or in real life, but I have. When I was just a little girl. It came out of a long black car with a door in the back.*

A soft and sinister UFO voice suddenly spoke up inside her. *Once upon a time, Jessie, when President Kennedy was still alive and all little girls were Punkins and the plastic body-bag had yet to be invented— back in the Time of the Eclipse, let us say—boxes like this were common. They came in all sizes, from Men's Extra Large to Six-Month Miscarriage. Your friend keeps his souvenirs in an old-fashioned mortician's body-box, Jessie.*

As she realized this, she realized something else, as well. It was perfectly obvious, once you thought about it. The reason her visitor smelled so bad was because it was dead. The thing in Gerald's study wasn't her father, but it was a walking corpse, just the same.

No . . . no, that can't be—

But it was. She had smelled exactly the same thing on Gerald, not three hours ago. Had smelled it *in* Gerald, simmering in his flesh like some exotic disease which can only be caught by the dead.

Now her visitor was opening the box again and holding it out to her, and once again she saw the golden glitters and diamond flashes amid the heaps of bones. Once again she watched as the narrow dead man's hand reached in and began to stir the contents of the wicker body-box—a box which had perhaps once held the corpses of infants or very small children. Once again she heard the tenebrous click and whisk of bones, a sound like dirt-clogged castanets.

Jessie stared, hypnotized and almost ecstatic with terror. Her sanity was giving way; she could feel it going, almost *hear* it, and there wasn't a thing on God's green earth she could do about it.

Yes there is! You can run! You have to run, and you have to do it now!

It was Punkin, and she was shrieking . . . but she was also a long way off, lost in some deep stone gorge in Jessie's head. There were *lots* of gorges in there, she was discovering, and lots of dark, twisty canyons and caves that had never seen the light of the sun—places where the eclipse never ended, you might say. It was interesting. Interesting to find that a person's mind was really nothing but a graveyard built over a black hollow place with freakish reptiles like this crawling around the bottom. Interesting.

Outside, the dog howled again, and Jessie finally found her voice. She howled with it, a doglike sound from which most of her sanity had been subtracted. She could imagine herself making sounds like that in some madhouse. Making them for the rest of her life. She found she could imagine that very easily.

Jessie, no! Hold on! Hold onto your mind and run! Run away!

Her visitor was grinning at her, its lips wrinkling away from its gums, once again revealing those glimmers of gold at the back of its mouth, glimmers that reminded her of Gerald. Gold teeth. It had gold teeth, and that meant it was—

It means it's real, yes, but we've already established that, haven't we? The only question left is what you're going to do now. Got any ideas, Jessie? If you do, you better trot them out, because time has gotten awfully short.

The apparition stepped forward, still holding its case open, as if it expected her to admire the contents. It was wearing a necklace, she saw—some weird sort of necklace. The thick, unpleasant smell was growing stronger. So was that unmistakable feeling of malevolence. Jessie tried to take a compensatory step back for the one the visitor had taken toward her, and found that she couldn't move her feet. It was as if they had been glued to the floor.

It means to kill you, toots, Ruth said, and Jessie understood this was true. *Are you going to let it?* There was no anger or sarcasm in Ruth's voice now, only curiosity. *After all that's happened to you, are you really going to let it?*

The dog howled. The hand stirred. The bones whispered. The diamonds and rubies flashed their dim nightfire.

Hardly aware of what she was doing, let alone why she was doing it, Jessie grasped her own rings, the ones on the third finger of her left hand, with the wildly trembling thumb and forefinger of her right. The pain across the back of that hand as she squeezed was dim and distant. She had worn the rings almost constantly across all the days and years of her marriage, and the last time she'd taken them off, she'd had to soap her finger. Not this time. This time they slid off easily.

She held her bloody right hand out to the creature, who had now come all the way to the bookcase just inside the entrance to the study. The rings lay on her palm in a mystic figure eight below the makeshift sanitary napkin bandage. The creature stopped. The smile on its pudgy, misshapen mouth faltered into some new expression which might have been anger or only confusion.

"Here," Jessie said in a harsh, choked growl. "Here, take them. Take them and leave me alone."

Before the creature could move, she threw the rings at the open case as she had once thrown coins at the EXACT CHANGE baskets on the New Hampshire Turnpike. There was less than five feet between them now, the mouth of the case was large, and both rings went in. She distinctly heard the double click as her wedding and engagement bands fell against the bones of strangers.

The thing's lips wrinkled back from its teeth again, and it once more began to utter that sibilant, creamy hiss. It took another step forward, and something—something which had been lying stunned and unbelieving on the floor of her mind—awoke.

"*No!*" she screamed. She turned and went lurching up the hallway while the wind gusted and the door banged and the shutter clapped and the dog howled and *it was right behind her,* it was, she could hear that hissing sound, and at any moment it would reach out for her, a narrow white hand floating at the end of a fantastic arm as long as a tentacle, she would feel those rotting white fingers close on her throat—

Then she was at the back door, she was opening it, she was spilling out onto the stoop and tripping over her own right foot; she was falling and somehow reminding herself even as she went down to turn her body so she would land on her left side. She did, but still hit hard enough to see stars. She rolled over onto her back, lifted her head, and stared at the door, expecting to see the narrow white face of the space cowboy loom behind the screen. It didn't, and she could no longer hear the hissing sound, either. Not that those things meant much; it could hurtle into view at any second, seize her, and tear her throat out.

Jessie struggled to her feet, managed one step, and then her legs, trembling with a combination of shock and blood-loss, betrayed her and spilled her back to the planks next to the wire-covered compartment which held the garbage. She moaned and looked up at the sky, where clouds filigreed by a moon three-quarters full were racing from west to east at lunatic speed. Shadows rolled across her face like fabulous tattoos. Then the dog howled again, sounding much closer now that she was outside, and that provided the tiny bit of extra incentive she needed. She reached up to the garbage compartment's low sloped top with her left hand, felt around for the handle, and used it to haul herself to her feet. Once she was up, she held the handle tightly until the world stopped swaying. Then she let go and walked slowly toward the Mercedes, now holding out both arms for balance.

How like a skull the house looks in the moonlight! she marvelled following her first wide-eyed, frantic look back. *How very like a skull! The door is its mouth, the windows are its eyes, the shadows of the trees are its hair . . .*

Then another thought occurred, and it must have been amusing, because she screamed laughter into the windy night.

And the brain—don't forget the brain. Gerald's the brain, of course. The house's dead and rotting brain.

She laughed again as she reached the car, louder than ever, and the dog howled in answer. *My dog has fleas, they bite his knees,* she thought. Her own knees buckled and she grabbed the doorhandle to keep from falling down in the driveway, and she never stopped laughing as she did it. Exactly *why* she was laughing was beyond her. She might understand if the parts of her mind which had shut down in self-defense ever woke up again, but that wasn't going to happen until she got out of here. If she ever did.

"I imagine I'll need a transfusion, too, eventually," she said, and that caused another outburst of laughter. She reached clumsily across to her right pocket with her left hand, still laughing. She was feeling around for the key when she realized the smell was back, and that the creature with the wicker case was standing right behind her.

Jessie turned her head, laughter still in her throat and a grin still twitching her lips, and for a moment she *did* see those narrow cheeks and rapt, bottomless eyes. But she only saw them because of

(*the eclipse*)

how afraid she was, not because there was *really* anything there; the back stoop was still deserted, the screen door a tall rectangle of darkness.

But you better hurry, Goodwife Burlingame said. *Yes, you better make like a hockey player while you still can, don't you think?*

"Going to make like an amoeba and split," Jessie agreed, and laughed some more as she pulled the key out of her pocket. It almost slipped through her fingers, but she caught it by the over-sized plastic fob. "You sexy thing," Jessie said, and laughed hilariously as the door banged and the dead cowboy specter of love came charging out of the house in a dirty white cloud of bone-dust, but when she turned (almost dropping the key again in spite of the oversized fob), there was nothing there. It was only the wind which had banged the door—only that and nothing more.

She opened the driver's door, slid behind the wheel of the Mercedes, and managed to pull her trembling legs in after her. She slammed the door and, as she pushed down the master-lock which locked all the other doors (plus the trunk, of course; there was really nothing in the world quite like German efficiency), an inexpressible sense of relief washed over her. Relief and something else. That something else felt like sanity, and she thought she had never felt anything in her life which could compare with its sweet and perfect return . . . except for that first drink of water from the tap, of course. Jessie had an idea that was going to end up being the all-time champeen.

How close was I to going mad in there? How close, really?

That might not be a thing you ever want to know for sure, toots, Ruth Neary returned gravely.

No, maybe not. Jessie stuck the key in the ignition and turned it. Nothing happened.

The last of the laughter dried up, but she didn't panic; she still felt sane and relatively whole. *Think, Jessie.* She did, and the answer came almost at once. The Mercedes was getting along in years (she wasn't sure they ever really got anything so vulgar as old), and the transmission had started doing some annoying little tricks lately, German efficiency or no German efficiency. One of them was a failure to start sometimes unless the driver shoved up on the shift-lever poking out of the console between the bucket seats, and shoved up hard. Turning the ignition key while pushing up on the transmission lever was an operation which would take both hands, and her right was already throbbing horribly. The thought of using it to shove on the transmission lever made her cringe, and not just because of the pain. She was quite sure it would also cause the deep incision across her inner wrist to break open again.

"Please God, I need a little help here," Jessie whispered, and turned the ignition key again. Still nothing. Not even a click. And now a new idea stole into her head like a nasty-tempered little burglar: her inability to start the car had nothing at all to do with the little glitch that had developed in the transmission. This was more of her visitor's work. It had cut the telephone lines; it had also raised the hood of the Mercedes long enough to rip off the distributor cap and throw it into the woods.

The door banged. She glanced nervously in that direction, quite sure that she had seen its white, grinning face in the darkness of the doorway for just a moment. In another moment or two it would come out. It would grab a rock and smash the car window, then take one of the thick slivers of safety glass and—

Jessie reached across her waist with her left hand and shoved the knob of the transmission lever as hard as she could (although it did not, in truth, seem to move much at all). Then she reached clumsily through the lower arc of the steering wheel with her right hand, grasped the ignition key, and turned it again.

More nothing. Except for the silent, chuffing laughter of the monster that was watching her. That she could hear quite clearly, even if only in her mind.

"*Please, God, can't I have just one fucking break?*" she screamed. The transmission lever wiggled a little under her palm, and when Jessie turned the key over to the Start position this time, the engine roared to life—*Ja, mein Führer!* She sobbed with relief and turned on the headlights. A pair of brilliant orange-yellow eyes glared at her from the driveway. She screamed, feeling her heart trying to tear itself loose of its plumbing, cram itself into her throat, and strangle her. It was the dog, of course—the stray who had been, in a manner of speaking, Gerald's last client.

The former Prince stood stock-still, momentarily dazzled by the glare of the headlights. If Jessie had dropped the transmission into drive just then, she probably could have driven forward and killed it. The thought even crossed her mind, but in a distant, almost academic way. Her hate and fear of the dog had gone. She saw how scrawny it was, and how the burdocks stuck in its matted coat—a coat too thin to offer much protection against the coming winter. Most of all she saw the way it cringed away from the light, its ears drooping, its hindquarters shrinking against the driveway.

I didn't think it was possible, she thought, *but I believe I've come across something that's even more wretched than I am.*

She hit the Mercedes's horn-ring with the heel of her left hand. It uttered a single brief sound, more burp than beep, but it was enough to get the dog started. It turned and vanished into the woods without so much as a single look back.

Follow its example, Jess. Get out of here while you still can.

Good idea. In fact, it was the *only* idea. She reached across her body again with her left hand, this time to pull the transmission lever down into Drive. It caught with its usual reassuring little hitch and the car began rolling slowly up the paved driveway. The wind-driven trees shimmied like shadow-dancers on either side of it, sending the fall's first tornado-funnels of leaves whirling up into the night sky. *I'm doing it,* Jessie thought with wonder. *I'm actually doing it, actually getting the puck out of here.*

She was rolling up the driveway, rolling toward the unnamed wheel-track which would take her to Bay Lane, which would in its turn take her to Route 117 and civilization. As she watched the house (it looked more than ever like a huge white skull in the windy October moonlight) shrink in the rearview mirror, she thought: *Why is it letting me go? And is it? Is it really?*

Part of her—the fear-maddened part which would never entirely escape the handcuffs and the master bedroom of the house on the upper bay of Kashwakamak Lake—assured her that it wasn't; the creature with the wicker case was only playing with her, as a cat plays with a wounded mouse. Before she got much farther, certainly before she got to the top of the driveway, it would come racing after her, using its long cartoon legs to close the distance between them, stretching out its long cartoon arms to seize the rear bumper and bring the car to a halt. German efficiency was fine, but when you were dealing with something which had come back from the dead . . . well . . .

But the house continued to dwindle in the rearview mirror, and nothing came out of the back door. Jessie reached the top of the driveway, turned right, and began to follow her high beams down the narrow wheelruts toward Bay Lane, guiding the car with her left hand. Every second or third August a volunteer crew of summer residents, fueled mostly by beer and gossip, cut back the underbrush and trimmed the overhanging branches along the way out to Bay Lane, but this had been an off-year and the lane was much narrower than Jessie liked. Each time a wind-driven branch tapped at the car's roof or body, she cringed a little.

Yet she *was* escaping. One by one the landmarks she had learned over the years made their appearance in the headlights and then dwindled behind her: the huge rock with the split top, the over-grown gate with the faded sign reading RIDEOUT'S HIDEOUT nailed to it, the uprooted spruce leaning amid a stand of smaller spruces like a large drunk being carried home by his smaller, livelier friends. The drunk spruce was only three-tenths of a mile from Bay Lane, and it was only two miles to the highway from there.

"I can handle it if I take it easy," she said, and pushed the radio ON button with her right thumb, doing it very carefully. Bach—mellow, stately, and above all, *rational*—flooded the car from four directions. Better and better. "Take it easy," she repeated, speaking a little louder. "Go greasy." Even the last shock—the stray dog's glaring orange eyes—was fading a little now, although she could feel herself beginning to shake. "No problems whatsoever, if I just take it easy."

She was doing that, all right—maybe a little *too* easy, in fact. The speedometer needle was barely touching the 10 MPH mark. Being safely locked in the familiar surroundings of one's own car was a wonderful restorative—already she had begun to wonder if she hadn't been jumping at shadows all along—but this would be a very bad time to begin taking things for granted. If there *had* been someone in the house, he (*it,* some deeper voice—the UFO of all UFOs—insisted) might have used one of the other doors to *leave* the house. He might be following her right now. It was even possible that, were she to continue puddling along at a mere ten miles an hour, a really determined follower might catch up.

Jessie flicked her eyes up to the rearview mirror, wanting to reassure herself that this idea was only paranoia induced by shock and exhaustion, and felt her heart fall dead in her chest. Her left hand dropped from the wheel and thumped into her lap on top of the right. That should have hurt like hell, but there was no pain— absolutely none at all.

The stranger was sitting in the back seat with its eerily long hands pressed against the sides of its head, like the monkey that hears no evil. Its black eyes stared at her with sublimely empty interest.

You see . . . me see . . . WE see . . . nothing but shadows! Punkin cried, but this cry was more than distant; it seemed to have originated at the other end of the universe.

And it wasn't true. It was more than shadows she saw in the mirror. The thing sitting back there was *tangled* in shadows, yes, but not *made* of them. She saw its face: bulging brow, round black eyes, blade-thin nose, plump, misshapen lips.

"Jessie!" the space cowboy whispered ecstatically. "Nora! Ruth! My-oh-my! Punkin Pie!"

Her eyes, frozen on the mirror, saw her passenger lean slowly forward, saw its swollen forehead nodding toward her right ear as if the creature intended to tell her a secret. She saw its pudgy lips slide away from its jutting, discolored teeth in a grimacing, vapid smile. It was at this point that the final breakup of Jessie Burlingame's mind began.

No! her own voice cried in a voice as thin as the voice of a vocalist on a scratchy old 78-rpm record. *No, please no! It's not fair!*

"Jessie!" Its stinking breath as sharp as a rasp and as cold as air inside a meat-locker. "Nora! Jessie! Ruth! Jessie! Punkin! Goodwife! Jessie! Mommy!"

Her bulging eyes noted that the long white face was now half-hidden in her hair and its grinning mouth was almost kissing her ear as it whispered its delicious secret over and over and over: *"Jessie! Nora! Goody! Punkin! Jessie! Jessie! Jessie!"*

There was a white airburst inside her eyes, and what it left behind was a big dark hole. As Jessie dove into it, she had one final coherent thought: *I shouldn't have looked—it burned my eyes after all.*

Then she fell forward toward the wheel in a faint. As the Mercedes struck one of the large pines which bordered this section of the road, the seatbelt locked and jerked her backward again. The crash would probably have triggered the airbag, if the Mercedes had been a model recent enough to have come equipped with the system. It was not hard enough to damage the engine or even cause it to stall; good old German efficiency had triumphed again. The bumper and grille were dented and the hood ornament was knocked askew, but the engine idled contentedly away to itself.

After about five minutes, a microchip buried in the dashboard sensed that the motor was now warm enough to turn on the heater. Blowers under the dash began to whoosh softly. Jessie had slumped sideways against the driver's door, where she lay with her cheek pressed to the window, looking like a tired child who has finally given up and gone to sleep with grandma's house just over the next hill. Above her, the rearview mirror reflected the empty back seat and the empty moonlit lane behind it.

35

It had been snowing all morning—gloomy, but good letter-writing weather—and when a bar of sun fell across the keyboard of the Mac, Jessie glanced up in surprise, startled out of her thoughts. What she saw out the window did more than charm her; it filled her with an emotion she had not experienced for a long time and hadn't expected to experience again for a long time to come, if ever. It was joy—a deep, complex joy she could never have explained.

The snow hadn't stopped—not entirely, anyway—but a bright February sun had broken through the clouds overhead, turning both the fresh six inches on the ground and the snow still floating down through the air to a brilliant diamantine white. The window offered a sweeping view of Portland's Eastern Promenade, and it was a view which had soothed and fascinated Jessie in all weathers and seasons, but she had never seen anything quite like this; the combination of snow and sun had turned the gray air over Casco Bay into a fabulous jewel-box of interlocking rainbows.

If there were real people living in those snow-globes where you can

*shake up a blizzard any time you want to, they'd see this weather all
the time,* she thought, and laughed. This sound was as fabulously
strange to her ears as that feeling of joy was to her heart, and it
only took a moment's thought to realize why: she hadn't laughed
at all since the previous October. She referred to those hours, the
last ones she ever intended to spend by Kashwakamak (or any other
lake, for that matter), simply as "my hard time." This phrase told
what was necessary and not one thing more, she felt. Which was
just the way she liked it.

No laughs at all since then? Zilch? Zero? Are you sure?

Not *absolutely* sure, no. She supposed she might have laughed in
dreams—God knew she had cried in enough of them—but as far
as her waking hours went, it had been a shutout until now. She
remembered the last one very clearly: reaching across her body
with her left hand so she could get the keys out of the right pocket
of her culotte skirt, telling the windy darkness she was going to
make like an amoeba and split. That, so far as she knew, had been
the last laugh until now.

"Only that and nothing more," Jessie murmured. She took a pack
of cigarettes out of her shirt pocket and lit one. God, how that
phrase brought it all back—the only other thing with the power to
do it so quickly and completely, she had discovered, was that awful
song by Marvin Gaye. She'd heard it once on the radio when she'd
been driving back from one of the seemingly endless doctor's appointments which had made up her life this winter, Marvin wailing
"Everybody knows . . . especially you girls . . ." in that soft, insin-
uating voice of his. She had turned the radio off at once, but she'd
still been shaking too badly to drive. She had parked and waited
for the worst of the shakes to pass. Eventually they had, but on the
nights when she didn't wake up muttering that phrase from "The
Raven" over and over into her sweat-soaked pillow, she heard herself chanting, "Witness, witness." As far as Jessie was concerned, it
was six of one and half a million of the other.

She dragged deep on her cigarette, puffed out three perfect rings,
and watched them rise slowly above the humming Mac.

When people were stupid enough or tasteless enough to ask about her ordeal (and she had discovered she knew a great many more stupid, tasteless people than she ever would have guessed), she told them she couldn't remember much of what had happened. After the first two or three police interviews, she began to tell the cops and all but one of Gerald's colleagues the same thing. The single exception had been Brandon Milheron. To him she had told the truth, partly because she needed his help but mostly because Brandon had been the only one who had displayed the slightest understanding of what she had gone through . . . was still going through. He hadn't wasted her time with pity, and what a relief that had been. Jessie had also discovered that pity came cheap in the aftermath of tragedy, and that all the pity in the world wasn't worth a pisshole in the snow.

Anyway, the cops and the newspaper reporters had accepted her amnesia—and the rest of her story—at face value, that was the important thing, and why not? People who underwent serious physical and mental trauma often blocked out the memories of what had happened; the cops knew that even better than the lawyers, and Jessie knew it better than any of them. She had learned a great deal about physical and mental trauma since last October. The books and articles had helped her find plausible reasons not to talk about what she didn't want to talk about, but otherwise they hadn't helped much. Or maybe it was just that she hadn't come to the right case histories yet—the ones dealing with handcuffed women who were forced to watch as their husbands became Purina Dog Chow.

Jessie surprised herself by laughing again—a good loud laugh this time. Was *that* funny? Apparently it was, but it was also one of those funny things you could never, ever tell anyone else. Like how your Dad once got so excited about a solar eclipse that he blew a load all over the seat of your underpants, for instance. Or how— here's a *real* yuck—you actually thought a little come on your fanny might make you pregnant.

Anyway, most of the case histories suggested that the human mind often reacted to extreme trauma the way a squid reacts to danger—by covering the entire landscape with a billow of obscuring ink. You knew *something* had happened, and that it had been no day in the park, but that was all. Everything else was gone, hidden by that ink. A lot of the case-history people said that—people who had been raped, people who had been in car crashes, people who had been caught in fires and had crawled into closets to die, even one skydiving lady whose parachute hadn't opened and who had been recovered, badly hurt but miraculously alive, from the large soft bog in which she had landed.

What was it like, coming down? they had asked the skydiving lady. *What did you think about when you realized your chute hadn't opened, wasn't going to open?* And the skydiving lady had replied, *I can't remember. I remember the starter patting me on the back, and I think I remember the pop-out, but the next thing I remember is being on a stretcher and asking one of the men putting me into the back of the ambulance how badly I was hurt. Everything in the middle is just a haze. I suppose I prayed, but I can't even remember that for sure.*

Or maybe you really remembered everything, my skydiving friend, Jessie thought, *and lied about it, just like I did. Maybe even for the same reasons. For all I know, every damned one of the case-history people in every damned one of the books I read was lying.*

Maybe so. Whether they were or not, the fact remained that she *did* remember her hours handcuffed to the bed—from the click of the key in the second lock right up to that final freezing moment when she had looked into the rearview mirror and seen that the thing in the house had become the thing in the back seat, she remembered it all. She remembered those moments by day and relived them by night in horrible dreams where the water-glass slid past her along the inclined plane of the shelf and shattered on the floor, where the stray dog bypassed the cold buffet on the floor in favor of the hot meal on the bed, where the hideous night-visitor in the corner asked *Do you love me, Punkin?* in her father's voice and maggots squirmed like semen from the tip of its erect penis.

But *remembering* a thing and *reliving* a thing did not confer an obligation to *tell* about a thing, even when the memories made you sweat and the nightmares made you scream. She had lost ten pounds since October (well, that was shading the truth a bit; it was actually more like seventeen), taken up smoking again (a pack and a half a day, plus a joint roughly the size of an El Producto before bedtime), her complexion had gone to hell, and all at once her hair was going gray all over her head, not just at the temples. That last was something she could fix—hadn't she been doing so for five years or more?—but so far she simply hadn't been able to summon up enough energy to dial Oh Pretty Woman in Westbrook and make an appointment. Besides, who did she have to look good for? Was she planning to maybe hit a few singles bars, check out the local talent?

Good idea, she thought. *Some guy will ask if he can buy me a drink, I'll say yes, and then, while we wait for the bartender to bring them, I'll tell him—just casually—that I have this dream where my father ejaculates maggots instead of semen. With a line of interesting conversational patter like that, I'm sure he'll ask me back to his apartment right away. He won't even want to see a doctor's certificate saying I'm HIV-negative.*

In mid-November, after she had begun to believe the police were really going to leave her alone and the story's sex angle was going to stay out of the papers (she was very slow coming to believe this, because the publicity was the thing she had dreaded the most), she decided to try therapy with Nora Callighan again. Maybe she didn't want this sitting inside and sending out poison fumes for the next thirty or forty years as it rotted. How much different might her life have been if she had managed to tell Nora what had happened on the day of the eclipse? For that matter, how much difference might it have made if that girl hadn't come into the kitchen when she did that night at Neuworth Parsonage? Maybe none . . . but maybe a lot.

Maybe an *awful* lot.

So she dialed New Today, New Tomorrow, the loose association of counsellors with which Nora had been affiliated, and was shocked to silence when the receptionist told her Nora had died of leukemia

the year before—some weird, sly variant which had hidden suc-
cessfully in the back alleys of her lymphatic system until it was too
late to do a damned thing about it. Would Jessie perhaps care to
meet with Laurel Stevenson? the receptionist asked, but Jessie remembered Laurel—a tall, dark-haired, dark-eyed beauty who wore
high heels with sling backs and looked as if she would enjoy sex
to the fullest only when she was on top. She told the receptionist
she'd think it over. And that had been it for counselling.

In the three months since she had learned of Nora's death, she'd
had good days (when she was only afraid) and bad days (when she
was too terrified even to leave this room, let alone the house) but
only Brandon Milheron had heard anything approaching the complete story of Jessie Mahout's hard time by the lake . . . and Brandon
hadn't believed the crazier aspects of that story. Had sympathized,
yes, but not believed. Not at first, anyway.

"No pearl earring," he had reported the day after she first told
him about the stranger with the long white face. "No muddy footprint, either. Not in the written reports, at least."

Jessie shrugged and said nothing. She *could* have said things, but
it seemed safer not to. She had badly needed a friend in the weeks
following her escape from the summer house, and Brandon had
filled the bill admirably. She didn't want to distance him or drive
him away entirely with a lot of crazy talk.

And there was something else, too, something simple and direct:
maybe Brandon was right. Maybe her visitor had just been a soupçon of moonlight, after all.

Little by little she had been able to persuade herself, at least in
her waking hours, that this was the truth of it. Her space cowboy
had been a kind of Rorschach pattern, one made not of ink and
paper but of wind-driven shadows and imagination. She didn't blame
herself for any of this, however; quite the opposite. If not for her
imagination, she never would have seen how she might be able to
get the water-glass . . . and even if she *had* gotten it, she never
would have thought of using a magazine blow-in card as a straw.
No, she thought her imagination had more than earned its right to

a few hallucinatory megrims, but it remained important for her to remember she'd been alone that night. If recovery began anywhere, she had believed, it began with the ability to separate reality from fantasy. She told Brandon some of this. He had smiled, hugged her, kissed her temple, and told her she was getting better in all sorts of ways.

Then, last Friday, her eye had happened on the lead story of the *Press-Herald*'s County News section. All her assumptions began to change then, and they had gone right on changing as the story of Raymond Andrew Joubert began its steady march from filler between the Community Calendar and the County Police Beat to banner headlines on the front page. Then, yesterday . . . seven days after Joubert's name had first appeared on the County page . . .

There was a tap at the door, and Jessie's first feeling, as always, was an instinctive cringe of fear. It was there and gone almost before she realized it. Almost . . . but not quite.

"Meggie? That you?"

"None other, ma'am."

"Come on in."

Megan Landis, the housekeeper Jessie had hired in December (that was when her first fat insurance check had arrived via registered mail), came in with a glass of milk on a tray. A small pill, gray and pink, sat beside the glass. At the sight of the glass, Jessie's right wrist began to itch madly. This didn't always happen, but it wasn't exactly an unfamiliar reaction, either. At least the twitches and that weird my-skin-is-crawling-right-off-the-bones sensation had pretty much stopped. There had been awhile there, before Christmas, when Jessie had really believed she was going to spend the rest of her life drinking out of a plastic cup.

"How's yer paw today?" Meggie asked, as if she had picked up Jessie's itch by some kind of sensory telepathy. Nor did Jessie think this a ridiculous idea. She sometimes found Meggie's questions— and the intuitions which prompted them—a little creepy, but never ridiculous.

The hand in question, now lying in the sunbeam which had startled her away from what she had been writing on the Mac, was dressed in a black glove lined with some frictionless space-age polymer. Jessie supposed the burn-glove—for that was what it was—had been perfected in one dirty little war or another. Not that she would ever have refused to wear it on that account, and not that she wasn't grateful. She was very grateful indeed. After the third skin-graft, you learned that an attitude of gratitude was one of life's few reliable hedges against insanity.

"Not too bad, Meggie."

Meggie's left eyebrow lifted, stopping just short of I-don't-believe-you height. "No? If you've been running that keyboard for the whole three hours you've been in here, I bet it's singing 'Ave Maria.' "

"Have I really been here for—?" She glanced at her watch and saw that she had been. She glanced at the copy-minder on top of the VDT screen and saw she was on the fifth page of the document she had opened just after breakfast. Now it was almost lunch, and the most surprising thing was she hadn't strayed as far from the truth as Meggie's lifted brow suggested: her hand really wasn't that bad. She could have waited another hour for the pill if she'd had to.

She took it nevertheless, washing it down with the milk. As she was drinking the last of it, her eyes wandered back to the VDT and read the words on the current screen:

No one found me that night; I woke up on my own just after dawn the next day. The engine had finally stalled, but the car was still warm. I could hear birds singing in the woods, and through the trees I could see the lake, flat as a mirror, with little ribbons of steam rising off it. It looked very beautiful, and at the same time I hated the sight of it, as I have hated the very thought of it ever since. Can you understand that, Ruth? I'll be damned if I can.

My hand was hurting like hell—whatever help I'd gotten from the aspirin was long gone—but what I felt in spite of the pain was the most incredible sense of peace and well-being. Something was gnawing at it, though. Something I'd forgotten. At first I couldn't remember what it was. I don't think my brain *wanted* me to remember what it was. Then, all at once, it came to me.

He'd been in the back seat, and he'd leaned forward to whisper the names of all my voices in my ear.

I looked into the mirror and saw the back seat was empty. That eased my mind a little bit but then I

The words stopped at that point, with the little cursor flashing expectantly just beyond the end of the last unfinished sentence. It seemed to beckon to her, urge her forward, and suddenly Jessie recalled a poem from a marvellous little book by Kenneth Patchen. The book was called *But Even So,* and the poem had gone like this: "Come now, my child, if we were planning to harm you, do you think we'd be lurking here beside the path in the very darkest part of the forest?"

Good question, Jessie thought, and let her eyes wander from the VDT screen to Meggie Landis's face. Jessie liked the energetic Irishwoman, liked her a lot—hell, *owed* her a lot—but if she had caught the little housekeeper looking at the words on the Mac's screen, Meggie would have been headed down Forest Avenue with her severance pay in her pocket before you could say *Dear Ruth, I suppose you're surprised to hear from me after all these years.*

But Megan wasn't looking at the pc's screen; she was looking at the sweeping view of Eastern Prom and Casco Bay beyond it. The sun was still shining and the snow was still falling, although now it was clearly winding down.

"Devil's beating his wife," Meggie remarked.

"I beg your pardon?" Jessie asked, smiling.

"That's what my mother used to say when the sun came out before the snow stopped." Meggie looked a little embarrassed as she held her hand out for the empty glass. "What it means I'm not sure I could say."

Jessie nodded. The embarrassment on Meggie Landis's face had lensed into something else—something that looked to Jessie like unease. For a moment she hadn't any idea what could have made Meggie look that way, and then it came to her—a thing so obvious it was easy to overlook. It was the smile. Meggie wasn't used to seeing Jessie smile. Jessie wanted to assure her that it was all right, that the smile didn't mean she was going to leap from her chair and attempt to tear Meggie's throat out.

Instead, she told her, "My own mother used to say, 'The sun doesn't shine on the same dog's ass every day.' I never knew what that one meant, either."

The housekeeper did look in the Mac's direction now, but it was the merest flick of dismissal: *Time to put your toys away, Missus,* her glance said. "That pill's going to make you sleepy if you don't dump a little food atop it. I've got a sandwich waiting for you, and soup heating on the stove."

Soup and sandwich—kid food, the lunch you had after sledding all morning on the day when school was cancelled because of a nor'easter; food you ate with the cold still blazing redly in your cheeks like bonfires. It sounded absolutely great, but . . .

"I'm going to pass, Meg."

Meggie's brow furrowed and the corners of her mouth drew down. This was an expression Jessie had seen often in the early days of Meggie's employment, when she had sometimes felt she needed an extra pain pill so badly that she had cried. Megan had never given in to her tears, however. Jessie supposed that was why she had hired the little Irishwoman—she had guessed from the first that Meggie wasn't a giver-inner. She was, in fact, one hard spring potato when she had to be . . . but Meggie would not be getting her way this time.

"You need to eat, Jess. You're nothing but a scarecrow." Now it was the overflowing ashtray which bore the dour whiplash of her glance. "And you need to quit *that* shit, too."

I'll make you quit them, me proud beauty, Gerald said in her mind, and Jessie shuddered.

"Jessie? Are you all right? Is there a draft?"

"No. A goose walked over my grave, that's all." She smiled wanly. "We're a regular packet of old sayings today, aren't we?"

"You've been warned time and time again about not over-doing—"

Jessie reached out her black-clad right hand and tentatively touched Meggie's left hand with it. "My hand's really getting better, isn't it?"

"Yes. If you could use it on that machine, even part of the time, for three hours or more and not be yelling for that pill the second I showed my face in here, then I guess you're getting better even faster than Dr. Magliore expected. All the same—"

"All the same it's getting better, and that's good . . . right?"

"Of course it's good." The housekeeper looked at Jessie as if she were mad.

"Well, now I'm trying to get the rest of me better. Step one is writing a letter to an old friend of mine. I promised myself—last October, during my hard time—that if I got out of the mess I was in, I'd do that. But I kept putting it off. Now I'm finally trying, and I don't dare stop. I might lose my guts if I do."

"But the pill—"

"I think I've got just enough time to finish this and stick the printout in an envelope before I get too sleepy to work. Then I can take a long nap, and when I wake up I'll eat an early supper." She touched Meggie's left hand with her right again, a gesture of reassurance which was both clumsy and rather sweet. "A nice big one."

Meggie's frown remained. "It's not good to skip meals, Jessie, and you know it."

Very gently, Jessie said: "Some things are more important than meals. You know that as well as I do, don't you?"

Meggie glanced toward the VDT again, then sighed and nodded. When she spoke, it was in the tone of a woman bowing to some conventional sentiment in which she herself does not really believe. "I guess so. And even if I don't, you're the boss."

Jessie nodded, realizing for the first time that this was now more than just a fiction the two of them maintained for the sake of convenience. "I suppose I am, at that."

Meggie's eyebrow had climbed to half-mast again. "If I brought the sandwich in and left it here on the corner of your desk?"

Jessie grinned. "Sold!"

This time Meggie smiled back. When she brought the sandwich in three minutes later, Jessie was sitting before the glowing screen again, her skin an unhealthy comic-book green in its reflected glow, lost in whatever she was slowly picking out on the keyboard. The little Irish housekeeper made no effort to be quiet—she was that sort of woman who would probably be unable to tiptoe if her life depended on it—but Jessie still did not hear her come or go. She had taken a stack of newspaper clippings out of the top drawer of her desk and stopped typing to riffle through them. Photographs accompanied most, photographs of a man with a strange, narrow face that receded at the chin and bulged at the brow. His deep-set eyes were dark and round and perfectly blank, eyes that made Jessie think simultaneously of Dondi, the comic-strip waif, and Charles Manson. Pudgy lips as thick as slices of cut fruit pooched out below his blade of a nose.

Meggie stood beside Jessie's shoulder for a moment, waiting to be acknowledged, then uttered a low "Humph!" and left the room. Forty-five minutes or so later, Jessie glanced to the left and saw the toasted cheese sandwich. It was now cold, the cheese coagulated into lumps, but she wolfed it nevertheless in five quick bites. Then she turned back to the Mac. The cursor began to dance ahead once more, leading her steadily deeper into the forest.

36

That eased my mind a little bit but then I thought, "He could be crouched down back there so the mirror doesn't show him." So I managed to get turned around, although I could hardly believe how weak I was. Even the slightest bump made my hand feel like someone was jabbing it with a red-hot poker. No one was there, of course, and I tried to tell myself that the last time I saw him, he really *was* just shadows . . . shadows and my mind working overtime.

But I couldn't quite believe it, Ruth—not even with the sun coming up and me out of the handcuffs, out of the house, and locked inside my own car. I got the idea that if he wasn't in the back seat he was in the trunk, and if he wasn't in the trunk, he was crouched down by the back bumper. I got the idea that he was still with me, in other words, and he's been with me ever since. That's what I need to make you—you or somebody—understand; that's what I really need to say. *He has been with me ever since.* Even when my rational mind decided that he'd probably been shadows and moonlight *every* time I saw him, he was with me. Or maybe I should say *it* was with me. My visitor is "the man with the white face" when the sun is up, you see, but he's "the thing with the white face" when it's down. Either way, him or it, my rational mind was eventually able to give him up, but I have found that is nowhere near enough. Because every time a board creaks in the house at night I know that it's come back, every time a funny shadow dances on the wall I know it's come back, every time I hear an unfamiliar step coming up the walk I know it's come back—come back to finish the job. It was there in the Mercedes that morning when I woke up, and it's been here in my house on Eastern Prom almost every night, maybe hiding behind the drapes or standing in the closet with its wicker case between its feet. There is no magic stake to drive through the hearts of the real monsters, and oh Ruth, it makes me so *tired.*

Jessie paused long enough to dump the overflowing ashtray and light a fresh cigarette. She did this slowly and deliberately. Her hands had picked up a small but discernible shake, and she didn't want to burn herself. When the cigarette was going, she took a deep drag, exhaled, stuck it in the ashtray, and returned to the Mac.

I don't know what I would have done if the car battery had been dead—sat there until someone came along, I guess, even if it meant sitting there all day—but it wasn't, and the motor started on the first crank. I backed away from the tree I'd hit and managed to get the car pointed down the lane again. I kept wanting to look in the rearview mirror, but I was afraid to do it. I was afraid I might see him. Not because he was there, you understand—I knew he wasn't—but because my mind might *make* me see him.

Finally, just as I got to Bay Lane, I *did* look up. I couldn't help it. There was nothing in the mirror but the back seat, of course, and that made the rest of the trip a little easier. I drove out to 117 and then up to Dakin's Country Store—it's one of those places where the locals hang out when they're too broke to go over to Rangeley or to one of the bars in Motton. They mostly sit at the lunch counter, eating doughnuts and swapping lies about what they did on Saturday night. I pulled in behind the gas pumps and just sat there for five minutes or so, watching the loggers and the caretakers and the power company guys go in and come back out. I couldn't believe they were real—isn't that a hoot? I kept thinking they were ghosts, that pretty soon my eyes would adjust to the daylight and I'd be able to see right through them. I was thirsty again, and every time someone came out with one of those little white Styrofoam cups of coffee, I'd get thirstier, but I still couldn't quite bring myself to get out of the car . . . to go among the ghosts, you might say.

I suppose I would have, eventually, but before I could muster enough courage to do more than pull up the master-lock, Jimmy Eggart pulled in and parked beside me. Jimmy's a retired CPA from Boston who's lived at the lake year-round since his wife died back in 1987 or '88. He got out of his Bronco, looked at me, recognized me, and started to smile. Then his face changed, first to concern and then to horror. He came to the Mercedes and bent down to look through the window, and he was so surprised that all the wrinkles were pulled out of his face. I remember that very clearly: how surprise made Jimmy Eggart look young.

I saw his mouth forming the words "Jessie, are you all right?" I wanted to open the door, but all at once I didn't quite dare. This crazy idea came into my head. That the thing I'd been calling the space cowboy had been in Jimmy's house, too, only Jimmy hadn't been as lucky as I had been. It had killed him, and cut off his face, and then put it on like a Halloween mask. I *knew* it was a crazy idea, but knowing that didn't help much, because I couldn't stop thinking it. I couldn't make myself open the fucking car door, either.

I don't know how bad I looked that morning and don't *want* to know, but it must have been bad, because pretty soon Jimmy Eggart didn't look surprised anymore. He looked scared enough to run and sick enough to puke.

He didn't do either one, God bless him. What he did was open the car door and ask me what had happened, had it been an accident or had someone hurt me.

I only had to take one look down to get an idea what had put a buzz under him. At some point the wound in my wrist must have opened up again, because the sanitary pad I'd taped around it was entirely soaked. The front of my skirt was soaked, too, as if I'd had the world's worst period. I was sitting in blood, there was blood on the steering wheel, blood on the console, blood on the shift-lever . . . there were even splatters on the windshield. Most of it had dried to that awful maroon color blood gets—to me it looks like chocolate milk—but some of it was still red and wet. Until you see something like that, Ruth, you just don't have any idea how much blood there really is in a person. It's no wonder Jimmy freaked.

I tried to get out—I think I wanted to show him I could do it under my own power, and that would reassure him—but I bumped my right hand on the steering wheel and everything went white and gray. I didn't pass out completely, but it was as if the last bunch of wires between my head and my body had been cut. I felt myself falling forward and I remember thinking I was going to finish my adventures by knocking most of my teeth out on the asphalt . . . and after spending a fortune to get the top ones capped just last year. Then Jimmy caught me . . . right by the boobs, as a matter of fact. I heard him yelling at the store—"Hey! Hey! I need a little help out here!"—in a high, shrieky old man's voice that made me feel like laughing . . . only I was too tired to laugh. I laid the side of my head against his shirt and panted for breath. I could feel my heart going fast but hardly seeming to beat at all, as if it had nothing to beat *on*. Some light and color started to come back into the day, though, and I saw half a dozen men coming out to see what was wrong. Lonnie Dakin was one of them. He was eating a muffin and wearing a pink tee-shirt that said THERE'S NO TOWN DRUNK HERE, WE JUST ALL TAKE TURNS. Funny what you remember when you think you're getting ready to die, isn't it?

"Who did this to you, Jessie?" Jimmy asked. I tried to answer him but couldn't get any words out. Which is probably just as well, considering what I was trying to say. I think it was "My father."

Jessie snuffed out her cigarette, then looked down at the top newsprint photograph. The narrow, freakish face of Raymond Andrew Joubert gazed raptly back . . . just as he had gazed at her from the corner of the bedroom on the first night, and from her recently deceased husband's study on the second. Almost five minutes passed in this silent contemplation. Then, with the air of one who starts awake from a brief doze, Jessie lit a fresh cigarette and turned back to her letter. The copy-minder now announced she was on page seven. She stretched, listened to the minute crackling sounds from her spine, then began to touch the keys again. The cursor resumed its dance.

Twenty minutes later—twenty minutes during which I discovered how sweet and concerned and amusingly daffy men can be (Lonnie Dakin asked me if I'd like some Midol)—I was in a Rescue Services ambulance, headed for Northern Cumberland Hospital with the flashers flashing and the siren wailing. An hour after that I was lying in a crank-up bed, watching blood run down a tube into my arm and listening to some country music asshole sing about how tough his life had been since his woman left him and his pickup truck broke down.

That pretty well concludes Part One of my story, Ruth—call it Little Nell Across the Ice, or, How I Escaped Handcuffs and Made My Way to Safety. There are two other parts, which I think of as The Aftermath and The Kicker. I'm going to scamp on The Aftermath, partly because it's only really interesting if you're into skin-grafts and pain, but mostly because I want to get to The Kicker before I get too tired and computer-woozy to tell it the way I need to tell it. And the way you deserve to have it told, come to think of it. That idea just occurred to me, and it's nothing but the bald-assed truth, as we used to say. After all, without The Kicker I probably wouldn't be writing you at all.

Before I get to it, though, I have to tell you a little more about Brandon Milheron, who really sums up that Aftermath period for me. It was during the first part of my recovery, the really ugly part, that Brandon came along and more or less adopted me. I'd like to call him a sweet man, because he was there for me during one of the most hellacious times of my life, but sweetness isn't really what he's about—seeing things through is what Brandon is about, and keeping all the sightlines clear, and making sure all the right ducks stay in a row. And that isn't right, either—there's more to him than that and he's better than that—but the hour groweth late, and it will have to do. Suffice it to say that for a man whose job it was to look out for a conservative law-firm's interests in the wake of a potentially nasty situation involving one of the senior partners, Brandon did a lot of hand-holding and encouraging. Also, he never gave me hell for crying on the lapels of his natty three-piece suits. If that was all, I probably wouldn't be going on about him, but there's something else, as well. Something he did for me only yesterday. Have faith, kid—we're getting there.

Brandon and Gerald worked together a lot over the last fourteen months of Gerald's life—a suit involving one of the major supermarket chains up here. They won whatever it was they were supposed to win, and, more important for yours truly, they established a good rapport. I have an idea that when the old sticks that run the firm get around to taking Gerald's name off the letterhead, Brandon's will take its place. In the meantime, he was the perfect person for this assignment, which Brandon himself described as damage control during his first meeting with me in the hospital.

He does have a kind of sweetness about him—yes, he does—and he was honest with me from the jump, but of course he still had his own agenda from the beginning. Believe me when I say my eyes are wide open on *that* score, my dear; I was, after all, married to a lawyer for almost two decades, and I know how fiercely they compartmentalize the various aspects of their lives and personalities. It's what allows them to survive without having too many breakdowns, I suppose, but it's also what makes so many of them utterly loathsome.

Brandon was never loathsome, but he was a man with a mission: keep a lid on any bad publicity that might accrue to the firm. That meant keeping a lid on any bad publicity that might accrue to either Gerald or me, of course. This is the sort of job where the person doing it can wind up getting screwed by a single stroke of bad luck, but Brandon still took it like a shot . . . and to his further credit, he never once tried to tell me he took the job out of respect for Gerald's memory. He took it because it was what Gerald himself used to call a career-maker—the kind of job that can open a quick shortcut to the next echelon, if it turns out well. It is turning out well for Brandon, and I'm glad. He treated me with a great deal of kindness and compassion, which is reason enough to be happy for him, I guess, but there are two other reasons, as well. He never got hysterical when I told him someone from the press had called or come around, and he never acted as if I were just a job—only that and nothing more. Do you want to know what I really think, Ruth? Although I am seven years older than the man I'm telling you about and I still look folded, stapled, and mutilated, I think Brandon Milheron may have fallen a little bit in love with me . . . or with the heroic Little Nell he sees in his mind's eye when he looks at me. I don't think it's a sex thing with him (not yet, anyway; at a hundred and eight pounds, I still look quite a bit like a plucked chicken hanging in a butcher shop window), and that's fine with me; if I never go to bed with another man, I will be absolutely delighted. Still, I'd be lying if I said I didn't like seeing that look in his eyes, the one that says I'm part of his agenda now—me, Jessie Angela Mahout Burlingame, as opposed to an inanimate lump his bosses probably think of as That Unfortunate Burlingame Business. I don't know if I come above the firm on Brandon's agenda, or below it, or right beside it, and I don't care. It is enough to know that I'm *on* it, and that I'm something more than a

Jessie paused here, tapping her left forefinger against her teeth and thinking carefully. She took a deep drag on her current cigarette, then went on.

than a charitable side-effect.

Brandon was right beside me during all the police interviews, with his little tape-recorder going. He politely but relentlessly pointed out to everyone present at every interview—including stenographers and nurses—that anyone who leaked the admittedly sensational details of the case would face all the nasty reprisals a large New England law-firm with an exceedingly tight ass could think up. Brandon must have been as convincing to them as he was to me, because no one in the know ever talked to the press.

The worst of the questioning came during the three days I spent in "guarded condition" at Northern Cumberland—mostly sucking up blood, water, and electrolytes through plastic tubes. The police reports that came out of those sessions were so strange they actually looked believable when they showed up in the papers, like those weird man-bites-dog stories they run from time to time. Only this one was actually a dog-bites-man story . . . and woman as well, in this version. Want to hear what's going into the record books? Okay, here it is:

We decided to spend the day at our summer home in western Maine. Following a sexual interlude that was two parts tussle and one part sex, we showered together. Gerald left the shower while I was washing my hair. He was complaining of gas pains, probably from the sub sandwiches we ate on our way from Portland, and asked if there were any Rolaids or Tums in the house. I said I didn't know, but they'd be on top of the bureau or on the bed-shelf if there were. Three or four minutes later, while I was rinsing my hair, I heard Gerald cry out. This cry apparently signalled the onset of a massive coronary. It was followed by a heavy thump—the sound of a body striking the floor. I jumped out of the shower, and when I ran into the bedroom, my feet went out from under me. I hit my head on the side of the bureau as I went down and knocked myself out.

According to this version, which was put together by Mr. Milheron and Mrs. Burlingame—and endorsed enthusiastically by the police, I might add—I returned to partial consciousness several times, but each time I did, I passed out again. When I came to the last time, the dog had gotten tired of Gerald and was noshing on me. I got up on the bed (according to our story, Gerald and I found it where it was—probably moved there by the guys who came in to wax the floor—and we were so hot to trot we didn't bother to move it back where it belonged) and drove the dog off by throwing Gerald's water-glass and fraternity ashtray at it. Then I passed out again and spent the next few hours unconscious and bleeding all over the bed. Later on I woke up again, got to the car, and finally drove to safety . . . after one final bout of unconsciousness, that is. That was when I ran into the tree beside the road.

I only asked once how Brandon got the police to go along with this piece of nonsense. He said, "It's a State Police investigation now, Jessie, and we—by which I mean the firm—have lots of friends in the S.P. I'm calling in every favor I have to, but in truth I haven't had to call in that many. Cops are human beings, too, you know. These guys had a pretty good idea of what really happened as soon as they saw the cuffs hanging from the bedposts. It's not the first time they've seen handcuffs after someone popped his carburetor, believe me. There wasn't a single one of those cops—state *or* local—who wanted to see you and your husband turned into a dirty joke as a result of something that was really no more than a grotesque accident."

At first I didn't say anything even to Brandon about the man I thought I saw, or the footprint, or the pearl earring, or anything else. I was waiting, you see—looking for straws in the wind, I suppose.

Jessie looked at that last, shook her head, and began to type again.

No, that's bullshit. I was waiting for some cop to come in with a little plastic evidence bag and hand it to me and ask me to identify the rings—finger-rings, not earrings—inside. "We're pretty sure they must be yours," he'd say, "because they have your initials and those of your husband engraved inside them, and also because we found them on the floor of your husband's study."

I kept waiting for that because when they showed me my rings, I'd know for sure that Little Nell's Midnight Caller had just been a figment of Little Nell's imagination. I waited and waited, but it didn't happen. Finally, just before the first operation on my hand, I told Brandon about how I'd had the idea that I might not have been alone in the house, at least not all the time. I told him it could have just been my imagination, that was certainly a possibility, but it had seemed very real at the time. I didn't say anything about my own missing rings, but I talked a lot about the footprint and the pearl earring. About the earring I think it would be fair to say I *babbled,* and I think I know why: it had to stand for everything I didn't dare to talk about, even to Brandon. Do you understand? And all the time I was telling him, I kept saying stuff like "Then I *thought* I saw" and "I felt *almost sure* that." I had to tell him, had to tell someone, because the fear was eating me from the inside out like acid, but I tried to show him in every way I could that I wasn't mistaking subjective feelings for objective reality. Above all I tried to keep him from seeing how scared I *still* was. Because I didn't want him to think I was crazy. I didn't care if he thought I was a little hysterical; that was a price I was willing to pay to keep from getting stuck with another nasty secret like the one about what my father did to me on the day of the eclipse, but I desperately didn't want him to think I was crazy. I didn't want him to even *speculate* on the possibility.

Brandon took my hand and patted it and told me he could understand such an idea; he said that under the circumstances, it was probably tame. Then he added that the important thing to remember was that it was no more real than the shower Gerald and I took after our athletic, bump-and-bruise romp on the bed. The police had gone over the house, and if there had been someone else in there, they almost certainly would have found evidence of him. The fact that the house had undergone a big end-of-summer cleaning not long before made that even more likely.

"Maybe they *did* find evidence of him," I said. "Maybe some cop stuck that earring in his own pocket."

"There are plenty of light-fingered cops in the world, granted," he said, "but it's hard for me to believe that even a stupid one would risk his career for an orphan earring. It would be easier for me to believe that this guy you thought was in the house with you came back later and got it himself."

"Yes!" I said. "That's possible, isn't it?"

He started to shake his head, then shrugged instead. "Anything is possible, and that includes either cupidity or human error on the part of the investigating officers, but . . ." He paused, then took my left hand and gave me what I think of as Brandon's Dutch Uncle expression. "A lot of your thinking is based on the idea that those investigating officers gave the house a lick and a promise and called it good. That wasn't the case. If there had been a third party in there, it's odds-on that the police would have found evidence of him. And if they'd found evidence of a third party, I'd know."

"Why?" I asked.

"Because something like that could put you in a very nasty situation— the kind of situation where the police stop being nice guys and start reading you the *Miranda* warning."

"I don't understand what you're talking about," I said, but I was beginning to, Ruth; yes indeed. Gerald was something of an insurance freak, and I had been informed by agents of three different carriers that I was going to spend my period of official mourning—and quite a few years after—in comfortable circumstances.

"John Harrelson in Augusta did a very thorough, very careful autopsy on your husband," Brandon said. "According to his report, Gerald died of what MEs call 'a pure heart attack,' meaning one uncomplicated by food poisoning, undue exertion, or gross physical trauma." He clearly meant to go on—he was in what I've come to think of as Brandon's Teaching Mode— but he saw something on my face that stopped him. "Jessie? What's wrong?"

"Nothing," I said.

"Yes there is—you look terrible. Is it a cramp?"

I finally managed to persuade him that I was okay, and by then I almost was. I imagine you know what I was thinking about, Ruth, since I mentioned it earlier in this letter: the double kick I gave Gerald when he wouldn't do the right thing and let me up. One in the gut, one smack in the family jewels. I was thinking how lucky it was I'd said the sex was rough—it explained the bruises. I have an idea they were light, anyway, because the heart attack came right on the heels of the kicks, and the heart attack stopped the bruising process almost before it could get started.

That leads to another question, of course—did I cause the heart attack by kicking him? None of the medical books I've looked at answer that question conclusively, but let's get real: I probably helped him along. Still, I refuse to take the whole rap. He was overweight, he drank too much, and he smoked like a chimney. The heart attack was coming; if it hadn't been that day, it would have been the next week or the next month. The devil only plays his fiddle for you so long, Ruth. I believe that. If you don't, I cordially invite you to fold it small and stuff it where the sun doesn't shine. I happen to think I've earned the right to believe what I want to believe, at least in this matter. *Especially* in this matter.

"If I looked like I swallowed a doorknob," I told Brandon, "it's because I'm trying to get used to the idea that someone thinks I killed Gerald to collect his life insurance."

He shook his head some more, looking at me earnestly all the while. "They don't think that at all. Harrelson says Gerald had a heart attack which may have been precipitated by sexual excitement, and the State Police accept that because John Harrelson is about the best in the business. At most there may be a few cynics who think you played Salome and led him on deliberately."

"Do you?" I asked.

I thought I might shock him with such directness, and part of me was curious as to what a shocked Brandon Milheron might look like, but I should have known better. He only smiled. "Do I think you'd have imagination enough to see a chance of blowing Gerald's thermostat but not enough to see you might end up dying in handcuffs yourself as a result? No. For whatever it's worth, Jess, I think it went down just the way you told me it did. Can I be honest?"

"I wouldn't want you to be anything else," I told him.

"All right. I worked with Gerald, and I got along with him, but there were plenty of people in the firm who didn't. He was the world's biggest control-freak. It doesn't surprise me a bit that the idea of having sex with a woman handcuffed to the bed lit up all his dials."

I took a quick look at him when he said that. It was night, only the light at the head of my bed was on, and he was sitting in shadow from the shoulders up, but I'm pretty sure that Brandon Milheron, Young Legal Shark About Town, was blushing.

"If I've offended you, I'm sorry," he said, sounding unexpectedly awkward.

I almost laughed. It would have been unkind, but just then he sounded about eighteen years old and fresh out of prep school. "You haven't offended me, Brandon," I said.

"Good. That takes care of me. But it's still the job of the police to at least entertain the possibility of foul play—to consider the idea that you could have gone a step further than just hoping your husband might have what is known in the trade as 'a horny coronary.' "

"I didn't have the slightest idea he had a heart problem!" I said. "Apparently the insurance companies didn't, either. If they'd known, they never would have written those policies, would they?"

"Insurance companies will insure anyone who's willing to pay enough freight," he said, "and Gerald's insurance agents didn't see him chain-smoking and belting back the booze. You did. All protests aside, you must have known he was a heart attack looking for a place to happen. The cops know it, too. So they say, 'Suppose she invited a friend down to the lake house and didn't tell her husband? And suppose this friend just happened to jump out of the closet and yell Booga-Booga at exactly the right time for her and exactly the wrong one for her old man?' If the cops had any evidence that something like that might have happened, you'd be in deep shit, Jessie. Because under certain select circumstances, a hearty cry of Booga-Booga can be seen as an act of first-degree murder. The fact that you spent going on two days in handcuffs and had to half-skin yourself to get free militates strongly against the idea of an accomplice, but in another way, the very fact of the handcuffs makes an accomplice seem plausible to . . . well, to a certain type of police mind, let us say."

I stared at him, fascinated. I felt like a woman who's just realized she has been square-dancing on the edge of an abyss. Up until then, looking at the shadowy planes and curves of Brandon's face beyond the circle of light thrown by the bedlamp, the idea of the police thinking I might have murdered Gerald had only crossed my mind a couple of times, as a kind of grisly joke. Thank God I never joked about it with the cops, Ruth!

Brandon said, "Do you understand why it might be wiser not to mention this idea of an intruder in the house?"

"Yes," I said. "Better to let sleeping dogs lie, right?"

As soon as I said it, I had an image of that goddamned mutt dragging Gerald across the floor by his upper arm—I could see the flap of skin that had come free and was lying across the dog's snout. They ran the poor, damned thing down a couple of days later, by the way—it had made a little den for itself under the Laglans' boathouse, about half a mile up the shore. It had taken a pretty good piece of Gerald there, so it must have come back at least one more time after I scared it away with the Mercedes's lights and horn. They shot it. It was wearing a bronze tag—not a regulation dog-tag so that Animal Control could trace the owner and give him hell, more's the pity—with the name Prince on it. Prince, can you imagine? When Constable Teagarden came and told me they'd killed it, I was glad. I didn't blame it for what it did—it wasn't in much better shape than I was, Ruth—but I was glad then and I'm still glad.

All that's off the subject, though—I was telling you about the conversation I had with Brandon after I'd told him there might have been a stranger in the house. He agreed, and most emphatically, that it would be better to let sleeping dogs lie. I guessed I could live with that—it was a great relief just to have told one person—but I still wasn't quite ready to let it go.

"The convincer was the phone," I told him. "When I got out of the handcuffs and tried it, it was as dead as Abe Lincoln. As soon as I realized that, I became sure I was right—there *had* been a guy, and at some point he'd cut the telephone line coming in from the road. That's what really got my ass out the door and into the Mercedes. You don't know what scared is,

Brandon, until you suddenly realize you might be out in the middle of the woods with an uninvited houseguest."

He was smiling, but it was a less winning smile that time, I'm afraid. It was the kind of smile men always seem to get on their faces when they're thinking about how silly women are, and how it should really be against the law to let them out without keepers. "You came to the conclusion that the line was cut after checking one phone—the one in the bedroom—and finding it dead. Right?"

That wasn't exactly what happened and it wasn't exactly what I'd thought, but I nodded—partly because it seemed easier, but mostly because it doesn't do much good to talk to a man when he gets that particular expression on his face. It's the one that says, "Women! Can't live with 'em, can't shoot 'em!" Unless you've changed completely, Ruth, I'm sure you know the one I'm talking about, and I'm sure you'll understand when I say that all I really wanted at that point was for the entire conversation to be over.

"It was unplugged, that's all," Brandon said. By then he was sounding like Mister Rogers, explaining that sometimes it surely *does* seem like there's a monster under the bed, by golly, but there's really not. "Gerald pulled the t-connector out of the wall. He probably didn't want his afternoon off—not to mention his little bondage fantasy—interrupted by calls from the office. He'd also pulled the plug on the one in the front hall, but the one in the kitchen was plugged in and working just fine. I have all this from the police reports."

The light dawned, then, Ruth. I suddenly understood that all of them—all the men investigating what had happened out at the lake—had made certain assumptions about how I'd handled the situation and why I'd done the things I'd done. Most of them worked in my favor, and that certainly simplified things, but there was still something both infuriating and a little spooky in the realization that they drew most of their conclusions not from what I'd said or from any evidence they'd found in the house, but only from the fact that I'm a woman, and women can be expected to behave in certain predictable ways.

When you look at it that way, there's no difference at all between Brandon Milheron in his natty three-piece suits and old Constable Teagarden in his satchel-seat bluejeans and red firehouse suspenders. Men still think the same things about us they have always thought, Ruth—I'm sure of it. A lot of them have learned to say the right things at the right times, but as my mother used to say, "Even a cannibal can learn to recite the Apostles' Creed."

And do you know what? Brandon Milheron *admires* me, and he admires the way I handled myself after Gerald dropped dead. Yes he does. I have seen it on his face time after time, and if he drops by this evening, as he usually does, I am confident I will see it there again. Brandon thinks I did a damned good job, a damned *brave* job . . . for a woman. In fact, I think that by the time we had our first conversation about my hypothetical visitor, he had sort of decided I'd behaved the way he would have in a similar situation . . . if, that is, he'd had to deal with a high fever at the same time he was trying to deal with everything else. I have an idea that's how most men believe most women think: like lawyers with malaria. It would certainly explain a lot of their behavior, wouldn't it?

I'm talking about condescension—a man-versus-woman thing—but I'm also talking about something a hell of a lot bigger and a hell of a lot more frightening, as well. He didn't understand, you see, and that has nothing to do with any differences between the sexes; that's the curse of being human, and the surest proof that all of us are really alone. Terrible things happened in that house, Ruth, I didn't know just *how* terrible until later, *and he didn't understand that.* I told him the things I did in order to keep that terror from eating me alive, and he nodded and he smiled and he sympathized, and I think it ended up doing me some good, but he was the best of them, and he never got within shouting distance of the truth . . . of how the terror just seemed to keep on growing until it became this big black haunted house inside my head. It's still there, too, standing with its door open, inviting me to come back inside any time I want, and I never *do* want to go back, but sometimes I find myself going back, anyway, and the minute I step inside, the door slams shut behind me and locks itself.

Well, never mind. I suppose it should have relieved me to know my intuition about the telephone lines was wrong, but it didn't. Because there was a part of my mind which believed—and believes still—that the bedroom telephone wouldn't have worked even if I *had* crawled behind that chair and plugged it in again, that maybe the one in the kitchen was working later but it sure as hell wasn't working then, that it was get the hell away from the house in the Mercedes or die at the hands of that creature.

Brandon leaned forward until the light at the head of the bed shone full on his face and he said, "There was no man in the house, Jessie, and the best thing you can do with the idea is let it drop."

I almost told him about my missing rings then, but I was tired and in a lot of pain and in the end I didn't. I lay awake for a long time after he left—not even a pain-pill would put me to sleep that night. I thought about the skin-graft operation that was coming up the next day, but probably not as much as you might think. Mostly I was thinking about my rings, and the footprint nobody saw but me, and whether or not he—*it*—might have come back to put things right. And what I decided, just before I finally dropped off, was that there had never been a footprint or a pearl earring. That some cop had spotted my rings lying on the study floor beside the bookcase and just took them. *They're probably in the window of some Lewiston hockshop right now,* I thought. Maybe the idea should have made me angry, but it didn't. It made me feel the way I did when I woke up behind the wheel of the Mercedes that morning—filled with an incredible sense of peace and well-being. No stranger; no stranger; no stranger anywhere. Just a cop with light fingers taking one quick look over his shoulder to make sure the coast is clear and then whoop, zoop, into the pocket. As for the rings themselves, I didn't care what had happened to them then and I don't now. I've come more and more to believe in these last few months that the only reason a man sticks a ring on your finger is because the law no longer allows him to put one through your nose. Never mind, though; the morning has become the afternoon, the afternoon is moving briskly along, and this is not the time to discuss women's issues. This is the time to talk about Raymond Andrew Joubert.

Jessie sat back in her chair and lit another cigarette, absently aware that the tip of her tongue was stinging from tobacco overload, that her head ached, and that her kidneys were protesting this marathon session in front of the Mac. Protesting *vigorously.* The house was deathly silent—the sort of silence that could only mean that tough little Megan Landis had taken herself off to the supermarket and the dry-cleaner's. Jessie was amazed that Meggie had left without making at least one more effort to separate her from the computer screen. Then she guessed the housekeeper had known it would be a wasted effort. *Best to let her get it out of her system, whatever it is,* Meggie would have thought. And it was only a job to her, after all. This last thought sent a little pang through Jessie's heart.

A board creaked upstairs. Jessie's cigarette stopped an inch shy of her lips. *He's back!* Goody shrieked. *Oh, Jessie, he's back!*

Except he wasn't. Her eyes drifted to the narrow face looking up at her from the clusters of newsprint dots and she thought: *I know exactly where you are, you whoredog. Don't I?*

She did, but part of her mind went on insisting it was him just the same—no, not him, *it*, the space cowboy, the specter of love, back again for a return engagement. It had only been waiting for the house to be empty, and if she picked up the phone on the corner of the desk, she would find it stone dead, just as all the phones in the house by the lake had been stone dead that night.

Your friend Brandon can smile all he wants, but we know the truth, don't we, Jessie?

She suddenly shot out her good hand, snatched the telephone handset from the cradle, and brought it to her ear. Heard the reassuring buzz of the dial-tone. Put it back again. An odd, sunless smile played about the corners of her mouth.

Yes, I know exactly where you are, motherfucker. Whatever Goody and the rest of the ladies inside my head may think, Punkin and I know you're wearing an orange jumpsuit and sitting in a County Jail cell— the one at the far end of the old wing, Brandon said, so the other inmates can't get to you and fuck you up before the state hauls you in front of a jury of your peers . . . if a thing like you has any peers. We may not be entirely free of you yet, but we will be. I promise you we will be.

Her eyes drifted back to the VDT, and although the vague sleepiness brought on by the combination of the pill and the sandwich had long since dissipated, she felt a bone-deep weariness and a complete lack of belief in her ability to finish what she had started.

This is the time to talk about Raymond Andrew Joubert, she had written, but was it? Could she? She was so *tired*. Of course she was; she had been pushing that goddamned cursor across the VDT screen almost all day. Pushing the envelope, they called it, and if you pushed the envelope long enough and hard enough, you tore it wide open. Maybe it would be best to just go upstairs and take a nap. Better late than never, and all that shit. She could file this to memory, retrieve it tomorrow morning, go back to work on it then—

Punkin's voice stopped her. This voice came only infrequently now, and Jessie listened very carefully to it when it did.

If you decide to stop now, Jessie, don't bother to file the document. Just delete it. We both know you'll never have the guts to face Joubert again —not the way a person has to face a thing she's writing about. Sometimes it takes heart to write about a thing, doesn't it? To let that thing out of the room way in the back of your mind and put it up there on the screen.

"Yes," she murmured. "A yard of heart. Maybe more."

She dragged at her cigarette, then snuffed it out half-smoked. She riffled through the clippings a final time and looked out the window at the slope of Eastern Prom. The snow had long since stopped and the sun was shining brightly, although it wouldn't be for much longer; February days in Maine are thankless, miserly things.

"What do you say, Punkin?" Jessie asked the empty room. She spoke in the haughty Elizabeth Taylor voice she had favored as a child, the one that had driven her mother completely bonkers. "Shall we carry on, my deah?"

There was no answer, but Jessie didn't need one. She leaned forward in her chair and set the cursor in motion once more. She didn't stop again for a long time, not even to light a cigarette.

37

This is the time to talk about Raymond Andrew Joubert. It won't be easy, but I'm going to do my best. So pour yourself another cup of coffee, dear, and if you've got a bottle of brandy handy, you may want to doctor it up a bit. Here comes Part Three.

I have all the newspaper clippings beside me on the desk, but the articles and news items don't tell all I know, let alone all there *is* to know—I doubt if anyone has the slightest idea of all the things Joubert did (including Joubert himself, I imagine), and that's probably a blessing. The stuff the papers could only hint at and the stuff that didn't make them at all is real nightmare-fodder, and I wouldn't *want* to know all of it. Most of the stuff that isn't in the papers came to me during the last week courtesy of a strangely quiet, strangely chastened Brandon Milheron. I'd asked him to come over as soon as the connections between Joubert's story and my own had become too obvious to ignore.

"You think this was the guy, don't you?" he asked. "The one who was in the house with you?"

"Brandon," I said, "I *know* it's the guy."

He sighed, looked down at his hands for a minute, then looked up at me again—we were in this very room, it was nine o'clock in the morning, and there were no shadows to hide his face that time. "I owe you an apology," he said. "I didn't believe you then—"

"I know," I said, as kindly as I could.

"—but I do now. Dear God. How much do you want to know, Jess?"

I took a deep breath and said, "Everything you can find out."

He wanted to know why. "I mean, if you say it's your business and I should butt out, I guess I'll have to accept that, but you're asking me to re-open a matter the firm considers closed. If someone who knows I was watching out for you last fall notices me sniffing around Joubert this winter, it's not impossible that—"

"That you could get in trouble," I said. It was something I hadn't considered.

"Yes," he said, "but I'm not terribly concerned about that—I'm a big boy, and I can take care of myself . . . at least I think I can. I'm a lot more concerned about you, Jess. You could wind up on the front page again, after all our work to get you off it as quickly and as painlessly as possible. Even that's not the major thing—it's miles from the major thing. This is the nastiest criminal case to break in northern New England since World War II. I mean some of this stuff is so gruesome it's radioactive, and you shouldn't plink yourself down in the fallout zone without a damned good reason." He laughed, a little nervously. "Hell, I shouldn't plink myself down there without a damned good reason."

I got up, walked across to him, and took one of his hands with my left hand. "I couldn't explain in a million years why," I said, "but I think I can tell you *what*—will that do, at least for a start?"

He folded his hand gently over mine and nodded his head.

"There are three things," I said. "First, I need to know he's real. Second, I need to know the things he did are real. Third, I need to know I'll never wake up again with him standing in my bedroom."

That brought it all back, Ruth, and I began to cry. There was nothing tricky or calculating about those tears; they just came. Nothing I could have done would have stopped them.

"Please help me, Brandon," I said. "Every time I turn off the light, he's standing across the room from me in the dark, and I'm afraid that unless I can turn a spotlight on him, that's going to go on forever. There isn't anybody else I can ask, and I have to know. Please help me."

He let go of my hand, produced a handkerchief from somewhere inside that day's screamingly neat lawyer's suit, and wiped my face with it. He did it as gently as my Mom used to when I came into the kitchen bawling my head off because I'd skinned my knee—that was back in the early years, before I turned into the family's squeaky wheel, you understand.

"All right," he said at last. "I'll find out everything I can, and I'll pass it all on to you . . . unless and until you tell me to stop, that is. But I have a feeling you better fasten your seatbelt."

He found out quite a lot, and now I'm going to pass it on to you, Ruth, but fair warning: he was right about the seatbelt. If you decide to skip some of the next few pages, I'll understand. I wish I could skip writing them, but I have an idea that's also part of the therapy. The final part, I hope.

This section of the story—what I suppose I could call Brandon's Tale—starts back in 1984 or 1985. That was when cases of graveyard vandalism started popping up in the Lakes District of western Maine. There were similar cases reported in half a dozen small towns across the state line and into New Hampshire. Stuff like tombstone-tipping, spray-paint graffiti, and stealing commemorative flags is pretty common stuff out in the willywags, and of course there's always a bunch of smashed pumpkins to swamp out of the local boneyard on November 1st, but these crimes went a lot further than pranks or petty theft. *Desecration* was the word Brandon used when he brought me his first report late last week, and that word had started showing up on most of the police crime-report forms by 1988.

The crimes themselves seemed abnormal to the people who discovered them and to those who investigated them, but the *modus operandi* was sane enough; carefully organized and focused. Someone—possibly two or three someones, but more likely a single person—was breaking into the crypts and mausoleums of small-town cemeteries with the efficiency of a good burglar breaking into a house or store. He was apparently arriving at these jobs equipped with drills, a bolt-cutter, heavy-duty hacksaws, and probably a winch—Brandon says a lot of four-wheel-drive vehicles come equipped with them these days.

The breaks were always aimed at the crypts and mausoleums, never at individual graves, and almost all of them came in winter, when the ground is too hard to dig in and the bodies have to be stored until the deep frost lets go. Once the perpetrator gained entry, he used the bolt-cutter and power drill to open the coffins. He systematically stripped the corpses of any jewelry they might have been wearing when they were interred; he used pliers to pull gold teeth and teeth with gold fillings.

Those acts are despicable, but at least they're understandable. Robbery was only where this guy got started, though. He gouged out eyes, tore off ears, cut dead throats. In February of 1989, two corpses in the Chilton Remembrance Cemetery were found without noses—he apparently knocked them off with a hammer and a chisel. The officer who caught that one told Brandon, "It would have been easy—it was like a deep-freeze in there, and they probably broke off like Popsicles. The real question is what does a guy do with two frozen noses once he has them? Does he put 'em on his keychain? Maybe sprinkle 'em with nacho cheese and then zap 'em in the microwave? What?"

Almost all the desecrated corpses were found minus feet and hands, sometimes also arms and legs, and in several cases the man doing this also took heads and sex-organs. Forensic evidence suggests he used an axe and a butcher-knife for the gross work and a variety of scalpels for the finer stuff. He wasn't bad, either. "A talented amateur," one of the Chamberlain County deputies told Brandon. "I wouldn't want him working on my gall-bladder, but I guess I'd trust him to take a mole off my arm . . . if he was full of Halcion or Prozac, that is."

In a few cases he opened up the bodies and/or skull cases and filled them with animal excrement. What the police saw more frequently were cases of sexual desecration. He was an equal-opportunity kind of guy when it came to stealing gold teeth, jewelry, and limbs, but when it came to taking sexual equipment—and having sex with the dead—he stuck strictly to the gentlemen.

This may have been extremely lucky for me.

I learned a lot about the way rural police departments work during the month or so following my escape from our house by the lake, but that's nothing compared with what I've learned in the last week or so. One of the most surprising things is how discreet and tactful small-town cops can be. I guess when you know everybody in the area you patrol by their first names, and are related to a good many of them, discretion becomes almost as natural as breathing.

The way they handled my case is one example of this strange, sophisticated discretion; the way they handled Joubert's is another. The investigation went on for seven years, remember, and a lot of people were in on it before it ended—two State Police departments, four county sheriffs, thirty-one deputies, and God knows how many local cops and constables. It was right there at the front of their open files, and by 1989 they even had a name for him—Rudolph, as in Valentino. They talked about Rudolph when they were in District Court, waiting to testify on their other cases, they compared notes on Rudolph at law-enforcement seminars in Augusta and Derry and Waterville, they discussed him on their coffee-breaks. "And we took him home," one of the cops told Brandon—the same guy who told him about the noses, as a matter of fact. "You bet we did. Guys like us always take guys like Rudolph home. You catch up on the latest details at backyard barbecues, maybe kick it around with a buddy from another department while you're watching your kids play Little League ball. Because you never know when you're going to put something together in a new way and hit the jackpot."

But here's the really amazing part (and you're probably way ahead of me . . . if you're not in the bathroom tossing your cookies, that is): for all those years all those cops knew they had a real live monster—a ghoul, in fact—running around the western part of the state, *and the story never surfaced in the press until Joubert was caught!* In a way I find that weird and a little spooky, but in a much larger way I find it wonderful. I guess the law-enforcement battle isn't going so well in a lot of the big cities, but out here in East Overshoe, whatever they're doing still seems to work just fine.

Of course you could argue that there's plenty of room for improvement when it takes seven years to catch a nut like Joubert, but Brandon clarified that for me in a hurry. He explained that the perp (they really do use that word) was operating exclusively in one-horse towns where budget shortfalls have forced the cops to deal only with the most serious and immediate problems . . . which means crimes against the living rather than against the dead. The cops say there are at least two hot-car rings and four chop-shops operating in the western half of the state, and those are only the ones they know about. Then there are the murderers, the wife-beaters, the robbers, the speeders, and the drunks. Above all, there's the old dope-ola. It gets bought, it gets sold, it gets grown, and people keep hurting or killing each other over it. According to Brandon, the Police Chief over in Norway won't even use the word *cocaine* anymore—he calls it Powdered Shithead, and in his written reports he calls it Powdered S******d. I got the point he was trying to make. When you're a small-town cop trying to ride herd on the whole freakshow in a four-year-old Plymouth cruiser that feels like it's going to fall apart every time you push it over seventy, your job gets prioritized in a hurry, and a guy who likes to play with dead people is a long way from the top of the list.

I listened to all this carefully, and I agreed, but not all the way. "Some of it feels true, but some of it feels a little self-serving," I said. "I mean, the stuff Joubert was doing . . . well, it went a little further than just 'playing with dead people,' didn't it? Or am I wrong?"

"You're not wrong at all," he said.

What neither of us wanted to come right out and say was that for seven years this aberrant soul had gone flitting from town to town getting blowjobs from the dead, and to me putting a stop to that seemed quite a bit more important than nabbing teenage girls who've been shoplifting cosmetics at the local drugstore or finding out who's been growing goofy-weed in the woodlot behind the Baptist church.

But the important thing is that no one forgot him, and everyone kept comparing notes. A perp like Rudolph makes cops uneasy for all kinds of reasons, but the major one is that a guy crazy enough to do things like that to dead people might be crazy enough to try doing them to ones that are still alive . . . not that you'd live very long after Rudolph decided to split your head open with his trusty axe. The police were also troubled by the missing limbs—what were those for? Brandon says an uncredited memo saying "Maybe Rudolph the Lover is really Hannibal the Cannibal" circulated briefly in the Oxford County Sheriff's Office. It was destroyed not because the idea was regarded as a sick joke—it wasn't—but because the Sheriff was afraid it might leak to the press.

Whenever one of the local law-enforcement agencies could afford the men and the time, they'd stake out some boneyard or other. There are a lot of them in western Maine, and I guess it had almost become a kind of hobby to some of these guys by the time the case finally broke. The theory was just that if you keep shooting the dice long enough, you're bound to roll your point sooner or later. And that, essentially, is what finally happened.

Early last week—actually about ten days ago now—Castle County Sheriff Norris Ridgewick and one of his deputies were parked in the doorway of an abandoned barn close to Homeland Cemetery. This is on a secondary road that runs by the back gate. It was two o'clock in the morning and they were just getting ready to pack it in for the night when the deputy, John LaPointe, heard a motor. They never saw the van until it was actually pulling up to the gate because it was a snowy night and the guy's headlights weren't on. Deputy LaPointe wanted to take the guy as soon as they saw him get out of the van and go to work on the wrought-iron cemetery gate with a spreader, but the Sheriff restrained him. "Ridgewick's a funny-looking duck," Brandon said, "but he knows the value of a good bust. He never loses sight of the courtroom in the heat of the moment. He learned from Alan Pangborn, the guy who had the job before him, and that means he learned from the best."

Ten minutes after the van went in through the gate, Ridgewick and LaPointe followed with their own headlights out and their unit just barely creeping along through the snow. They followed the van's tracks until they were pretty sure where the guy was going—the town crypt set into the side of the hill. Both of them were thinking Rudolph, but neither one of them said so out loud. LaPointe said it would have been like jinxing a guy who's throwing a no-hitter.

Ridgewick told his deputy to stop the cruiser just around the side of the hill from the crypt—said he wanted to give the guy all the rope he needed to hang himself. As it turned out, Rudolph ended up with enough to hang himself from the moon. When Ridgewick and LaPointe finally moved in with their guns drawn and their flashlights on, they caught Raymond Andrew Joubert half in and half out of an opened coffin. He had his axe in one hand, his cock in the other, and LaPointe said he looked ready to do business with either one.

I guess Joubert scared the hell out of them both when they first saw him in their lights, and I'm not a bit surprised—although I flatter myself that I can imagine better than most what it must have been like, coming on a creature like him in a cemetery crypt at two in the morning. All other circumstances aside, Joubert suffers from acromegaly, a progressive enlargement of the hands, feet, and face that happens when the pituitary gland goes into warp-drive. It's what caused his forehead to bulge the way it does, and his lips to pooch out. He also has abnormally long arms; they dangle all the way down to his knees.

There was a big fire in Castle Rock about a year ago—it burned most of the downtown—and these days the Sheriff jugs most serious offenders in Chamberlain or Norway, but neither Sheriff Ridgewick nor Deputy LaPointe wanted to make the trip over snowy roads at three in the morning, so they took him back to the renovated shed they're using as a cop-shop these days.

"They *claimed* it was the late hour and the snowy roads," Brandon said, "but I have an idea there was a little more to it than that. I don't think Sheriff Ridgewick wanted to turn over the *piñata* to anyone else until he'd taken at least one good crack at it himself. Anyway, Joubert was no trouble—he sat in the back of the cruiser, chipper as a chickadee, looking like something that had escaped from an episode of *Tales from the Crypt* and—both of them swear this is true—singing 'Happy Together,' that old Turtles tune.

"Ridgewick radioed ahead for a couple of temp deputies to meet them. He made sure Joubert was locked up tight and the deputies were armed with shotguns and plenty of fresh coffee before he and LaPointe left again. They drove back to Homeland for the van. Ridgewick put on gloves, sat on one of those green plastic Hefty bags the cops like to call 'evidence blankets' when they use them on a case, and ran the vehicle back to town. He drove with all the windows open and said the van still stank like a butcher's shop after a six-day power failure."

Ridgewick got his first good look into the back of the van when he got it under the arc-lights of the town garage. There were several rotting limbs in the storage compartments running along the sides. There was also a wicker box, much smaller than the one I saw, and a Craftsman tool-case full of burglar's tools. When Ridgewick opened the wicker box, he found six penises strung on a length of jute twine. He said he knew it for what it was at once: a necklace. Joubert later admitted that he often wore it when he went out on his graveyard expeditions, and stated his belief that if he'd been wearing it on his last trip, he never would have been caught. "It brung me a power of good luck," he said, and considering how long it took to catch him, Ruth, I think you'd have to say he had a point.

The worst thing, however, was the sandwich lying on the passenger seat. The thing poking out from between the two slices of Wonder Bread was pretty clearly a human tongue. It had been slathered with that bright yellow mustard kids like.

"Ridgewick managed to get out of the van before he threw up," Brandon said. "Good thing—the State Police would have torn him a new asshole if he'd puked on the evidence. On the other hand, I'd have wanted him removed from his job for psychological reasons if he *hadn't* thrown up."

They moved Joubert over to Chamberlain shortly after sunrise. While Ridgewick was turned around in the front seat of the cruiser, reading Joubert his rights through the mesh (it was the second or third time he'd done it— Ridgewick is apparently nothing if not methodical), Joubert interrupted to say he "might have done somefing bad to Daddy-Mummy, awful sorry." They had by that time established from documents in Joubert's wallet that he was living in Motton, a farming town just across the river from Chamberlain, and as soon as Joubert was safely locked up in his new quarters, Ridgewick informed officers from both Chamberlain and Motton what Joubert had told them.

On the way back to Castle Rock, LaPointe asked Ridgewick what he thought the cops headed for Joubert's house might find. Ridgewick said, "I don't know, but I hope they remembered to take their gas masks."

A version of what they found and the conclusions they drew came out in the papers over the following days, growing as it did, of course, but the State Police and the Maine Attorney General's Office had a pretty good picture of what had been going on in the farmhouse on Kingston Road by the time the sun went down on Joubert's first day behind bars. The couple Joubert called his "Daddy-Mummy"—actually his stepmother and her commonlaw husband—were dead, all right. They'd been dead for months, although Joubert continued to speak as if the "somefing bad" had happened only days or hours ago. He had scalped them both, and eaten most of "Daddy."

There were body-parts strewn all over the house, some rotting and maggoty in spite of the cold weather, others carefully cured and preserved. Most of the cured parts were male sex-organs. On a shelf by the cellar stairs, the police found about fifty Ball jars containing eyes, lips, fingers, toes, and testicles. Joubert was quite the home canner. The house was also filled— and I do mean filled—with stolen goods, mostly from summer camps and cottages. Joubert calls them "my things"—appliances, tools, gardening equipment, and enough lingerie to stock a Victoria's Secret boutique. He apparently liked to wear it.

The police are still trying to sort out the body-parts that came from Joubert's grave-robbing expeditions from those that came from his other activities. They believe he may have killed as many as a dozen people over the last five years, all hitchhiking drifters he picked up in his van. The total may go higher, Brandon says, but the forensic work is very slow. Joubert himself is no help, not because he won't talk but because he talks too much. According to Brandon, he's confessed to over three hundred crimes already, including the assassination of George Bush. He seems to believe Bush is actually Dana Carvey, the guy who plays The Church Lady on *Saturday Night Live.*

He's been in and out of various mental institutions since the age of fifteen, when he was arrested for engaging in unlawful sexual congress with his cousin. The cousin in question was two at the time. He was a victim of sex abuse himself, of course—his father, his stepfather, and his stepmother all apparently had a go at him. What is it they used to say? The family that plays together stays together?

He was sent to Gage Point—a sort of combination detox, halfway house, and mental institution for adolescents in Hancock County—on a charge of gross sexual abuse, and released as cured four years later, at the age of nineteen. This was in 1973. He spent the second half of 1975 and most of 1976 at AMHI, in Augusta. This was as a result of Joubert's Fun with Animals Period. I know I probably shouldn't be joking about these things, Ruth—you'll think I'm horrible—but in truth, I don't know what else to do. I sometimes feel that if I don't joke, I'll start to cry, and that if I start to cry I won't be able to stop. He was sticking cats in trash barrels and then blowing them to pieces with the big firecrackers they call "can-crushers," that's what he was doing . . . and every now and then, presumably when he needed a break in the old routine, he would nail a small dog to a tree.

In '79 he was sent away to Juniper Hill for raping and blinding a six-year-old boy. This time it was supposed to be for good, but when it comes to politics and state-run institutions—especially state-run *mental* institutions—I think it's fair to say that nothing is forever. He was released from Juniper Hill in 1984, once more adjudged "cured." Brandon feels—and so do I—that this second cure had more to do with cuts in the state's mental health budget than with any miracle of modern science or psychiatry. At any rate,

Joubert returned to Motton to live with his stepmother and her commonlaw, and the state forgot about him . . . except to issue him a driver's license, that is. He took a road-test and got a perfectly legal one—in some ways I find this the most amazing fact of all—and at some point in late 1984 or early 1985, he started using it to tour the local cemeteries.

He was a busy boy. In the wintertime he had his crypts and mausoleums; in the fall and the spring he broke into seasonal camps and homes all over western Maine, taking anything that struck his fancy—"my things," you know. He apparently had a great fondness for framed photographs. They found four trunks of them in the attic of the house on Kingston Road. Brandon says they are still counting, but that the total number will probably be over seven hundred.

It's impossible to say to what extent "Daddy-Mummy" participated in what was going on before Joubert did away with them. It must have been a lot, because Joubert hadn't made the slightest effort to hide what he was doing. As for the neighbors, their motto seems to be, "They paid their bills and kept to themselves. Wasn't nothing to us." It's got a gruesome kind of perfection to it, wouldn't you say? New England Gothic, by way of The Journal of Aberrant Psychiatry.

They found another, bigger, wicker box in the cellar. Brandon got Xeroxes of the police photos documenting this particular find, but he was hesitant about showing them to me at first. Well . . . that's actually a little too mild. It was the one and only place where he gave into the temptation all men seem to feel—you know the one I mean, to play John Wayne. "Come on, little lady, jest wait until we go by all them dead Injuns and keep lookin' off into the desert. I'll tell you when we're past."

"I'm willing to accept that Joubert was probably in the house with you," he said. "I'd have to be a goddam ostrich with my head stuck in the sand not to at least entertain the idea; everything fits. But answer me this: why are you going on with it, Jessie? What possible good can it do?"

I didn't know how to answer that, Ruth, but I did know one thing: there was nothing I could do that would make things any worse than they already were. So I hung tough until Brandon realized the little lady wasn't going to get back into the stagecoach until she had gotten her look at the dead Injuns. So I saw the pictures. The one I looked at the longest had a little sign saying STATE POLICE EXHIBIT 217 propped up in the corner. Looking at it was like looking at a videotape someone has somehow made of your worst nightmare. The photo showed a square wicker basket standing open so the photographer could shoot the contents, which happened to be heaps of bones with a wild collection of jewelry mixed in: some trumpery, some valuable, some stolen from summer homes and some doubtless stripped from the cold hands of corpses kept in small-town cold-storage.

I looked at that picture, so glaring and somehow bald, as police evidence photographs always are, and I was back in the lake house again—it happened right away, with no lag whatsoever. Not remembering, do you understand? I'm there, handcuffed and helpless, watching the shadows fly across his grinning face, hearing myself telling him that he is scaring me. And then he bends over to get the box, those feverish eyes never leaving my face, and I see him—I see *it*—reaching in with its twisted, misshapen hand, I see that hand starting to stir up the bones and jewels, and I hear the sounds they make, like dirty castanets.

And do you know what haunts me most of all? I thought it was my father, that was my *Daddy,* come back from the dead to do what he'd wanted to do before. "Go ahead," I told him. "Go ahead, but promise you'll unlock me and let me out afterward. Just promise me that."

I think I would have said the same if I'd known who he really was, Ruth. Think? *I know* I would have said the same. Do you understand? I would have let him put his cock—the cock he stuck down the rotting throats of dead men—into me, if only he would have promised me I didn't have to die the dog's death of muscle-cramps and convulsions that was waiting for me. If only he would have promised to SET ME FREE.

Jessie stopped for a moment, breathing so hard and fast she was almost panting. She looked at the words on the screen—the unbelievable, unspeakable admission on the screen—and felt a sudden strong urge to delete them. Not because she was ashamed for Ruth to read them; she was, but that wasn't it. What she didn't want to do was *deal* with them, and she supposed that if she didn't delete them, she would have to do just that. Words had a way of creating their own imperatives.

Not until they're out of your hands, they don't, Jessie thought, and reached out with the black-clad index finger of her right hand. She touched the DELETE button—stroked it, actually—and then drew back. It *was* the truth, wasn't it?

"Yes," she said in the same muttery voice she'd used so often during her hours of captivity—only at least now it wasn't Goody or the mind-Ruth she was talking to; she had gotten back to herself without having to go all the way around Robin Hood's barn to do it. That was maybe progress of a sort. "Yes, it's the truth, all right."

And nothing but, so help her God. She wouldn't use the DELETE button on the truth, no matter how nasty some people—including herself, as a matter of fact—might find that truth to be. She would let it stand. She might decide not to send the letter after all (didn't know if it was even fair to send it, to burden a woman she hadn't seen in years with this ration of pain and madness), but she would not delete it. Which meant it would be best to finish now, in a rush, before the last of her courage deserted her and the last of her strength ran out.

Jessie leaned forward and began typing again.

Brandon said, "There's one thing you're going to have to remember and accept, Jessie—there's no concrete proof. Yes, I know your rings are gone, but about them you could have been right the first time—some light-fingered cop could have taken them."

"What about Exhibit 217?" I asked. "The wicker box?"

He shrugged, and I had one of those sudden bursts of understanding the poets call epiphanies. He was holding onto the possibility that the wicker box had just been a coincidence. That wasn't easy, but it was easier than having to accept all the rest—most of all the fact that a monster like Joubert could actually touch the life of someone he knew and liked. What I saw in Brandon Milheron's face that day was perfectly simple: he was going to ignore a whole stack of circumstantial evidence and concentrate on the lack of concrete evidence. He was going to hold onto the idea that the whole thing was simply my imagination, seizing on the Joubert case to explain a particularly vivid hallucination I'd had while I was handcuffed to the bed.

And that insight was followed by a second one, an even clearer one: that

I could do it, too. I could come to believe I had been wrong . . . but if I succeeded in doing that, my life would be ruined. The voices would start to come back—not just yours or Punkin's or Nora Callighan's, but my mother's and my sister's and my brother's and kids I chummed with in high school and people I met for ten minutes in doctors' offices and God alone knows how many others. I think that most of them would be those scary UFO voices.

I couldn't bear that, Ruth, because in the two months after my hard time in the house by the lake, I remembered a lot of things I had spent a lot of years repressing. I think the most important of those memories came to the surface between the first operation on my hand and the second, when I was "on medication" (this is the technical hospital term for "stoned out of your gourd") almost all the time. The memory was this: in the two years or so between the day of the eclipse and the day of my brother Will's birthday party—the one where he goosed me during the croquet game—*I heard all those voices almost constantly.* Maybe Will's goosing me acted as some kind of rough, accidental therapy. I suppose it's possible; don't they say that our ancestors invented cooking after eating what forest fires left behind? Although if some serendipitous therapy took place that day, I have an idea that it didn't come with the goose but when I hauled off and pounded Will one in the mouth for doing it . . . and at this point none of that matters. What matters is that, following that day on the deck, I spent two years sharing space in my head with a kind of whispering choir, dozens of voices that passed judgment on my every word and action. Some were kind and supportive, but most were the voices of people who were afraid, people who were confused, people who thought Jessie was a worthless little baggage who deserved every bad thing that happened to her and who would have to pay double for every good thing. For two years I heard those voices, Ruth, and when they stopped, I forgot them. Not a little at a time, but all at once.

How could a thing like that happen? I don't know, and in a very real sense, I don't care. I might if the change had made things worse, I suppose, but it didn't—it made them immeasurably better. I spent the two years between the eclipse and the birthday party in a kind of fugue state, with my conscious mind shattered into a lot of squabbling fragments, and the real epiphany was this: if I let nice, kind Brandon Milheron have his way, I'd end up right back where I started—headed down Nuthouse Lane by way of Schizophrenia Boulevard. And this time there's no little brother around to administer crude shock therapy; this time I have to do it myself, just as I had to get out of Gerald's goddam handcuffs myself.

Brandon was watching me, trying to gauge the result of what he'd said. He must not have been able to, because he said it again, this time in a slightly different way. "You have to remember that, no matter how it looks, you could be wrong. And I think you have to resign yourself to the fact that you're never going to know, one way or the other, for sure."

"No, I don't."

He raised his eyebrows.

"There's still an excellent chance that I can find out for sure. And you're going to help me, Brandon."

He was starting to smile that less-than-pleasant smile again, the one I bet he doesn't even know is in his repertoire, the one that says you can't live with 'em and you can't shoot 'em. "Oh? And how am I going to do that?"

"By taking me to see Joubert," I said.

"Oh, no," he said. "That's the one thing I absolutely will not—can not—do, Jessie."

I'll spare you the hour of round-and-round which followed, a conversation that degenerated at one point to such intellectually profound statements as "You're crazy, Jess" and "Quit trying to run my life, Brandon." I thought of waving the cudgel of the press in front of him—it was the one thing I was almost sure would make him cave in—but in the end, I didn't have to. All I had to do was cry. In a way it makes me feel unbelievably sleazy to write that, but in another way it does not; in another way I recognize it as just another symptom of what's wrong between the fellers and the girls in this particular square-dance. He didn't entirely believe I was serious until I started to cry, you see.

To make a long story at least a little shorter, he got on the telephone, made four or five quick calls, and then came back with the news that Joubert was going to be arraigned the following day in Cumberland County District Court on a number of subsidiary charges—mostly theft. He said that if I was really serious—and if I had a hat with a veil—he'd take me. I agreed at once, and although Brandon's face said he believed he was making one of the biggest mistakes of his life, he stuck by his word.

Jessie paused again, and when she began to type once more she did so slowly, looking through the screen to yesterday, when last night's six inches of snow had still been just a smooth white threat in the sky. She saw blue flashers on the road ahead, felt Brandon's blue Beamer slowing down.

We got to the hearing late because there was an overturned trailer truck on I-295—that's the city bypass. Brandon didn't say so, but I know he was hoping we'd get there too late, that Joubert would already have been taken back to his cell at the end of the County Jail's maximum-security wing, but the guard at the courthouse door said the hearing was still going on, although finishing up. As Brandon opened the door for me, he leaned close to my ear and murmured: "Put the veil down, Jessie, and keep it down." I lowered it and Brandon put a hand on my waist and led me inside. The courtroom . . .

Jessie stopped, looking out the window into the darkening afternoon with eyes that were wide and gray and blank.

Remembering.

38

 he courtroom is illuminated by the sort of hanging glass globes Jessie associates with the five-and-dime stores of her youth, and it is as sleepy as a grammar school classroom at the end of a winter day. As she walks forward down the aisle, she is aware of two sensations—Brandon's hand, still on the incurve of her waist, and the veil tickling against her cheeks like cobwebs. These two sensations combine to make her feel strangely bridal.

Two lawyers stand before the judge's bench. The judge is leaning forward, looking down into their upturned faces, the three of them lost in some murmuring, technical conversation. To Jessie they look like a real-life re-creation of a Boz sketch from some Charles Dickens novel. The bailiff stands to the left, next to the American flag. Near him, the court stenographer is waiting for the current legal discussion, from which she has apparently been excluded, to be over. And, sitting at a long table on the far side of the rail which divides the room between the area set aside for the spectators and that which belongs to the combatants, is a skinny, impossibly tall figure clad in a bright-orange jailhouse overall. Next to him is a man in a suit, surely another lawyer. The man in the orange jumpsuit is hunched over a yellow legal pad, apparently writing something.

From a million miles away, Jessie feels Brandon Milheron's hand press more insistently against her waist. "This is close enough," he murmurs.

She moves away from him. He's wrong; it's *not* close enough. Brandon doesn't have the slightest idea of what she's thinking or feeling, but that's okay; she knows. For the time being, all her voices have become one voice; she is basking in unexpected unanimity, and what she knows is this: if she doesn't get closer to him now, if she doesn't get just as close as she can, he will never be far enough away. He will always be in the closet, or just outside the window, or hiding under the bed at midnight, grinning his pallid, wrinkled grin—the one that shows the glimmers of gold far back in his mouth.

She steps quickly up the aisle toward the rail divider with the gauzy stuff of the veil touching her cheeks like tiny, concerned fingers. She can hear Brandon grumbling unhappily, but the sound is coming from at least ten light-years away. Closer (but still on the next continent), one of the lawyers standing before the bench is muttering, ". . . feel the State has been intransigent in this matter, your honor, and if you'll just look at our citations—most notably *Castonguay* vs. *Hollis* . . ."

Closer still, and now the bailiff glances up at her, suspicious for a moment, then relaxing as Jessie raises her veil and smiles at him. Still holding her eye with his own, the bailiff jerks his thumb toward

Joubert and gives his head a minute shake, a gesture which she can, in her heightened emotional and perceptual state, read as easily as a tabloid headline: *Stay away from the tiger, ma'am. Don't get within reach of his claws.* Then he relaxes even more as he sees Brandon catch up with her, a parfit gentle knight if ever there was one, but he clearly does not hear Brandon's low growl: "Put the veil down, Jessie, or I will, goddammit!"

She not only refuses to do what he says, she refuses to even glance his way. She knows his threat is empty—he will not cause a scene in these hallowed surroundings and will do almost anything to avoid being dragged into one—but it would not matter even if it weren't. She likes Brandon, she honestly does, but her days of doing things simply because it's a man doing the telling are over. She is only peripherally aware that Brandon is hissing at her, that the judge is still conferring with the defense lawyer and the County Prosecutor, that the bailiff has lapsed back into his semi-coma, his face dreamy and distant. Jessie's own face is frozen in the pleasant smile which disarmed the bailiff, but her heart is pounding furiously in her chest. She has now come within two steps of the rail—two *short* steps—and sees she was wrong about what Joubert is doing. He is not writing, after all. He is drawing. His picture shows a man with an erect penis roughly the size of a baseball bat. The man in the picture has his head down, and he is fellating himself. She can see the picture perfectly well, but she can still see only a small pale slice of the artist's cheek and the dank clots of hair which dangle against it.

"Jessie, you can't—" Brandon begins, grabbing at her arm.

She snatches it away without looking back; all her attention is now fixed on Joubert. "Hey!" she stage-whispers at him. "Hey, you!"

Nothing, at least not yet. She is swept by a feeling of unreality. Can it be she, doing this? Can it really? And for that matter, *is* she doing it? No one seems to be noticing her, no one at all.

"Hey! Asshole!" Louder now, angry—still a whisper, but only just barely. "*Pssst! Pssst!* Hey, I'm talking to you!"

Now the judge looks up, frowning, so she is getting through to *somebody*, it seems. Brandon makes a groaning, despairing sound and clamps a hand on her shoulder. She would have yanked away from him if he had tried to pull her backward down the aisle, even if it meant ripping off the top half of her dress in the process, and perhaps Brandon knows this, because he only forces her to sit down on the empty bench just behind the defense table (all the benches are empty; this is technically a closed hearing), and at that moment, Raymond Andrew Joubert finally turns around.

His grotesque asteroid of a face, with its swollen, poochy lips, its knife-blade of a nose, and its bulging bulb of a forehead, is totally vacant, totally incurious . . . but it *is* the face, she knows it at once, and the powerful feeling which fills her is mostly not horror. Mostly it is relief.

Then, all at once, Joubert's face lights up. Color stains his narrow cheeks like a rash, and the red-rimmed eyes take on a hideous sparkle she has seen before. They stare at her now as they stared at her in the house on Kashwakamak Lake, with the exalted raptness of the irredeemable lunatic, and she is held, hypnotized, by the awful rise of recognition she sees in his eyes.

"Mr. Milheron?" the judge is asking sharply from some other universe. "Mr. Milheron, can you tell me what you're doing here and who this woman is?"

Raymond Andrew Joubert is gone; this is the space cowboy, the specter of love. Its oversized lips wrinkle back once more, revealing its teeth—the stained, unlovely, and completely serviceable teeth of a wild animal. She sees the glimmer of gold like feral eyes far back in a cave. And slowly, oh so slowly, the nightmare comes to life and begins to move; slowly the nightmare begins to raise its freakishly long orange arms.

"Mr. Milheron, I would like you and your uninvited guest to approach the bench, and immediately!"

The bailiff, alerted by the whiplash in that tone, snaps out of his daze. The stenographer looks around. Jessie thinks Brandon takes her arm, meaning to make her comply with the judge's order, but she cannot say for sure, and it doesn't matter in any case, because she cannot move; she might as well be planted waist-deep in a plug of cement. It is the eclipse again, of course; the total, final eclipse. After all these years, the stars are once again shining in the daytime. They are shining inside her head.

She sits there and watches as the grinning creature in the orange overall raises its misshapen arms, still holding her with its muddy, red-rimmed gaze. It raises its arms until its long, narrow hands hang in the air about a foot from each of its pale ears. The mimicry is horribly effective: she can almost see the bedposts as the thing in the orange jumpsuit first revolves those splayed, long-fingered hands . . . and then shakes them back and forth, as if they are being held by restraints which only he and the woman in the turned-back veil can see. The voice that comes out of its grinning mouth is a bizarre contrast to the gross overdevelopment of the face from which it drifts; it is a reedy, whining voice, the voice of an insane child.

"I don't think you're *anyone!*" Raymond Andrew Joubert pipes up in that childish, wavering voice. It cuts through the stale, over-heated air of the courtroom like a bright blade. "You're only made of moonlight!"

And then it begins to laugh. It shakes its hideous hands back and forth within manacles only the two of them can see, and it laughs . . . laughs . . . laughs.

39

Jessie reached for her cigarettes, but succeeded only in knocking them all over the floor. She turned to the keyboard and the VDT again, without making any attempt to pick them up.

I felt myself going insane, Ruth—and I mean I really felt it happening. Then I heard some voice inside me. Punkin, I think; Punkin who showed me how to get out of the handcuffs in the first place and got me moving when Goody tried to interfere—Goody with her wistful, counterfeit logic. Punkin, God bless her.

"Don't you give it the satisfaction, Jessie!" she said. "And don't you let Brandon pull you away until you do what you have to do!"

He was trying, too. He had both hands on my shoulders and was pulling on me as if I were a tug-of-war rope, and the judge was hammering away with his gavel and the bailiff was running over and I knew I only had that one last second to do something that would matter, that would make a difference, that would show me that no eclipse lasts forever, so I . . .

So she had leaned forward and spit into his face.

40

And now she leaned back suddenly in her desk chair, put her hands over her eyes, and began to weep. She wept for almost ten minutes—great noisy shaking sobs in the deserted house—and then she began to type again. She stopped frequently to swipe her arm across her streaming eyes, trying to clear her blurred vision. After awhile she began to get ahead of the tears.

. . . so I leaned forward and spit in his face, only it wasn't just spit; I hit him with a really fine gobber. I don't think he even noticed, but that's all right. It wasn't him I did it for, was it?

I will have to pay a fine for the privilege and Brandon says it will probably be a hefty one, but Brandon himself got out from under with only a reprimand, and that's a hell of a lot more important to me than any fine I might have to pay, since I more or less twisted his arm up behind his back and then lockstepped him to the hearing.

And I guess that's it. Finally it. I think I'm really going to mail this, Ruth, and then I'm going to spend the next couple of weeks sweating out your reply. I treated you shabbily all those years ago, and while it wasn't strictly my fault—I've only come to realize lately how often and how much we are moved by others, even when we are priding ourselves on our control and self-reliance—I still want to say I'm sorry. And I want to tell you something else, something I'm really starting to believe: I'm going to be okay. Not today, not tomorrow, and not next week, but eventually. As okay as we mortals are privileged to get, anyway. It's good to know that—good to know that survival is still an option, and that sometimes it even feels good. That sometimes it actually feels like victory.

I love you, dear Ruth. You and your tough talk were a big part of saving my life last October, even though you didn't know it. I love you so much.

Your old friend,

Jessie

P.S.: Please write me. Better yet, call . . . please? *J.*

Ten minutes later she laid her letter, printed and sealed within a manila envelope (it had proven too bulky for an ordinary business-length envelope), on the table in the front hall. She had gotten Ruth's address from Carol Rittenhouse—*an* address, anyway—and had written it on the envelope in the careful, straggly letters which were all she could make with her left hand. Beside it, she put a note carefully written in the same straggly letters.

Meggie: Please mail this. If I should call downstairs and ask you not to, please agree . . . and then mail it anyway.

She went to the window in the parlor and stood there for awhile before going upstairs, looking out over the Bay. It was starting to get dark. For the first time in a long time, this simple realization didn't fill her with terror.

"Oh, what the fuck," she told the empty house. "Bring on the night." Then she turned and slowly climbed the stairs to the second floor.

When Megan Landis came back from running her errands an

hour later and saw the letter on the table in the front hall, Jessie was deeply asleep beneath two down comforters in the upstairs guest room . . . which she now called *her* room. For the first time in months her dreams were not unpleasant, and a tiny cat's smile curled the corners of her mouth. When a cold February wind blew beneath the eaves and moaned in the chimney, she burrowed deeper beneath the comforters . . . but that small, wise smile did not fade.

November 16, 1991
Bangor, Maine